The Vampire Queen's Servant

Joey W. Hill

HEAT
New York

THE BERKLEY PUBLISHING GROUP
Published by the Penguin Group
Penguin Group (USA) Inc.
375 Hudson Street, New York, New York 10014, USA
Penguin Group (Canada), 90 Eglinton Avenue East, Suite 700, Toronto, Ontario M4P 2Y3, Canada (a division of Pearson Penguin Canada Inc.)
Penguin Books Ltd., 80 Strand, London WC2R 0RL, England
Penguin Group Ireland, 25 St. Stephen's Green, Dublin 2, Ireland (a division of Penguin Books Ltd.)
Penguin Group (Australia), 250 Camberwell Road, Camberwell, Victoria 3124, Australia (a division of Pearson Australia Group Pty. Ltd.)
Penguin Books India Pvt. Ltd., 11 Community Centre, Panchsheel Park, New Delhi—110 017, India
Penguin Group (NZ), 67 Apollo Drive, Rosedale, North Shore 0745, Auckland, New Zealand (a division of Pearson New Zealand Ltd.)
Penguin Books (South Africa) (Pty.) Ltd., 24 Sturdee Avenue, Rosebank, Johannesburg 2196, South Africa

Penguin Books Ltd., Registered Offices: 80 Strand, London WC2R 0RL, England

This is an original publication of The Berkley Publishing Group.

Cover art by Don Sipley.
Cover design by George Long.

First edition: July 2007

Library of Congress Cataloging-in-Publication Data

Hill, Joey W.
The vampire queen's servant/Joey W. Hill.—1st ed.
p. cm.
ISBN 978-0-425-21590-6
1. Vampires—Fiction. I. Title.
PS3608.I4343V36 2007
813'.54—dc22

2007006591

PRINTED IN THE UNITED STATES OF AMERICA

10 9 8 7 6 5 4 3

Praise for the novels of Joey W. Hill

"Sweet yet erotic . . . will linger in your heart long after the story is over."

—*Sensual Romance Reviews*

"Erotic sex, amazing characterization, a budding romance . . . a highly enjoyable and recommended read."

—*Romantic Times*

"One of the finest, most erotic love stories I've ever read. Reading this book was a physical experience because it pushes through every other plane until you feel it in your marrow."

—Shelby Reed, author of *Holiday Inn* and *Seraphim*

"The perfect blend of suspense and romance . . . will linger in the mind long after it's finished."

—*Road to Romance*

"Wonderful . . . the sex is hot, very HOT, [and] more than a little kinky . . . erotic romance that touches the heart and mind as well as the libido."

—*Scribes World*

"A beautifully told story of true love, magic, and strength . . . a wondrous tale . . . A must read."

—*Romance Junkies*

"A passionate, poignant tale . . . the sex was emotional and charged with meaning . . . yet another must-read story from the ever-talented Joey Hill."

—*Just Erotic Romance Reviews*

"This is not only a keeper but one you will want to run out and tell your friends about."

—*Fallen Angel Reviews*

"Not for the close-minded. And it's definitely not for those who like their erotica soft."

—*A Romance Review*

"All the right touches of emotion, sex, and a wonderful plot that you would usually find in a much longer tale."

—*Romance Reviews Today*

Berkley Heat Titles by Joey W. Hill

THE VAMPIRE QUEEN'S SERVANT

THE MARK OF THE VAMPIRE QUEEN

A VAMPIRE'S CLAIM

BELOVED VAMPIRE

Berkley Sensation Titles by Joey W. Hill

A MERMAID'S KISS

A WITCH'S BEAUTY

Anthologies

UNLACED

(with Jaci Burton, Jasmine Haynes, and Denise Rossetti)

The Vampire Queen's Servant

1

LYSSA wanted a meal. Preferably something muscular, a man whose long, powerful body would serve her well as she took his blood. She would hold him down, drink her fill and ride him hard. Take him deep, making him give up his rich blood and hot seed to her body at the same time. She'd push him to exhaustion, beyond rational thought. All those wonderful muscles would be taut and slick as he pounded into her with single-minded urgency, his most primitive instincts making him into a fierce, beautiful rutting animal. Just imagining it made heat shimmer over her skin. As she gazed out the window from the shadows of the backseat of her limo, her lips parted, her tongue caressing the backside of her fangs as if she could already taste him.

For months she'd made herself take blood functionally, letting it nourish her the way freeze-dried packets would keep a lost camper alive. But like most vampires, her desire for blood was intertwined with her need to dominate her victim sexually. Without that, the blood had no taste. No vitality.

She missed taking alpha males. She enjoyed the fight, their resistance, the sweet taste of heated blood. The perception, if only for a moment, that the hunt would be a challenge. A vampire didn't survive by being ruled by her compulsions, any more than a woman survived by being consumed by her most private desires. But tonight she needed release, and she was feeling reckless enough not to care about the consequences to her fragile heart.

Her nails were just the beginning. A manicure, then a man.

It irritated her that the car in the deserted parking lot of the salon was not Max's. Maybe her manicurist had experienced car trouble and borrowed someone else's vehicle. Still, it set off alarm bells in Lyssa's head. But since her limo was an evening's rental while she stayed in Atlanta, she couldn't very well ask the driver to scope out the area for signs of rival vampires. Of course, if she'd had a marked human servant, he could have performed the task for her.

Leave me be, Thomas. I've made my choice on that. For now.

She studied her nails by the light thrown into the car from the parking lot lamps. Hellhound that he was, her Irish wolfhound Bran had torn one when she was indulging his incessant need for attention. It had grown back to the half-inch length she preferred in no time, but the glossy burgundy polish could not be regenerated. Perfection was essential, particularly these days when showing any vulnerability could create dangerous situations. Though she easily could afford to pay a manicurist to come to her home, her enemies needed to know she wouldn't hesitate to go out to seek simple indulgences.

The hell with it. So it wasn't Max's car. If it was a trap or trick, she was ready to prove to any enemy or potential suitor foolish enough to challenge her that she was not to be trifled with—particularly not when she teetered on the edge of full-blown bloodlust.

She nodded to the driver, indicating she was ready. Throughout the trip from her mansion on the outskirts of Atlanta to the downtown area, the fifty-something black man had watched her closely in the rearview mirror. From her research into his background and her request from the rental company she knew he was ex-military and used regularly for high-risk clients. Add to that, perhaps somewhere in his southern past he had a grandmother into voodoo or witchcraft, or some other path that believed in the otherworldly. For it was obvious he sensed there was something different about her. Something that warned him not to turn his back.

Getting out, he opened her door. When she stepped onto the pavement, she noted his large hand tightened on the top of the window as he apparently controlled an urge to draw away from her.

"I'll be two hours," she said. "You're welcome to do as you wish during that time."

"I'll likely just sleep in the car, ma'am."

"No." His brows lifted as she turned, pointed. "If you do that, there's a hotel parking deck two miles that way. You'll go there. It's not safe to sleep in a car downtown late at night, Mr. Ingram." It was possible someone might slit his throat and pose as her driver, a twisted attempt to gain her favor or capitulation. The pressure on her to remarry since Rex's death was fierce, and courtship in the vampire world had all the romance to it of a terrorist cell planning to blow up a preschool.

She didn't want the driver's blood spilled on her account. Particularly since blood spilled on the ground was wasteful. "Do as I say." Withdrawing some money from her small purse, she handed the folded bills to him. "That's three hundred dollars. Lock up the car, eat dinner in the hotel and pay for a room to take your nap. Come back for me at midnight."

He nodded. She could see her actions created many questions in his mind, but she appreciated that he didn't ask them, choosing to sort them out himself. Perhaps this driver would consider . . . No, his fear was too palpable.

Even while she discarded the idea of hiring him as her permanent driver, for hiring staff was something she'd recently shied away from doing, her mind was admonishing her as she knew Thomas, her last human servant, would have done. *You must have staff. Most importantly, you need a servant. Who will take care of you, my lady*?

Only a human servant would ask that question and sincerely mean it when talking about his Mistress, a vampire over a thousand years old. It was moot in this case. Lyssa had no interest in Mr. Ingram as anything but a driver.

A marked human servant was different from an employee or domestic staff person. It was a person who served her by choice, binding himself to her by blood for much more intimate reasons than just to drive her car. One who accepted the demands of the role out of desire rather than fear, a form of submission that brought her a deep, lasting pleasure.

She just hadn't found anyone yet. A year was not a long time to wait when one had her life span. She still missed Thomas too much. It was that simple.

As she walked toward the high alabaster archway of the Eldar Salon and Spa, the sight of the familiar security guard waiting for her made her relax somewhat. Unless there was serious cause, she didn't believe in canceling an appointment at the last minute or being significantly late, like a movie or rock star who believed the world revolved around her schedule. People who worked had families, lives. Short lives at that. Rex had pointed out to her more than once that it didn't matter since humans frequently squandered the time they had. But that was their decision. Hers was to be reasonably prompt so they would have that choice to make.

She looked back at Elijah Ingram. She supposed most clients who rented a limo for the night didn't even know the name of their drivers, but she'd known much more than that about him before he'd come to pick her up. Enough to be reasonably certain he'd go to the hotel, pay for parking and take just enough of the change to get himself a soda and a Danish from the vending machine. He'd doze in the car and stash away the rest of the money to pay for his grown son's many mistakes. Other than purchasing that guilty snack, he wouldn't spend the money on anything for himself.

Elijah Ingram was a decent, hard-working man. A man who knew the dangers of taking money from the damned.

~

Her standing arrangement with the Eldar to open for her at ten o'clock in the evening whenever she came to her Atlanta home and requested it had cost her a fortune, giving the proprietors the not unjustified impression she was obscenely wealthy. As a result, the staff acted with the appropriate deference. Not overly chatty, attentive to her moods. They'd always been careful not to surprise her with the unexpected.

For that reason alone, Lyssa knew she should turn on her heel and walk back out. The man who stepped into the foyer to meet her was not Max.

However, she didn't turn around and leave. In fact, she brushed away the warning to do so the way she'd impatiently push a cobweb aside as she passed into a darker, deeper cave where unknown things—possibly treasure—awaited her.

This man did not look the least bit like her manicurist. For one thing, he was blatantly, solidly heterosexual, a condition easily detected by a person with her heightened senses.

His body was a feast. An absolute feast.

Men scoffed at hose, because in the Industrial Age they'd become associated with women's wear only, but she well remembered the way men had looked in them when they'd been the fashion. She'd favored the short tunics of the Renaissance period, particularly in Italy. They'd allowed a full view of the leggings from calf to groin. When men strode down the cobbled street in them, their swords at their hips, the air ringing with the flowing speech of a language meant to seduce . . . There was no woman who wouldn't have felt a stirring in her loins at such a virile sight.

This man wore such a garment easily, without self-consciousness, though she suspected he'd worn street clothes to the salon. He'd chosen a modified version of the hose, no codpiece, so his heavy cock and testicles cambered intriguingly beneath the tan fabric, framed between the columns of his muscular thighs. The top of the hose was rolled down so it rode low on his hips, low enough she could see his hip bones, the diagonal slope of the muscles above them that formed a *Vee* as they arrowed toward the genitals. His feet were bare. Since he was drying his hands on a towel, the motion drew her attention to the solid, compact muscle of his bare upper body. The man was a fighter, a cross between an Irish boxer and a medieval knight.

His fair, reddish brown hair had copper highlights from exposure to the sun. Loose, it fell to his shoulders. A neatly trimmed moustache and short beard following his chin outlined his firm lips. Set well on either side of a nose that had been broken at least once, his blue eyes had fine blond lashes with the same hints of copper. His skin was pale but ruddy, too Celtic to tan.

He'd executed a short bow when he stepped into the foyer, but he'd not yet spoken. His overly firm grip on the towel revealed some tension. When she registered the steady thud of his heart, smelled his heat and the life pulsing through him, a response rippled through her. She countered it with irritation, trying to force herself to be sensible. Careful.

"Are you mute?"

"No, my lady. I would never speak before you gave me leave."

Despite her intention to remain inscrutable, she couldn't help the way her interest rose when he spoke so formally. "Tell me who you are," she said, giving him a mental nudge to ensure a truthful answer.

His broad shoulder twitched, a corner of his mouth curving up. "There's no need to use compulsion, my lady. I'm Jacob Green. Thomas sent me."

At that shocking statement, he slowly raised his hand, making it obvious he intended no threat. From one of the display tables, he picked up a small envelope embellished like a suitor's calling card, complete with a red wax seal and a curl of gold ribbon.

Emotion flooded her chest at the sight of it. For a moment she couldn't speak, could do nothing but look at something Thomas had touched, recently.

Jacob stepped forward. Most men were taller than she was, and he was no exception at a little over six feet. "He died at peace, with great regard and affection for you until the end."

Taking the envelope from his hand, she felt the warmth of his skin even though she made sure their fingers did not touch. Somehow she felt reassured by that heat, by him standing so close. Not improperly, just close enough to feel his support, an unspoken offer of assistance. That was what it felt like to have a human servant, to go to ground during daylight and know he was nearby. Watching over her.

She shrugged off the unexpected thought. Turning the envelope over and over in her hands, she suppressed the sudden need to crush it as if she could absorb the essence of the man who had sent it, feel the way she'd felt when Thomas had been with her. *Not completely alone.*

He'd been her companion for a hundred and fifty years. Then, after all they'd been through together, she'd abandoned him to die alone.

Aware of her audience, she got a grip on herself and broke open the seal.

~

As she bent her head over the note, Jacob fought the urge to reach out to her, touch the rippling satin of her straight black hair. Thomas had shown him sketches, a portrait. He'd described her with the emotional eloquence only a dying man could conjure, but he'd admitted nothing would come close to meeting Lady Elyssa Amaterasu Yamato Wentworth in person.

He'd pictured her taller, likely because Thomas had told him vivid, heart-stopping tales of her battles with other vampires during the early territory wars. But she'd been born a vampire, and her Asian mother had apparently given her the petite build. Lady Lyssa was considered one of the most powerful and ancient vampires still living, fully in command of her faculties and abilities, not a common occurrence for any vampire over five hundred, much less one over one thousand years old.

Even while cursing the memory of her dead husband, Rex, Thomas had attributed a portion of her uncanny aptitude for survival to him. An aptitude that had grown exponentially in the last fifty years due to the lessons Rex had taught as well as inflicted upon her.

She looked barely out of girlhood, a young woman in her early twenties. That impression vanished the moment Jacob looked into her eyes, a startling jade green rimmed with a solid black line around the irises. Generation upon generation of women were there, layered like rock strata. The energy of it emanated from her, mingling with her other-than-human power to influence and destroy. Despite that, the man in him noticed the bow of her lips, touched and glossed in burgundy, the way her soft black sweater clung to her upper body.

Her skirt was layers of gauze in hues of gold and green, reminiscent of a fairy. That, as well as the eyes, reminded him her father had been a Fey lord. She was a slim woman with perfectly shaped small breasts and nicely curving hips. Her slender legs teased him, a glimpse of knee or calf appearing between the points of the skirt as she moved.

Stirring and magnetic, she riveted his attention just by existing. She'd had that effect on him the very first time he'd seen her, over two years ago. But what made the strongest impression on him now was the flash of naked emotion in her eyes when she took the envelope from his hands.

> *My gracious lady, please accept this last offering from your humble servant. Something I know you will not go out and obtain for yourself. I give you Jacob. You and he need one another, I promise you. He will serve you well, far better than a feeble, bookish monk.*

Lyssa was cognizant of Jacob's intent study as she read, as well as every motion he made. She was used to scrutiny by humans when she chose to walk among them, but his regard was different. Far more personal, as if he was memorizing every detail of her appearance and expressions.

He'd moved a step closer, a gesture of comfort, but he respected her privacy by facing her so he looked beyond her shoulder, not down at her note. The heat of his body shimmered over her skin like the dangerous brush of sunlight.

Damn you, Thomas.

"Do you know what's in this?" She gestured with it. He stood so close the ribbon under the wax seal fluttered against his pectoral, the light covering of hair on his chest. It made her fingers itch to stroke. To curl in and tug.

He gazed down at her with those clear and steady blue eyes. "I know it was my introduction. Thomas said I'd need it. But I didn't read it."

The seal had been unbroken, applied with Thomas's particular method for the times she'd needed to be certain information was not compromised.

"I want my manicure. Where's Max?" She straightened, not backing away. When she tilted her head, she noted his attention was distracted by the proximity of her lips. She felt his gaze there like the teasing caress of a tongue, and had to quell the urge to moisten them. *Try something improper, Sir Knight, and you'll regret it.*

But would *she*? She pushed the sly voice away. She was used to men being overwhelmingly attracted to her. It was the vampire allure. But she liked the look of this man. Of course, she'd intended to cap off her night by finding a dinner with similar specifications. Only this one far exceeded those specifications, tempting her to skip the whole spa experience and take him home for several days. She'd chain him spread-eagle on her bed and bite, scratch and suckle to her heart's content. While she wasn't willing to immediately capitulate to Thomas's recommendation of this man as a servant, she had his word she could trust him. It made her imaginings grow even more dangerously attractive.

"Max is fine, my lady. Sleeping quite deeply at his apartment, the aftereffect of his usual Chinese takeout . . . with a little bit of sleep aid added. I'll perform your manicure as well as a pedicure. If you'll permit it."

Add to that he'd somehow convinced Martin, the security guard, that he was an approved substitute for the evening. Not an easy feat. Clearing her throat, she managed to sweep a scornful glance over him. Enjoyed the journey immensely. "What training have you had to give me a manicure?"

"Thomas taught me."

His lips curved in that half smile again. Reassurance or humor she didn't know, but the reaction of her body took her by surprise. A hard shudder just below the level of muscle, like a simmering in her blood no human eye could see. Also unexpected was the fact he registered it. The smile disappeared. After a moment's hesitation, he pulled back the curtain dividing the waiting area from the private rooms of the salon. "Please let me attend to you, my lady."

She creased the fold of the note, frowning. Glanced down at the nail that had no polish.

Yes, her wounds healed quickly. Unfortunately, despite the myth that vampires were invincible, she could and did have bad hair days just like anyone else. One could use vampire glamour to make humans think they were seeing perfection, but it didn't work on other vampires without an exceptional level of effort. Unable to see her own face, she missed having a human servant to ensure she'd done her hair and makeup properly. To do quick fixes on her nails between full manicures. To help her dress and bathe.

The fact of the matter was, whether or not a reflection was needed, she liked being attended. Thomas had teased her about it, once he'd known her well enough to know when she was in the mood to be teased. He would have known this was *not* one of those moments.

The monk had relied heavily on her regard for him and her sentiment about his passing. It did not mollify her that he'd been right on both counts. While she knew she was taking petty revenge on the man who should not be the target of her ire, she couldn't stop herself.

"We shall see," she said at last, sweeping past him.

2

As she moved past, he touched the small of her back, a guiding hand. It almost brought Lyssa to a freezing halt. When her gaze flickered up to his profile, she realized the gesture hadn't been calculated. Whatever Thomas had taught him of the deference she demanded was intertwined with an automatic instinct to project protective body language toward a woman. It didn't displease her, but it startled her, for she intimidated most men enough they'd never dare contact without invitation. He'd already moved into her personal space as if the boundary did not apply to him. Apparently it didn't, for nothing he'd done yet had bothered her. In fact, the way she hadn't reacted negatively to his nearness was the only thing that *did* bother her.

The sameness about her preferred room served to soothe her—the occasional chair and the mosaic tile table beside it, topped with an array of tools. The low stool pulled close for the manicurist. Warmth emanated from the gas log fire, which she required regardless of the season because she chilled easily. Its dim light was the room's only illumination. She glanced at the antique pine china cabinet that held more manicure supplies and the bronze pedestal sink, making sure nothing was out of order, before she focused on her favorite feature of the room. The two bare walls had life-sized female nudes drawn in simple black brushstrokes. Titillating, dreamy impressions that aroused yet relaxed the viewer, one depicted the curve of a woman's back and hip, a fall of gem-sparkled hair as she reclined. On the other wall the woman sat on the point of her bottom, legs drawn up and crossed against her body, hair again sweeping the ground.

Lyssa loved the small room. Understated opulence, set off by the images that were more about substance than form, as if the artist had captured the simplest rendition of a woman's quiet but complicated soul.

"My lady." Jacob extended his hand. "I believe you usually prefer to remove your shoes?"

Nonplussed, she took his hand as he went to one knee. Guiding her hand to his shoulder to balance her, he bent and slid off one heeled slipper, then the other. Absorbing the sensation of his fingers gliding along her ankle bone and her instep, she studied the shape and feel of his shoulder under her hand. Solid bone and muscle, telling her he was disciplined about what he put into his body, as well as how he conditioned it. When he took her hand, his pulse had begun to race beneath her touch. An urge swept over her to trail her fingers under his hair, feel the individual strands slide through them, see the way they looked tangled in her grasp.

I give you Jacob. Thomas's note, offering her a man whose motives were as yet unknown to her.

"Stay on your knees."

He stilled, his hand hovering over her right foot as he remained on one knee, his elbow propped on it.

Wondering at herself, for she hadn't indulged such a romantic notion in a long time, she moved her hand to his ear, tracing the shape of it. Then she curled her fingers into his hair as she'd desired.

If she exercised her enjoyment of such things with her prey it could be dangerous, giving a sharp edge to her hunger. While she was experienced enough to control it, it was disruptive, an appetite that only grew stronger as she fed. Her mind said she was going to discard Thomas's offer as a presumption, tolerated only because it was now made beyond the grave. The sensation drifting through her fingers and up her arm was saying something else entirely.

The wide expanse of his shoulders had tensed, the smooth cords of muscle displayed well. While his hand was now curled above her foot, one forefinger was extended, the scoundrel daring to brush the top of her foot in a very light caress.

Her gaze followed the line of his spine, marking each vertebra, noting the shallow dip in his lower back. Her brow furrowed at the crisscrossing of scars. Lash marks, deep ones that would still be sensitive, probably a month or two old at most. There was the tempting swell of his buttocks well defined by the hose. Because of the low ride of the rolled waistband, she could see the hint of the indentation between his buttocks. She wanted to place her finger in that shallow valley, caress the tip of his spine there.

She wondered if his cock was swelling to even greater proportions against the crotch, testing the limits of the fabric. Since she could smell his arousal, she suspected it was, his reaction wetting the tip of his broad head. Her tongue touched her lip as she imagined it.

Just that instance of desire and she remembered a different image. Rex lying on the bed, his fist in her hair, forcing her mouth down roughly on his length. One hand clamped on her thigh as she faced away from him, his fingers bruising her, communicating his intention to break her thigh bone if she didn't make him come quickly enough. Or to do so anyway as part of the rush of pleasure of his climax. One of the lovers' games they'd played.

Withdrawing her hand, she wondered how it was possible to hate and love someone equally. To miss him desperately in the dead hours of the night and yet be relieved to be without him. So relieved that the idea of having another like Rex had kept her unusually chaste ever since she'd lost both him and Thomas.

"Why did you dress this way?" she asked.

When Jacob raised his head, his face was at the level of her breasts. She was aroused just from touching him, so her nipples were drawn to hard points. Since she was small in that area, she only wore a bra when she deemed it necessary.

He deliberately studied the curves, the upward thrust of the nipples, the way they pushed against the stretched yarn of her sweater, before he raised his gaze. She didn't feel he was being vulgar, improper. Instead, she felt wholly desired, a woman's need that the passage of time never diminished. She couldn't deny the potency of it when it was offered by the right man. From the aching hardness of her nipples, she concluded he was apparently the right man.

"Thomas told me you'd want to see as much of me as possible. He said that you had a fondness for this style and it might intrigue you enough to give me a chance." The dim firelight shadowed his face, but she was almost sure there was a hint of that attractive smile again.

You deceitful, conniving monk. I don't think you made it to Heaven after all.

"I would have stepped out naked, but . . ." He lifted a shoulder, and now she was the one who couldn't take her gaze off his lips. "I figured the security guard might take exception."

"What if I'd wanted you to strip before me right there, regardless?"

"I suppose he would've had to get over it, wouldn't he, then?"

From the shockingly teasing glance he gave her, the hint of Irish brogue that tempered his words, she realized he thought she was offering a jest. It appeared Thomas had not apprised him of everything being a human servant meant. Or that she didn't have much of a sense of humor.

~

Would a smile on her lips banish the lonely melancholy Jacob saw in her face? Such sadness would have made a mortal woman look drawn, detracting from her beauty. On her it added to the haunting, mysterious quality. Mixed with a fuck-me-now sensuality, that air of mystery was turning his compass upside down. Vulnerability, an intimidating, imperious manner and an erotic aura that would register on the hellfire side of red hot mixed together to drive him crazy. A man could be torn in half by the desire to have her body and the need to protect it with every ounce of strength in his own.

Thomas had been so concerned about her not having a human servant, Jacob sometimes thought the man had hastened his own passing when Jacob had refused to leave him until the end. It had seemed absurd that a creature as formidable as Lady Lyssa was supposed to be could be at risk from the simple absence of a mortal companion. During these first few minutes, he understood Thomas's concerns better. She was so tightly wound up the stress pulsed off her like a force field. Though he couldn't identify whether the cause was emotional or physical in nature, he sensed she was in desperate need.

The first step in the manicure was supposed to be massaging the hands to loosen and relax the joints, easing tension in the wrists. But after the intimate caress she'd bestowed on him several moments ago it seemed too personal to start with that. Not to mention his body was already inflamed by that proprietary touch. She'd been testing him to be sure, giving him the barest taste of what it would be like to be considered hers.

"I want you to do my feet first," she said, gazing at him with those dark eyes that revealed nothing of her own thoughts.

Apparently, he was to have no choice in the matter. She was determined to drive him to insanity. He gave himself a mental shake, steadied himself. "Yes, my lady."

Lyssa settled into the occasional chair, taking it to a half-reclining position so her feet were lifted from the floor, but still pointed on a slope toward it. As she did so, she watched his reaction in her peripheral vision. She wanted him to perform the pedicure on his knees. If Thomas had trained him, he would obey the unspoken command her body language was projecting, but she wondered if Jacob truly understood the significance of it. It was not an easy lesson for most strong-willed men to comprehend. Even Thomas had occasional difficulty with it, and he'd spent his life learning obedience to his God.

Jacob moved away from the stool. Kneeling with simple grace, like a knight before a queen in an Edward Blair Leighton painting, he took her right foot in his hands to begin the massage. He handled the move with the same relaxed familiarity with which he wore the hose and spoke to her. Mixing it all easily with more modern mannerisms and speech, he roused her curiosity about him further. Was he a stage player of some type?

Lyssa tried to ignore the tremor that ran through her at his touch and studied his hands instead. He had clean nails. A dusting of fine hairs lay along the upper part of the long fingers that handled her with gentle but firm assurance. He didn't grip her as if she were a doll, but he didn't clasp her too firmly either.

It was evident he was experienced and confident when touching a woman's body. That perfect balance could not help but evoke in her mind the way his hands would feel upon her thighs, along the valley of her spine, sliding down to her hips. Because of their height difference, when she stood before him and those arms closed around her, drawing her near if she desired it, the sensation would be sheltering, provocative. His throat would be warm beneath her lips as he lifted his jaw, trusting. Offering. Submitting.

His hands moved over the arch of her foot, caressed her heel and worked the top of her foot, his fingers whispering up her ankle in a way that shot signals of hard lust up the insides of her thighs to her core, dampening the silken fabric covering her there. The feel of her own arousal, warm and slippery, drove her desire even higher.

Was she losing her mind? She'd met the man five minutes ago. What had Thomas been thinking? She knew her own reactions and desires well enough to know her response to this man was out of proportion, even for the cravings for blood and sex she'd been experiencing before coming through the door. Thomas would have been very ill at the end. Would he have been ill enough to make a poor judgment call? Been compelled to do something he did not wish to do? Had someone found him, despite her best efforts to ensure everyone thought he was dead, killed by her own hand? Was Jacob a trap?

The thoughts helped her rein in her wayward responses. She narrowed her gaze on the man at her feet, a hawk targeting her prey.

"I can't believe Thomas would do something like this behind my back."

"He didn't intend disrespect. He—"

"I know how Thomas felt about me." She spat it. "You, on the other hand, I know nothing about."

"Thomas's introduction—"

"I read it. Why do you want to become a human servant? Are you running from death? Or are you one of those idealistic idiots who believe vampires are misunderstood creatures, issuing pretentious threats while we cling to the shadows and whine out our angst over our lost mortality?"

The description made Jacob smile. Too late, he realized he should have curbed the urge. He'd been warned her moods changed as quickly as the snap of a whip.

In a blink, the room closed in on him with a suffocating energy. Making the chamber much warmer than the gas log fire, the power raised the hairs on his neck.

"Do you realize, mortal, I could rip you apart limb by limb? Tear out your entrails and take your blood while you watch, choking on your last breath? Don't play games with me, and do not speak false, or those words will be your last."

When Jacob raised his gaze, he saw her eyes had taken on a reddish cast as she spoke, a hint of fang pushing over the right side of her full lip. The humanity had disappeared from her expression.

A wise man would have taken his hands off her foot. Put about a hundred feet between him and the threat he knew she was capable of executing. But Jacob knew that would be it. Game over. The last nine months of his life a waste. Most importantly, he would fail her, something he'd sworn to a dying man he would not do.

"I know you can destroy me," he said quietly, staring down at that shapely foot. "My reasons for wanting to be your servant are complicated and personal, my lady. My tongue isn't clever enough to explain them as you wish me to do. But I can prove myself to you, if you'll give me the opportunity."

It took Herculean effort to manage the words in an even tone, to raise his attention back to her face and hold that preternatural gaze without flinching, though his muscles tensed in an involuntary readiness he knew would be futile if she chose to strike. "I suspect if you truly intended to tear my limbs off, you wouldn't take the time to threaten me."

"Perhaps I feed on fear."

"There are other, more satisfying meals I can offer you." Daring or just plain stupid he didn't know, but going with his gut, Jacob bent and placed his lips against the top of her foot.

3

SMALL, fine-boned, cold. Like his mother's china. When he was little he'd been forbidden to touch it. As a man, he'd learned how to handle delicate things, enjoying the sensation while taking the proper care to keep them from harm.

Despite her strength, which could tear out the concrete foundation of the Eldar if she chose to exercise it, he thought of her as delicate. There were many formidable women, with or without vampire strength. But it was his experience that all of them had a need for love, unless damage to their heart had caused them to wall it off. They all desired to be cherished emotionally, and the art of conveying that through physical touch was one of the most potent ways to do it.

His lady appeared to have some sizeable fortifications around her heart for reasons he knew too well. Even so, he thought he could see a light guiding him through the crevices that still remained in those walls, toward the dark center of her soul.

Perhaps that intuition came from Thomas's many insights into her. Or maybe it wasn't intuition at all, merely the rationalizing stupidity that came with a man's lust. But though he'd woken countless times in the middle of the night bathed in sweat, his cock spent like a teenager's over the dreams he'd had about her, as many or more times the dreams had been about other things. Things that created a deeper-than-physical yearning unable to be assuaged with a grip on his cock. Only the feel of her in his arms would be enough. He let that guide him now.

Thomas had exaggerated nothing, even the way she made this abrupt transition from haughty goddess to merciless sorceress. As overwhelming as she was, he wanted to please her, to give her the gift of losing herself in her own desire. She was so lonely. He felt it from her like a labored heartbeat that made his own chest ache.

So he shifted his lips to her instep, tasted her there, his tongue flicking along the curve as he nuzzled the sole of her foot. When she placed her other foot against his shoulder, he figured she was about to shove him back on his ass. Or through a wall. But when he lifted his lashes, he found she'd gone motionless and was watching him. Turning his head, he brushed his hair along her ankle before he put his mouth against her calf. Slowly, so he conveyed his respect and his intention, he gripped her ankle and lifted her foot from his shoulder, supporting her calf in his other palm as he tasted her, all along the length of that fine limb.

The gauzy points of the skirt brushed his forehead. His nostrils flared when he smelled her response, which spurred his cock like a shot of adrenaline. *Steady, mate. Make it about her.*

He didn't suppress the male passion that made him nip at her as he reached her knee, her thigh. She arched, a gasp leaving her at the rougher contact, and he did it again, marking her lightly with his teeth. Her other foot moved, rested on his thigh as he squatted before her. Then, not content with that, she slid it under his arm, bent her knee so her leg curved around his bare back, drawing him in. He made himself take his time though, nuzzling the thigh of the leg he still held, working his way up in millimeters. A tiny caress of his tongue, a quick suckle from his lips, then that scoring again, tasting her flesh in his mouth, feminine, silky skin.

Always ask permission.

The recollection of Thomas's instruction was an irritating intrusion. Jacob didn't ask women's permission to drive them to pleasure. He took his cues from their bodies, their gasps, the clutch of their fingers. With her response, he felt an aggressive need to prove he could take over her senses. Perhaps it was because she was challenging him in a way no woman ever had. Or perhaps it was because he sensed against all logic and Thomas's teachings she needed him to try to take her over. But for the moment, he chose to obey Thomas's directive. In his own way.

He made himself look up at her. "My lady, you don't need to tear me limb from limb to destroy me. Just deny me the taste of you now. May I give you pleasure?"

He was already giving her pleasure, on so many levels all Lyssa could think was she wanted his lips to be doing far less talking. But the part of her that still hung grimly to a shred of rationality was reassured by such hard-core evidence of Thomas's tutelage. She suspected her answer was obvious to him, since her eyes could not help but drift down his bare upper body to the hard and impressive evidence of his own desire, revealed by his spread thighs. His cock was a long hard ridge against the hose, held against him only by the tight constraint of the fabric. There was a small wet area marking the tip as she'd suspected.

"Put your mouth on my cunt, Jacob," she said softly. "Prove to me you want to be my slave."

Most human servants were not fond of the term, but that was

what they were. Bound to her service forever, compelled by an oath to serve whatever need his Mistress demanded of him, a servant could not deny the true nature of the role. So she used it deliberately, watched his gaze flicker, a flare of resistance. But as she moved, intending to push him back from her, he wrapped his arm over her bent knee, his palm hot on the inside of her thigh as he levered it outward and followed the line of it beneath her skirt, the gossamer fabric drifting over him as he worked his way ever closer, his tongue now on that tender pocket of bone and flesh at the joining point of thigh and hip, his jaw brushing the outer labia beneath her soaked panties.

"Vanilla," he murmured against her flesh as he turned his head. His mouth nuzzled her fully, still separated from her flesh by the panties. She quivered at the contact. "Powder. Perfume. So sweet, m'lady."

His voice was husky, muffled by the fabric rucked up onto his broad shoulders. She curved her legs up on those shoulders, resting her heels along the slope of his back. However, she clutched the arms of the chair, not daring to allow herself the intimacy of touching him with her hands. It had been two years since she'd allowed a man to touch her like this. This was simply bottled up lust, being released with the uncontrolled explosion of anything kept too long under pressure. But God, now she wanted him to keep talking. The trace of Ireland was there the more he got aroused, and it vibrated against her flesh.

Talk, don't talk. Smile, don't smile. My lady, your moods are as mercurial as the weather, and ten times as hard to predict.

Shut up, Thomas. It was her mind imagining what the monk would be saying to her now, but the recollection was so strong she could almost believe he might be standing here, watching them with amusement. She'd no wish for a third party at the moment.

Jacob worked his hand beneath the skirt, hooked her panties, pulling the crotch aside so he could lick and nuzzle her flesh. She sucked in a breath, moved against him. Shoved actually, pressing her wet heat into his mouth, his nose and chin, unable to prevent undulating against the friction of that soft beard. It and the tickle of the moustache were a rough contrast to the moist texture of his mouth, his invading tongue.

Ah, gods . . . deep inside of her. He plunged, working her, his lips moving on the outside while that tongue thrust, caressed.

Jacob Green. I give you Jacob . . .

He knew her clit better than her own fingers, alternating light butterfly touches of his upper lip against it with the rougher abrasion of his moustache, even as he sealed his whole mouth over her, brought his tongue out to play with her clit before delving in again, fucking her with his mouth in a way that made her think of that big cock prominently outlined in those indecent hose plunging into her cunt, stretching her.

The orgasm detonated in her body as if he'd tripped mines strategically placed at every erogenous point. Her breasts, her lower abdomen, her arched throat, her brain, heart, soul. Even in the soles of her feet, pressed hard against the taut skin of his back, her toes curled into him. Everything screamed with the release so that she had to bite down on her tongue to prevent her vocal cords from doing the same.

Even so, a long moan broke from her, a quiet, broken sound that almost sounded . . . pleading.

More, more, more . . . If I could just be lost like this for a decade, forget everything that's happened . . .

She wanted to ride that furious wave far out into the ocean so when it melted back into the sea, she'd be left in a place of quiet peace and wild beauty, where nothing was required but simple existence.

He made it easy to imagine such a resting place. As she forced herself to come down in convulsive shudders, her body jerking, he overlooked nothing. He kept going, slowly suckling her sex, alternating with teasing licks, nursing her through the aftershocks and then cleaning her with his mouth, making sure he took every drop of her juice before he gently pulled the crotch of her panties back in place, kissing her over top of them in a way that made her close her eyes, shudder again. Even then he didn't just pull away and leave her immediately without the close heat of his presence. His mouth drifted back over her thigh, down toward her knee as his hands followed the same path, straightening her skirt as he came from beneath it.

She couldn't let herself get so far off shore. Off balance. She had to regain control. This was happening too fast. This wasn't a dinner she'd picked up in a bar.

"Keep your head bowed. Don't look at me."

She could tell the quick snap of the command startled him as his head began to rise. But she didn't want him to see her in this half-reclined pose, her legs open to him as a woman would with her lover, showing him how he'd taken her to a boneless aftermath.

"Did I not please you, my lady?" He obeyed her, though she noted the tension in his shoulders, the splay of his fingers taut on his thighs as he dropped out of the squat onto his knees. He kept his spine straight and shoulders back even as he bowed his head. A warrior being deferential to his queen, but not necessarily submissive. She was aware of the difference, and it confirmed what she'd sensed. Thomas had taught him the proper motions, but Jacob did not truly understand what it meant. Only she could teach him that. *If* she accepted him.

A human servant could be a lover when she wanted one, someone who met her needs large and small. This man, physically powerful by mortal standards but helpless as a newborn to a vampire, nevertheless had a quiet confidence that made her feel feminine. As if she didn't always have to be strong, the way a woman was supposed to feel around a man she trusted. Yet she could lift him with a finger or rip him apart as she'd threatened.

It had been a long time since she'd felt a violent desire that could drive her hunger to a pleasurably uncomfortable level. But his words, those blue eyes, his impudent caresses, even that inappropriate need to smile so often, were rousing a different sort of hunger. One she'd been willing to forget and do without. Until now.

She was going to take him home.

Damn you, Thomas.

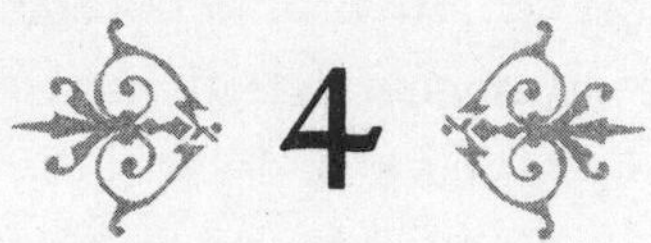

4

SHE didn't fall into daydreaming, losing sense of place and herself. She didn't act on impulse. Despite those warning signs, she impulsively reached for him now, curling her nails into the firm skin of his biceps, exerting pressure.

She wanted to know how he'd respond to a woman's desire without her commanding it. She almost wished he would fight her, struggle, but he gave her something as satisfying. More so.

Without hesitation, he surged up from the floor. Taking her by her upper arms, he lifted her to her knees on the chair as he erased the distance between them, closing his mouth over hers in a hard, demanding kiss.

All that desire he'd kept banked roared over her in full, raging force, goaded she was sure by the things she'd made him do against his nature.

As a woman, she'd missed this. God, how she'd missed this. She avoided the intimacy of lips when taking a man for her meal. Their kisses came off weak, disappointing, giving her dinner a distracting, unpleasant taste.

This was distracting, but not the least bit disappointing or unpleasant.

Kissing her way deeper into his mouth, she let him feel the shape of her fangs against his tongue, a deadly expression of pleasure. As she raked her nails up his back, there was the satisfying gouge into flesh. Cutting into one of the lash scars, she found the river of life that flowed beneath it.

His breath was hot in the cavern of her mouth, his tongue tangling with hers as his hands gripped her hair. He pressed her body between the back of the chair and the pounding of his heart.

Tracing his lips with her tongue, she opened her eyes to look up into his. They were open as well, filled with desire and determination both. Glory yes, he was a dominant man. In his touch, in the way he held her, kissed her, she felt it. It was instinctive to him to take over, lead and protect. He would whisper things in her ears only fit for a creature of the night to hear. Dark desires, ways he would try to claim her. For a moment she imagined it, trembled with the feel of it, even knowing her own desires were even darker, her will stronger than any mortal man's.

But for this moment there was only dizzying sensation. Waves of it turning colors in her mind, overwhelming her. Tightening his hold on her hair, he yanked her head to the side and gripped her throat with his teeth, his tongue licking a pulsing artery.

She stiffened against him, her fingers digging into the gouges in his back she'd made as her body rippled in uncontrolled response.

"Jacob." When she spoke his name in a breathless whisper, his hand slid down her back, molding over the curves of her ass before he slid between her braced thighs, seeking her heat. Just the tips of his fingers brushed her clit as he sealed his palm over her throbbing cunt, her skirt bunched up between his touch and her skin. The heel of his hand pressed against the sensitive base of her buttocks.

He didn't break her skin, but he kept that hypnotic hold on her throat. His blue eyes blazed fire over the fragile skin of her face. Her fingers were sticky with him and she wanted that blood in her mouth. Wanted him in her bed. Accessible for play, for a snack, for a full-course meal . . . She yearned for his arms to encircle her in the middle of the night.

A companion.

"My lady." His voice was a hoarse rumble against skin as he eased his bite. She closed her eyes, sliding her hand up so it cupped his face even as her body quivered under the touch of his slowly kneading, clever fingers.

She could send him through a window and rolling into the street. She could lay her hands on his skull and crush it with a thought. But at this moment she reveled in the way his hands held her, so powerfully. He had the suggestion of Rex's strength, but none of the cruelty that had kept her from completely surrendering to the passion of her husband's embrace.

Colors. Spiraling colors. She'd ignored the warning sign as well as the dizziness because she'd been impatient for the sensation of the climax, of Jacob's kiss. But now the disorientation was increasing exponentially, clearing the sensual haze over her mind with the cold wind of apprehension.

Lowering her hands to his arms, she began to push, enough that he couldn't resist it. When he tried to maintain a hold on her, a simple additional exertion was all she needed to slam him back down on his knees before her, his grip dropping clumsily but quite pleasantly to the outside of her thighs. He tried to pull back but she merely tightened her hold on his shoulders. Staring at him unsmiling, she waited for him to understand.

A first lesson.

Jacob's eyes narrowed, betraying temper and not a small amount of frustrated lust, an energy she absorbed with pleasure, savoring it almost as much as she would blood.

"You haven't displeased me, Jacob," she said. "I admit I'm intrigued. But you won't come home with me tonight. You need to think some more. At the moment you're standing in the surf. If you submit to me, you'll be taken deep into the ocean and never touch solid ground again."

"I came prepared to go with you, my lady." He spoke low, obviously struggling for the earlier tones of smooth courtesy. "With respect, I think it's you who needs time to think. Not I."

Arrogant, even if he was also right. She didn't know enough about him, and unfortunately now was not going to be the moment for her to learn more. Time was short. Regardless, she lifted a disdainful brow. "So if it was my will to take you home tonight and make you serve me with your mouth while another man fucked *you* from behind, that would be fine?" At his startled reaction, she gave a sharp nod. "I will take you far past what you think your limits are, to the level *I* find acceptable. After that, I might go even further. See how you handle pain, how loyal you would be to me under torture."

She knew how to do such things, but the thought made her a little sick, especially when her body was still shuddering from that kiss and the orgasm that had surged up like a violent seizure at his barest touch.

"I'm committed to your service, my lady. Whatever it might be."

But she heard the rage against it in his voice. "I think you're rash and foolish," she said in sudden anger. "Driven by your cock and your male ego. You're romanticizing the situation, blinding yourself."

The world was becoming a wavering rainbow. Nothing was as it seemed. She needed to go. Was it time for her driver to return? She couldn't remember when she'd said for him to come. She used her dwindling reserves of strength to send out an urgent compulsion to him, a mental shove that would have him turning the key in the ignition and heading this way before he even thought about the fact he was earlier than she'd suggested.

She'd known the danger of going out like this. It was too much . . . But she'd wanted a manicure, damn it. One pleasure. But there were no easy pleasures anymore.

"My lady?"

By his alarmed expression she knew her irises had gone blood red, her pale face even paler. Her fangs had elongated and now pricked her lips, lancing the skin and drawing blood. Salty blood that tasted metallic on her tongue.

It was too late. The chair became green, then purple. The fire was now olive drab, with blue flickering lights. She had to trust Thomas's choice and see how Jacob performed under fire. Hopefully not literally.

"Vial . . . in my bag. I need it."

After a quick look at her face, he retrieved it from the side table, searched and found the medicine. The room spun. When it righted itself, he was holding her, easing her back into the chair. "My lady, what's the matter?"

"That's not your concern." His skin was so hot, so alive. She felt the richness of his blood as if she was bathing in it, but the snakes of pain were there too, coiling in her lower stomach.

"I need blood. Fresh."

"Direct from the source, or mixed with this?" He gestured with the glass tube.

"Mixed." Though the idea of sinking her fangs into his throat was enough to make her arch off the chair with a cry of yearning, pain tearing at her.

Snatching up a pair of razor clippers, he sliced a line across his forearm with the blade. The arterial blood was quick and red. She wondered how he knew a finger prick wasn't sufficient.

Picking up the vial, he removed the cork and brought the tube against his skin so the blood flowed into it without further waste. It turned black upon contact with the potion. He capped the tube and shook it to accomplish the mix, caught up the towel and swiped it across the outside to keep the blood spilled there from dripping on her clothes.

"Hand it to me. Please." Propping her head on the back of the chair, she attempted to rest her hands on the arms in a position of dignity, though she wanted to curl in a ball around the pain.

He brought it to her lips instead, cradling her face with his hand. Those vivid eyes and appealing lips were close. She wondered if he knew his eyes turned different shades depending on his moods. Sapphires, a summer sky, the Mediterranean right before sunset . . .

She drank the bitter stuff but reveled in the taste of him, wishing she hadn't had to spoil her first sampling with this. The way he touched her face, with his palm so close to her fangs . . . He didn't fear her in the way she hated. Despite her mockery, she didn't sense that obsessive unrealistic fascination with her kind she found contemptuous. She could teach him to fear her in ways that would bring her pleasure, though. Ways that would bring them both pleasure.

Thomas. This is insanity. Who is this human, that he makes me feel this way? Does he understand it? Is that what he hides from me, or is he as confused as I am?

The colors were steadying, reforming. Objects reflected a less surreal perspective. She needed to get to the car, but the potion left her with a hazardous temporary lassitude. She could simply abide here, let Thomas watch over her . . . No, not Thomas. This was Jacob. She blinked. No, she couldn't stay. She'd been here too long, was too exposed.

Jacob had no idea what the hell was happening. This wasn't the effect of hunger. He was certain of that. This was illness. The woman whose power had nearly blasted him into the next room several times during their brief interaction was now almost ghostlike in her fragility. After she'd consumed the medicine, her fangs had slowly retracted, her gaze returning to that midnight darkness and jade that watched him as if she wore the soul of the night itself. The part that beckoned to a man even as it froze his bowels in fear.

"Trust. Thomas said trust." There was a feverish quality to her eyes.

"Trust must be earned, my lady. If you allow me, I'll start earning it."

She looked down. Following her gaze, Jacob saw the arm she grasped was the one he'd cut for her medicine. Now his blood was on her skin and her skirt. When he picked up the towel from the table again, she didn't object as he wiped her palm down. There was nothing he could do for the stain on the skirt. "My apologies."

She nodded, watching him with an oddly mesmerized expression. "You're fortunate I didn't wear white. I would have taken great pleasure in punishing you for staining it."

Such a threat from a vampire should have been terrifying. So why did he only feel arousal as the fingers of her free hand drifted over the cut?

Get a grip. She needs more than your cock at the moment. Thomas had warned him she had an astounding and often infuriating way of bringing a man's lust into every situation. Right now though, worry was taking precedence.

Her hand stopped drifting, clutched in a sudden spasm. Though she was a petite woman whose head barely reached his shoulder, he was sure he'd have the imprints of her fingers on his forearm and possibly the bones beneath for some time. Pain was part of being a human servant, though. When he'd stood before the altar in the monastery chapel, the blood clotting on his back and making him lightheaded, his body screaming for relief, he'd understood that. Thomas had been preparing him with the flogging. Physical suffering would be part of accepting his lady's regard, and never allowed to distract him from her care.

Therefore, despite the increasing strength in her grip, it was the convulsive movement and the trembling in her hand which shot his attention back to her face. The lines around her mouth had deepened, giving him warning. "My lady."

When she slumped in the chair, he caught her. Her hair tangled in his fingers.

"Take me to the door, Jacob." Her lashes fluttered, showing him her green eyes briefly. "It will be all right then. Driver . . . Mr. Ingram, should be out there. He'll get me home."

5

SHE wasn't inviting him to go with her. He could get her to the door, maybe to the car, and that was all. He could hardly contain his frustration.

Thomas had said it might take time to gain entry into her household. He'd come up with several different strategies for Jacob to execute over time, the manicure being just the first. So while Jacob had not planned to be unsuccessful this night, he'd been prepared to deal with it if he was. However, Thomas hadn't known there was something wrong with her. Having seen the strange disease which had taken her servant, Jacob felt his heart clutch with dread, his mind filled with questions. All of his plans to be patient were blown away by the fact she obviously needed a protector far more than Thomas had realized.

But the way she'd looked up at him, trusting him at least for this moment, pushed away the disturbing thoughts. He propped her gently in the chair and retrieved from the pine cabinet several things not necessary for a manicure. Forearm gauntlets carrying a variety of silver-tipped wooden shafts and small knives, and a nine millimeter handgun. He shucked the hose, thrust his legs quickly into a pair of worn jeans and tugged on a pair of boots under them before putting the gun in its belt holster on his back waistband. Quickly he laced the gauntlets to his forearms and checked the triggering mechanism. Shrugging on a long-sleeved navy blue shirt, he buttoned enough buttons to hold it on and conceal the gauntlets and gun, though it was loose enough to allow him access to them.

At least there was one good thing about her loss of consciousness. He was certain when he reached for the weapons she would have put his face through a wall, suspecting he was a trap sent by her enemies. The truth might elicit the same reaction. He just didn't feel their first meeting was the appropriate time to mention that among his many past career choices he'd been a vampire hunter. He'd hoped for a more casual and affable moment to interject that into the conversation, though now he was wondering if the woman ever had a relaxed moment.

This one had been forced upon her. Bending, he scooped her up in his arms. As her head rolled inward, her cheek pressing to his chest, he had the gratifying and humbling experience of knowing she'd relinquished all control to him. The gods always had a backwards way of offering opportunities to prove oneself.

When he got to the foyer, he found the limo was in the middle of the parking lot under a lamp. Prompt and ready as she'd said.

"Is she okay?"

Martin, the security guard, spoke from the reception desk. Jacob nodded. "She drifted off. I'm going to make sure she gets home." Trying to sound casual, as if it were nothing unusual. He'd worked it out that Martin had accepted him as Max's replacement for the evening, but he knew this could easily stretch the boundaries if he acted as if anything were amiss. "Max warned me sometimes she nods off like this. Late hour and all. Think she's on some of those designer mood drugs for anxiety."

"She's an odd one, she is. Rich folk." The guard shook his head.

"Her limo's here. Can you go out and ask him to come right to the door?"

Martin immediately rose. "Sure. Be right back."

As the guard left through the glass doors, Jacob felt his charge rouse.

"Put me down."

Glancing down, he saw she was looking at him like an irritable cat who'd found herself in the jaws of a drooling Labrador.

"You fainted, my lady."

A self-mocking smile touched her lips. "Just like a Victorian heroine. Put me down, Jacob."

He let her feet drop to the floor but kept his hands at her waist, supporting her as she swayed. "I'm not living up to the formidable image I'm sure Thomas described," she commented.

"He said you were harmless as a kitten." He recalled vividly the way she'd shoved him to his knees earlier with barely the pressure of two fingers. Responding to her arch look, he added, "I'm sure your past is littered with men foolish enough to underestimate you, my lady. I won't be one of them."

He still saw the traces of red in her eyes like the banked fires of Hell. "It seems I should learn not to make the same mistake about you," she said. "Only time will tell, for both of us. Your hose . . . where did you learn to wear them?"

It was an odd question for the moment, but he responded automatically. "I used to work the Faire circuit, my lady. As a jouster and sword fighter. Sometimes a juggler and a fool. I've been in the circus as well."

"That's where you picked up your courtly mannerisms." She blinked at him, and he nodded.

"Yes, my lady."

"You're a drifter, then. Did Thomas explain this isn't a job for a vagabond?"

It riled him, perhaps because he couldn't deny it, but he managed an even tone. "I've never left a person who needed me by their side. Or at their back." *Except my own brother.* He shoved that thought and everything that went with it away. "I won't fail you in that regard, my lady."

The lights of the limo passed over her as it turned into the covered entranceway. Instinctively he shifted before the glaring light could strike her sensitive eyes.

"I'm walking you to the car at least."

"Not taking me all the way home? You still owe me my manicure."

He stopped. "That's what I'd like to do," he said, barely daring to hope. "If you would allow it."

"Are you up to the challenge? For what it could mean? There will be consequences, whether I end up accepting or rejecting you."

Her green eyes were suddenly quite sharp and focused on his. In their depths, he saw the very real threat, but beyond that he saw a wealth of possibilities. Things that made her warning similar to a tree falling across the mouth of a waterfall. The water of his desire would simply rush under and over to fling itself over the edge in order to experience the euphoria of the descent.

Over the months of training, Thomas had forced him to thoroughly analyze all the paths his life had taken to be absolutely sure he wanted to embark upon this one. Jacob had come to the conclusion all those paths had converged to lead him to Thomas's door. But now he wondered if Thomas suspected her illness. Had he hoped Jacob would lose his heart to her so quickly that when the truth was known he would be willing to lock his destiny with hers, no matter the consequences? Or had Thomas known Jacob had lost his heart to her long ago?

She was gazing at him. He realized they'd been standing there looking at one another for several minutes. "Perhaps I'm rushing you?" she asked.

"No. *No*, my lady." Without hesitation now, he took her hand and raised it to his lips, feeling how much colder she'd gotten in just the past few moments. When he registered the rigidity of her limbs, he understood. *Pain*. She was fighting pain and likely the overwhelming desire to succumb to unconsciousness to escape it. Keeping his grip on her hand, he tried to convey with warm pressure she had someone in her corner.

"I'm going out to the car now," she said. "Follow two paces behind. Appear a bit besotted, as if you're someone I'm taking home to feed me."

"My lady, you can't walk without help."

She straightened, though he saw her features tighten with the effort. He had to stomp on the compulsion to override her protests and carry her to the car. She was too weak. He could feel it.

"I must never appear vulnerable to my watching enemies, or even those who call themselves my friends, Jacob. Do you understand? It's the most important rule of my world."

"Then let me try this, my lady. I think it will serve your purpose."

Standing in the doorway, in full view of the parking lot, he reached out his other hand. Bemused, Lyssa took it. He drew her to him, closer, closer, until he brought her all the way to him, their fingers loosely linked so she was brushing his thighs with her nails. Bending his head, he nuzzled her cheek with his lips, her fair skin with that knightly fringe beard and moustache. It smelled faintly of coconut oil, explaining the unexpected and appealing softness of it.

"I can do 'besotted' quite easily with you, my lady."

His eyes were brilliant, almost too painful for her to look at in her present state. "You're making me . . . dizzy," she whispered. Leaning into him, she felt his pulse hammer against her like a mob pounding at a castle gate. He was right. She wasn't going to be able to walk to the car. The medicine was kicking in fully and it would rob her of her full strength for at least two hours. Her consciousness as well. She'd truly been a fool to go out tonight. It was getting so much harder to predict when the attacks would come.

"Jacob . . . if I can trust you, if you have any regard for me, for the promises you offered . . . get me home."

"Put your arms around me," he said with sharp urgency. She complied, gripping his shirt as her strength deserted her. Did he know where she lived? Had she told him that? What about Bran? Oh, sweet Jesus, she hadn't told him about Bran.

Jacob caught her up in his arms a moment before she sagged, a fluid movement that would appear like the impulse of an impassioned lover. Keeping her tilted in to him, he tucked his head over hers so it wouldn't drop back and show she'd truly lost consciousness this time, something he knew by her boneless weight. He took small nibbles at her lips, breathing on her lashes as he strode to the limo, nodding reassuringly to an intrigued Martin as he passed him. "Lock it up. I'll get my things from Max tomorrow. I'm taking her home."

And hopefully by tomorrow he'd have his lady's help in reassuring Max with a plausible story when the man called in a panic after learning some stranger had taken his place for her manicure.

The driver, Mr. Ingram he assumed, was a black man of intimidating size and about fifty years. He'd opened the car door for them. His brow knitted at the picture they made, but Jacob did not acknowledge him as he eased her across the backseat and ducked in after her.

Ingram blessedly didn't say anything, just shut the door. It gave Jacob a moment to settle Lyssa against his side and take another quick glance at their surroundings through the black-tinted windows. The salon was located off of a reasonably quiet downtown side street, a good distance from the nightlife that would be kicking into high gear as they approached midnight. But his sixth sense was fully active, telling him her concerns were warranted. There might not be vamps out there, but their spies surely were.

Lady Elyssa was *the* Vampire Queen, the last living descendant of the original royal clan of the Far East. Her relationship to the ruling Vampire Council was similar to the British royal family to Parliament, for the vampire monarchies had died out several centuries ago, but she had significant clout due to her physical prowess, extensive Region and wide variety of powers. She had helped create the Council and the delicate network of laws that kept the predatory nature of vampires from ensuring their own extinction.

In the vampire world, brutality and civility constantly played a chess game for influence. Low-level war games were common and acceptable ways to prove oneself and acquire more territory. Without the influence of vampires like her, there would be no balance. Even now, a new threat was rising. There was increasing dissatisfaction among the ranks of "made" vampires with the established order set by the "born" vampires who ran the Vampire Council and most of the Regions.

However, despite her great value to the vampire world and the enemies she'd accumulated, the stubborn woman kept no entourage, living a life of relative solitude, particularly since the shocking death of her husband, about which only she and Thomas had known the truth. And now Jacob, entrusted with the information before Thomas's death.

"Ma'am? Do you wish to go home now?" Jacob looked up at the driver, whose gaze encompassed both of them. "Ma'am?" he repeated.

"She's sleeping," Jacob responded. "Yes, she wants to go home."

"All due respect, sir, you're not my client. She doesn't look asleep. She looks like she passed out. A lady like that has a lot of secrets. I don't want to know any of them, but I aim to see her home safely."

When Jacob shifted, the driver's eyes sharpened, warning him.

"Son, I've got a Beretta up here, pressed against the seat cushion. You can get out of the car without her, or you can tell me something that will convince me you should stay. You and that semiautomatic you have under your shirt."

"Good . . . driver."

Jacob glanced down and saw Lyssa's catlike eyes were open, fixed on the man. When she lolled her head around to look at Jacob, her features were so perfect and delicate she could be set on a shelf with a trio of china dolls. He would have to look twice to make sure she was real. But when a man felt the energy around her, it was forcibly clear how alive she was.

"He's . . . mine. Okay. Take us home. Keep me safe. Good driver. Must sleep now. Won't wake for a while."

Her eyes drifted closed, her head falling back on Jacob's shoulder. In the same movement she nestled in under his chin, letting him tighten his hold over her shoulders. One hand latched loosely inside his shirt front, her fingers brushing his bare skin. The other hand drifted into his lap across his thigh, her touch an inch or two from his groin.

Whether her affectionate body language was done strategically to reassure the driver or from her own desire, Jacob didn't know, but it did the trick.

As the driver raised a brow, Jacob heard the Beretta uncock. Mr. Ingram shook his head. "If you ain't hers, son, you're soon going to be. Hope you know what the hell you're doing."

Jacob wondered the same thing himself. As they pulled out of the parking lot, he felt burned to ash by her touch and those two simple words.

He's mine.

LYSSA's sleep was deep and long, filled with interesting dreams. Of a knight with pale blue eyes who tucked her in before he went off to battle. She dreamed long enough that her dream brought him back to her. Wearing full-skirted chain mail with a tunic of the Crusades over it, the field of white bearing a red cross as pure as blood. She helped him out of it in the sanctity of their chamber, removing his gauntlets from his large hands, massaging her fingers over the calluses he'd earned from wielding sword and mace.

When she unlaced the mail and he lifted it off, she noted the dirt in the creases of his knuckles, the lines that heat, wind and cold had etched on his handsome face. Reaching up, she touched his lips, framed by the soft down of his beard and moustache. He kissed her fingers, his tongue playfully teasing her skin.

A bath steamed behind him. As he stood before her gloriously nude, muscular, powerful, aroused, she tried to tease, to slip away. But he was having none of that. He seized her waist in hands as gentle with her as they were powerful in the service of his Lord. Drawing her into his arms, he pulled her full against him, her breasts pressed into his skin, rising above the velvet and ribbon edge of her scooped-neck dress. His lips sought hers when he pushed her gown away and held her. Tighter. Even tighter.

Too tightly. He was hurting her, and she couldn't get free. She threw her head back, crying out. It was Rex's dark face, his lips pulled back in a snarl as he crushed her, her ribs breaking beneath the iron band of his arms while her heart beat frantically like a bird trapped in a cage getting smaller and smaller.

It's astounding the pain a vampire can endure, isn't it? Almost nothing can actually kill us.

He would not take her in her dreams. Not there, not in her life, not anywhere. Pulling her lips back in a matching snarl, she met his gaze.

As you found out. Didn't you, dearest?

His eyes glowed red. With a roar, he broke her rib cage like a frame of matchsticks, his touch separated from her heart by shards of shattered bone and so much more . . .

Lyssa woke, opened her eyes. Well, the first part of the dream had been nice. She could still feel that knight's rough palm, the strength of an eager male lover instead of a . . .

No, she wouldn't dishonor Rex's memory by venting her rage on him with name-calling. She dwelled instead on the knight, as if the other part of the dream had not existed. His blue eyes and copper hair.

Her fingers moved down her body, bare beneath the sheets. Finding her smooth sex wet, she shuddered at just the touch of her fingers. That knight of her dreams had reminded her of someone. Of . . .

She bolted upright in the bed, a motion too rapid for the human eye to follow if any humans had been present. She was alone in her bedchamber, which was an appropriate name for it, since she had it appointed like a medieval fantasy. Heavy canopy drapes for the large bed. A massive stone fireplace, the tapestry hung near it depicting hunting scenes in the bold colors and poor drawing style of the early centuries of the second millennium. Stained glass on her windows kept light filtered during daylight hours. Lit candles on the dark wood dresser and the faint smell of smoke lingering from matches being struck told her she hadn't been alone for long.

He'd gotten her home somehow. Gotten her to her own bedroom. Had Thomas described it to him, or had he wandered through the rooms, carrying her in his arms until he found the one that felt just right, like the fairy tale?

Well, Goldilocks she surely wasn't. As she turned and put her feet on the floor, she grasped the tall post, feeling the carvings of clematis flowers and leaves twining around it. Her hair fell forward, tangling in her nails as she swept it from her eyes. If she was cast in a fluffy animated retelling of one of those grim fairy tales, her character would be a wicked witch, a darkly dangerous stepmother. The thought almost made her smile.

She wondered what her knight would do when she took him to her bed. Chained him as she'd imagined, making him wait upon her pleasure. Even when he was allowed to sleep in her bed less encumbered, she'd still require him to sleep with one wrist cuffed and chained to the bed, a nominal reminder of his devotion, of the fact that he was her property.

Or perhaps she wouldn't chain and cuff his wrist, but his fine cock and scrotum. Jacob. When she thought of the personality he'd shown, the temper, her hunger stirred. She was ravenous. A side effect of the powder, she knew, but it was further stirred by her dream and memories of the things that had happened between them before she fainted.

While the malady she suffered had many drawbacks, including the inability to predict these attacks, one of its better aspects was that the spells, like the tides, fully receded after they'd run their course.

Her strength and potency had returned with her hunger. As well as the sharpness of her faculties, her ability to think and question.

Bran? How had Jacob gotten past him? How had he gotten in, period? Why was she thinking of him as if she'd already made the decision to keep him? He hadn't even told her the full truth of why he wanted to be her servant. She knew almost nothing of him. Thomas's endorsement held great weight, but normally she would have investigated far more about the man before bringing him into her home. Perhaps desperate times called for desperate measures, though she disliked thinking of her situation as desperate.

After brushing out her hair and sliding on a black satin robe and some jewelry to armor herself, she left the room and the west wing for the stairwell. She liked her Atlanta mansion, built in a fortress style with stone. While she'd have preferred it situated even more deeply in the woods than it was, at least it backed up to thirty acres of forest she'd had fenced, the outer perimeter regularly patrolled.

As she walked down the stairs, she knew it was still night. Probably about two thirty in the morning, given that the medicine usually knocked her out for two hours. The outside landscaping lights mounted beneath the stained glass windows threw light before her on the curving stairwell and into the foyer. Reds, blues and golds merged with the shadows.

Stopping halfway down the staircase, she cocked her head, her exceptional senses picking up music from a radio and voices. And . . . aromas.

He was cooking eggs. Speaking to someone. Who? She deepened her probe, the possible need for aggression rising in her. Then she relaxed. It was Mr. Ingram. The driver. With Jacob. Brow furrowed, she went to the base of the stairs and headed for the kitchen.

Since she hadn't sent a compulsion to Bran to conceal his response when he sensed her approach, there was a sudden thunderous bark, followed by several slightly less vocal ones and a surprised yelp from what sounded like Mr. Ingram. Then there was the clatter of toenails. Many toenails.

Stopping in the wide hall, she braced herself for canine assault.

Her hellhounds, Rex had called them. He'd actually been fond of the two girls. Not as fond as she was of all of them though, finding herself unable to suppress a smile as the pack of Irish wolfhounds came racing out of the kitchen. Graceful as deer when they had traction, they galloped pell-mell down the slick wooden floor of the long hall that was the central feature of her home. She winced as Maggie skidded into one of the mounted suits of armor and knocked the pike loose, sending it clattering to the floor after it bounced off of Fionn's head, which deterred his speed not a bit.

She suspected Rex's affection had to do with their reputation from ancient times of being able to rip an enemy's head off in battle. Plus the fact that, at one time, only royalty could keep them. Even when Irish nobility had been allowed to have them, the quantity of the dogs they were allowed depended on rank. While she found their ferocity very useful, their heritage noble, she'd found many other reasons to love them.

Bran was in the lead of course. The pack of nine dogs, seven males and two females, varied in color from black to brindle, fawn to red, but he was her ghost, a rare pure white. He came to a skidding halt just short of making contact, showing respect. Since he was nearly a yard tall at the shoulder, Bran was level with her breastbone when he raised his head as he did now. She stroked his head first as the pack leader, acknowledging him, then dispensed touches and reassuring words to the others. As she heard footsteps approaching, she raised her voice.

"You've been a very bad dog, Bran. Letting riffraff into my house."

Lifting her head, she studied Jacob, coming down the hallway toward her. Yes, he was just as appealing now as he'd been at the salon. The edge of lust she carried made her want to sink her teeth into him before another blink of time had passed. He still wore a shirt, but he'd buttoned a couple more buttons and wore it loose over the jeans, impeding her view in a manner that didn't entirely please her. But for the moment she was content to study him as he was. The blue eyes assessed her, concerned. The confident stride, the loose hands said he'd made himself comfortable in his surroundings.

She could intimidate or seduce a man with a look without any magical power. She'd had time to practice, after all. But Jacob had a self-possession that made an impression. Perhaps it was his colorful past and the secrets he'd yet to divulge to her that made him handle himself so well. Since he had Thomas's confidence, she acknowledged those secrets might be nothing to concern her, just the history behind his private revelations and struggles. A man at ease with himself, who knew where he'd been, what it meant and where he wanted to go. Which annoyed her exactly because of how much it appealed to her.

"I promise he ate at least three Jehovah's Witnesses to redeem himself," he responded.

"Bran would never eat my dinner if it delivered itself to my door. He has manners. How did you get past him?"

"Thomas taught me the command he used with them. He also gave me a handkerchief with his preserved scent. The two together seemed to do the trick."

"Fortunately for you." She fondled Fionn's ears, feeling the soft silk of the undercoat mixed with the rough top layer. It reminded her somewhat of the softness of Jacob's lips, mixed with the stimulation of his facial hair. "Why is the driver still here?"

"I think you should hire him, my lady. He's very competent, and he's had military training."

"He would never work for the likes of me."

"I think he'd consider it, if an offer was made."

"What lies have you been telling him?"

His eyes narrowed. "I would never lie about you, my lady. I will lie *for* you, if needed for your well-being."

"Hmm." He was showing that edge of irritation he'd demonstrated when she'd accused him of being a drifter, stimulating her in a way he likely wouldn't expect. It brought back all the things the dream had roused as well. "Come with me, then."

"The driver—"

"Will wait without question if he is indeed the type of person I can use. For now, you'll follow me and keep silent, and that is all. Bran, take your brothers and sisters back to the kitchen. On guard."

Immediately the dog spun, his siblings in pursuit. They parted around Jacob, a river of fur and flashing eyes, and galloped back down the hall, leaving the two of them standing ten feet apart. To Lyssa, the distance didn't seem so much like the distance of strangers as the paced-off field of potential combatants.

When Jacob hesitated, she raised a brow. "If you can't follow my commands without question, you're also not the type of person I can use."

He would think her uncharitable for not thanking him, for not answering the many questions she could see he had about her welfare, about the house, about his role in it. But she was not his companion. He was applying to be hers. Despite their unfortunate beginning, it was time to see if he would accept a full understanding of what that meant. Only then could she decide whether to allow him to serve her under one mark. Maybe two. She knew he would be discontent with anything less than three, but it was not her role to make him content. He needed to accept that as well.

~

This was not the same woman he'd helped into the limo. It was another intriguing version of her. At the salon, she'd been a temptress. Here she was that, but also obviously queen. He felt it in her assessing gaze, the imperious tone and the restless lust that moved in her eyes and had his cock jumping eagerly even as his mind balked at being treated as chattel.

She was walking away, leaving him the choice. Once he followed, he was agreeing to be what she was requiring at this moment and perhaps ever after. He struggled with it, the independence of a lifetime warring with the image Thomas had given him of a woman who needed him, who intrigued his mind and fantasies.

She stopped at the stairwell, laying her hand on the banister. Slim, elegant fingers, the middle one bearing a ring with a sapphire set in silver, the gem as large as a fingernail. He wondered if her husband had given it to her, and unexpected displeasure surged at the thought. Lifting that hand, she freed her hair from a clip that held part of it away from her face. As the strands dropped, she ran her hand through the silken weight of it, an ebony tide that pulled his gaze to the hips it brushed. The black satin robe clung to her, the fit and loose neckline telling him she wore nothing beneath it.

"Jacob." Her voice was a purr. Her eyes were as dark as the shadows clustering around the stairwell. "Every moment you hesitate will make your punishment much more intense."

"I'm not afraid of pain, my lady."

She chuckled. "Then you've not experienced it intensely enough. But there are punishments far worse than pain."

"Worse than losing your sense of yourself?"

She cocked her head. "Sometimes that is the most pleasurable part of pain. Come. I'd say I don't bite"—her lip curled up slightly at one corner—"but we both know that to be untrue."

When she ascended the stairs, he found himself following, taking them two at a time to her one. As he caught up, an instinct contrary to his nature kept him a pace behind her.

She took him to her bedroom where he'd laid her less than two hours before, hoping he was doing the right thing, that he was overlooking nothing for her care. He hadn't wanted to leave her side. But when her face had eased into a peaceful expression, he'd returned to Mr. Ingram to keep him company. The driver had refused to leave until she presented herself to him fully lucid and assured him Jacob was welcome in her home. If Jacob had dallied over her, he was certain the man would have come looking for him with that Beretta, a situation certain to have disturbed his lady's much needed rest.

While he'd followed Thomas's direction to get past the dogs, even Bran had not given him an unconditional green light. He'd stood stiffly by the front door, his stock-still posture and the watchful eyes seeming to say, "*Well, then. Do you have the stones, mate?*"

Now in the present, as Lyssa glanced over her shoulder at him, he had the feeling the same challenge was being issued.

Do you have the stones, mate?

7

As he stepped over the threshold she was moving to the walls, switching on small spotlights to highlight the room's artwork. "Stand in the center of the room, arms at your sides."

A Matisse. A Titian. A Van Gogh. Deep expressions of the soul in a multitude of colors, like the woman who lived here. While he had many questions for her, he knew the spur of curiosity was not why he wanted to ask them right now. A part of him wanted to deny she could order him to be silent. But he had to understand the unfamiliar before he could determine if it needed to be rejected or defied. What was swirling through him now as he obeyed her command was definitely unfamiliar. His loins tightened with every quiet sound he heard. Her feet sinking into the carpet. The soft swish of her robe moving on her legs. She fluttered at the corner of his vision and then disappeared.

Before he could turn in surprise and look for her, her hand touched his back.

"That's a neat trick," he said.

"Jacob." Her voice was a whisper along his spine. "I know you're nervous. I can hear your pulse. You've never submitted before. When you make love to a woman, you take her over. You let her feel your strength, your desire. If there is any surrendering, she surrenders to you. When you let yourself go, it's only when you're certain she's become lost in you. In the passion you've given her."

Did he detect a certain edge to her tone, as if she resented the women he'd had before? That would be absurd. Almost as absurd as his relief when he saw no evidence of Rex's presence in this room. Nothing to remind him she'd been alive long enough to have been touched not only by her husband, but by many other men.

She caressed his hips, holding him as she rose on her toes to press her mouth under his ear. "If you wish to be my servant, you must learn what surrender truly means." Her hands slid under his arms and she began to toy with one of the shirt buttons, the color on her nails shining faintly in the soft light. "So don't make me gag you. I want to make use of that pretty mouth of yours, that clever tongue. You'll stay silent from this point forward unless I command you to speak. Remain still."

He'd begun to raise his hands, intending to clasp them over hers on his abdomen, but at that he stopped, battling his own will. Taking a deep breath, he made himself lower his hands back to his sides.

"Good. Very good."

As she opened his shirt, she moved closer, the barest brush of her body against his back, his buttocks. Her breath tickled his spine through the light fabric.

Though he knew it was a defense mechanism, Jacob tried to sort out the questions he had, mundane and less mundane, as if writing them down in his head for later reference. Anything to keep himself motionless as her fingers tormented him with nothing more than the unfastening of his shirt and her command to be still. Why did she breathe? Did she like coffee? Max had said she preferred a pot brewing in the foyer of Eldar, but she hadn't even asked for a cup. Was it the aroma? Should he make her breakfast? What was the driver doing? Had she ever had a man self-combust and die, incinerated by the fire she ignited in him?

Placing her palms on his now bare stomach, she kept one there while moving the other up to find his nipple. He swayed, leaning back into her as sensation shot through him. Her arms tightened, holding him. He felt her pleasure in his response, in the way she touched her lips to his neck. While he'd never thought of the throat as an erogenous zone for him, it apparently was now, for his cock became harder every time she went near it.

"Perhaps you're thinking this will be like those times when you *let* a woman control the moment. *Let* her ride your cock to climax while you held onto the bed rails and pretended you were bound. Soft games of pleasure with no real risk, the dark areas of yourself untouched, vulnerabilities unchallenged."

She came around to face him, her fingernails scraping his skin as she followed the waistband of his jeans, just inside the band of fabric. "Lovely musculature. Mature, lean. Not the body of an untried boy. There are scars here. You've fought battles."

"I've—"

"Hush. You do not have my leave to speak."

A sharper command this time, in a tone that shot resentment through him. She began to hum softly to herself. As if her dialogue was intended to be a one-way conversation, like a potential buyer examining a thoroughbred racehorse. He suspected she was doing it that way deliberately to goad him.

On the other hand, her expression was focused, fascinated, as if she'd been given a private viewing of a special work of art and was standing alone in a room with it, envisioning it as hers. The look in her eyes was enough to make him want to reach for her, hold her against his aching want.

That response grew even more intense when she unbuttoned his jeans and opened them, reaching in to clasp his hard cock and adjust it, bringing it out of the recesses of the pants. Moving closer, she let go to run her hands back along the inside of the jeans to palm his bare ass. Pushing her knuckles against the hold of the fabric as she kneaded him, she rubbed the satin of her robe against his cock where it was taut and erect, revealed by the open fly.

His hot flesh felt the bite of the open teeth of the zipper, but it couldn't dampen the inferno of desire raging through his blood like the sudden rise of lava in a smoking volcano. When she tilted her head, her lips were so close he couldn't resist any longer.

"No," she murmured.

"Yes," he insisted.

When he closed the gap, he stumbled forward at the lack of contact. She was no longer there, empty air the only thing in front of him.

"Take off the rest of your clothes, Jacob."

He spun awkwardly and saw a flash of her, then she vanished like mist with that rapid speed vampires had. His gaze went to the ceiling, knowing gravity didn't necessarily limit them, but he found nowhere for her to perch.

"Clothes off. Lie across the bed with your feet on the floor, your arms stretched over your head as far as they can go. If I have to tell you to do it again, I'll *make* you do it and crush your male ego." Her voice was a sensual caress, coming from several places in the room, moving like a capricious wind, disorienting him. "But even worse, I'll tie you down and leave you like that for several days, until you realize what belonging to me truly means. Enough to regret it."

Jacob lifted a lip, curled it in a snarl. "Give it your best shot, my lady."

He couldn't say why he did it. Maybe because he didn't want to capitulate so easily. Maybe because he had no game plan for this other than his intuition and unwillingness to be controlled.

He didn't see her coming. A shove knocked him to his knees and the shirt was ripped off his shoulders. When he flipped to his back, it was floating down to the floor. The candles flickered with the passage of her flight.

Rolling into a crouch, he didn't bother removing the pants. They were a tactical disadvantage open and low on his hips, but by the time he lifted a hand to remove them, she could be on him. He waited for it, that sense of impending air movement. Guessing her next direction based on her last strike, he ducked away, twisted back and grabbed, managing to seize a portion of her robe and tumble her across his legs.

Anticipating the lightning move of her hand, he reared back and dodged the grasp. He clamped down on her wrist, a move he knew she could easily counter by breaking his arm. But he had to believe the point of this impromptu match was not to injure. While he understood she was trying to prove something to him, he was just as determined to get his own message across.

He would be her servant. He wouldn't be livestock. At least that was what his pride told him, drowning out the voice of his psyche that said there might be darker issues involved in his resistance.

She'd frozen in a half-standing position, her slender forearm cuffed by his grip while she stared at him, two feet between their faces, her foot planted between his knees. He'd pulled her robe off her shoulder, exposing most of her right breast. Even as the pleasure of seeing that milk white curve made his body respond, a sense of shame swept him at this evidence of rough handling. Knowing how much stronger she was, he nevertheless eased his grip at the feel of those fragile female bones. With his other hand, he reached out and slid the satin back up on her shoulder, his fingers whispering along the collarbone, itching to trail down her sternum to cup one of those soft curves.

She straightened, drawing back from him. Her gaze narrowed. "You've fought vampires before."

"Yes, my lady."

"In the limo, you were wearing weapons. Several. I don't remember that Thomas had any particular skill with weaponry. In fact, I worried about his fingers when he handled kitchen knives."

"He told me of your enemies, of your world. My brother is a vampire hunter. He taught me how to fight them. But I quit. Thomas felt that was another reason I was qualified to be your servant in a way he wasn't. His words, my lady. Not mine." He added it quickly at her expression. "My brother and I . . . our paths separated some time ago. I'd rather not speak of him."

He didn't want to think about Gideon, who would be apoplectic if he knew what his younger brother was doing.

"You neglect to mention your brother is a vampire killer, that you worked with him, and you're refusing to tell me more than that? When I can crush your windpipe before you can blink?"

"Killing me is your choice, my lady. What I tell you of my life is mine."

She made a noise somewhere between irritation and disgust, a Japanese curse that sounded as if she'd compared him to an earthworm, if he'd gotten the translation right. Being fluent in a handful of languages was another part of his resume he'd not yet been able to cover, though he didn't think revealing that now would appease her. She stepped back several more feet, her expression merciless, hard.

"A rather significant omission, from both you *and* Thomas."

Now he was glad for the command not to speak unless requested to do so. Nevertheless, he braced himself for the uncomfortable questions. However, after several tense moments, one of those pauses she seemed to favor, she simply said, "You're a fool to worry about chivalry when it comes to a female vampire."

"I'll never raise a hand to you, my lady. If you tell me my choice is to be bound on that bed or to strike you, then I submit. There is no choice then."

"I won't make it that easy for you. You may go lie on the bed. Or you may leave and never see me again."

On that note, she was gone from his sight again. Multidirectional, her voice filled the room. It was as if he were in the inner sanctum of a goddess's temple, hearing her voice coming from the elements, making him unsure if it emitted from the whisper of water in the fountains, the mysterious rustling of the trees, the flicker of firelight in the braziers, or the stones that came from the earth itself.

"If I forced you to go to the bed after you fought me, whether by hiding behind your chivalry or my physical force, you'd take some comfort in that. It's harder to do it willingly, not knowing what to expect or what it will do to you, what I'll expose. But you'll discover far greater pleasure in the torment if you go willingly than if you fight."

His knee-jerk reaction was that she was trying to inflict some misguided lesson upon him. But perhaps submitting also unlocked certain vulnerabilities in his lady. Would it give her greater pleasure as well, to see him submit? In her voice he could detect her urgent desire to see him go down by his own volition, though he had the conflicting suspicion his resistance teased the sharp edge of her lust.

Trying not to think about it too much, Jacob made his decision. Leaning his hips against the footboard to keep his balance, he removed one boot, then the other. While he was aware of her regard from somewhere in the room, he knew it would be pointless to seek her out. Pushing off the jeans, he retrieved his shirt and laid both garments over the arm of a chair, placing his boots in front of it.

As he stood completely nude, deliberating his next move for several charged moments, he wondered what she was thinking. He was throbbing, enormous. He hoped she took pleasure in that. Life in a circus had helped him get past modesty about personal nakedness, but he found himself somewhat self-conscious under the circumstances.

"You think you can commit over three centuries to me, Sir Vagabond?"

"As long as you need me."

"You say that, but you resist me. Did Thomas tell you the oath to a vampire of my rank?"

"I am sworn to your service. Compelled by absolute loyalty, I safeguard your well-being before my own or any other ties of family or friendship. I swear it by the giving of my blood to you and before all of Divinity, may my life be cursed and my soul be damned if I speak false or ever betray the vow."

A pregnant silence filled the room. "Thomas made you take the oath," she said at last.

"It was the last step in my training. I stood vigil in the monastery chapel for three days and three nights before he spilled my blood on the stones to consecrate the words."

Fifty lashes across his back. Required when administered in conjunction with the oath, they were part of the Ritual of Binding to a vampire queen. It was a ritual so ancient most vampires under three hundred years old didn't know it. Lyssa moved through the shadows outside of his vision, staring at those crisscrossing lines that would have turned his back into a mass of blood when they'd occurred, causing enough pain to make the strongest man sick, lose control of his bowels. Then the monks would have made him scrub those stones clean on his hands and knees, naked, before they would offer to tend his wounds. The Master always came first.

"Did Thomas use my whip?"

"Yes, my lady. He said you'd used it on him when you accepted him."

She closed her eyes. She'd given it to Thomas as a gift years before. He'd apparently carefully preserved it. Once a human became a servant, most wounds he'd received even previous to his acceptance would not leave permanent scarring, unless his Mistress anointed the weapon with a drop of her own blood first.

Without knowing if she would accept him, Jacob had subjected himself to torture and permanent disfigurement. An exceptional act of loyalty. It moved her far more than she wanted him to know.

"I'd like you to put your boots under the bed," she said at last.

Odd. From the tone of her voice, Jacob could tell that had been a request, not a command. He suspected Lady Lyssa never intimated words except exactly as she intended. She could likely orchestrate any nuance she wanted in her speech.

"Under the bed. Just like the country song?"

She didn't respond. He didn't expect her to do so, but at least he didn't sense she was offended by him forgetting himself and speaking out of turn. Putting the boots neatly just under the bed, he eyed the expanse of mattress.

From the corner of his eye, he realized she was behind him now, almost three feet back. Close, reminding him of the temptations that might wait for him if he complied. Far enough back so the decision was his, as she'd said. After that, his choices would be limited.

He turned around to face her. Keeping his gaze on hers, he took a step back, then another. The anticipation that rose in her expression resulted in a taut, indefinable anxiety in his gut as he sat down on the bed. As tall as he was, he'd still have to flex his feet to keep his toes grazing the floor if he slid back to where the crook of his knees met the mattress as she wished. Lying back, he felt the soft quilting of the cool bed linens give beneath him.

She hadn't made the bed, so he smelled her, felt the rumpled waves of the quilted blanket beneath him. He'd undressed her for her comfort, trying not to take advantage of her unconscious state to ogle, but now her scent taunted back to life the vision of smooth, pale flesh and curves he'd briefly glimpsed, the bare folds of flesh between her legs, for vampires only had hair above the neck. He raised his arms over his head, his knuckles brushing the covers.

"See if you can reach the opposite edge of the mattress."

He stretched out his arms as far as he could and came within a few inches of reaching the other side if he strained.

"Hold that position. I want you to pretend your arms are already bound. In a moment, they actually will be."

When he heard the clank of metal, he wanted to roll away, leap up. With a force of will that took more effort than he expected, he kept still. *A beautiful woman wants to tie you up and have her way with you. You've played soft bondage before.* But only as she'd described, where it would have been easy to get loose. Where the emotional stakes were nowhere near as high as they would be here.

Now her robe brushed his leg. There was the sound of metal touching metal again. Her hand slid around to his calf, her fingers stroking the hair there before moving down to his ankle. She took her time about it, turning her hand over as if it were the page of a book to rub her knuckles along the same area. The electrical reaction ran up the inside of his thigh, prodded his cock up another notch.

Apprehension had affected his erection, but it was quickly being restored with the magic her fingers were creating. He didn't want to admit lying still at her command might also be contributing. He'd never considered it a sexual act, making himself helpless to a woman.

Thomas had told him there was no end to the things she could teach him. The crafty son of a bitch hadn't gone into these kinds of specifics, though. He wouldn't have bolted if he'd known. Probably. But it would have been nice to be prepared, as much as a man could be for something like this.

Of course, Thomas had been a monk. Which made Jacob add another question to his list. Had *Thomas* done this type of thing with her? Because he'd assumed the monk was under the vow of celibacy, he'd never even thought to ask.

Cold steel locked around his ankle. A loose fit, but not enough that he'd get it off without shearing off his heel. Trailing her hand down his foot, over his toes, she traced the lines between them. Her lips were soft and warm on his knee, the area just below it. He wanted to see her, but by holding the position she'd ordered he could only feel her and strain his ears to hear her movements.

The contact of her mouth tickled, making him quiver. Her lips curved against him. A smile, maybe. He felt a prick, just the touch of a fang, and then her weight shifted. Putting her back against his bound leg, she sat, letting his leg and the bed support her as she took hold of the other foot and restrained it in the same manner. There were chains attached to the manacles and she made some adjustment to them which widened the spread of his legs with the pressure of her shoulder against one of his calves.

Air touched his balls as she made him that much more defenseless by somehow anchoring the chains to the corner posts. He swallowed, told himself he could lie here. That he'd done this willingly. He wasn't afraid of her hurting him, so why was a well of panic trying to cloud his brain, take over his body and make it tremble as if he were some type of untried virgin?

"Very nice." She caressed the inside of his leg, dragging her nails over his thigh. His cock was at full attention now as if it knew she'd straightened to look at it.

"Even better," she murmured. Her body rubbed against his leg as she rose. She appeared like the unexpected touch of a breeze up near his head, standing on her knees on the mattress to the right of his straining hands. The neckline of her robe was loose, showing him the crescents of her breasts. At his avid gaze, she spread the upper part of the robe open, revealing her bosom completely. She had curves like firm, juicy apples, the pink nipples capturing his attention and making saliva pool in his mouth.

She pulled another set of manacles on the bed. As she balanced herself, her hands closed on his wrists and the metal snapped onto them, a series of clicks and pressure that told him they were locked with a key like the ones on his ankles. Crossing his wrists, she hooked the manacles together, avoiding contact with his fingers. A hard quiver ran through his muscles as she used the key to sweep a lock of hair off his forehead.

"You've stopped straining. Reach for the edge of the bed as far as you can."

"Come down here."

"Obey me and perhaps I will."

8

HER voice was breathless.

He swallowed the urge to reach up before his hands were anchored and make her come down to him. For one thing, she could easily slip away. But he was recalling her words.

If you can't obey me, I have no use for you.

He wasn't sure that was true, but some iota of good sense told him he'd better not test his theory at this moment. So he reached as far as he could, feeling the muscles of his upper body sliding up his ribs, stretching taut over his stomach. Her eyes reflected her enjoyment in the show.

The arch in his back increased as she moved away to tether the manacles with chain to the bed rail, drawing up the slack further. Taking hold of the joining point of the manacles on his wrists, she pulled on him, one sharp, decisive move that elicited a grunt from him and stretched out his body several more inches. It would have taken a rack borrowed from the Spanish Inquisition—or a vampire's strength—to extend his body this far, and he felt the strain in his joints as she held him with one hand, tightening the chains with the other to keep him that way.

The floor was gone beneath his toes. She'd just made him completely helpless. The room had gotten exponentially smaller, warmer. With his thighs spread, nothing protected his genitals. His cock had no sense at all, staying high and stiff, calling all sorts of attention to itself. The stretched position put pressure on the gnawing hunger in his lower abdomen.

"Does looking at me make you wetter, my lady?" Fighting panic, he asked the question with rough demand, driven mad by watching her gaze course over him, linger.

"It does, Jacob. Would you like to taste?"

"I would. If it pleases my lady."

"You've learned your manners well. I'll have to attend more Faires in the future." However, rather than granting his desire, she sat on the bed, spread out the hem of her robe's skirt in a half moon before her and smoothed it. Sitting there with her dark hair falling on her creamy shoulders, she was bewitching, her breasts bare and taunting him with their proximity. "My cunt is a hot, wet sheath, but small and tight, my courteous knight. You seem generously endowed."

"Well, my lady, perhaps you should let me make your silken walls more so with my tongue, for an easier fit." He swallowed. "Christ, let me fuck you, Lyssa. Let me give you pleasure."

His fingers closed into fists as he braced himself for what might come next. Protecting her he'd been prepared to do. Taking care of her. But he hadn't expected to be at her total mercy.

"Not just yet. I think you need a test in obedience first. You're talking out of turn again. I'd also advise you to think twice before you ever call me familiar again." Rising to her knees, she spread the hem of her robe out like a curtain just above her knees as she straddled his forearms. As she looked down at him, he had to fight the urge to crane his neck back, see if she had spread open the garment enough to give him a glimpse of heaven.

"I'm going to move over your body now. If you don't remain still, I'll stop, get off the bed and leave you this way for an hour as punishment before we start again."

In this position he could fondle the base of her bare ass with his fingertips, for the back of the robe was draped over his hands. But as she stared down at him, he didn't.

She walked on her knees, as delicate in her movements as a crane through water. Watching the hem lift above him as she moved toward his head, he felt the wave of trapped heat beneath. He inhaled her a moment before she released the robe and it drifted over his face, closing him into darkness. The soft fabric brushed his jaw, the lines of his shoulders and biceps as she moved along the length of his arms, now like a wild cat gliding slowly over a fallen tree. When she straddled his head, her thighs brushed his temples, the heat of her cunt just above him as she progressed.

He registered wetness on his forearm. Warmth. Arousal she'd left there.

All intentions to obey dissipated. Perhaps she'd do as she'd threatened. Perhaps not. That was her decision. This one was his, and he was going to make it damn hard for her to make hers.

He eased upward so she'd know his action was premeditated and began to lap at her, his tongue making the second sweet contact of the night with those slick lips. He didn't rush, didn't try to devour her in one bite. Didn't want to nip at her like a dog and make her jump away. He teased, stroked, made her hesitate on the point of decision of what to do about his disobedience. Whether to follow her own mandate or decide it was worthwhile to take some time to mull it over.

In this position his chin and lower lip had the best access to her clit and so he rubbed her, letting her feel the rough friction of the trimmed fringe of his beard as he delved deeper with his tongue, using his neck muscles to strain higher. Oh, sweet Jesus in heaven. That was a shudder of response against his mouth. As he clamped his lips more tightly over her, starting to suckle around his thrusting tongue, he nuzzled the tiny puckered entrance to her backside with his nose.

She dug her hand into his chest and the upper part of his abdomen for balance. The imprint of all five fingers seared his skin like a tattoo. She began to rub herself against his mouth, the wet heat of her body lubricating her movements so he felt his cheeks, mouth and chin getting damp. He reveled fiercely in it, her taste. He might have sold his soul to take her just once in the quiet, magical dimness of her bedroom.

She started to move toward his feet again, leaving his face. Turning his head, he bit the inside of her leg gently, trying to hold her through persuasion, but she kept going, the skirt of the garment whispering over his face, a trail of pitch black filled with her scent. Her knees moved over his shoulders, then back to the bed on either side of him. When the robe slipped from his face she'd reached his hips. She turned to face him, swinging her leg over his cock and giving him the incredulous hope she'd impale herself, give him that welcoming glove.

Instead, she seated herself on his stomach and untied the robe, letting it drop off her shoulders and pulling it free so she sat upon him completely naked. His gaze moved over her. His lady. His Mistress. Why it was so easy to think of her that way had to be more than just Thomas's training, and he knew it. While he couldn't explain it, he couldn't deny the swirl of primitive desire taking him over, making him willing to do whatever she wanted to accept him.

As all born vampires were, she was perfect. Not a blemish to her pale skin, no memory evoked by childhood scars. Now he could see what he'd known from tasting the sweetness of her pussy, that she had no silky black hair between her legs to match the God's bounty spilling over her shoulders and down her back.

As he watched, she reached between her legs with both hands and came away with wet fingers. Starting to rock her hips again, she stroked herself against his stomach. Bumped his cock with each undulation of her ass, performing a sinuous dance upon him.

His throat was dry as she arched back, a lithe move to trace her damp fingers along the inside of his right leg and then his left. Her backside pushed his cock down with the crescent angle of her body. She ran her hands along the outside of his calves, then his thighs, marking him with the honey she'd gathered on her hands. In that position, if he could ignore the screaming in his neck, he could look down his body to an unimpeded view of her pussy in its glistening state.

She continued to rock upon him in that relentless, slow-rolling motion, creating friction between them. He groaned as more of her juices made tiny tracks over the petals of flesh. Still arched, she brought one hand back there—holy Christ—penetrated herself, thumb rubbing her clit. Then she stretched almost as far as she'd made him do to paint a circle of her fluids on his ankles, the arches of his feet.

When at last she rose, her pale face was flushed. She sank her fingers into herself again, oiling herself all the way to her top knuckles. Sweeping her hands behind her once more, she gripped his cock. Using her dew to lubricate his shaft, she pressed her buttocks around him, rubbing. Slow, up and down.

"Did you know when cats rub their faces against you, they're marking you with their scent?" she asked.

He didn't have a clue as to the price of a newspaper or who was president. He was hypnotized by the glide of her body. The feel of her ass pressed around his cock, sliding up and down, aided by the response leaking from him. Her upper body tilted up, the small breasts quivering, her glossy hair whispering on her shoulders.

"If I decide to keep you, I'll mark you this way often so other vampires know you're claimed. We have a very keen sense of smell."

She released herself abruptly and leaned down over him, her breast just over his mouth. "Please me, Jacob."

He wanted to bite down like a rabid animal, but somehow he remembered himself enough to close his lips over the nipple with a gentle sucking pressure. His cock was hard and large, sliding along the back of her thigh, so close to her pussy it made him want to groan. He'd never focused on using his tongue so persuasively. Suckling a woman's breast was as much of a complicated art as eating her cunt. If a man could get past his fascination with nipples and only stimulated them when the timing was right, the rewards were great.

So he licked her slowly, methodically, almost like a cat bathing her, and was rewarded by her purr. Catching her fingers in his hair for just a moment, she released him to stretch her arms the length of his bound ones, closing her hands on his wrists below the manacles. He marked *her* now, with the wetness of his mouth on her breast, with the liquid on the tip of his cock, bumping insistently against her buttocks, her thighs.

As the purr became a growl and her movements became more urgent, he began to use his teeth. Now he seized the nipple, bit down, held it with rigid pressure as he flicked it rapidly with his tongue, released it to let the blood rush back into it, then did it again.

Her pussy was slick against his abdomen as she stroked her clit against his cut stomach muscles. Feeling her against him, he couldn't keep himself from fucking the air to communicate how much he wanted to be inside her.

She shifted, pushing the other breast into his mouth. He was even rougher now, nipping, pulling hard as her hip movements became more frenetic. When he heard the incoherent plea in the back of her throat, he knew he was hearing a woman on the edge of losing control. He lashed her with his tongue, strained to reach her with his cock as she moved wildly on him, using his stomach with the singular fierceness of a woman doing laundry on a washboard.

As she began to climax, he snarled his desire against her but kept up his sensual torment on her breast, feeling the hard nipple of the other one brushing the stubble of his cheek and the curve of his ear as she surged forward, humping herself on him with abandon, her thighs spread wide to bring her clit in full contact with his hard stomach, knees sinking into the bed. Her flesh spasmed against him when she cried out, a pure note of pleasure that gripped his cock and made it throb futilely for what she held just out of reach.

She went for a long time. The climax wrung cry after cry out of her, then small harsh moans of aftershocks that kept her shuddering, her head bowed and hair covering her face. The soft strands draped over him like a curtain. Like the climax at the salon, it was the release of a woman who'd denied herself for far too long. As if she'd just been freed from a prison of her own making and had given herself leave to find the type of pleasure in a man's body she hadn't received in quite a while.

There was an emotional component to it, too, in the way she fell over him, her body arched over his face and fingers gripped on his forearms again. When she drew back, pressed her temple into his shoulder, she nestled her cheek into his armpit as if she were getting as close as she could. Close as she could get to having his arms around her.

So when she shifted, trying to match every part of her upper body to the corresponding parts of his, he followed his intuition. When she stretched out her arms far enough to brush his bound hands with her fingers this time, he twined his own with hers, holding them with simple, loose intimacy. Her lashes fanned his skin as she closed her eyes, pressed her temple to his. The searing, almost spiritual pleasure he felt for her was enough to distract him from the agony of the most intense erection he could ever remember having.

At length, the last shudder passed through her. He stayed still beneath her, quivering, his head turned so his breath was on her hair, lips pressing there. Feeling her breasts against the upper part of his chest. While he was in torment, in some odd way he wished they could stay like this forever, knowing he'd brought her pleasure, feeling her quiet joy in lying on top of him.

Untangling herself from his grip with reluctance, Lyssa pushed herself up, pressing her bottom back against his turgid cock. Studying the blue eyes that held so much lust she couldn't quell a hard quiver of response, she ran her fingers with deliberate casualness over the hardened nubs of his nipples, the muscles damp with her climax.

"I did warn you, Jacob," she said softly. "You disobeyed."

"Aren't you glad I did, then?" His voice was husky, so unconsciously sexy in his own desire Lyssa wanted to take him all over again.

"Yes," she said simply. "But you won't be. I'll be back in an hour."

Rising to stand over his naked body, she saw understanding dawn. A surge of fierce temper flooded his expression, goaded by the razor edge of a sexual frustration so high it would exceed even a male wolf's chained near a pack of females, every one of them in heat.

"Before you say a word," she said in an even softer voice, "remember you're here by choice, for the moment. If obeying my commands is too much for you to handle, then I'll free you and let you be on your way. Is that what you want, Jacob?"

She kept her expression unreadable, impassive, while inside her a voice was shrieking at her to relent. *He'll leave, and you want him. You want him worse than you've wanted anything in a while. Damn Thomas.*

If she said that phrase too many times, could it impact where the monk had gone when he crossed over? She was superstitious enough to say a prayer to take it back, though it felt strange to pray in a moment like this, with her body still vibrating with the orgasm, aching for something more fulfilling.

She wanted nothing more than to kiss Jacob's snarling mouth, taste herself on his lips and ride that engorged cock, feel a sense of connection. She'd just relieved a need without giving herself the intimacy she truly craved. He was so angry he obviously didn't trust himself to respond to her question. *Good.* It gave her the excuse to regain her sense, to put some space between them.

"Since you don't know your answer, I'll leave you alone to think about it."

She could use a variety of excuses for the reasons she found herself wanting Jacob. Enforced celibacy, Thomas's knowledge of what attracted her, loneliness for a mate, and perhaps some of all of it held truth. But she knew it was more. When he looked at her, she felt like she'd found something precious she'd be insane to relinquish. Perhaps Thomas had cast a dark spell, something to compel her to take Jacob as her servant. If she hadn't known the monk's devotion to his God so well, she'd have given the idea more merit.

He had picked a man for her who was everything she wanted and nothing she needed. But if she was crazy enough to keep him, he had to learn the basic lesson she was trying to teach him. Otherwise his time in her world would be cut short for reasons far more serious than the loss of a position in her household.

9

JACOB wanted to strangle her. Strangle her then roll her beneath him, feel her trembling body open, trusting him to give her pleasure with his hands on her.

Fuck this. And fuck Thomas for not explaining this better.

But as he thought back, he realized the dying man had indicated that *all* vampires lived by the code of hierarchy established by dominance. Even as their queen, Lyssa had to continually earn the title. Otherwise, she would have become a pawn long ago, political currency trotted out by anyone who could take her and use the value her blood gave her.

When she'd made the decision to marry Rex, sealing a political alliance between the ancient Asian royal house and the more distant remnants of the Western European one, it had been her decision. Jacob was dealing with a woman who'd lived long enough to know exactly what she had to do to protect what was hers. No matter the trappings of culture and civilization with which they surrounded themselves, vampires brought a level of brutality to their personal and public politics that made the machinations of human governments look like schoolyard antics.

He just hadn't understood how deeply that sentiment pervaded vampire society, even into the sanctity of the bedroom. He'd also made the mistake of arrogance, thinking all the long hours with Thomas had prepared him. Those hours had been like kindergarten, the barest concept of what education would require of the student.

He wasn't the type of man who surrendered lightly. He too had a code of honor he'd clung to grimly, even when every other decision in his life had seemed haphazard, no real plan. Many things had made him leave Gideon, but primarily it had been a shadow that had haunted his dreams since sexual awakening. He'd gone into the world to seek it as if he were looking for a grail. Gideon had scoffed at him, told him he'd read too many Irish folktales.

Jacob doubted the nagging feeling himself at times, up until the night he first saw Lady Lyssa. The shadow memory had shattered, drawing him to the actual woman behind it. The feeling had only grown stronger under Thomas's tutelage. Yes, he was a drifter, a dreamer. A man who'd been in search of a hazy sense of destiny for the almost thirty years of his life. But that destiny was her. He was certain of it.

This, though—he glanced up at the manacles, felt the scream of his muscles—hadn't exactly been part of the picture.

Okay. He made himself think past the ache, lingering panic, fury and—holy God—unabated lust. He had a lot to learn about Lyssa's world. But she'd wanted him free there at the end so he could touch her. He'd felt it. He knew it.

He had to earn her trust. Maybe then she'd learn to respect him. Curl up in his arms and fall asleep with ease, knowing he was there to care for her.

That one visual summed it up, a physical gesture of trust meaning so much more. It had the ability to assuage some of the emptiness inside of him, just by imagining it.

Everything else was what he had to learn to get there.

~

He'd have been surprised to know Lyssa did respect him. Enough to think she should boot him out on his handsome ass with the driver she was preparing to meet again.

Mr. Ingram sat at the kitchen island on a stool, yesterday's paper open. The empty plate that had held the eggs Jacob had prepared for him was at his left. As Ingram finished each section of the paper, he'd folded it neatly to his right. She wondered if he was normally that meticulous or if he was trying to stave off panic at being left with no instruction or direction while effectively imprisoned by her wolfhounds. It was the dogs' favorite room regardless, due to its warmth and proximity to food. Bran lifted his head in greeting but didn't move otherwise. The floor appeared littered with long hairy rugs tossed about to land in doglike shapes. The radio had been left on her preferred jazz station, Russ Freeman's stirring melody about a woman with gypsy eyes filling the room.

"Your man was kind enough to leave me a paper. It's kept my mind off my bladder, though I'll admit I was close to using cookware. Your main fellow there likes to show his teeth every time I shift."

"The closest bathroom is down that hall." She nodded. "Please take as long as you wish. Bran, off guard."

The driver jumped when the dogs erupted as if she'd run an electric current through the linoleum. They leaped for the dog door and charged out with repetitious thumps, yips and growls. In less than a moment, they were alone.

He cleared his throat. "I guess they needed to go, too."

"They tend to approach everything with zeal," she said with a tight smile. "Please. Go take your comfort and then I'd like to speak to you. At the very least to thank you for your professionalism. It's been awhile since I've had one man take such care for my well-being, let alone two in the same night."

He nodded, sliding off the stool. From his stiff movements, she suspected he'd hardly dared shift. Apparently his circulation had suffered as his bladder grew more insistent.

"I apologize for causing you discomfort," she added, feeling a pang. "It wasn't my intention."

"Well, that's reassuring." He made his way gingerly toward the hallway. "I'd started thinking my decision to stay and make sure that fellow hadn't kidnapped you had ended up with me being the prisoner."

"Jacob thought I would want to speak to you. I must feel that way, otherwise the dogs wouldn't have kept you." When he turned, meeting her gaze with trepidation in his eyes, she said, "They tend to understand my needs before I do."

"Sounds like the boy's got some of that, too, if he asked me to wait."

When she didn't choose to respond to that, he nodded and disappeared around the corner. Lyssa turned to the bowl of fruit on the counter, picked up an orange and held it, enjoying the feel of the rind, the smell of the juice beneath as she brought it to her nose.

The boy. As if the driver intuited there was a vast difference between their ages, despite the fact she appeared a handful of years younger than Jacob. How would he look when his hair got threads of gray in the reddish brown, turning it silver in certain lights? She imagined the deepening crow's feet enhancing his smiling eyes, the laugh lines around his mouth sculpting into the deeper character lines of a man in his fifties. Inscrutability was necessary for the politics in her life, and everything showed in Jacob's face. Anger, passion, tenderness, concern. All of it at intense and alive high volume. He was too impulsive, too uncensored.

These thoughts might not matter. He could even now be counting the minutes until she released him so he could turn his back on his offer of an oath to her, considering the never-sealed contract dissolved.

No. If Jacob had made an oath to Thomas, he would keep it unless she released him from it. She knew that as well as she knew the slices of orange would glisten like clusters of teardrops when the outer skin was gently removed, every one of them a burst of sensation capable of eliciting a response from her.

"Ma'am?"

She opened her eyes and found the driver in one doorway. Jacob leaned against the other.

She'd left the key on the bed. But the manacles had been drawn taut. Even if he'd managed to get his fingers on the key it would have been impossible for him to position it to open the cuffs. Yet there he stood.

He studied her for a moment, perhaps two. Whatever the driver had intended to say, he held it now, apparently picking up on the tension. Jacob had put his jeans back on, but not the shirt. She'd thought she could read his face, and she did read a variety of emotions there. Simmering anger, frustration, the bite of desire. But mixed together they made something she couldn't interpret, like a language she recognized but didn't understand.

Straightening, he moved toward her. One step. Two. There was a rolling grace to his gait, a trained power. Her gaze traveled over the smooth glide of muscle along his shoulders, his waist, the way his hips moved, drawing her eye to the curve of his groin area demarcated by the thighs she'd felt flex beneath her own not too long ago.

When he reached her, he dropped to one knee, surprising her no small amount. Lifting his hand, he opened it to offer her the key.

"I may not understand the games you feel you must play, my lady. But this is no game to me. I've offered myself willingly to you and will continue to do so."

She didn't look at clocks, for she knew what time of day it was to every minute. The ebb and flow of her life force was dependent on the rising and setting of the sun. So it seemed to her time skipped a beat. She lost a moment or two, just studying the mystery of the man on his knees before her.

"I'll continue to consider it," she said at last. "But you need to think as well. The life you enter with me would be all about games, strategizing to a level of viciousness I suspect your soul is too pure to understand. If you stay with me, it's likely to be corrupted. At worst, mortally wounded. I will be no friend to you. I can be crueler than anything you've ever imagined."

"This makes you different from any other woman, how?" His blue eyes glinted, but he held his firm mouth in a resolute line. "A man who doesn't test the mettle of his soul isn't much of a man, my lady. My offer to serve you stands." His gaze held hers. "I promise I won't make it easy to refuse me."

10

"HMMM." She turned dismissively to look toward the driver. "There's a phone here if there's someone you need to call."

She'd felt his attention shifting between her and Jacob during their exchange. Probably trying to determine which of them was more in need of a mental ward. She sensed a melting pot of reaction from Mr. Ingram, but it was as uncomplicated as a homemade soup. With Jacob, it was a potion of intricate response and intent affecting her with its provocative scent.

"I called my boss on my cell while I was waiting on you. Told him I'd be late, didn't know how long. Gave him the address in case he needed to come reassemble my body from a basement freezer."

He said it matter-of-factly, amusing her again. He was an anachronism—competent, discreet, diplomatic but not insincere. The room was full of anachronisms, and three very disparate ages at that. Fate was an interesting creature.

"I'd like to offer you a job as my full-time driver," she decided. "It would involve a great deal of travel. I move around the southern states quite a bit. The living area and bedrooms down that hallway, where the bathroom is, are quarters for my staff. There are similar accommodations in my other homes.

"I know you don't have family, except a grown son who doesn't deserve to carry your name." He started, but she pressed on. "I'll pay you what you're worth, which is about four times more than your current annual income, and I'll cover whatever expenses you need. Food, gas, et cetera. Your salary will be entirely unencumbered by daily living expenses."

"Sounds like a much better deal than she's offering me," Jacob commented, moving to the center island to take a seat on a stool.

"Him I have a use for." She gave Jacob a deprecating look. "You I intend to chain in the yard and give the scraps the dogs don't want."

"I don't get to sleep at the foot of the bed?"

"The floor, if you're good."

Her words brought that half smile out to play on his lips. When he sat down, he crossed his arms over his bare chest. His knees were splayed, one foot braced on the floor and the other hooked in the rung of the stool. He looked as enticing as first blood from a wound. She wanted to pour herself a glass of her favorite wine and chase her first swallow down with a bite of him.

When she swayed at the power of the feeling, it reminded her that feeding was a decision she needed to make soon. Steadying herself, she didn't think she'd displayed any weakness, but a quick glance showed Jacob's eyes had narrowed. He obviously had an exceptional attention to details. Usually a blessing in a servant, but a curse at the moment.

"What do you think, Mr. Ingram?" she said.

The driver came a step closer at her gesture, but kept the island between them. "I'm not sure if my soul is as strong as the boy's," he said carefully. "You want more than a driver, that's the way it seems to me. It wouldn't be fair to commit to a job and then back out, so I need to know what it is I'm really dealing with."

She understood clearly the "what" was referring to her.

"I'm a vampire," she said simply. "You may not believe that. You may decide I'm a mentally unstable person and make your polite though hasty farewells. But you asked for honesty." She inclined her head. "I have enemies. Many. Which is why I take so many precautions on my property and when I go beyond its boundaries. As long as I appear ready for them, it's unlikely they'll ever attack. They wait for the moment of weakness only. It is the way of our world. My enemies also rarely target staff unless staff members get between them and me. I'll never ask you to do that."

"That's gracious, ma'am. But I'm not a coward. I'm also not so easy to kill." His dark eyes glittered.

"I don't doubt your courage, but they'd kill you with as much effort as swatting a fly and it wouldn't even slow them down on their way to me," she said bluntly. "Good staff is hard for a vampire to find, so we don't sacrifice them frivolously. It's not unheard of for a vampire to slay another and then promptly turn around and offer the dead vampire's staff positions in his own household. After all, you've already worked for one, what's the difference in working for another?" She lifted her shoulder in a casual shrug. "Though I admit, some of them wouldn't give you a choice. There is some danger involved."

The black man removed his cap, scratched his head. There was gray in the close-cropped cotton of his hair. "I suspect a person in your circumstances has to break a few laws to live under the radar. So what I need to know, ma'am, is if you dishonor what I consider one of the more important Commandments. Do you kill?"

At her ironic look, he set his jaw. "I've broken it myself, when I served. Even had to do it once or twice in this job. I know it's not something a person should break lightly, which is why I'm asking."

Lyssa pursed her lips. "An extraordinarily honest question. Are you asking to give yourself time to think your way out of a crazy woman's house? Because if that's the case, the door is there. Neither I nor my dogs will keep you from leaving, and I'll wish you no ill will."

Ingram glanced at the door, then at Jacob.

"He's not yet bound to my service," she said in an even tone. "He's also still free to go. If I decide to keep him, I'm sure I'll regret him for the nuisance he is."

Jacob wisely chose not to comment on that. Ingram cleared his throat, met her gaze squarely. "I knew when you got into my car tonight you weren't human, ma'am. I got a sense for it. You're not the first of your kind I've driven."

That was a surprise. "Indeed. Yet you drove me. Most wouldn't after recognizing it."

"I thought about driving away. But when I say I'll do a job, I do it. Never left anybody who paid my boss for a ride without one."

They studied each other for a few minutes in silence. The night was waning. Lyssa wanted to go to bed. She rarely let physical factors impair her judgment, but it was possible this was one of those infrequent times. She'd made several very impetuous decisions tonight. However, seeing Elijah Ingram's large hands turning his cap in that methodical way as if it represented the cog of his mind, she knew her intuition was sound. She just needed to speed up the interview process and hope the loss of finesse wouldn't lose her the possibility of his service.

"All right then." Perching on the stool at the end of the counter, she took the seat directly across from him. "When I have a human servant, I take blood from him. If he maintains his health and diet adequately, that sustains me and I don't crave additional blood. If I'm somewhere he's not and I need it, I can seduce and temporarily command the mind of a person to draw blood from him. Not in a lethal dose. We prefer to know the history of our donors, though, so that's usually an unexpected event."

She paused, her glance shifting between the two of them. "Once annually, in order to retain my full strength, I have to take a healthy adult in the prime of his life and drain him dry. I take his life," she added quietly, so there was no misunderstanding. "He has to be a good person, not the dregs of society. Blood infected with evil impacts a vampire . . . negatively."

"Draining him doesn't make him a vampire?"

The question came from Mr. Ingram, because of course Jacob would know all this. However, she saw the forced strain around his mouth, the sharp focus of his eyes. He might know it, but it didn't make hearing it any easier. And she wouldn't dress it up for either of them.

She shook her head. "You do have to drain the body to do that, but to convert a human requires a special secretion from the fangs. You have to prep the person with three different marks, like a servant, and make them drink from the sire first as well."

"You always take a man? For your kill, I mean."

She rolled it over a moment. His generation held to certain moral tenets that he would never dismiss no matter his own circumstances. That suggested not only what motivated the question, but the proper answer for it.

"Always a man. Never a woman. Absolutely never a child."

She didn't add she chose a healthy male because she was a female vampire. As such, the taste of a male was just preferred. Sweeter to her palate.

From Jacob's expression, she saw he understood the nuances in her response in a way Mr. Ingram would not. He wasn't pleased with the revelation. She decided to ignore the ridiculous twinge of lust his possessive reaction sent through her vitals. Obviously a lingering side effect of her medicine.

"I try to pick a person with few ties, but that's not easy when you're seeking a person of integrity. When I go on the hunt, my driver and servant—for it's best to have both to do this though not completely necessary—help me with transportation and disposal of the body."

Had Jacob truly understood what would be required of him during her annual kill? Or like the requirement of sexual submission, had the significance been lost on him because it was so far from what he knew the world to be? If he'd truly hunted vampires, he wouldn't be completely naive about her kind. But she wondered.

Drawing herself up straight in the chair, she spoke unapologetically. "If I don't do this once a year, I weaken. Within ten years I'd become a living corpse, even with regular feedings. It's a form of what you would think of as rigor mortis. Unable to move, I'd suffer an eternity of starvation. It's likely from that state some of the myths about our being dead have sprung. A human, stumbling upon a vampire in that condition, gets too close and the vampire is just strong enough to grab hold and restore some of his vitality by draining him. But he will have lost some of his faculties from the deprivation, and control of his bloodlust will be much harder. Human blood in a terminal quantity from a living donor once a year is the only thing that prevents imbalance in our constitution."

"Are there those who do it more than once a year?"

Apparently, Elijah had kept his wits about him enough to catch the subtle notes of what wasn't being said as well as what was. "Yes." Lyssa nodded. "For the pleasure of it. For the added strength they perceive it gives them, like taking an overdose of vitamins. But I am not one of those vampires."

There was a cap on the number of humans that could be killed by a single vampire in the course of a year. The number was higher than she liked, but she was not Council and her influence had kept the quantity lower than initially proposed. She'd had to be satisfied with that.

Ingram swallowed. His jaw flexed. "The explanation's appreciated. I understand from your way of thinking you're just treating that one person the way I have to treat my dinner. But when you're the same as that dinner, it's different."

"We may be human in appearance, but vampires are a different species. We exist and thrive in very different environments. There are many mysteries we don't understand about one another."

Her voice was becoming more flat, her body language minimal. Feeling Jacob's close regard again, Lyssa knew she was showing her weariness. While she didn't have to retire at the first glimpse of the sun, this evening, including her fainting episode, had drained her. She'd done her best for now. If they wanted to leave, well, that would be fine. But even as she had the thought, her gaze drifted back to Jacob, his bare shoulders and firm mouth. When a pang of yearning clenched a cold fist in her belly, she had to push it away with a surge of effort.

"That's my philosophy on it," she continued. "But it's not shared by all my kind. Many view you as tools, fodder for entertainment, food, experiments. The same as many of you view other species. Not equals in any sense, not deserving of any rights we haven't given you. Beings who have the simple misfortune of being treated as a product instead of a sentient being with its own right of existence."

She lifted a shoulder. "It's an understandable deduction. For the most part, the weakest of us is superior to you in strength and longevity. Most of us that live to one hundred years outstrip your experiential intelligence, because if we don't, we don't live to see two hundred."

"So you don't agree with that viewpoint?" This from Jacob, his mind working over her words so hard she could see it in his expression.

"Yes. And no." She leaned back in the chair. "I'm a predator, Jacob, and humans are my prey. I'll never view them in a way comfortable to you or your kind. But like the hunter who's finally learned to respect the stag enough to kill few and far between, and only when necessary for food, I've learned there's far more to you. An essence whose value is separate from my needs. However, while a human may sit down to a burger, despite the fact there's a salad bar nearby with enough lower food chain nutrition to fully sustain him, for a vampire there is no salad bar. There is only human blood."

Time ticked away for a quarter of a moment as she waited. Jacob picked up Ingram's keys from the counter as the driver at last raised his gaze, meeting hers with visible effort. "I'll think about it awhile, but if you're . . . interviewing elsewhere, I'll tell you it's likely I'll say no. There are just some things it's hard for a human to do. It's hard to watch a cat catch a mouse and not help the mouse, isn't it? I could maybe drive you around while you're here, for your manicures and errands. I'd have to think about that, too. I'm just not sure I'm your man for the rest."

"I understand. I appreciate your honesty, more than you realize." Rising, she came around the counter and extended her hand. "Thank you for considering it."

He hesitated. When she began to lower her hand, her gaze frosting, he surprised her by reaching out, albeit awkwardly. A light shake, the way a big man tended to handle a woman's fingers. It almost made her smile, though his honest words had stung. Not because she was ashamed of what she did to survive, but because she liked him.

"I'm finding it hard to believe you're letting me go so easy after telling me all that."

"Well, again, Mr. Ingram, who would believe you? But there's another reason." She withdrew her hand. "No one serves me except by choice."

She shifted her attention to Jacob so he would not miss the warning note in her voice. "Once the choice is made, I become far more territorial."

11

Jacob remained in the kitchen while she escorted Mr. Ingram to his limo. He wasn't sure what to make of all the images she'd put in his head, all the feelings she'd stirred in him in less than one night's time. Whether it was emotional overload or something else he didn't know, but he realized he needed to shut the tornado of thoughts down. Put them in a room where they might work out to some kind of sense next time he opened the door to look at them.

So he took an orange out of the fruit bowl and began to roll it across the table top between his callused palms. Back, forth. Back, forth. A simple mind-clearing exercise ironically taught to him by Gideon to help him fight vampires, to combat their overwhelming physical and mental presence.

When she returned, he was still doing it. As he lifted his head, he saw she was looking at his wrists, which still bore the light imprint of the manacles. She wet her dry lips, making something tighten in his chest. But he watched her, waiting for her to make the next move. Trying to hold on to a sense of calm.

She moved around the island. "How did you get free?"

"If I tell you that, my lady, you'll know all my secrets. I won't be able to employ the same tactic to get free again."

She stopped, a foot between them. Shifting on the stool so he faced her, he released the orange and laid one arm on the counter, his other hand braced on his thigh in an open, casual pose he was sure she knew was deceptive. A bowstring drawn as taut as he was could send an arrow to the moon.

"So does it get you off, playing the all-powerful Oz?" he asked.

Placing her hand on one of his knees, she exerted pressure until he widened the space between them. She moved in, her gaze on his face. "Is that what you think? That this is about ego?"

"It's got to be, in one form or another. You want me to hand mine to you on a platter."

"I want you to let go of it, so it doesn't stand between me and the rooms of your soul." She blinked. Once. "There's a pleasure in that, I'll not deny it. But there's more to it." When she cupped his jaw, Jacob couldn't help the tension in his neck, resisting the movement. "If you don't learn how to be submissive, Jacob, you won't survive in my world. It's not complicated to understand. The only thing complicated, the only thing to solve, is your refusal to accept it even after all your training with Thomas."

As Jacob had watched her conduct her macabre discussion with the driver, he'd noted there was an eerie stillness to her which became more pronounced as dawn approached. She didn't even shift when she spoke now, no facial expressions. As if the closer it came for her to take her rest, the less effort she put into maintaining human characteristics. Ironically it underscored the point she'd been trying to make about the difference in their status, from a vampire's perspective. An explanation echoing in his mind now.

But as he gazed at her, fighting his simmering irritation, something raw and painful surfaced in her expression, a sudden flash of anguish too powerful for her to contain. It was a stark contrast with the blankness of her features, like a slash of red paint against a white canvas. "I can't bear to lose another human servant," she said. "Do you understand that?"

Jacob blanketed her fingers with his own without hesitation then, his heart easing. "I know, my lady. But obedience is no guarantee. Thomas was far more obedient than I'll ever be, I'm sure. In the end, he defied your rules. He loved you enough to know when it was time not to obey anymore."

"So he's dead," she said flatly. "Exactly my point. He didn't need to be. Your life will depend on your absolute obedience to my will. Do you at least understand that?"

"I understand you think so." He sobered at her frustrated expression. "I told you I offer myself willingly, my lady. If you'll be patient with me, this isn't something I'm used to. Being told to—"

"Trust without question? When your mind and heart are shrieking at you to do something different from what I'm telling you to do?"

There was no arguing with the truth. He inclined his head, mouth tight. "I'm not intending disrespect, Lady Lyssa. In my own defense, you're not telling me everything going on here. Things I think Thomas didn't know about you."

"You want too much, too fast. Do you think I don't understand? This would be difficult for most people, but for a man like you it's almost impossible." She leaned in, breath touching his face as she spoke. "I've been alive long enough to see every form of foolish bravery and abject cowardice, Jacob. True submission is not only the most courageous act a person can commit to another, it's an act of faith. Of trust. After only a few hours together, you laid yourself on my bed and let me chain you. That intrigued me."

She softened somewhat, though she drew her hand away from his. "I make no apologies for anything I demand. I require the type of devotion most people think only God should be given." At his startled look, she allowed herself a tight smile. "God's definition of submission is far more merciful than mine. I want to keep you alive. God has less concern about which side of the Curtain his creations are on.

"Don't touch me," she said as he began to reach for her again. Jacob's jaw hardened, his eyes flashing, but he obeyed, surprising her. Tilting her head, Lyssa pursed her lips, blew a soft line of air down the column of his neck and watched the reaction shiver through him. "Try to offer me everything. Don't move until I give you permission."

She heard his breath catch in his throat as he apparently made a conscious effort to breathe deeply, relax. Slowly his fingers opened as his eyes closed and he gave up his other senses to the moment, stirring her.

Cradling his jaw still, she used her thumb now to ease his head to the right so she had a clear path to her goal. Dropping her other hand, she cupped him, her fingers curving under the round shape of his testicles, the heel of her hand pressing against his hardening cock.

She didn't have to do it this way, but she wanted to make him understand what power she could and would wield over him.

Exposing her fangs, she aligned them with the artery she wanted in his throat and applied pressure. Harder, harder, until she felt the skin give way and his body tighten with reaction to the pain. Warm blood, warm heat, flooded her mouth. Sustenance. She made a sound of pleasure, kneading him with her other hand. Releasing the aphrodisiac through her fangs, she ensured his pain would mix with something worth the discomfort.

Within seconds his fist was clenched on the counter, his cock leaping full and huge against her touch. He began to push helplessly against her as she locked her grip around his shoulders, holding him. Fifteen seconds later she heard his incredulous, guttural curse against her ear, felt his futile resistance and the vibration of his harsh groan as his seed spilled, dampening his jeans against her hand. The orgasm ripped through him like lightning. He was obviously struggling not to lift his hands as she'd commanded, but suddenly she wanted him to do so.

"Touch me," she whispered. The words were garbled with her fangs still in him, her tongue lapping at his skin, nourishing her with the flow of his blood. He heard her, though.

She'd expected him to grip her about the waist or hips, the clumsy gropings of a man in the throes of one dying climax, already starting to climb the hill to the second she would give him.

He did put his hands on her waist, fingers digging into her hips, but only to anchor her to him as he surged up from the stool and turned them. As she wrapped her legs around his waist, bringing her wet heat against damp denim, the robe fell down her bare legs, exposing her hips. He slammed her down on the wood counter of the island, his hands sliding to her thighs, pushing the robe even further out of his way to grasp flesh. She kept one arm around his shoulders, the other hand on the side of his neck, holding him as she drank, laving him with her tongue. Tearing away her panties, he got his hands between them to unfasten his jeans and shove them out of the way.

She could have stopped him, cut his legs right out from under him, literally or figuratively, but she wanted to feel him inside her as she drew in his blood and let it sustain her.

When she felt the tip of him rub over her clit, his minute hesitation at the moment of irrevocable decision, she clamped her thighs over his buttocks and drove him into her. She almost wished she wasn't so wet so his entry would have been rougher, for she wanted to feel every incremental push forward. However, despite his impressive size he sank deep and fast through her slickness.

It had been so long, he stretched her to the point of pain. She welcomed it, arching into his body.

His palms slapped down on either side of her head on the countertop to keep his balance. He didn't know he didn't need his balance. She had him. She wouldn't let him fall.

With the clamp of her limbs, fingers and fangs upon him, she would make sure he had bruises on his thighs and neck. While she slept the day away, he would finger those places and think of her, the visible claims she'd put on him. The first of many.

She'd never desired to bond with someone so quickly. Perhaps it was her prolonged self-enforced loneliness. Perhaps Thomas had known her needs too well. Perhaps the Three Fates had intervened because they delighted in driving Lyssa to distraction. Any reason was less disturbing than this incomprehensible need to be so immediately close to him that she wanted to meld their souls.

Regardless, the moment Jacob was buried deep within her, sensation exploded throughout her body. The blood in her mouth grew sweeter, more vibrant. She took a hard pull instead of a sip, rewarded with a groan from Jacob as he reacted to the flood of erotic sensation it sparked. His cock was hard as a ramrod inside her but blissfully much thicker.

She stroked, pumping her hips as she stimulated her pussy with it, again and again, using the hold of her legs to use him as she desired, up and down. Stroke, stroke, that wonderful ridged head deep inside and the heavy weight of his testicles bumping the tender base of her ass outside as she tongued his neck, tasted his blood and felt the pure pleasure of possession. Perhaps even in a small, safe way, the feeling of being possessed herself, the feel of a man's weight pressing her down.

The orgasm surprised her, for it had been a long while since she'd had one during sex with a human, no matter the stimulation. Too often, when she was nourishing herself from a stranger, she didn't want to feel the emotional emptiness accompanying a physical climax. Unprepared for the violence of the unexpected release, she increased the force of her bite, driving her fangs in deeper.

As if her soul suddenly had an agenda all its own that disregarded the shrieking warning from her mind, she obeyed its desire and released the precious drops of venom of the first mark into him. It coursed through a human's veins like a lick of flame. Instead of crying out from the searing pain, Jacob growled in response, lifted one hand from the table and cupped the back of her head. From his reaction it was obvious he knew what she had done. Exultation filled her at his obvious fierce pleasure in her decision.

He held her there, supporting her neck and skull with his large palm. The muscles of his other arm strained as he bore his weight and the movement of hers, helping him rock against her tight clasp of his body just above the hips. With a primal male sound, he came again, the heat of him filling her, making her moan against his throat. It was an agonizingly sweet pleasure, the sensation of blood and seed entering her from different points.

Even as the orgasm went from powerful waves to pleasurable ripples, slowing her movements, it took some time for her fangs to retract. He also rocked to stillness upon her reluctantly, but he was obviously spent as she drew out the feeding, enjoying the pleasure of nourishing herself with a willing lover. His body quivered with a shuddering aftermath, making her convulse with aftershocks. When at last she pulled out, she licked the wounds, holding pressure there with her lips as she put her forehead to his jaw, his mouth.

Neither of them spoke or moved for some time. Lyssa wondered at the feeling of quiet communion. As she finally laid her head back and he raised his, their eyes met, but she couldn't think of anything to say. The significance of the moment could not be denied.

On a surge of pure impulsiveness, she'd given him the first mark. The first step toward making him hers forever.

12

SHE pushed against him. As he straightened, he took her with him so she sat on the counter's surface and he stood between her spread thighs. Gripping her hips to slide her forward, he effectively kept them joined and changed the angle, rubbing against the dense spot inside that female vampires and humans shared as a pleasure spot. When she arched in response, he took advantage of that, taking a firmer hold on one buttock, his fingers teasing in the cleft beneath her robe.

"Enough," she said softly. She didn't shove him away, she wouldn't be that cruel, but she wanted to be certain he understood. No matter the intensity of the moment, she didn't stop being his Mistress.

Jacob met her gaze. Removing her fingers from his throat, she saw she'd done a good job. All sorts of dark feelings of pleasure ran through her at the two swollen marks there. "Your hands by your sides."

Slowly, with great visible reluctance, he withdrew his touch, resting his hands alongside his thighs. When he started to pull up his jeans, she shook her head. Reaching down between her still spread thighs, she gripped him, caressed his wet testicles and brushed the hot sticky skin between their heavy weight and the musky dampness on his thigh. "If I choose to give it, my next mark will be here. I'll command you to spread yourself, hold yourself open to me. Without restraints, you'll have to remain still and trust my fangs will find your thigh and not other tempting areas. But now it's almost dawn. I want you close. Get dressed and follow me."

She set the house alarms before she took him back to her room. He watched carefully. The majordomo duties of a servant were extensive, particularly for a vampire with a Region like hers. From his close attention, she was reassured that Thomas had prepared him adequately for that, at least.

When she led him through the house and stepped back over the threshold of her bedroom, she realized it might be a mistake to bring him here instead of to a guest bedroom. The nested intimacy of the room, the rumpled covers, the lingering scent of what had been done here earlier, distracted her. As did the manacles still on the bed, tossed there when he'd freed himself.

She spoke the chant of opening and the wood floor shimmered. The colors of the Persian rug melted, buckling and evolving into the shape of a flight of stairs disappearing into the darkness of a lower chamber.

Jacob studied it, his brows raised. "I don't remember this in the catalog of vampire powers."

"There's much you don't know. You'll join me below. When I rise, we'll speak about your interim duties."

"You intend to test me. Again."

"Yes." She glanced at him without apology. "Thomas's endorsement means a great deal, but I must be fully convinced. Perhaps you'll flaunt this test as you did my last one. Or perhaps you'll suffer it despite your tricks. Spend the time thinking about who I am and what I want from you. Perhaps by tomorrow night, you'll decide you want your freedom and that will be the end of it."

"Or not, and it will be the beginning of something else. Perhaps you'll learn to trust me, my lady. Not every man who desires your soul for his own wants it for the power, or to delight in your pain. There are some who want only the honor of caring for you. Of being called your champion. Your protector."

Her heart tightened into a defensive fist, his words digging into the tender area like nails.

"My protector." Touching a hand to her brow absently, she smoothed her own skin, the tendrils of her hair he'd loosened brushing her knuckles. The sun was rising. Weariness closed around her like a trap. At one time she could stay up well past sunrise in the quiet darkness of this upper bedroom. She'd watch the sliver of light glitter between the frugal gap in the curtains. Sitting a foot away from where it laid its bright line on the floor, making the threads of the rug glitter, she'd read. Or think. Or simply be.

Even as she relearned how to breathe air that did not contain either the threat or the promise of Rex, she remembered the longing that came with his gentle touch on her neck when she dozed. Lonely versus alone. Rex represented both emotions. When she was tired, it could tear her apart anew to remember.

I always had the power, Thomas. You didn't understand that until the end, did you? I ripped out his heart as easily as I'd crush a peach in my hand. But it was too late for you then. Knowledge of my strength provided you nothing, used too late. That's why I must be cruel, make Jacob understand, even when my strength is not what it once was.

"Follow me or not. It's your choice." She started down the stairs. "If it were me, I'd go home."

He followed.

The bedroom in the hidden room was almost a mirror image of the one above. She wanted to feel she was in her room, not in a pretend chamber, regardless of which one she used. This one had more space, however, for times when she might need or decide to remain out of sight indefinitely. A sitting area and a library were here. There was also an eye-catching centerpiece. A St. Andrew's cross carved of teakwood, the grain smooth as a woman's silken thighs or the velvet shaft of a man's erect cock.

She ran her hand down one of the arms, then exerted pressure. The hinges were well oiled, so it lowered smoothly from an upright to a horizontal position.

"Take off all your clothes. There's a bathroom over there. You'll be restrained on this until I wake, about ten hours from now, so I encourage you to make use of it."

She didn't look toward him, but she could feel the conflict vibrating off him.

"Jacob." One quiet word, but she infused it with everything. Not only command, but the threat of taking away what he said he wanted. Perhaps she could have injected a hint of reassurance, but in this room particularly she remembered who and what she was, and her voice chilled accordingly.

"My patience is thin as the skin covering all your pleasing muscles and just as easily stripped away. I don't want to hear a word from you right now. The stairs are there. If you walk up them, the door will open and Bran will make sure you're escorted off the grounds. You won't be issued an invitation to return."

Moving to the armoire, she began to slide off her own clothes as she heard him go into the bathroom and close the door. Probably to stare at himself in the superfluous mirror and question whether he'd lost his mind.

At least you have a physical reflection, she thought. The mental one can be so much more frightening.

~

He was losing his mind. Jacob yanked off his clothes, folded them on top of the commode and looked at himself in the mirror. Something felt off about this whole scenario, as if there were huge pieces of the puzzle missing, a whole script he'd only been given a portion of to read before rehearsal. Access to this chamber, for example. No vampire he'd ever heard of had telekinetic attributes, let alone the ability to transfigure floor and carpet into a stairwell. It wasn't illusion. He'd walked over that exact portion of floor earlier and felt and seen nothing to indicate a chamber below the surface.

She was determined to force him to submit to her on a lot of levels, and sexually was the least of them. He wasn't stupid. As she herself had implied, he knew that was just the gateway to the deeper layers of himself. Perhaps if he knew she would eventually give him some answers, he'd feel a little less nervous about walking back out there, but she hadn't offered that bone. She was making him follow on faith. His head had never been so messed up, and all the things he knew about vampires were taunting his mind, making his gut clutch.

Do you realize, mortal, I could rip you limb from limb. . . .

With a curse, he turned away from his image in the mirror and opened the door. Fuck it. Gideon always said he was fatally impetuous. He might just prove him right.

She'd raised the cross upright again and was leaning against it, wearing a nightgown of sheer black lace, nothing under it from low neckline to midthigh. He saw her nipples, the folds of her sex, all of her curves and the slender shapes of her thighs defined in the provocative pose. As he watched, she threaded her hands through the adjustable cuffs and held onto them as if bound there.

When she slid her feet into the loosened ankle cuffs like slippers, she gripped the hand cuffs to raise and balance herself for the maneuver. As she held most of her weight that way, her legs spread and hip cocked at a defiant angle, he was dry mouthed just looking at her. Even contemplating what was ahead, his cock couldn't help but be semi-erect. At the sight of this it rose to full mast, flooded with immediate, gut-wrenching lust as she licked her lips, showing him tiny fangs. It made a throb of reaction go through his neck, just below where she'd bitten him, and heat sear straight to his groin. Her dark hair hung loose, reaching almost to her waist, blending with the black lace like a silk curtain over a teasing transparent panel.

"Come to me."

He knew all about the way a fly would blunder into the glistening strands of a spider's web. Though her position was one of self-restraint, the sensual splaying of her arms and legs and the way she watched him approach told him he was looking at a predator. No question on who was prey in this room.

Nevertheless, he came forward, the heat of her gaze twining around him like the sticky strands of a web in truth.

A man who doesn't test the mettle of his soul isn't much of a man. . . .

His hunger rose even further as he reached her and she didn't free herself. Instead, as he leaned in, putting his hands on her hips, the flesh separated from him only by thin lace, she strained toward him as if bound in truth. "Touch me. Please. Tease me as you would if I were your prisoner, yours to torment."

He went on instinct. Sliding his arm around her waist, he splayed a hand between the wood and her body, gripping her ass to rub her against him, pushing her forward further against her restraints as he nudged her face to the side and used his teeth to mark her shoulder, right at the juncture of her throat. He clamped down much harder than he'd done it before.

She gasped, shuddered. In his peripheral vision he saw her eyes widen in shock. She strained against the bonds, pressing her breasts into his bare chest. He brought his other hand up to squeeze her there as he would if he were fulfilling his own desires only, using her body to slake his lust. The ripple of reaction got even more violent. When she dropped her head back on her shoulders, he moved from his bite to suckling her throat, tonguing the narrow valley at her collarbone while she quivered. Dropping one hand, he cupped her through the gown, found her hot and soaking.

"You're wet for me, my lady." He stared into her dark, fathomless eyes. The pupil had all but swallowed the green, so it was just a ring of glowing emerald. "Your pussy wants me again."

Her lips parted at the crude talk. He noticed she didn't take as much care to hide her fangs when she was aroused. That reddish tint was back in her eyes, and there was a tautness to her features hinting at some other face he'd yet to see. As if he were seeing brief glimpses of a different being, a metamorphosis, here and then gone.

"It makes you hard, having me this way, does it?" Her voice was a breathless whisper. When she moved her body urgently against him, he curled his fingers in the gown, holding her still with a touch on her spread thighs as he guided his tip to her to rub her clit with slow, small movements. She went still and trembling, as if feeling the intensity of it.

"Yes," he said low. "It makes me want to fuck you until you can't walk. I want to hear you scream my name, my lady."

"Then you understand the power of it," she said in that same whisper. "Having something you want so much as your willing captive." She closed her eyes and rocked against him. The feeling was too much. He backed off, intending to ruck up her skirt, find her beneath it and feel the sweet honey of her pussy run over his cock again, smell it in his nostrils.

Instead he was spun in a circle, a flash of black disorienting him as his body was bumped, turned so fast he stumbled and couldn't get his bearings. She was moving around him, gripping an arm, an elbow, his hip, making him dizzy like a child twirled to stagger after a piñata.

Only she wasn't intending him to chase after anything. He was thrust backward against the St. Andrew's cross and his feet swept from beneath him as he and the cross were taken to a horizontal position. His wrists and ankles yanked apart, spread and cuffed. Not held loosely as she'd done it to herself. In no more than a few blinks, while his head was still off balance, she had his limbs buckled down tightly, no keys this time, adjusted so he was stretched out in the *X*-shape, fully extended as she'd done on the bed. Then she brought him upright again, the world tilting, his stomach dropping.

"It's even more pleasurable when that can be done slow. When a Mistress makes her slave stand still, watch her thread each strap, tighten it. Make him feel his loss of freedom an increment at a time, his lust growing and stirring her own. But for your first time we'll do it a bit differently."

He managed to focus on her, just in front of and below him. With that inscrutable gaze in place again and no further conversation, she sank down and put her mouth on his cock, letting her fangs scrape him.

He reacted violently, throwing back his head so it rapped against the wood hard, but he barely felt it.

Her location shot his mind to the thought of where she'd said she'd put the second mark. Each of the marks had a serious functional purpose. The first mark was a tracking mechanism, allowing her to know his whereabouts at any time. So while at the time he'd felt triumph at her decision to give the first mark, he now understood it was the least impulsive of the marks to give, because it safeguarded her against betrayal. The next mark would link their minds, allowing her to speak to him without words. Even more significantly, it allowed her to tap into his thoughts whether he wanted her to do so or not. From the past few hours, Jacob was beginning to think it was that mark he needed to be most apprehensive about, despite the ominous significance of the third. The final mark linked him to her immortality, prolonging his life three or four times its normal span. However, as with the other marks, it came with a darker side. Much darker. If she was killed, he died as well.

He'd asked if the first and second marks were two-way. Thomas's cryptic reply had been, "when she allows it." He'd told Jacob she could block his awareness of her whenever she chose to do so. In short, the marks tilted the scales all her way.

But perhaps there might come a time when he would know her mind, her heart, whether she willed it or not. When she would let her defenses down for him. The thought helped steady him.

Nothing else did. Her tongue teased the underside of his cock, licking as she nuzzled his balls. She didn't go fully down on it, though he ached to feel the sucking pressure of that petite, perfect mouth. She rose, her gaze heavy lidded, lips moist.

"You have a nice taste. You've no idea how it feels to me to see you restrained, going to bed knowing your cock will ache and leak for me, your dreams full of me . . ."

Turning away, she went to the armoire and opened it. Sliding open a narrow drawer, she trailed a finger through the contents. He heard clinking sounds like metal.

When she turned she had something in her hand that looked like the double-looped wire harness put on the neck of a bottle of wine to hold the cork securely. It had three circles in progressive sizes. The widest one was made of chain and threaded with pewter beads. The middle circle was a silver cuff, and the smallest of the loops had a decorative convex cap made of bronze. On the concave side of the cap there was a two-inch-long thin rod of surgical steel, slightly wider than pencil lead, except it flared to a bulb-shaped end similar to a Q-tip.

When she opened the door of a small cabinet in the armoire, a dim light activated within it, apparently to help her see the array of glass bottles. His lady seemed to have a penchant for stained glass in her home.

A home he assumed was still above them, unless she'd distorted space and time so they were in a bubble somewhere, floating in the universe beyond the range of help or anything he'd ever known. A man began to have some desperate and strange thoughts when bound so he couldn't move.

13

PUTTING down the object she'd retrieved from the drawer, she picked up a bottle and poured a thick clear gel in her hand. When she used it on the small piece of jewelry, he began to understand, enough to be very concerned about that two-inch slender rod under the concave cap.

She came back to him then, her nipples dark smudges, her breasts quivering erotically with her movements under the stretched hold of the lace, her sex taunting him. As she moved, she unlatched the three loops, her fingers glistening with the oil.

"Your lack of piercings didn't surprise me, but the lack of tattoos did." She cocked her head. "It's rare to see a completely unmarked man your age. Why is that?"

He pulled his attention away from the thing she was treating as jewelry and he was viewing as a potential torture device. From the slight smile on her lips, he suspected she recognized his struggle to focus.

"My brother always said if you mark your body with a symbol, it means you stand by it forever. Only things branded on the soul can be branded on the body. So far I've found the only constant is that everything changes."

"You always have yourself."

He managed a half smile, even as his body tensed when she reached for him. "It seems *you* have me now."

"I do," she agreed. "This rod," her finger caressed it, "is no wider than your opening, actually a bit smaller, and it's going no further than the length of my smallest finger. There are ways to relax the opening if you focus, take deep breaths. Just let it slide in."

He nodded, but kept his eyes on her face. Her hands gripped him, a cool, slick feeling evoking a moment of panic he could do nothing about. She outlined the tiny slit at the tip of his cock with the rod. "Did you know this opening is called the meatus? Do you think that's why women think of men's penises as pieces of meat?"

He took a breath, then another.

"I won't hurt you, Jacob. Not past bearing. Trust me, Sir Vagabond. Let go."

He tried. It was startling, invasive and therefore uncomfortable, but she eased it in with gentle fingers. The metal bar was as smooth as the arms of the cross beneath his body. She used her thumb to position the cap on the head of his cock, like pushing in the head of a tack. Then she ran the chains along his outside length. The quiet *snick* of the broader cuff of the second loop made him jump as she fastened it snugly just behind the ridge of his head. When the third chain loop cinched around the base of his cock and scrotum, his balls drew up at the unusual feeling of restraint. Brushing against his thighs, the extra chain dangled down beneath them, adding weight to the sensation because of the beads added there for that purpose.

"Look down now," she commanded softly.

When he did, he saw her hands playing with his now well-lubricated cock. He'd lost some of his arousal to trepidation, but her touch and the intense look in her eyes, reflecting her great pleasure in adorning him, made it strain back against the chains, causing pinching. Not unbearably painful, but apprehensively close. She'd made it tight enough to hold him if he wasn't erect, so increasing the size increased the feeling of binding. The discomfort reminded him he was hers, as he was sure she intended.

The bronze disk with a pewter inlay was centered at the tip of his cock, anchored there by the slender rod inserted inside him. A pinwheel of chains ran from it to the silver cuff she'd clasped behind the flare of his head. The longer chains running down his cock to the base and his scrotum were interspersed with uncut gems that dug into his shaft. He was going to pass a difficult day waiting for her to wake.

"You're beautiful." She said it softly, barely a breath of sound. She sank to her knees and considered him from eye level, coming close to run her tongue just under the cap, touching his invaded slit.

Jacob groaned, a primitive wave of response rolling through his body. He winced as the hold of the jewelry tightened further. But he couldn't stop himself. Oh, holy Jesus . . . she was lapping, nipping at him, her oiled hands stroking over him, squeezing his balls, fingering at his ass though he reflexively clenched there. Her oiled finger and the nail stabbed at him, wriggled, got past the tight muscles of his buttocks to play around the rim.

"Lady . . . Mercy." He had no idea what coming with that rod inside him would do, but he'd never been so aroused and uncomfortable at once. Over all of that, the greatest ache came from the coil of need in his lower belly, which made him want to bury himself in her willing cunt as he had earlier. If the past several hours were what daily life with her would be like, he suspected she'd kill him long before they ever got to the second mark, let alone the third.

"Do I strike you as a merciful creature, Jacob?" She nipped at him again, tugging on one of the chains and inciting a jolt of reaction he felt deep in his testicles. "Do you know you can get much longer rods? They can vibrate, even make musical tones when they vibrate against you, like the rims of wine glasses."

"Someone has too damn much time on their hands," he said desperately.

Rising with a glint in her gaze, she pushed on the cross. With the release of a lever, she reclined him back to a forty-five-degree angle. "So you can sleep," she explained the adjustment. "Perhaps join me in my dreams."

"You're going to leave me like this."

"Yes." She nodded. "As I said, it leaves you nothing but time to think." She bent over him, her hair falling so it brushed his bare chest. Reaching through the strands, she caressed him again, tapped on the top of the jeweled adornment for his cock. "But if you sleep, I may come to visit you in your dreams."

He couldn't find words to answer that, not with the desire hot in her eyes, filling him with the unfamiliar desire to beg for something. Her mercy . . . her cruelty. Maybe just her. But he bit it back. When he said nothing, she turned away with a bemused look. Extinguishing all but one of the candles in the far corner of the room provided enough light that when she walked toward the bed, the snug grip of the lace on her hips showed him the movement of her ass, the shadow of the cleft in between. Putting a hand to the heavy carved bedpost, she used it to lift herself onto the high bed. For one agonizing moment, she was on all fours, her knees wide enough to show him the lips of her pussy beneath the pattern. Turning on one hip, she stretched out, fanning her hair across her left shoulder as she lay down on her right side. When she flipped it back, it created a shining wave on the creamy linen expanse of the pillow.

"I think I'll sleep on top of the covers." Her gaze lingered on him like a cat enjoying her dinner. "I expect my dreams will keep me warm enough."

Balancing accounts, memorizing household duties . . . Thomas should have drowned him in all the forbidden pleasures of a Spanish bordello so she couldn't so effectively destroy his concentration with things he'd never experienced before. Somehow, however, he doubted that would have helped. What affected his body when it came to her was far more than physical, and she seemed to exploit that at every turn. On how many men had she honed the skill?

She tucked her hands under her cheek like an innocent child preparing to take her repose, unfettered by sins. When her eyes immediately began to droop, the siren's mask slipped, the shadows etching out an exhaustion too startling to be false.

Thomas said she could stay up even to the midmorning hours as long as she wasn't in direct sunlight, and it was barely past dawn. Maybe there was a reason she'd used distraction more than physical exertion to get him onto the cross. It managed to drive back his frustrated lust and tangled emotions enough to realize she'd actually been as tired as she'd said.

She turned on her back, giving him a different view of her body in that scrap of lingerie.

"Tell me who Jacob is." Her voice, sleepy, surprised him. "I like bedtime stories."

"Should *Arabian Nights* come to mind?"

She smiled. "Only if you tell me a bad story."

He chuckled, but Lyssa heard the strain in the tone. His current condition was weighing heavily on his mind. She wanted him thinking, particularly while his connection to her was still limited to one mark. No matter what happened, she didn't mind giving him the one that would let her know where he was, that he was alive. She'd like to keep track of him.

It was another of the many things being alive so long had taught her. A person could make a lasting impression in less than a moment. She cultivated those impressions as if they were physical relationships, visiting with them in her mind when she wanted company, imagining words they might have said intertwined with what they did say during their brief interaction with her.

"Tell me about you, Jacob. I want to see the pictures in my head. Who were your parents?"

"My parents are dead, my lady."

"Will you tell me how? You don't have to, if it's too painful."

"I can refuse you nothing, my lady. When you ask."

She acknowledged the barb, but waited, cognizant of his hesitation.

"It was a lightning strike on the water while we were all at the beach. My brother knew CPR, worked on Dad and talked me through doing it on Mom, because I was eight and didn't know how. It didn't matter, they were both gone within a few minutes."

She studied the darkness, the way it closed around her but still gave her the sense of him, just to the right of her bed. For Christmas one year, Thomas had given her a set of plastic stars that glowed in the dark. He'd put them on her ceiling for her. She watched them glow above her now. "I asked you who they were, and you told me how they died. You don't like to talk about them, then."

"When you're eight, your parents are the center of your universe. It's a shitty age to learn the universe can be turned into a donut with nothing more than a thunderstorm."

"So it was you and your brother. The vampire hunter."

"Gideon."

"He's a story for another night. But start the story for me, so I can look forward to it another time."

"How much time passes before you trust someone, my lady? Before I can sleep next to you, hold you in my arms to keep you safe as you slumber?"

His voice had the rough quality of anger, the edge of panic that overcame a strong man when he realized he was completely helpless.

There was a unique type of alpha who could fight through it, who had the capacity to find the pleasure on the other side of pain. She'd recognized it in him easily, such that the rough edge sent shivers of pleasure through her body.

Lifting a hand, she touched the darkness that held the shape of him as if she were touching him. "That will be up to you, Jacob. But I've never trusted anyone. Not even Thomas. Until the end, when he sacrificed his life for me."

When he drew in a breath, she discovered another thing Thomas hadn't shared, but that didn't surprise her. "That, too, is a story for another night. Besides which, I keep my human servant too busy to laze around in bed with his Mistress during the daylight hours." Though the mental picture was far too pleasing. "Where did the accent come from? The Irish."

"My parents were from Ireland. I was born and raised here, but being around them and my aunt and uncle . . . well, I picked it up. I guess it was something like knowing two languages. I could switch between them both, and sometimes the accent feels more comfortable to me. It made me feel closer to memories of them. For the first three years after their death, I spoke that way all the time. It also went over well at the Faire, so I guess it comes automatically now, in certain situations."

"I like it, too. The way it comes and goes." Like a lover's fingers gliding up her spine when they weren't expected. "Give me something about Gideon, since I'm already disposed to dislike him."

"In terms of force of will, you two are matching brick walls." His tone was dry. "But because of him I saw you for the very first time."

When he shifted as much as his bindings allowed, she noticed his cock had dropped to a semierect state. She ran a hand over her hip, idly cupped her breast to play with the nipple, and watched his organ stiffen, lengthen. Heard him stifle a groan.

"When did you see me for the first time?"

She smiled at his whispered curse, but he answered her. "I trained and worked with Gideon into my early twenties. College wasn't for me. Never did take to the idea of having someone else teach me what I could pick up a book and learn for myself, making my own impressions. We were at a bullfight down in Mexico, because he was on the trail of a male vampire who liked blood sports, as many vampires seem to do."

"Mmm."

"You were there. With Thomas and . . ."

"Rex." She whispered the name, not wanting to call his image into the room. She didn't want Jacob saying his name, as if it would bring harm to him, like the calling of a curse.

"He seemed very into it. Very amused at how you weren't."

Lyssa's gaze rose. While he was obviously stimulated by her body, Jacob had his clear blue gaze focused on her face in a way that told her he saw the woman behind the seductive pose. The woman he'd seen that day. "When you got up to leave, he caught hold of your arm. From a distance, even to someone close by, that's all it would have looked like. A man grasping a woman's arm. He never stopped smiling, but he broke your forearm, just crushed the bone and it gave. You went white, but you didn't sit back down. You stared at each other, a stalemate. I remember Thomas was completely expressionless, but something vibrating from him said if he could have called the bull up into the stands he'd have staked Rex on those horns."

Lyssa turned her attention toward the ceiling. She had a mural painted there. A moonlit night, shadows of clouds chasing the full, pale beauty of the orb. Thomas's stars gleamed among the images. "It's difficult for mortals to understand relationships between vampires," she said at last. "He was almost invincible. There was no move he couldn't anticipate. He'd read almost every book I'd heard of, and he never slept well. It was as if his mind was constantly accelerating. What did your brother say?"

"He told me it wasn't our business. That you were a vampire, too. As if that made a difference."

"It does, Jacob." She ran her fingertips up her throat, tracing the arteries, feeling the scrape of her own nails. "We never did finish our manicure. I have what you need here. You can finish it tomorrow night."

"Whatever my lady wishes." The tone of his voice indicated he was frustrated by her unwillingness to say more. She could ignore that, of course. But something made her want to give him something, just a piece.

She turned back on her hip, one hand draped on it so his gaze could not help but be distracted by where her fingers rested, inches from the folds of her sex beneath the lace. It allowed her the pleasure of looking at him without that too perceptive gaze on her face. Her Irish knight had fine definition in his arms and across his stomach. She'd likely have him shave off all his body hair except on his skull, if she kept him. But she wasn't displeased by the thatch of hair gleaming on his broad chest. She liked the idea of stroking through its softness, tugging. Plus, he'd already proven the worth of his beard and moustache. She didn't go back to his eyes, preferring the sense of physical stimulation only.

"Not all vampires are sexual dominants, but most are. We have very strong sexual compulsions, and we live by a stringent pecking order. You maintain your place on the ladder by proving you can repel any threat to it. Rex had wanted me since we first met. I knew we were meant to be together, for many reasons. But we never could reconcile that part of our relationship. I would not become his slave, for I knew the depths of his cruelty and his need. If I had ever relented, he would have killed me, for he'd have had no use for me. But because I never did . . ."

She'd become the enduring passion in his life. The one thing he'd loved, as much as he understood what love was. She'd thought loving her could help him become the man she'd sensed he was capable of being. A memory rose in her mind, of Rex sprinkling rose petals over her bare body. While she'd slept, he'd gathered them, every rose from miles around it seemed. She'd wakened from a dream into a snowstorm of petals while he'd stood over her, showering her in them. Pale pink, white, bloodred . . .

When he'd sunk between her parted knees, she'd scooped up two handfuls and poured them over his head, watching them tumble over his shoulders. He'd looked at her in what for Rex had been a vulnerable moment. Wondering at her, not understanding her. So different from himself but in that blink of time content to know she accepted him. No doubt, no challenge. When she exposed her throat in invitation, he sank his fangs into her, his body penetrating her as well. She'd wrapped herself around him, holding him. Though she'd known it was a fleeting moment, the capriciousness of time was something she understood and accepted as well. Hours later, he created a crown of the thorns and made her wear it so he could lick the blood that trickled down her forchcad off her cheeks, her lips.

There'd been only one creature powerful enough to kill him. She had.

"My lady?"

"I'm tired, Jacob. No more stories for now. But . . . why didn't you and your brother hunt us that day?"

"We were there for another vampire. It was odd, though." Jacob paused. "He said he would hunt Rex in time, but he would never hunt you."

"Because I'm a woman?" She was amused at the thought. "That kind of foolishness must be a family trait."

"No. He's killed female vampires before. He didn't say why, just made sure I saw you so I'd recognize you were off-limits. Once I saw you . . . I knew that would never be a problem. I could never cause you harm, my lady."

Her attention moved deliberately over his bindings, underscoring his helplessness with a mocking look. "I agree. It's also a good thing Rex is gone. He would have killed your brother with as much effort as blinking."

A muscle flexed in Jacob's jaw and he shifted his hips, giving her the pleasure of watching his cock and testicles move with his body while bound in the uncomfortable jewelry. "I wouldn't underestimate Gideon."

"I don't. There was no overestimating Rex. Whatever you believe he was capable of, he was. Plus far more."

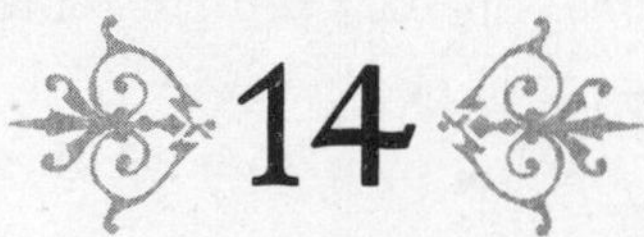

14

THE dampening effect of her mockery and the serious turn of their conversation gave him little relief. The purr of her voice rubbed like soft fur against his cock, which made that contraption she'd put on him even more excruciating. As she lay on the bed not ten feet away, the flickering candlelight reflected on her nipples, made the cleft of her cunt shift behind the pattern of her nightgown like the shadow of an elusive creature.

He'd never been forced to submission by a woman, never gotten aroused by it as she'd made him respond. At least to himself, he was forced to admit the thing imprisoning his cock made him hard mainly because she'd wanted to put it on him. It made him think of how she'd described the pleasure of slowly binding a servant, letting him feel his gradual descent into helplessness. The clasp of the cock harness kept the image of her hands there. The fascinated desire in her eyes ran through his mind, over and over.

She was a witch, sorceress, Medusa, vampire. He suspected he'd seen only the surface layers of a woman with more faces than the thoughts wrestling in his mind.

He'd never cared for feeling trapped. He supposed no one did, but to keep the frissons of panic down, he reminded himself this was his choice, that he wanted to be here.

Throughout his training with Thomas, the servant had used the word *defenses. You must have no defenses with her. You must lower all your defenses to be a servant.* Jacob thought he'd understood. But he hadn't. Whatever his expectations of this past night and the months of planning and preparation, it had far exceeded them. She'd challenged him, infuriated him, roused him more than any woman, real or imagined, ever had. She'd elicited protective feelings in him, erratic waves of fierce loyalty. Jacob realized Thomas's grueling training had been the same as that inflicted on a grunt in basic training. Grilled until he knew how to respond to conditions the monk couldn't have anticipated. Like learning what it meant to be a sex slave.

Uncomfortable with the thought, he nevertheless made himself take a closer look at it. She was a master politician, focused, deliberate. While he had no doubt she'd taken sexual pleasure in dominating him, she said she was teaching him what it was to be a human servant in her world. If she was really doing that, it meant there was a real chance she intended to accept him, even if she hadn't admitted it fully to herself yet.

He thought of her again in the car, the way she'd looked up at him, that brief look out of those mesmerizing green eyes. *He's mine.*

He was fucked. That was all. No help for it. He discovered a strap between the open arms of the upper *X* that could cup the back of his head so he didn't have to sleep with his temple propped awkwardly against the wood, straining the hell out of his neck.

He was exhausted and she obviously felt they were safe here, in a chamber that didn't exist to prying eyes. She would need his energy when she woke. Though God knows in what form she'd demand it. A dozen new images went through his brain, most of which brought him to full aching hardness again.

He could have closed his eyes, but he didn't. He watched her make soft noises in her dreams, studied every feature of her face, the fall of her hair, the curves of her body, letting his eyes do what his body wanted to do so much. Now deep in her sleep, she turned away from him, giving him another cock-teasing view of her body, her heart-shaped ass. The hem of lace rode up, skimmed the base of it an inch or two from where her pussy nestled between the press of her thighs. His thoughts drifted, sensual motes in the air as his lids reluctantly drooped, capturing and taking the vision of her into his dreams.

~

Hands molded over the muscular curves of his ass, nails digging in as soft lips traveled a path up his spine. The same fingers moved around his waist, playing with his navel and the flat of his belly, teasing the line of silky hair, drifting upward to his nipples, leaving his cock hungering for a touch.

The candle had burned down only halfway. He hadn't been asleep that long. She appeared to be in as deep a slumber as she'd been before he'd nodded off. Or was she?

He blinked. As she came into focus, he saw her stretched on her back, her jade green eyes gone almost black as the pupils dilated in the meager light.

He swallowed as her right hand rose, plucking at the nightgown, inching it up her legs. Displaying pale thighs, more and more of them until she reached the apex and touched herself, rising into the contact, a shudder racking her.

The invisible hands were descending. As her gaze followed their track he knew somehow she was doing it, this velvet clasp over his cock that dug those chains and uncut gems into him, making him grunt and jerk against his bindings. A skirt brushed against his legs as if a woman knelt before him. A groan tore from his throat when a hot, wet mouth closed over him, slid down his shaft, taking all of him.

On the bed, his lady's legs were parted, her head tilted back, but her attention was still on him while she manipulated her clit, dipped her fingers into her cunt to spread the slick honey over her lips.

Hands gripped his buttocks again, allowing the mouth to increase its suction on his dick and give a ruthless steadiness to the strokes. He could imagine her here, suckling him, serving him even as she lay a few feet away controlling it all, giving him a male fantasy all on her own terms.

He writhed in the restraints as the tongue on him teased his underside, sucked his testicles one at a time into that illusory mouth, licked them, and then came back up to take his cock again. Trembling against the cross, he realized he might find out how it felt to come with that rod inside him, his cock chained to restrict the flow of the fluids. As he watched her masturbate, the undulations of her body became more frenetic, an agitated snake coiling and uncoiling, writhing, seeking a bearing. The impressions of the lace on her skin, flickering in the candlelight, even reminded him of the sinuous patterns of a serpent.

Feeling like the tide whipped by the wind, he couldn't stop from pitting himself against it. "Spread your legs for me," he whispered. "Let me see the sweetness you won't let me taste. Let me watch you come."

Her eyes widened at his outburst, delivered in a low voice full of husky demand. Triumph surged through him as the unexpected stimulus began to pull her over the edge. The mouth left his cock. At first, he thought she couldn't maintain the magic this close to losing control herself, but then the invisible fingers thrust between his lips with the exotic scent of her cunt on them. He sucked the taste off them, watching with burning eyes as she bucked on the bed, gasping, crying out, her pussy contracting beneath her fingers as she tugged furiously on her clit hood.

He hadn't known if she would flush or not, given a vampire's paleness, but there it was. A pink blush sweeping her throat, her cheeks, the insides of her thighs, a heat that felt like a furnace blast.

Pain seared through his cock as the sight feeding his eyes made him bigger, thicker. As she came down and her eyes rested on him, he knew he was going to be punished for taking the game away from her. Fine. He could bear it. With this level of discomfort, his erection should be cooling in no time.

He hadn't counted on those hands. They slid beneath the cross-piece of the frame and two fingers dove deep between his buttocks to milk him with slow movements guaranteed to keep him hard while her fancy cock ring denied him a climax. But when pre-cum leaked around the bronze disk on the head of his cock he felt panic, wondering if that tiny rod would be like a finger stuck in a dam. Eventually the water pressure would build up and explode through the minute spaces around the plug, creating an excruciating flood of sensation. He could die from the agonizing pleasure of it.

He'd never thought of using sex as a weapon. His seducing her to climax with words had been more emotional than calculated, an attempt to regain some control. But he'd gotten in a lucky shot with a master swordswoman. The master now thought she was dealing with an equally skilled opponent and would no longer hold back. She'd slice him to ribbons.

Though she'd come down from climax, she kept her legs spread, playing with herself where he could see the glistening folds, the wet gleam of her knuckles, the post-climax dampness trickling down the base of her ass. At a particularly deft squeeze deep in his own, he let out a guttural snarl and cursed his own weakness.

"I told you I could be crueler than anything you could imagine," she whispered. It resounded through the chamber and inside his head. "You think about it, Jacob. Think."

He blinked in darkness. The candle had burned out, so the only illumination was the light on the clock and those glowing stars on her ceiling. Almost five hours had passed. He could barely make out her form, but it was in the same position, resting on her hip and turned away from him, the way she'd been before he'd drifted off. Though there were no hands touching him, his cock didn't care. The thin layer of flesh stretched over his ironlike erection suffered in the tight clasp of the cock rings and chains. His urethra burned from the invasion of the anchoring rod.

Think, Jacob.

He couldn't *think*. No one who used his rational mind about this would stay. It didn't matter if his brother, Mr. Ingram and even his lady thought he was fucking crazy. Maybe he agreed with them, but again, that didn't matter. This was where he was supposed to be.

~

Lyssa dreamed of storms. Wild whipping winds beneath her leathery wings. Her eye was turned toward the ground for prey, but in this type of storm everything had taken cover. She spun, the wind whistling over and under her, the vibration of the thunder and electric static of lightning skimming along her skin.

There. A duck paddled in a marina, unconcerned by the storm because she lived in the shelter of Man's harbor. While wild ducks often found such a port because so many of the wild places were disappearing, this was a domesticated duck, released or lost from somewhere. Living alone during the winter months because she was too weak and less capable of migrating with her wild brethren. Nature weeded out. Nature provided.

Lyssa tucked in her wings and dove with single-minded intent. The noise of the storm and the darkness provided her cover. The reflection of lightning gleamed off her talons as she unfurled them like landing gear, only she would use them to snatch dinner and be aloft again, never touching the ground.

Thirty feet from her goal, another movement caught her eye. She veered off sharply, somersaulted in a controlled move and dropped in a hover.

The white duck, having seen her now, had panicked. However, her mate, a brown and black wild duck and the distraction Lyssa had seen, now shepherded his snowy female into the shadow of the floating docks. She was not alone after all, and Lyssa would not kill one of a mated pair. Nature weeded out. Nature provided. But Lyssa could choose what offering to take.

A piercing scream split the air. She spun to see the wiser, wild-born mate snatched by a hawk who'd apparently been marking Lyssa's prey as well. The duck had been focused on Lyssa and getting his mate to shelter. The hawk had been noticed too late.

The white duck squawked her distress as the hawk pulled her mate into the air and broke his neck in an easy movement, carrying him away.

Over in less than a breath. The clouds boiled in the sky behind Lyssa. The white duck swam in circles out in the open, lost, in anguish. Confused by what had just happened.

The hawk's approach had been covered by the storm, just like her. Opportunists. The world of men was turning birds of prey into opportunistic scavengers. As civilization often did, it turned wild creatures into what they were never intended to be. Perhaps it did the same thing to men.

She flipped, dropped and pulled the white duck from the water, ending her life in the same economical movement.

You won't have to learn how to live without him.

~

Lyssa opened her eyes to see Jacob sitting cross-legged on her bed, watching her. Wearing a T-shirt and clean pair of jeans, he'd apparently taken the time to shower and change.

On the unrumpled side of the bed where he sat, he'd laid her satin robe and a pair of slippers. He balanced her brush on his knee and had a basin of hot water with a facecloth sitting within reach behind him.

As the time of her rising drew near, if nothing set off the warning spells she had guarding the upper room, the staircase would reopen. Apparently Jacob had made good use of that effect when he'd managed to free himself again.

His blue eyes were steady, bluer than the daytime sky she'd never seen, the analogy coming from the imitation of it in picture books. But she sensed his were a reflection of the actual color, perhaps pieces of the sky itself, they were so vivid and real.

"I did spend the night thinking, my lady. Fully bound as you left me." He inclined his head. "I chose to free myself an hour before dusk to prepare for your care. I ask your forgiveness and pray you won't view that as flaunting your will."

Lyssa pushed herself up, blinking. Wetting the cloth and squeezing out the excess hot water, he spread it out over his hands. "May I, my lady?"

When she nodded, he brought it to her face, pressing comforting heat to her skin. She drew in a breath, letting it wake her up and drive grogginess away. She smelled the scent of the lotion she used to remove traces of makeup and realized she'd forgotten to remove it as she customarily did before she slept. Apparently he'd noticed and so did it for her now, withdrawing the cloth after a moment to wipe the lids, over and under, pass the cloth over her cheeks, her lips, so she could feel the touch of his fingers through it. He brought the basin onto the bed then, rinsed it out a couple times. When he was done, he put cloth and basin back to the side and lifted the robe. "If you'd like to slip into this, my lady, I'll brush and pin up your hair before you bathe. Unless you'd like me to help you wash it today."

Once when she'd been angry with Thomas over something she couldn't even remember, she'd told him she was going to toss him over the next available cliff. Unruffled, he'd assured her she'd never do that. "If my usefulness to you expires on every level, you'll still need a mirror." Perhaps that's why he'd taken such extra care to teach Jacob all the things involved in her daily toilette, and overlooked some of the other things that seemed so much more significant.

"What if I told you I'd make you leave if you don't tell me how you keep getting loose?"

"That threat is wearing thin, my lady. I need to have some secrets from you or I'll bore you within the first century."

He held the robe by the shoulders. Lyssa pulled the black nightgown over her head. In a fit of petulance, she tossed it to the floor. Let him have his secrets. He could keep them while he picked up after her.

His gaze flickered to it, then back to her, but he didn't comment. His attention did slide down her throat though, to the slopes of her bare breasts, the nipples that tightened under his regard as she remembered his mouth there.

Sliding out of the bed, she turned her back to him. She expected him to rise, but he didn't. He moved down the bed until he was behind her, his knees close to the back of her legs. Touching her hands lightly with his, he guided them into the sleeves. When he brought the satin up, he stopped just short of pulling it onto her shoulders, restricting the movement of her arms unless she wanted to tear the garment. He'd adjusted his position so his long legs were on either side of her, his left foot next to her bare one on the floor. His heat was on three sides of her, his touch conveying a sense of reassurance.

Whatever she sensed from him, it wasn't censure for her treatment of him yesterday evening. She felt no emotional withdrawal from him at all. Intriguing.

"My lady, will you tell me what happened last night?"

"Not yet," she said after a long moment. With renewed energy simmering in her blood, last night's episode was deceptively remote in her mind. "For now, you'll carry a backup for the powder I have. I'll show you the ingredients. As you saw last night, once I take it, I require a recuperation period."

Even saying that much to him was difficult. She hated the necessity of it. So she didn't look at him. She gazed at the painting on the wall. Van Gogh's *Café Terrace on the Place du Forum*. It always made her slightly dizzy, in a good way. It also reminded her of one night Rex had danced with her in a quiet deserted street under a jeweled sky in Italy.

"You now know when an enemy could kill me, Jacob. It would be child's play. Just a matter of waiting and watching."

Ironic as well, considering the things she hadn't told him yet.

When he rose, she drew in a breath as his body touched her back. He finished easing the robe onto her shoulders and freed her hair with a brush of his big hands on her nape beneath it. Drawing her hair to one side, he bent his head and his lips grazed the side of her neck where he'd bitten her, making her shudder. Gods, did the man know nothing of showing a servant's respect?

"It will not be child's play for anyone as long as I watch over you, my lady."

She closed her eyes, overcome by a sense of guilt. She needed to send him away, refuse him before his life was lost.

Thomas, you wouldn't have sent him if you'd known. It was pointless. Of course, she had already given him the first mark herself, so how could she cast stones? She wanted him, though it was the height of selfishness to do so.

"I didn't think vampires could hold their breath. Or had breath at all."

He was actually teasing her for her reaction to that kiss on her throat. The scoundrel.

"Of course vampires breathe," she said impatiently, covering the warm rush of response that went through her skin. "You can't speak without breath. Cough, or yawn. It's just that the lack of breath won't kill us. We don't require oxygen to live."

Pulling the robe closed, she tied the sash and turned to face him.

Jacob sitting was distracting. Standing before her with those vivid eyes studying her face and firm mouth within touching distance, he was overwhelming. It made her need oxygen, despite what she had just said.

It infuriated her suddenly, the frustration of having to be one thing and say another, of having him not understand and take it all so lightly. Of course, that was likely because she hadn't told him the things he really needed to know. He was having trouble understanding the full impact of the situation because she herself didn't want to accept it.

"My lady." His hands touched her face. He'd stepped forward to close the small gap between them, and she hadn't even noticed the movement. "Sometimes you look so sad. Please let me help you."

Raising her lashes, she looked up at his concerned expression. "You are too good-hearted for this task, Sir Vagabond. I think you need to move on, continue your wanderings."

He shook his head. "My feet have grown heavy and clumsy since yesterday, my lady. I'd trip over them and fall flat on my face if I got more than a hundred paces from you." When he traced her brow with a finger, something passed through his eyes. "I'm not as good as you think, Lady Lyssa. I'm no saint, and I'm far from harmless."

"My mind does not tell me false, knight. You're too pure a soul for this work. So was Thomas. That's why he's dead."

She walked away from him, the staircase opening so she could ascend to the upper level where she could see the light of the moon glittering through the stained glass.

He'd collected the items from her bed and was following, so she sat down at her vanity, drawing her robe around her ankles in a sweeping fan. She needed to have Jacob remount the mirror on the wall. Since she showed no reflection, she hadn't been able to bear the absence of Thomas in the glass standing behind her, dressing her hair, his hands moving in an odd mime over empty space while she felt every touch. So she'd removed it, putting Edward Hughes's *Midsummer Eve* there, the human girl daring to stand among the fairies, foolishly bent over as if she thought she'd happened upon charming miniature children.

She heard his footsteps, let the tension flow out of her shoulders as he began to brush her hair. Firm, full strokes, easy pressure to remove tangles. He didn't speak again, apparently picking up on her mood.

"I'm having a dinner party here three weeks from now," she said, looking at that girl. At the fairies studying her, amused with her naïveté. "A party of eight. The two of us, and three other vampires and their servants. Once I get bathed and dressed, we'll go over the details, the contacts. You'll call their servants directly as well as send it by sealed invitation. I'll prepare the invitations."

Suddenly, she couldn't handle his touch a moment longer. Rising abruptly, she turned to face him. "We'll select the catering choices together. I'll tell you what I want and how I want it done, and it will be your responsibility to coordinate it."

When he laid the brush on the vanity, her gaze strayed to the long fingers, the way they handled such a feminine object with ease. "As my lady wishes."

She didn't see any apprehension in his expression, so he obviously knew how to do this part. "Go to the kitchen. You'll need to familiarize yourself with everything to instruct the caterers properly. The same goes for everything else in the house. If I have overnight guests, you should be able to provide them whatever they need."

The original works of art in the room mocked her with their realism, their value, as she spouted nonsense she was sure Thomas had gone over with him a hundred times.

"I'll provide you an allowance to do whatever you need to serve my household, and you'll let me know whenever more needs to be transferred into that account. I check the books once a week. You'll be given a salary for your own needs, of course."

He nodded. "Do you want me to help you bathe, my lady?"

She blinked. She'd fired words at him intended to point out his inferior status and he'd rebounded with something that reminded her of the intimacy she could require from him. That he offered freely and so temptingly.

"No," she snapped. "Go to the kitchen. Do as I've asked."

Pivoting on her heel, she strode to the bath and closed the door, turning the key in the lock with a decisive, unmistakable click.

Because the first mark told her where he was, she knew he stood in the same spot several minutes before leaving to do her bidding. When she turned her gaze to the tub, her forehead still pressed against the cool wood of the door, she saw steam rising from it. It brought her the scent of lavender and rose petals, telling her he'd sprinkled oils for both in the water. He'd also placed a vase of flowers on the foot of the tub, artfully strewing a handful of the mixed petals down along the damp side of the porcelain. It created a pale pink and lavender-colored path that made her dizzy, much like the Van Gogh. In the rising steam she could imagine herself dancing with Jacob, twined around him, immersed in him.

Thomas, who the hell is this human?

15

"WHY would vampires want food? Or care about it at all?" Jacob asked.

The butcher-block kitchen table had more space than the center island, but Jacob discovered Bran tended to get bored and plant his huge front paws on the table's surface, dragging everything on it to the floor. He wondered if Lyssa had ever had the same urge he had, to tie the animal's ears in a painful knot. Or ended up as he had, in a wrestling match with Bran for one of the cookbooks, laughing at them both. It turned out the island was more comfortable for Jacob's long legs anyway, and easier to circle and examine the various items he'd spread out over the counter.

Catering catalogs, cookbooks, several legal pads and pens. When she'd joined him about an hour ago, he'd seen her glance over the three proposed menus he'd already laid out, including appetizers, salad, soup, main course, dessert, and wine selections. He'd made notes in the margins on other household issues. The dogs' schedule, where the switchboxes were, flashlights, a list of things he hadn't found he might have to get at the hardware store. He hadn't let her curt dismissal rattle him, hadn't spent his time sulking. He hoped that had impressed her. Or maybe annoyed her just a little bit. He couldn't tell, but it cheered him to imagine either one.

"Vampires like food," she responded. "We can't digest it in great quantities, but we love the taste, the aroma. The main purpose of having a five-course meal is to delight them with different flavors and scents."

"So why don't we choose a mixture of flavors they haven't experienced before, together with things they have, so they can enjoy the new and familiar together? Like fresh brownies, with a side of raspberry cream sauce. A salad made out of fresh produce from local farmers. Nothing smells as good as a garden tomato that's never seen the inside of a refrigerator." He made a notation. In the corner of his eye, he noted she appeared fascinated by the way he held a pen. He was left-handed, so he had an awkward scribble barely legible to himself. "Will there be any politics to deal with?" he asked.

"Are we both breathing?"

Jacob glanced up in time to see a look of amusement cross her face. It helped ease the ball of apprehension he was carrying in his gut, anticipating that any moment she was going to do something else to test his limits. The way he felt around her was worse than it had been with his high school history teacher who'd loved surprise pop quizzes. In the microcosm of totalitarianism that could only exist in a classroom, to fail on even one of the tests would be 25 percent of the student's grade for the semester. A passing grade on the test was simply discarded, proof he was paying attention. He was finding some definite correlations between Lyssa and Mr. Winstead.

He'd had mixed feelings about the way she'd shut the door in his face. Thomas had helped her far more with her morning toilette than she'd allowed him to do this morning. Her dismissal rankled, but on the other hand, he was realizing how difficult it was to maintain self-control around a woman who kept him in a near constant state of wanting. She looked at him one moment with naked desire glittering in her eyes, her body trembling at his briefest touch. A blink later, she shoved him away, shut him out. Now here she was in a pair of tailored brown slacks and a soft cream sweater he supposed she thought of as simple and demure. Still, he longed to close his hands over the band of the sweater on her hips, pet the curve of her breasts. She'd pulled her dark, fine hair back with a barrette so it lay on her shoulder blades. Spun silk he'd had the pleasure of touching, so just looking at it made his fingers itch.

"The purpose of the dinner is to mark a new vampire for my Region. Thomas explained the structure of our holdings, I assume?"

He had. The vampire world was divided into Regions, groupings of territories won through battle or influence during the formation of the current vampire society, before the Council had been appointed. The heads of those Regions were known as Master vampires. A vampire who accumulated enough wealth and influence might be awarded an overlord title and a territory inside a Region by the Council, preferably with the consent of the Region Master. Vampires lacking the power or experience to be an overlord applied to reside in a territory. The overlord then put them in charge of different business interests. In return the vampires gave the overlord a percentage for his protection and backing. The overlords served the Region Master.

Jacob remembered asking Thomas if it was similar to racketeering. He'd earned an affectionate smack with the book the monk was reading, Thomas knowing when his student was yanking his chain. Understanding the class-conscious formality of vampire society, Jacob thought it made perfect sense they'd chosen a feudal structure.

She was the southern Master. The southern states were hers, everything from Virginia to Texas.

At Jacob's nod, Lyssa continued. "Brian Morris, my guest of honor, is a scientist. He's a born vampire who's petitioned his Regional

Master, who also happens to be his natural father, to immigrate to the States to continue his research. The facility is in my Alabama territory. The overlord of that territory is actually a couple, Lady Tara and Lord Richard. They'll be invited to the dinner to witness the marking and accept responsibility for his protection."

"What would have happened if he'd moved out of his territory without permission?"

She paged through one of the cookbooks, stopping on a lasagna dish. As she followed the lines of text with the unpolished finger, it reminded him he owed her a manicure.

"Well, since he's the Region Master's son, it would have been handled a bit differently. However, in a normal case, you either serve a vampire or you're a loner, and vampires don't tolerate a loner. The point of the system we have is to ensure protection, prosperity, secrecy and a support network for our activities. Any vampire in a territory may appeal a decision to the Region Master if they feel they're being treated unfairly by the overlord. There are different management styles," she acknowledged with a tilt of her head. "Some are more brutal than others. If a vampire can't find resolution, he or she might seek refuge in another Region, but if that Master isn't willing to offer asylum, the vampire would be considered rogue. Welcome in no territory, his original Master or overlord would quickly catch up to him. The most common punishment is interring him in a sealed container as punishment or warning to others."

"But you said you don't need air."

She nodded. "A vampire can live that way for eternity, with great suffering. Most vampires have strengths of value, so the Master or overlord would likely only prolong the lesson a month or two."

"Have you . . ." Jacob swallowed, wondering if he really wanted an answer to the question.

When she met his gaze, he noticed she'd chosen tiny gold hoop earrings and small diamond studs for her ears. With their healing abilities, vampires pierced their ears anew each time they chose to wear them. Other than his knowledge of that fact, to all appearances she could have been standing at the head of a board meeting, discussing a change in stock prices. "How would it make you feel about me? If those who have displeased me are screaming hopelessly underground for a release that will only come at my pleasure?"

Jacob sat back, crossed his arms. "You've never done it, my lady. Thomas would never have served you if you had such cruelty."

"A lot can happen between two people on a journey through life together." Her dark eyes dwelled on his face, intent and unwavering. "By the end, there were many things Thomas did without thought he wouldn't have considered before we met. In my world, it's a delicate balance, fear and respect, obedience and free will. No vampire respects compassion if he interprets it as weakness. If you find the right balance, you'll command the loyalty of those in your territory. If you're too brutal, you push them into hatred. That is not my way."

Jacob wryly noticed it was not a direct yes or no, but something to help him sleep at night. Or day, as the case might be. Regardless, he'd no doubt she'd calculated her answer that way.

"You have the largest Region. But you're not part of the Council. Thomas said that was your choice."

She nodded. "I have three hundred vampires in my area. I helped form the Council and the rules that govern our world, but I'm the last queen of the Far East clan. While that doesn't mean a great deal anymore, symbolically it means enough to tip the scales of power adversely if I sat on the Council. You'll get to meet them later this year. All the overlords and Masters meet once every five years to pay them our respects. What else did Thomas tell you about the vampires in my Region?"

Though her voice was flat, her eyes were still intently focused. He knew what she was asking as if it had been whispered in his ear. "That there are thirty-nine fugitives you've granted asylum."

She studied him for a moment more. "There are fifty now. When a vampire is accepted into my Region, I mark him or her so I know their whereabouts at all times. That's what I'll be doing with Brian. With the fugitives, it also gives them a limited ability to let me know if they're in distress and who is causing that distress. I may not get there in time, but I will hunt down the perpetrator and make him regret his actions. As long as my reputation holds, they are safe here."

A sixth of the vampires in her Region were fugitives and yet no overlord or Region Master dared challenge her asylum for them. Jacob was starting to pick up on the reason for her reticence about her illness. *I cannot ever show weakness before my enemies, Jacob. It is the first rule of my world.*

"Any new territory disputes I should be aware of?"

"None right now. When Rex died, I had to prove I could defend my Region alone. That process is never quite over, but I've had several decisive and somewhat brutal victories recently." When she tilted her head, considering some dust on the light fixture, he saw the hint of red deep in her irises, like crimson silt at the bottom of an emerald sea. "It's been quiet," she commented.

It stirred a memory Thomas had given him. Of a time when several vampires, including one of her own overlords, had trapped her in an alley. Or so they'd thought. Three bodies had been left behind, and hers had not been one of them. In fact, after making a brief stop to freshen up, she'd met Rex as planned for a theater production of *Peter Pan* and seemed to thoroughly enjoy the play.

"You've had a pretty big jump in fugitive numbers since Thomas left. So the conflict between the made and born vampires is getting worse?"

"You're paying attention," she observed. "Yes." She spread out her hands, the long nails making it a graceful motion, though it conveyed tension. "As Thomas probably told you, the number of born vampires has dwindled over the past several centuries. To balance that, the Council has allowed more vampires to be made. Unfortunately, these vampires often lack the perspective a born vampire has. They tend to be more resistant to our laws. It's not a popular opinion, but I believe that made vampires have genetic weaknesses, specifically poorer impulse control and a greater level of bloodlust, not a good combination."

"Almost as though making a vampire is incestuous."

"You also catch on quickly." The compliment warmed him, but she didn't raise her attention from the cookbook she was studying again. "There are some, including myself, who have suggested it would be best to stop making vampires altogether until we can better understand why." She snorted. "We are shouted down. It is apparently better to let rabid dogs loose on the populace than to be perceived as politically incorrect. Most of the Region Masters and not enough of the overlords understand the world works best if humans believe we're the product of overactive imaginations in filmmaking. Sometimes it seems the more 'civilized' we get, the more immature and childish we are. We think we are somehow owed whatever we wish, rather than needing to impose limits on our own behavior. The truth becomes relative to our own experience only."

There were shadows in her eyes now, telling him the subject had taken a personal and perhaps painful turn for her. "At least there are strict rules on siring a vampire," she continued. "If you make a vampire without consent, your life is forfeit. The fledgling is spared, but fledglings often die without the sire to watch over them in the first decade. Vampires are not generally nurturing to children not their own. Of course, there is no restriction on trying to create a born vampire." She allowed herself a tight smile. "Otherwise known as trying to conceive a child."

Vampires did not use birth control. Becoming pregnant with a vampire child was rare, and treasured. Lyssa had never conceived, but Thomas had sometimes sensed she would have liked to have been a mother. While the monk had been thankful it had not occurred with Rex, and based on what Jacob knew of his lady's husband at this point, he had to agree, he thought he heard a wistful note in her voice. He wondered if she'd ever hoped . . .

Bran came and pushed against her leg, earning an ear rub. As she leaned over to do so, her clipped hair fell over her left shoulder, brushing the top of the dog's head. "In short, we live by ancient rules," she said in a crisper voice. "Our natures unleashed would result in a full-scale war with the human race. We may be far superior to humans, but your numbers are far vaster, and your grasp of technology more advanced. We must strike a harmonious balance."

"It sounds very civilized."

"Does it?" She considered that. "Then I've left a great deal out."

He bit back a smile, though his mind was still turning over her words, interpreting the personal nuances behind them. Trying to figure out how her mind worked. To cover his ruminations, he bent his head back over the open catalog. "How about this? It's a non-bake version of a fruit cake. It has marshmallows, raisins, graham crackers—"

"That sounds far too mundane."

Jacob pointed to a paragraph. "Except it says that it smells like freshly made candy."

Coming around the corner of the island, she laid a hand on his shoulder. When she leaned forward to look, her breast brushed the side of his arm. It wasn't the first time she'd touched him since she'd joined him in the kitchen. Possessive touches, as if he was hers to absently stroke as she was doing now, her hand shifting to his neck to play with the hair he'd queued back. Even without being told, he knew the liberty was not two-sided. Her demeanor, those touches aside, was all business. Even now she was segueing on other things Thomas had taught him about preparing for guests, while offering him points of etiquette specific to these guests and throwing in domestic instructions.

As he listened, a part of his mind wondered if he dared to test it, see if it was just a surface façade. Give in to the desire to run his hand down her back and feel the slight bump of her bra strap under the plush sweater. Play with the tips of her hair with his fingers. Risk a rebuff, or the tempting possibility of *not* being rebuffed.

In the end, he remained still. For one thing, the information she was giving him was critical to running her house. The way he handled it would determine if he could be the human servant Thomas said he could be with his last dying breath. Based on the things she'd told him thus far, her responsibilities were considerable. It underscored why Thomas had been concerned about her having someone who could watch her back during daylight hours. She was a protector herself, his Mistress.

Even more important, a quiet wonder flitted through her concentrated expression each time she touched him this way. He instinctively kept his head bent over the task of writing now as she stared at his profile and traced the hair at his temple, the curve of his ear. If he chose not to remain passive, he suspected he would take that joy away from her. While he might succeed in replacing it with a different, more volatile pleasure, his Mistress's desire at this moment appeared to be having him quietly submit to her caresses. Surprisingly, he found he *could* curb his own sexual desire, assuaging it with the pleasure of watching her rediscover the intimacy of casually touching a man who called himself hers, giving her that right.

"You've made four dessert selections so far," she observed. "While vampires don't eat, we do like a balanced olfactory diet. I think you have a sweet tooth, Jacob."

"A whole mouth of them," he agreed. "We'll have a total of four vampires and their servants. I'm thinking we can do a sampler for each of them."

"Hmm. Not a bad idea at all. But remember we'll only have four place settings. Servants don't eat with us. They stand behind the chairs of their Masters and Mistresses."

"Through the whole meal?"

Her green eyes glittered. "The more obedient servants hardly blink. They're like statues."

He had a variety of responses to that, but he managed to swallow them and look down at the catalogs again. "Here's what I have in mind for salads and the soup . . ."

She examined his choices, approved most. As he watched her, another idea captured his imagination, something which thankfully distracted him from his annoyance at the picture she'd painted. His purpose wasn't to be an activist to revamp vampire society. Instead, he'd taken his oath to serve every need of the vampire queen who was one of the most powerful figureheads in it. "Have you ever smelled fresh candy, my lady?"

She'd gone back to the kitchen counter, for she was providing Bran scraps from a bowl in the fridge. "In over a thousand years, I suppose I have. It's been awhile, though."

"There's an old-fashioned candy shop at the new mall."

"Good. Pick us up a selection there for the dessert."

"I was actually thinking you might want to come with me. I need to pick out some clothes for the dinner. The new mall's open 24/7." As she turned to look at him, a refusal already evident in her expression, he pressed on. "In the center of the building, there's a Ferris wheel in a glass atrium five stories tall. The wheel turns on a ball, so it not only goes in circles straight up and down, but spirals like a top. They do a light and fog show, so when the wheel tilts at an angle, it's like you're going through a waterfall, all air currents and colors."

When she made a demurring noise in her throat, he continued doggedly. "Waterfalls are the theme of the mall's design, so there are displays throughout the complex. Not just in-house designs. Some of them are sculptures on loan from museums for this first month of the mall's opening. I notice you've got quite a few fountains on your grounds. You might see one you'd like to purchase, or an artist you'd like to commission."

As he described the Ferris wheel, Lyssa watched the movement of his hands, the sparkle in his eyes, the half smile on his firm mouth. She'd started the morning by ordering him out of her presence. A moment ago, she'd made sure he understood that not only would he be viewed as inferior in the presence of other vampires, he would be required to act accordingly. His response to that dampening information was to invite her on a date. Her lips twitched. Perhaps she should have told him everything he could expect at the dinner, though she wanted the element of surprise to see how he'd handle himself. He'd encounter far worse at the Vampire Council Gathering.

Bran put his paws up on the island's edge to get Jacob's attention, managing to snag one of the legal pads.

"You great mop. Begone." Jacob shoved the paws off and gave him a thump on the head with a rolled-up catalog. Bran answered with a loud woof and beat the side of the cabinet fiercely with his heavy tail, setting off a cacophony from the pots and utensils hanging off the two ends.

"Geez. Here." Jacob picked up an orange out of the fruit bowl and sent it in an impressive sizzling straight line drive across the kitchen. It hit the dog door with enough force to send it through. Bran dashed after it. She heard the barking of the other dogs, startled by the appearance of the orange, initating a mass chase.

Jacob winced. "Well, I'll be restoring the landscaping on the back walkway tomorrow. You know, I don't think he's half as tough as he'd like you to believe."

"Most males aren't." Lyssa crossed her arms. "I don't usually go out in public. Not in an uncontrolled environment like that. I attract too much attention and make a target of myself."

"You just said you're at somewhat of a lull. What if I got you a disguise of sorts? Planned to get us there in a way we're less likely to be followed. You're interested, right?"

She cocked her head. "Yes. But can you escort me on this excursion and still have everything prepared for my party?"

"Yes, wicked stepmother. I'll have everything planned to the last detail while the mice sew my dress together." He tapped the top of the legal pad with the menu. "You'll have the full proposal with all the details by tomorrow when you rise."

She narrowed her eyes at the reference and pressed her lips together at his unrepentant grin. "What kind of disguise?" she demanded.

His pleased expression warmed her far more than it should have. "Will you trust me to surprise you, my lady?"

Studying him, she was sure she saw mischief simmering behind those clear blue innocent eyes.

"I'm going to regret this," she decided. "But I can still tear off your arms and beat you with them if you make a mockery of me."

He gave her a quick, absent smile as something caught his attention and he bent his head back over a magazine. Lyssa wasn't sure if his reaction made her want to make good on her threat now or eat him alive, but either way, she knew she was in perilous waters. But then, she'd been in those for so long, she should have fins by now. Was Jacob somehow Thomas's version of a personal flotation device?

How much did you know, monk?

16

FOR the next few nights, she made herself keep her distance. She assigned him a well-appointed room in the servants' quarters, making it clear he needed an invitation to join her in her bedroom.

She met with him for an hour during the early part of the night to answer any questions, but after that she would dismiss him from her presence, indicating her need to handle business away from the mansion where he was not invited, or to work on her own matters that were none of his concern.

However, instead of going on her errands or sequestering herself in the room he could not access without her help, she watched him. With the one mark, she could locate him anywhere, but the preternatural stillness and swiftness of a vampire allowed her to be in the same room with him undetected, a shadow dancing at the edges of his peripheral vision.

She told herself she was verifying his competency, his trustworthiness, his discipline when unsupervised. She also needed to know the man, and one of the best ways to know a man was to see what he was when he thought he was alone.

He took meticulous notes. Not only when she spoke to him, but as he learned other things on his own. He'd scribble the information in the dozen multicolored composition books he had. Gazing over his shoulder when he was deep in thought over them, she saw dates and notes he'd made under Thomas's tutelage. She had four houses and eight safe havens. He'd coded them all with names known only to her and Thomas, the addresses not written down anywhere. Then there were scrawled references to the security systems, the more mundane aspects of utility bills, landscape scheduling, winterizing and maintenance issues. Most of those items were handled by trusted companies, usually owned and operated by other vampires or their servants, but it was her servant's responsibility to oversee it all, make sure they did what they were paid to do.

He didn't waste any time proving his competence in that regard. Her Atlanta home was her favorite, but in the months without Thomas, things had fallen behind. She forced herself to stay up later one morning to watch him inspect the grounds from a crack in the curtain, out of the line of sunlight, despite the exhaustion it imposed on her. When she retired to her bed, he was on the phone. By the time she woke in early evening, the grounds were overrun. He was finishing up with the window company that had come and spent the day pressure washing the house and professionally cleaning the stained glass windows. He'd also ridden herd on the landscaping company, having them tidy up areas they'd not kept as well as they should. At twilight, while both companies loaded up their trucks, he was among her roses with a master gardener. From his gestures, she suspected they were discussing if the soil composition was optimal for the spring, and what type of pruning needed to be done at this point.

As he squatted down sifting the soil, he tilted his head to hear what the gardener said, squinting his eyes against the sunlight, his soft hair ruffled over his forehead by the breeze. She liked the way his jeans fit his body, the stress points all where they should be. In that T-shirt his almost thirty years sat very lightly on his shoulders. Very lightly. She'd think he'd lied to her, except the man had no artifice to him. She didn't need a second mark to know that. If he felt it, he said it. Another reason she was insane for even entertaining the idea of him as a servant.

So she kept telling herself. Yet she kept giving him more information, more to do, knowing he would prove competent in all ways except the ones most vital. She was keeping him around purely for how he made her feel, and that was dangerous to the point of absurdity.

He'd moved a small side table to the edge of the Persian rug, so each evening when she rose, she found an offering waiting for her at the top of the stairs. A single cut wildflower in a water glass. A piece of Belgian chocolate in the shape of a seashell, the white and dark swirled flavors teasing her tongue, her sense of smell. A tiny empty snail's shell that gleamed a light pink. It was then she realized he was using the items as a way to make sure she was all right, since she would take them back below with her or otherwise move them.

Such gestures had revealed something particularly unique about Thomas's choice. On the second night when she'd risen, she'd had a strong thirst for cold water, one of the few things other than blood that vampires needed for sustenance. Next to the Belgian chocolate had been a pitcher of ice water and a glass.

She'd noted it repeatedly during her observations, even now. As the gardener turned to ask for something, Jacob already had the soil tester he wanted in his hand.

At the Eldar, he'd caught her a moment before she fainted, before she even realized she was going to do it. In the kitchen, he'd handed Mr. Ingram his car keys a blink before Ingram had made his choice not to work for her. Jacob was precognitive, anticipating thoughts and desires before they occurred. Intriguingly, he didn't seem to realize it, probably considering it intuition or luck. Which also explained his brother's disappointment in losing him as a vampire hunter. A mortal precog had an advantage, using it to replace what his vision could not give him, the direction from which the vampire would strike. Of course, precognitive ability was hereditary, so the fact Gideon still lived despite his risky profession suggested both brothers had it.

After the gardener and the landscaping crew left, he took out her gardening tools and clipped a few blooms from each bush. Trailing him to the kitchen, she watched as he made up several vases. He placed one by her tub for her to enjoy during her bath. Then he did the same in her library and her upper bedroom. After that, he called a florist and ordered up special bouquets for the upcoming dinner. He also placed a standing order for weekly bouquets to be delivered every Monday, everything from wildflower groupings to more formal, elegant arrangements. He was bringing her house back to life.

When he went back to her garden box and put away her cleaned clippers, he picked up her gloves, held them in his hands. A faint smile crossed his face as he straightened one out on his knee and compared the size of their hands. Then he closed his hand over the glove, brought it to his nose.

She was back at the window by that time. She put her hand on the glass as if she were touching his shoulder, unable to stop herself while he did such an intimate thing. Swallowing, she let the curtain fall back in place. Perhaps her home wasn't the only thing he was reviving. The thought made her throat ache with emotions she couldn't afford to have.

The next night when she rose, she told herself she needed to go to her library and do some paperwork. She managed a half hour before she slipped into the kitchen and studied him as he laid out several selections of plates and compared them to the food choices they'd made for artistic presentation. After he chose some colors she didn't expect but found she liked, he placed them on the sideboard for the caterers to set the table. Cinderella was in fact making sure everything was in place so he could go play with her on Friday. She told herself the "wicked stepmother" comment didn't amuse her, even as her lips twitched at the recollection.

She admitted she was impressed by how competently he did everything, his large hands comfortable handling such delicate things as flowers and china. At the same time, he could pick Bran up around the midsection and wrestle with him in the grass. Or repair the work shed, the muscles of his bare back sculpted beautifully with light perspiration as he sawed wood or hammered nails into it. She'd almost burned a line down her forearm trying to get close enough to the window to watch that before the sun fully set.

Later that same night, she found him in her study, where he'd apparently spent most of the afternoon checking her accounts and familiarizing himself with the transactions and business conducted in her Region.

She knew she was seeing the result of Thomas's rigorous training, but to create a perfect sculpture, the clay had to be right. Her monk had found her a Renaissance man, a jack-of-all-trades confident enough to teach himself whatever he needed to learn, or find someone to teach him by experience.

As engaging as he was to watch at work, the way he spent his leisure time intrigued her even more. When he chose to take a couple hours off, most of the time he read from the books in her library. The choices he made over the several days included a seafaring novel written in the seventeenth century, a Louis L'Amour western and the latest James Patterson novel. There was also a compilation of Leonardo da Vinci's notes on his inventions and a complete how-to on gardening. His absorption in those was a different angle in the same mirror of enthusiasm when he found an X-Men comic sandwiched between two books. She had no idea how it got there but resolved to pick up some more when she saw how he sat cross-legged and barefoot on the library carpet to read it, his back a tempting naked curve, each vertebra coaxing the touch of her fingertips.

When he checked out her cable channels, he made expressions of horror when he found she had nothing but basic service, but he seemed mollified by her DVD player.

So on this fourth night, she reclined near the ceiling, stretched out on top of the custom crafted bookshelves in her office and watched him go through manuals at her desk. As he looked over the maintenance list for her indoor pool system, she wondered if the problem wasn't that he wasn't suitable, but that she didn't *want* him to be suitable. After all, being a precog would only enhance his strength to serve her, and perhaps balance some of his deficiencies.

Gods, she was giving herself a headache. A normal one, though that didn't abate her irritation.

A furrow creased over his brow. Pursing his lips, he closed the file and rose, headed out of the study toward the pool area. Of course, she followed him.

Most vampires did not like water, but her Fey father had been related to water sprites, so she supposed that explained why she'd always been attracted to the element. While she rarely ventured into it, she'd wanted the pool. It had a curving lotus shape surrounded by tropical vegetation and fountains activated by switches. Jacob played with them, checking the way the lighting worked, making sure no bulbs were out. When he figured out the different control settings on the fountains, he fetched his notebook and made some more notes. Intrigued, she watched as he sat down at the pool's edge and let his feet dangle in the water as he wrote, despite the fact he was immersing his jeans to just below his knees.

After a while he rose and hit the switch to roll back the cover shield on the glass ceiling, allowing the night sky to unfold above him.

Tipping his head back on his shoulders, he looked at the scattering of stars and slice of moon. He closed his eyes and rolled his shoulders, the first time she'd seen him let the demands of the past few days show.

Her concern with that was replaced by something entirely different when he stripped off his shirt. His jeans and underwear came off then, and he toed off his worn loafers. It brought her the scent of earth, for he'd apparently worn them out in the garden earlier and some of the aroma of the dirt had clung to the heels.

Telling herself she had things to do and needed to go, she stayed motionless among the foliage of the tropical plants. The moonlight played across his bare back, the curve of thigh and buttock. It also made the hair brushing just the top of his shoulders gleam. The ends were uneven, suggesting he cut it himself. She wondered if he was planning a haircut before the dinner. He probably would. He seemed to be anticipating everything else.

Apparently the only way she was going to win the pleasure of punishing him again was to poke a stick into those areas where she knew he'd slap back at her. Stirred by the thought, she wanted to reach out and stroke her hand down his back to the dip in his spine, venture to that firm buttock.

Turning his head, he held the pose a moment, apparently listening. For her? But she wasn't breathing, so only the echo of the pool lapping quietly at its edges and the gurgle of the pair of fountains he'd turned on broke the silence.

When he dove in, she watched the wavy line of his body stroking beneath the surface, his hair becoming copper-colored silk. She could imagine him as a merman, the sculpted upper body and a powerful tail gleaming in the moonlight as he lay on his back, tempting her to swim with him. To become something she could not be, losing herself in the pleasure of his company such that she could fool herself into thinking it was possible.

He did about fifty laps. By the time he'd finished, she'd sunk down on folded legs among the ferns, silently marking every stroke of his arms, the sinuous twists he did for the turns. When he came to a rest at her end of the pool, he folded his arms on the edge. Propping his chin on them, he gazed at one of the fountains, a Roman girl pouring water out of an urn onto her female lover's reclining nude body. "Would you care to join me for a swim, my lady?"

Tilting his head, he looked unerringly toward where she was. It surprised her enough she didn't think to move, to be gone before his glance could flicker that way. Was it a lucky guess, a sense he'd tested by speaking aloud? Or another example of that psychic ability?

She masked her reaction, rising to move out of her screened spot. "Vampires don't float, so we don't swim."

He stretched out an arm, flattening a wet palm on the concrete. "I'll hold you up, my lady. The water feels good."

"I'm not dressed for swimming."

Laughter rose in his eyes. "I suspect you're wearing the same type of suit under your clothes that I have on now."

She sighed, eyed him with a hint of exasperation. "I know Thomas didn't teach you impertinence."

No, he didn't. Thomas had admired her, cared for her, but Jacob wasn't sure if the monk had ever truly seen her as a woman. Jacob understood that, for his lady had an otherworldly presence that diminished illusions of human superiority. But at times like this, she was as female as any woman he'd known. He could tell she wanted to join him. He'd sensed her nearby most of the week, and it had nearly driven him mad at times. Smelling the slight hint of her perfume, knowing her silky skin might be within touching distance, her jeweled green eyes studying everything he did. Her moist lips close, parted to breathe air on his skin.

"Please, my lady."

When she came farther out of the screen of tropical plants, the desire he'd kept banked with difficulty sparked at finally seeing the body he'd been imagining all week. She shrugged out of the blouse she'd been wearing, unhooked her skirt and let it drop, leaving her in a pale pink lace bra and panties. The color was nearly transparent, blending with her flesh. He could see the shape of her nipples. When she came to the edge of the pool beside him, he held his position as she lowered herself to the edge and sat, dipping her feet into the water. Carefully at first, testing the temperature, then more confidently as she found it heated. It was far warmer than Jacob preferred, but he knew his lady disliked the cold. For the pleasure of her company, it could be boiling for all he cared. Her foot touched his side under the water, her toe whispering across his hip bone. An invitation.

He took it, clasping her ankle and moving around it to stand between her knees. His lady allowed him to reach up, unpin her hair and set aside the hand-carved wooden barrette holding it. Jacob stroked his hands through the dark locks, his fingers diving deep to find her scalp. Her feet curved around his hips, bringing him closer. Lowering his touch to her waist, he slid her off the edge and into the water, pulling her against him. He wanted to tell her how much he'd missed her, but he didn't.

Feeling his wet, muscular body against hers was the closest thing to contentment Lyssa had felt in several days. Her nerves sighed in relief. She'd given her body just a taste of him and now all it wanted was more, even knowing denial was in their mutual best interest. With his cock hard and insistent and pressed between their bodies, she suspected she was going to lose that battle with her will. At least tonight. Her clit was already quivering in little spasms at the contact, begging her to rub.

She avoided his lips, the tender intimacy of a kiss. Instead, she pressed her cheek against his, wrapped her arms around his back to anchor herself there. "Fuck me, Jacob," she whispered in his ear. "Now. No foreplay, no seduction. Just obey your Mistress."

His hand went between them, found the crotch of the panties and pulled them to the side, the other hand going behind to palm her ass and press, pushing her down upon him, driving into her slow and strong, making her breath leave her in a little gasp as his thickness invaded her, widening her legs, bringing her down more deeply on him. She tightened her calves on his back.

"Put your hands on your head." She ordered "Fingers laced."

As she let go of him, lying back in the water, using the movement of her arms to keep her above the surface of the water, she waited to see if he would obey. Did he know how it goaded her, the rebellious flare of fire in his eyes? Reluctantly, he complied, lacing his hands behind his head and giving up the use of his body entirely to her.

Using the strength of her thighs and upper body, she began to pump herself slowly on his length. Up and down. Stroke after stroke. Not permitting him to move so she could watch the response build in a hard quivering that jerked all the pleasing muscles of his upper body and his thighs, a response she could feel vibrating through her, adding to the sensations she was experiencing. Water rolled over his upper body, sculpting the pectorals, the curved biceps. She wanted to suck the water out of his collarbone, brush her cheek along the side of his wet throat.

"You have a marvelous cock." Her voice had gone throaty, and she saw his arms tighten in reaction to it. His cock grew even harder inside her, making her gasp. She felt the soft brush of his testicles against her ass as she moved. His buttocks were clenched beneath her heels. His gaze was on her face, moving down her throat, lingering on the way the pink lace clung to the curves of her breasts, her nipples now sharp points. Down the slope of her stomach to her stretched sex, joined with his, the silk of the panties and the movement of the water interfering with the view but not dampening his absorption in the distorted picture.

"I want to touch you," he said, his voice a growl caressing her nerve endings. It alone made her pussy ripple on him. In the flex of his jaw, the flare of his eyes, she knew he felt it. "That's what you want, too."

"Don't tell me what I want, servant," she responded lightly while her heart hammered against the wall of her chest. "You stand still while I fuck you. That's all I've given you leave to do."

It was wrong, she knew it was. He'd invited her into the water. When he'd touched her foot and moved between her legs, she'd looked at the beads of water rolling down his body and wanted to kiss every drop. She wanted to lift her chin and let him suck the moisture from her throat as well. Take her under and take over, and she couldn't do that. She had to do it this way, even as she knew she wasn't fulfilling either of their desires. But it would get some hormones out of the way. A clear head was the most important thing.

The orgasm was rolling up, making her lower body rigid. She squeezed him hard, milking his cock with her inner muscles, and heard him curse. "You'll come for me," she managed. "At the same time I come."

"No. Not like this."

"Any way I wish. That's what you must learn. You have no will. No choices but what I give you."

Oh, God, the sensations were swamping her. She wanted so much more. But this was what she could have. What she could handle.

The climax was a brutal shove over the edge of an abyss. Emptiness yawned below but she took what it could offer, pulling him with her with her skill, hearing him snarl in frustration as he let go, his body shuddering, his feet trying to hold them steady as the physical response unbalanced him.

The heat of his semen jetting seared her, took her up even higher. She pistoned her hips on him hard and fast now, drawing out his climax as well as her own, gasping out her pleasure, the rippling spasms passing through tender flesh.

When she opened her eyes, his chest was rising and falling with the exertion, his hands still laced on his head, his gaze burning on hers. He was beautiful, every muscle etched out with his tension, a powerful male animal held only by her will. She withdrew from him, reaching down to rearrange her panties back over herself. As she thought of their fluids mingling in her body and the water, the thought made her flush.

"If you can't look at me with respect, you won't look at me at all," she said sharply. "Lower your gaze."

"Make me."

She'd pushed him as far as his pride could stand, apparently. She turned her back on him, moved toward the edge of the pool. Damn him. Damn Thomas. Damn this emptiness in the pit of her belly even as her cunt wept with a desire only sated physically. Damn herself for a fool.

"Goddamn it . . ."

A splash of water as he lunged, caught her wrist, turned her around. She could have resisted him, but when he slid his arm around her waist and brought her up hard against him for the kiss she'd denied them both, she didn't. He lifted her off her feet, her toes brushing his calves as he held her by the nape and the waist, his palm pressing against her hip and buttock. When he covered her wet lips with his own, she tasted chlorine and man, cooler pool water mixing with the heat of his mouth.

She didn't put her arms around him. They rested in the water on either side of her, her whole weight held by him until he guided her thighs up around his hips, taking her back into a position where she was wrapped around his body, his buttocks under her calves, heels pressed to his thighs.

"Hold me, my lady," he muttered against her lips. "I won't betray your trust."

It wasn't about that. It was about him learning what the limits of their relationship were, a difficult obstacle for almost any servant. Most vampires gave their servants more time to learn it, to understand that the relationship was something different from anything defined in the mortal world, but she would be asking a great deal of him very soon, and he had to learn it now. She had to hammer it into him on every interaction.

But was he partly right? Was her concern a façade for her unwillingness to open her heart again? It was not inappropriate to be fond of one's servant, to show him physical affection.

When he lifted his head, he kept his intense gaze close to her face so it felt as if his eyes had a power to touch her like his fingers, only deep below the skin.

"Jacob, we're not lovers. We never will be. You serve my needs. Do you understand that?" She had to force the words out when all she wanted was for him to cover her mouth with his again, his tongue testing the sharpness of her fangs.

"Serving your needs fully is what I intend to do. It's my only desire."

She glanced at him sharply, but she didn't let him go. Instead, her hands curled around his neck under his wet hair, her fingertips playing along the steel cords of his shoulders. "Thomas should have made you understand what that means far better than he did."

"He knew . . ." Jacob paused, and Lyssa wished she couldn't tell how honest he was trying to be with her, to give her information without hurting her. "Time was short, my lady. He said he was teaching me what he was most suited to teach."

"Like manicures." Her tone was brittle even to her own ears. "Oh, Thomas."

"Your proper care was his primary concern."

"As opposed to his life." Her fingers clenched, her nails digging into his flesh, seeking to give pain to balance her own.

"Will denying yourself true pleasure with me change that?" Jacob's hands increased their pressure on her hips. "Change anything other than your happiness?"

Happiness was irrelevant at this point. Pushing out of his arms, she backed to the edge of the pool and turned away from him, closing her eyes. She stiffened as his hand touched her waist, slid around her from behind. His cheek rested against her temple as he enclosed her in the warmth and strong shelter of his body. Nothing sexual, just a connection of flesh to flesh. "What are you doing?"

"Comforting you, my lady." His tone, ever patient, telling her what to anyone else would be obvious. But people did not offer her comfort.

She leaned back into him, testing it out, even as her mind ordered her to leave his company. She couldn't regain her balance with him this close. Not in her current state of mind. She'd commanded armies. Run households the size of a town. Killed when killing was needed. But her woman's heart could still drive her to her knees, plant a knife between her shoulder blades.

"You wouldn't serve me if I wasn't like this," she said suddenly, desperately. "You wouldn't want to be with me at all."

"I don't understand, my lady." His fingers stroked her hip bone. "What do you mean?"

"If I wasn't beautiful. Desirable to men."

He shook his head against her temple. "No, my lady. That's not the reason. There are many women far more beautiful. In fact, I'd say you're plain as a fence post. I've seen women with much nicer breasts. Bigger. Long legs. Fine, firm asses that make a man wish his hands were permanently glued—"

When he reached down with his other hand to apparently take advantage of his description, she shoved him under the water, held him down. Shrieked as he grabbed her legs and hips and took her under with him. She struggled, thrashed, and he brought them both up, tossing his head to get the hair out of his eyes, laughing.

"You are impossible," she accused, even as she let him hold her about the waist as he treaded backward.

"I've heard that all my life, my lady."

"No doubt." She couldn't keep up with him. His moods were like the gentle waves of the tide on a shoreline, each cycle rinsing away what was left from the last one, leaving no remains to mar the next new moment. Why was it was so easy for him to slip beneath her defenses in ways even Thomas hadn't been able to accomplish?

"What are you doing?"

"Taking you past where you can touch, my lady. You'll have to cling to me, depend on me for your life."

"I can walk on the bottom. I can't drown," she added.

"I can pretend I'm rescuing you."

Knowing the moment to make her point had passed, she let it go. Maybe she'd gotten it across, but he was refusing to accept it. Again, that wasn't unusual for a new servant. What was unusual was her reluctance to push the issue, knowing the time factors involved.

The dinner would be the true test. With others there, it would eliminate the trap of intimacy she kept stumbling into with him and remind her of her responsibilities. Even though she suspected it would tear something vital in herself, she had to give him the scars he would need to survive the strikes inflicted upon him in her world. She had to know how tough he truly was. But for now . . .

"I want my manicure, Sir Vagabond."

17

HE set up his tools for her in the sunroom. She called it the moon room, since she only visited it on moonlit nights like this. The glassed area gave her a view of her rose garden and the statue in the middle, a fountain with water sprites cavorting around Pan.

"Doesn't he seem a little overendowed?" Jacob glanced toward the large appendage on the bronze statue.

Lyssa bit back a smile. "Are you envious, or worried you might suffer in comparison?"

Jacob snorted. "An elephant would suffer in comparison. I suspect most women would run screaming if they saw that."

"Some women are aroused by pain." She took a seat as he gestured her to it. "Some men as well. You found pleasure in the pain I inflicted on you, that first night."

She'd taken an hour alone to re-marshal her defenses while he prepared. When she walked away tonight she intended to have the upper hand. But he'd changed into the tight hose he'd worn at the Eldar. No shirt and bare feet, recreating everything as she could wish it. He'd set up an occasional chair for her comfort across the table from the stool he'd chosen for himself. The chair did not recline as the one at the Eldar did, but would provide her a more relaxed seat while he did her nails.

He'd risen the moment she'd come into the room, underscoring the fact he was hers. Stimulating her when she did not want to be stimulated. Gods, was she a teenager again?

"With respect, I think it was your pleasure that goaded my desire, my lady."

"Silver-tongued devil," she commented coldly. "Start my nails and tell me about your first conversation with Thomas. How you convinced him to train you."

Giving her a searching look, he picked up a file, apparently realizing it was best to start with filing her nails instead of the more intimate act of massaging her hands. "That first night I saw you, I wanted to speak to you, but Thomas prevented me from that. Quite smoothly, I might add. I ended up talking to him. He told me nothing of the truth of who he was, of course, but he must have seen something . . . different, in how I was drawn to you. You were occupied, so we shared a bottle of wine, an evening together. At the end of it, he gave me his card, told me to call him if I ever felt a compulsion to do so. About a year ago, I found that card in my dresser behind some other things. I called. He was in Madrid, and I joined him there."

Lifting a shoulder, he moved to the next finger, filing in one direction as was proper, brushing away the dust with a thumb that caressed her knuckle. She watched his lashes fan his cheeks, thickened by the shadowing of the moon, drawing her attention to the slope of his cheekbones, the sensuality of his mouth. "Once we established trust, he started telling me about you. At a certain point, he accepted I'd be here when he couldn't any longer."

Again, his gaze rose, lingered on her face. Not for the first time, she thought he didn't look at her the way a human servant looked at his Mistress. He looked at her the way a lover would, one who knew things about her needs, her fears.

He was a *human*. She should tell him to lower his gaze. But would she be doing so to teach him a lesson, or because of the way that look was making her feel?

She frowned. "You had no woman?"

"Of course not, my lady. I wouldn't come to you attached."

But he'd had women before. That was obvious. She found she wasn't interested in hearing about them, however. She didn't particularly care for the fact he'd had them, no matter how skilled it made him now.

His fingers were larger than hers, deceptively stronger-looking, and she was hyperaware of every place they touched her hand, how they held it. "Do you still prefer oval tips, my lady?"

"A little sharper than that." She tilted her head, let her voice lower into a purr. "I like being able to scratch a man's back, leave scars there when I drive my fangs into his throat, when his cock spurts into my body."

She was spitefully delighted to see the flash of lust in his eyes, a flare of jealousy at the implication of other lovers. When he bent his head back over his task, she continued lashing at him, unable to stop herself. Unable to push down the desire her own words were stoking in herself. "I also like to restrain a man when I feed or take any other sort of pleasure with him. Spread his arms and legs wide, leave him no defense against me. Did Thomas tell you that amid all his many pearls of wisdom? Were you prepared for how I treated you that first night, Sir Vagabond? The way I may treat you every night if I so choose?"

"He told me some of your preferences, my lady. Is that sharp enough?"

She moved her glance down, but before she could study the shape of the nail, he lifted her hand. Gripping her wrist, he brought her fingertip to his throat, pressing down so it punctured the skin, welled blood. Keeping his gaze on hers, he lifted his chin higher.

Jacob knew when he was being taunted. Defiance wasn't the best strategy when it came to vampires, but instinct as well as a good deal of male ego drove him to stand up to her now.

Because his experience had been that vampires were very ritualized and formal in their own interactions, he'd envisioned his first days with Lady Lyssa as a transition period, like a knight swearing allegiance to a chosen lady. Awe and reverence. A certain amount of formal detachment between them, not too messily intimate or personal.

So much for that idea. His cock was going to explode if she kept masturbating it with nothing more than her sultry voice and provocative words. She'd brought him to climax less than a few hours before, in another almost equally uncomfortable situation.

A trickle of blood itched along his throat. She'd gone so still that Jacob blinked to make sure she was still real. He couldn't tell if he'd offended her or if he'd done . . . something different. The way those jeweled eyes centered on him now, unmoving, unblinking, made him vote for something different. He tried to ignore the sly voice that suggested his aggressive response was to ignore his reaction to her words. The way hot lust licked up his cock, tightening his balls as he imagined the picture her words painted. Accessible to her touch whenever she willed it, his legs restrained. His blood pounded hard under the touch of her fingers.

"You do get aroused by pain, Sir Vagabond." The same question was delivered as a statement, uttered in that temptress's voice. Her green eyes were like a predator's, waiting for the right answer before she moved in for the kill.

"No, my lady. Except when you're the one administering it." Tightening his hand on her wrist, he leaned in. "When Thomas flogged me, he told me to imagine it was your hand wielding the whip. Damn if I didn't get as hard as the stones beneath my bare feet, even as I felt the blood get slick under my heels. The night you put that cock ring on me, it burned like fire, but all I could think about was how wet your cunt was getting while you watched my discomfort. You could have rammed a railroad spike up my ass and if it got you off, I'd still be hard as a rock, mesmerized by your nipples stiffening, your legs spreading so you could taunt me with your soaked pussy. No other woman has ever done that to me. It's you. Whatever you choose to do to me."

Desire knocked into Lyssa like an ocean wave hitting her midbody, spraying her senses. It was not just the smell of his blood, his heat. It was his defiant look, wrapped up with a gesture that offered her everything. He was challenging her control, recognizing full well she was testing him. He was testing her right back.

Jacob knew it was coming, could envision it happening before it actually did with that curious sense of déjà vu he got, but he forced himself to stay still. She surged up from the table. It was like going over the edge of a roller coaster, too fast to follow, everything out of his control as he was slammed up against the side of the sunroom, against the edge of a cabinet there.

He opened his hand, releasing the file so it made a muted tinny sound as it hit the floor. When he swallowed against her hold on his throat, he noted her grip was under his jaw rather than on his windpipe. Apparently he wasn't the first she'd trapped against a solid surface like a mad scientist with a pin and a hapless butterfly. The corner of the cabinet stabbed into his back and hip bone.

Her expression was merciless, hard. "Did you know vampires secrete something like a pheromone that makes mortals unable to resist us? The younger vampires can't control it at first. When they go out at night they avoid crowded areas so they don't cause a spectacle like the Pied Piper. I rarely use it. After so many centuries, if a woman blessed with a vampire's immortal looks hasn't honed her seductive powers to the same potency as a chemical reaction, then she has no right to use either."

"I'll deny you nothing, my lady."

"You deny me your submission." Her eyes glittered, her voice dropping to that cock-teasing whisper.

When he'd faced vampires with his brother, they'd intended to kill him before he could do the same to them. They'd discarded a civilized veneer, becoming 100 percent the savage predators they were. While hurting Lady Lyssa was the last thing he would ever do, he could not deny her sudden ferocity provoked his fighting instinct, which pissed him off. Closing his hands into fists, he suppressed the urge to struggle. Then it occurred to him a different strategy might be needed here.

You must go with your gut. Thomas's words. Lady Lyssa was a master of deception, even above the level of most of her peers. He would be of no use as a servant unless he learned how to cut through all that and get to what she really wanted from him, what she needed him to be. But what if what she wanted and needed was something she herself might not know? Something that might change from moment to moment.

After all, she is female.

"You like the fact I resist," he responded. He matched her seductive purr with a husky growl. He could take disobedience to an art form if it gave her the type of shuddering orgasms that made her keep coming back for more. "That's what's making you wet even now. You want to sink your fangs into me and invade my mind, make even more of me your slave."

Oh, he is such a handful.

Teaching a strong man to submit to her will by his own choice had always enthralled her. Under normal circumstances, that was important. While each vampire handled time differently, all vampires with an iota of wisdom knew the dangers of stagnation. The dreadful, often psychopathic effect of the Ennui took more of their numbers than anything. Ultimately, it was what had taken Rex. The thought disrupted the moment, reminded her that stagnation was irrelevant to her, like so many other things.

Easing Jacob down off the wall, she withdrew her hand, but in a motion that allowed her to trace his collarbone. The man had beautiful, firm skin. A delicious body. Thomas had given her substance and candy both. *You bad, bad monk. You learned things from me no monk should know.*

Turning away, she returned to her chair and deliberately laid her hand on the towel that was on the table, wiping off the blood that had collected on her fingers. Jacob approached a moment later, rubbing his neck and eyeing her warily as he straddled the stool again.

"I feed on my own terms," she said coolly. "I'll give you the second mark only if that's *my* desire. If I bind you to me and you prove tiresome, I'd likely kill you rather than exert the energy to sever our link. Therefore, I wouldn't rush me."

A grudging smile tugged at his lips, stirring her further. The man did not have enough control to suppress a smile. How on earth could he exercise the restraint to be her servant? Never mind she was fascinated by the way his lips curved, the appeal of his clever mouth, the genuine intelligence and affability his expression revealed.

"Fair enough, my lady."

They maintained a companionable silence while he finished the filing. When he placed her hands in a basin of warm water, the fragrant oils with which he'd infused it closed over her skin, filled her nose.

"Did Thomas tell you how long he was with me?"

"Yes. And that he would have served at your pleasure for as much as two hundred more years if your husband had not punished him for his loyalty to you." He gave her an even look. "For which you—"

Her hand was out of the water, her fingers pressed against his lips before he could say anything further. "We don't discuss that. Ever."

Despite her sharp command, she took advantage of the contact to trace the oil along his lips. Watching them part in surprised response, she felt her heart twist in a knot of nearly unbearable pain at the simple beauty of it. His fingertips pressed into the table, whitening with the suggestion of a man's rising desire. It made things quiver low in her stomach. So she took her hand away.

"We never speak of that, Jacob. Not unless I bring it up."

And I won't, because if any vampire or anyone connected to my world knows you know about it, your life would be forfeit.

Thomas had obviously had enormous confidence in this man. If she didn't trust her former servant's judgment so much, she'd be cursing the situation far more than she was doing. Thomas had never been dim-witted, far from it. If he'd told Jacob the second most precious secret she guarded, he'd done it to bind his candidate to her even more securely. If he entered her service, Jacob would need the full protection provided by all three marks to keep another vampire from compelling him to tell what he knew of her.

It had been a rather Machiavellian move on the part of her former servant. But if she rejected Jacob, refused to give him the second mark and sent him away, he would not become part of her world. The risk would be far less. *You didn't think of that, Thomas, did you? You didn't know my most important secret, the one that makes it impossible for me to give him three marks. A fine dilemma you've given me, my friend.*

But she found she couldn't be angry with Thomas's bold presumption. Not when she knew he'd been motivated by love, wanting to impose Jacob on her out of concern for her well-being. She supposed that was part of what had hurt so much about losing him, one of many things. They'd been a family unit, the two of them. Far more than she and Rex had ever been able to be.

If Thomas had sent a clone of himself—quiet, self-effacing, brilliant—she could have easily turned him away. But there was a sensual edge to Jacob that called to her, a fascinating complexity.

He was looking at her too intently, so she brushed a fingertip over his lashes, compelling him to lower his gaze, giving her the sole privilege of scrutiny, as was a Mistress's right. While he didn't deliberately disobey her by lifting his gaze, his hand covered hers in the basin, his thumb stroking the wet dip between her middle and index fingers.

"You know what a sexual submissive is, Jacob?" she asked, forcing indifference into her tone. Turning her hand, she closed it around his fingers, stilling him. "It means you submit to my will in all things. Even if that will is to watch you couple with another woman . . . another man . . . or share you with another vampire and his or her servant. It means if my desire is to chain you to a wall and torment you until you beg me for release, and even then deny you for the pure pleasure and amusement of seeing your hard cock suffer for hours, you will willingly do it."

Being whored out to others as she desired, allowing men to touch him the way he'd only allowed women to do. Or to have men *or* women do things to him he'd not permitted anyone to do. She'd threatened such a thing on their first meeting, but she knew at that point Jacob hadn't believed it was anything more than an attempt to intimidate him. She wondered what he thought now.

It was a long moment before he disengaged himself to wrap her hands in terry cloth. There was a tense pressure as he dried her fingers.

"You're right, my lady. I don't understand what a sexual submissive is."

That he admitted it impressed her. And moved her in a disturbing way. "I'm not surprised," she said without inflection. "I suspect for all your worldly travels, you're a bit old-fashioned, Jacob. A traditionalist. A knight protects a woman. He doesn't allow her to control him."

His hands stilled, his head bowed so the fine silk of his hair shadowed the bearded jaw. "I don't understand what a sex slave is, my lady, but I do understand what an oath of service is. A knight swears fealty to a queen. His life is hers to command. Whether it is to send him to his death or to a worse fate."

Catching him by the jaw, she dug in a little with her sharp nails, bringing his head up. "That would be a worse fate, what I described?"

"Would it, my lady?" The fine lashes lifted so his blue eyes met hers directly, creating a quiver of reaction low in her belly. "Would suffering for your pleasure be so awful? Should I be prepared to bear it the way a political prisoner fears torture?"

As Lyssa stared at him, she resisted the urge to lift his hand to her face. Press it against her cheeks, the bridge of her nose, her lips and chin. Feel her face through a man's sensual touch. He'd claimed he had no gift for words, but either he was a liar or simply unaware of his appeal.

"I leave that for you to decide, Sir Vagabond. I want my massage now."

A muscle flexed along his jaw, but he inclined his head and drew her hand into the clasp of his.

Lyssa closed her eyes at the sensation. Touch was a basic need. Babies had proven it. Though a vampire's body did not need the therapeutic effects of a massage, she loved the petting, the manipulation of her joints under capable fingers. Jacob had very capable fingers. Thomas obviously had taught him what she liked, but the pacing, the *feeling* conveyed through the touch, had to be genuine or it wasn't effective.

Making herself push aside the intensity of their conversation, she cleared her mind. She focused on the quiet of the room, the way the moonlight filled it. It was a warm night and the room had trapped the heat of the day's sun. It would hold it through most of the night, which was one of the reasons she liked this space. She was so rarely, truly warm. The only thing that seemed to warm her sufficiently was a man's body.

Jacob switched off the cosmetic light so moonlight was the only illumination. It also gave her sensitive eyes a rest while he did the massage. Her seizure of the other night notwithstanding, Thomas had chosen his protégé's debut well, a situation where he could prove his attention for detail while bringing his unique, attractive style to one of her private indulgences.

Perhaps Thomas had hoped it would be enough to overlook the deal breakers. The fact Jacob was a former vampire hunter, and that he wasn't very accomplished at sexual submission or unquestioning obedience in general. Or maybe Thomas knew the contrasts would intrigue her. Absolute loyalty. Resourcefulness. Beautiful body, clever fingers. The mystery mixed with the pleasure offered. Razor edge intelligence, perhaps only equaled by the monk himself.

When she closed her eyes to escape, she found it was a mistake to do so. These past few days, Jacob had served to distract her, but the quiet tranquility called forth the image like a séance. The ghosts of both Rex and Thomas tended to do that, slip into the still spaces whether invited or not, taking advantage of moments when she didn't want to focus her mind, like now.

Brown eyes. Brown hair gone gray too soon for a human servant's extended mortality. A face with so much character and intelligence it defied artistic rendering. "Strong bones" didn't cover it. In her mind, she could touch each plane of that face. The deep set of the eyes, the line of his brows, his firm, determined mouth.

My friend. My truest friend. I should have protected you.

The softness of a handkerchief brushed her face. Her lashes wet, she raised her gaze and saw Jacob touching the cloth to the corners of her eyes, carefully protecting her makeup.

"I'm not crying."

"I know. Vampires don't cry. Thomas told me." He was indescribably gentle. It fascinated her, how easily he could do tenderness when so much lean musculature embellished his shoulders, the broad chest. She'd been so used to Rex using gentleness as a distraction for his planned brutality. She couldn't deny there was something . . . remarkable about the ease with which Jacob touched her and how she accepted it. Even Rex had never achieved that level of familiarity, in all the years they'd been together.

"You know how he liked word games?" Jacob asked.

She'd said nothing to indicate she was thinking of Thomas. But she nodded.

"One day, when I was trying to distract him from his pain, I asked him to describe you using just one sentence." His quiet voice, the compassionate quality to it, soothed the ache, gave her an anchor in the helpless sense of loss that suddenly threatened to swamp her and produce more mortifying tears. "He said, 'She has the mindless courage of a predator, the broken heart of an angel, and a woman's unconquerable soul.' "

"Always the overly sentimental poet."

"He was that." When she looked away, he put the kerchief to the side and began to massage the joints of her other hand as he'd done with the first, saying nothing further. She watched the moon and her roses as his touch soothed the pain of the memories, distracting her with other things.

"Will you choose your polish, my lady?"

She chose the wet burgundy again. He remained silent, applying the base coat. She shifted her perusal to him, noting small scars, birthmarks, the movement of his body as he performed his task. The deft way he managed it with those large hands. How the hose fit his lower body.

She liked his abdomen, the flat expanse of it with sectioned stomach muscles and a light covering of hair. She liked knowing she could reach out and touch any of him if she chose to do so.

"Did you win at the joust, Sir Vagabond?"

The corner of his mouth curved as he opened up a box holding tiny piles of glittering gem chips. Rubies, diamonds, topaz, amber. "I did, my lady. Quite often."

"Ever defeated?"

"Every man can be defeated if he meets a better opponent. It's been some time since I've met one, though."

She appreciated his cleverness. "I've found myself a Lancelot, then. Perhaps the only thing that can defeat him is a woman."

Jacob chuckled. "I don't claim to be exceptional in that regard, my lady. A woman can bring me to my knees quite easily."

"I certainly hope so. But can she make you want to be there?"

He didn't even blink. "One look from you and I believe you could make a man want to do anything."

Sitting back with a smile, she tapped the section holding the white diamond chips. "You're well versed in courtly love to boot."

"One of the more effective defenses against women's cleverness." Giving her a wry look, he snapped off the nail dryer and pushed it to the side to work on the next coat of polish.

She said nothing after that, turning her attention back to her rose garden. She let her mind wander among the blooms even as she remained hypercognizant of his touch, keeping her half aroused even as it lulled her into this quiet peacefulness.

You need a regular clean donor. You need . . .

A companion. You knew I needed a companion. Someone who would give me the will to live. To want to be alive. All of a sudden she wished she hadn't burned Thomas's note. She'd kept the ribbon under her pillow, though. She wanted it in her hand now.

"My lady?" Jacob's soft question drew her out of the recesses of her memories. She focused, seeing with amazement time had ticked away over an hour. When she'd fallen into her reverie, her right hand rested in the nail platform on the table. At some point she'd curled up in the chair, her shoulder and cheek pressed into the crevice of the winged back, propping herself for more comfortable gazing. Her right hand rested on the chair arm now and her left hand was on the table. The nail platform and his tools were cleared away. She looked down and saw the ribbon trailing out from under the palm of her right hand, against the chair cushioning.

"When . . ."

"I thought you might want it, since you were thinking about him." Jacob gestured. "Are your nails to your satisfaction, my lady?"

Against the wet burgundy color, he'd added a feathered brush of silver on the three longest fingers of each hand, setting in place a tiny black diamond chip at the point of each feather.

"Forgive me, but I thought you'd like to try the black diamond against the color instead of the white. You were so relaxed, I didn't want to disturb you."

They were perfect. The female in her was well pleased, both with the manicure and the manicurist, as much as she didn't want to be. He bent toward her now, his blue eyes close, that beautiful mouth. That body, meant to please.

"Why is there no woman, Jacob?" she asked softly. "Have you been married?"

"No." He was holding her hand, ostensibly to check her manicure, but pressing on her ring finger, stroking the soft skin above where a circlet would have fitted. She'd never worn one for Rex. It was a mark of ownership she couldn't allow. "I don't really know why. There've been women I've cared about. I've enjoyed their company. At a certain point, I just know it's time to let go and move on. I think I loved a couple of them, but it wasn't the type of love that would have kept me with them. Love . . ." He paused, lifted a self-conscious shoulder.

Despite his training in the Faire and circus as a performer, she could tell he had a man's reluctance to talk about his deepest feelings. "Tell me what's in your heart," she murmured. Vampires were unapologetically selfish. Demanding every secret from their servants, offering their own only when absolutely necessary. That was the way it was, the way it had always been.

From his look, she knew virtually the same thought had passed through his own mind, but he responded after a long, thoughtful moment. "I've always believed love is more than just a feeling. It may start that way, but eventually it rips the fabric of what you know, becomes something far more than you expect."

"Pain and pleasure wrapped so tightly together that trying to separate the two will make you insane, as if you're unraveling a DNA strand meant to hold the universe together." She offered it quietly, as if she'd picked up the thread of the thought. As if they already shared a second mark. "It helps explain the reason for chaos. It's the alpha and the omega, beginning and end."

"Creates all the important questions and answers anything." An ironic smile curved his mouth. "Like why I have no woman."

18

LYSSA looked down at herself critically. "I certainly *hope* nobody recognizes me at the mall, because if they do I'm going to do something equally humiliating to you. Three times over."

He chuckled, came out of the bathroom. "With your permission, my lady, I'd like to put this on your lower back."

He pulled back the wet towel to show her a temporary tattoo, a black rose and thorns done in artistic interwoven loops. She'd seen versions of the design riding on the lower backs of young women, revealed by their jeans. Jeans much like she was wearing now. Blue and riding low on her slim hips, for which he'd provided a pair of equally low-riding black panties. The pants had been worn at the stress points and were embellished with a scattering of painted pewter roses just below the front pockets, highlighted with a touch of silver pink. She had to admit the decoration was pretty, whimsical. He'd combined it with a snug midriff-baring tie-dye T-shirt, also in swirls of pink. On the front was an image of several kittens with jade eyes like hers. Two of the kittens cavorted across her breasts. There was a third kitten napping between them and they were all perched on top of the shirt's lettering: "Not everyone is a morning person."

Her scoundrel, teasing her.

He'd pinned up her raven tresses and covered them with a shoulder-length wig of expensive quality. The human hair feathered naturally around her face with a red brown coloring.

Her comment notwithstanding, she allowed him to kneel behind her, pressing the tattoo to her lower back. As he held it there with one hand, he smoothed over it with the wet, warm cloth in the other. Tendrils of the water trickled down the curves of her buttocks beneath the jeans, an intimacy that made her very aware the points of his wrists were pressed against her denim-covered ass.

Despite her lapse at the pool, she'd continued her self-imposed abstinence. Five days now since that night. She couldn't trust herself to take advantage of the delights of his body and skill as a lover and resist the desire rising exponentially in her each day to give him the second mark. It was too soon. He had to at least get through the dinner to prove to her he was up to what they would face at the Council Gathering.

A mall was public. She could enjoy him without taking the risk. That, despite the fact she suspected he was deliberately testing her resolve as he brought his other hand to her front. His wide palm settled over her abdomen to anchor her as he increased the pressure on her lower back. He fanned his fingers so his smallest finger was under the waistband, just to the left of the button, perhaps a bare inch from the elastic of the panties. Which, given the style of the garments, did not put him far from a part of her body all too aware of him.

"You look lovely, my lady. But unless someone is expecting you to dress like this, you'll be very safe even without the wig. Plus we're taking other precautions."

The paper now sticking on its own, he rose but didn't take his hand from her waist. She knew she should move as she felt his thigh press against the back of hers, the line of his hip against the curve of her buttock.

"So you like the way I look then?" she managed. "You seem as if you're thinking about taking liberties you've not been invited to take."

"I welcome my lady's punishment," he murmured. The provocative words set off volts of current through every needy part of her body. The whisper of a moan escaped her as his chin nudged away the red brown hair and his lips closed on her collarbone. His hand slid up under the T-shirt, under the fabric stretched taut over the curves of her breasts. She wasn't wearing a bra, and his thumb and forefinger curved under the left one, gently squeezing as her whisper became a true sound of need. Saliva pooled in her mouth, and she felt the prick of her fangs on her lips.

Control. An easy word to bring to mind and equally easy to ignore in the face of the blatant erection he pressed against her buttocks. His arms were now both around her, one grasping her breast, the other hooked in that waistband. His thumb teased the line of her panties, his fingers curved low on the outside, stroking her mound through the denim just above her clit.

"How long will you refuse me, my lady, when I can tell you want me in your bed? Why deny yourself what belongs to you?"

That formal courtesy and language Thomas knew she found so appealing in a man, especially during this vulgar century, combined with Jacob's unique confidence and aggression, gave him the ability to seduce her, a woman who knew everything there was to know about seduction.

His voice was against her ear, his breath teasing the side of her neck. She'd noted his bite there had lingered a day or so, like the love bite of a teenage lover. That was unusual, for wounds, let alone blemishes, healed almost instantly on her. While it could be a progression of the illness she still refused to discuss with him, it could also be the fact they shared at least one mark. She'd heard of such things, though she hadn't noted it with past servants.

"I have my reasons. Be patient, Jacob, and don't press me."

"But I have a much shorter life span than you, my lady. By the time you make up your mind, I may no longer be able to live up to your demands."

She elbowed him in the ribs, giving him an exasperated snort. "Perhaps if I wait until you're old and doddering to give you another mark, you'll be more manageable. I can always find myself a young and energetic lover."

"Can you, then?"

She stepped back, turned and faced him. The Irish had slipped into his tone, this time she suspected without conscious awareness. For some reason the way he uttered it, softly, a little threateningly, ran a ripple of reaction through internal areas already experiencing some turbulent seas when it came to him. Tamping it down, she focused on more important matters. "Is there anything someone who knows me well would recognize?"

Though he obediently shifted his attention to serious contemplation of her question, it didn't make her body tingle any less, watching his eyes course over every part of it. She wondered what he was seeing. It had been a long time since she'd thought about that. Of course she knew by human standards she was stunning. But beauty could be surface. Drawing the eye before it tired of the display and then wandered on. Did he see anything worth looking at for several centuries?

What a ridiculous thought. While there was a sexual component to the vampire–servant relationship, she'd never denied her past servants the right to pursue a human lover as long as it didn't interfere with her own needs. So why did the idea of Jacob being with another woman displease *her* so much?

She reminded herself that a vampire–servant relationship had phases just as any other. Since Thomas had been her last servant, she'd simply forgotten about that. Sometimes servants were possessive at first. They learned the foolishness of that in time, but it could affect the vampire, too. It was just the newness of the attraction, of course. As they settled into it, it would become what it should be. She should enjoy this fun, flirtatious phase, the sharp pleasurable bite of sexual tension, anticipation.

And for heaven's sake, she hadn't *made* him her servant yet, officially. She kept threatening to throw him out every other day. It was alarming that she seemed to be reminding herself of the same things she was reminding him.

"Just your eyes. Here." He offered a pair of sunglasses suited to the rest of the attire, with pale silver pink frames and fashionable tinting. "They'll also help if there are any bright lights in the mall."

"So how does it look? The tattoo?"

"I'm reconsidering. Every male in the place will have his gaze glued to your backside. I'll have to stick close." As she slipped them on, Jacob wondered at how she could make anything appear beautiful, even a pair of cheap sunglasses.

"How are we getting there?"

"In the limo, at least part way." He lifted a full-length, cowled cloak. "Ingram's bringing two people with him who are roughly our height and build. He'll drop them off at the opera, they'll get out, her in your cloak and him dressed like me, and go enjoy our opera tickets. When Mr. Ingram parks the limo to wait for them, we'll slip out the passenger door and go get my bike where I've parked it."

"You have a motorcycle?"

He nodded. "Assuming we've not been followed, my lady, I'm going to treat you to a bike ride in the woods. I hope you're not faint of heart."

She took the cloak, haughtily ignoring that comment, and settled it over her shoulders, lifting the cowl and drawing it down over her face. "It seems you've thought of everything. Have you had the silver cleaned for our dinner?"

"Yes, my lady." He shrugged into a dark suit coat emphasizing his wide shoulders. He was wearing a white button-down shirt and dark dress jeans that fit his groin nicely, making the palm of her hand itch. "Did it myself. Not a spot on it."

"Food all ordered?"

"Catering service prepped and food ordered. Linens have been dry cleaned, fresh flowers will be delivered that afternoon, complete with a special bouquet I picked out myself for my lady's table setting."

"Music?"

"Done." When she paused, he cocked his head. "Are you playing wicked stepmother again? Can I please go to the mall now?"

She bit back a smile, gave him a severe look instead. "Thomas trained you well. But again, he did not teach you to be impertinent."

"That's an art form I cultivated all on my own to please my lady."

The lights of the limo went by the kitchen window as Mr. Ingram pulled into the drive. She nodded to him through it, pleased to see him again. When he got out, raised a hand, she was glad to see he appeared equally amiable.

"You've gone to a great deal of effort for this outing."

"You're a high-maintenance woman, no one's denying that," he agreed. As he began to turn away, she captured his hand, stopping him.

"Jacob, do you take nothing seriously?"

Leaning in, he brushed his lips over her nose, hesitated, then touched her lips as well. Just a simple contact. Because it was so simple, no attempt to push and claim her mouth more thoroughly, she felt the impact of it down to her toes, how much he held back.

"Yes, my lady. There are things I take very seriously. You know what they are."

When he drew the cowl forward to further cover her face, she turned her head, kissed his wrist, her fangs grazing him. He stilled, those blue eyes riveting on her gesture. His intensity sent frissons of excitement through her lower vitals, as if the excitement of new love awaited her tonight. Rather than just an evening's diversion provided to her by a precocious, intriguing and altogether exceptional male.

A *human* male, she reminded herself.

As he watched the thoughts course across her face, Jacob hoped he'd accomplish his primary objective tonight. He wanted to see his lady smile without thought. Perhaps even coax a giggle out of her and get her to engage in some innocent flirtation with the man who wanted to see her unfettered by shadows for one night.

For that gift, he could even force back his current, aching desire to have her body beneath him, feel her wet folds closing over him, the clutch of her hands on his shoulders.

"After you, my lady."

As she nodded, sweeping out the door toward the limo, he could well imagine what she'd look like without the cloak, her ass defined by those jeans, the provocation of the tattoo. "God help me," he muttered, following her out.

~

Oddly enough, one of the first places she wanted to go at the mall was the Mirror Maze, a dimly lit maze of mirrors confusing the mind. It disoriented the giggling and shrieking participants, causing them to bump into the mirrors they thought were open hallways and into each other. As a result, Jacob waited until the previous group had gone somewhat ahead of them before he led her through the curtains.

There were of course ghoulish sound effects, maniacal laughter and props to misdirect. Though he knew it was a game, he kept a firm grip on her hand as he watched her reach out and touch the glass. When she slid her fingertips along it, her brow raised in reaction to his image layering with the images of the others up ahead that were reflected back to them.

"Any dragons hiding in here, Sir Vagabond?"

"Worse," he said in a low voice. "Teenagers."

She chuckled. He noted as they caught up and passed other groups that only a brief glimpse of his lady was enough to have the young men running into walls, even more than they were already doing. She did have an undeniable effect on the male gender. He couldn't claim himself exempt.

When he took her to the exit to the maze, Lyssa hid a satisfied smile. Without a reflection, getting through the maze would have been easy for her, but she'd let him lead. He hadn't hesitated, had hardly even glanced at the cues or stopped to consider choices. "The luck of the Irish, indeed," she murmured.

She couldn't remember the last time she'd had an outing like this. Falls Harbor Mall was an octagon, with corridors forming a pinwheel to the central feature of the mall, the Ferris wheel Jacob had described. At each of the eight points there was a different fantastical water display to engage the imaginations of the shoppers.

For a while they just wandered by the storefronts and she considered different purchases. At first she was wary, scanning her surroundings, but logic kicked in and she knew among this mass of humanity she would feel the presence of a vampire a mile away. Further, she noted that Jacob, though attentive to her, never stopped casually scanning the crowd, looking for anything unusual. She found herself touched by it, the way she'd been by his protective guidance in the maze.

But when he bought her ice cream, she sent him into a men's store to pick out the clothes he said he needed for the dinner. In a mood to placate him, she took a seat in front of the store on a marble wall surrounding a two-story-high fountain. The fountain simulated a mountain, complete with animated goats butting their heads against rocks, a holographic image of salmon leaping up the falls, and a grizzly bear up to his ankles in the rushing water.

Jacob had bought the ice cream with his own money, insisting everything tonight was his treat. She'd chosen strawberry, mixed with chunks of the fresh fruit and topped with Godiva chocolate fudge. As she inhaled the mixture of flavors, she enjoyed the experience of smelling it among the cacophony of echoing sounds. People moving in surges like the rush of water. Wanting to spend money or just enjoy the sights among the nearly two hundred stores. Young people prowling, here to be seen.

When a little girl and her mother sat down near her, she offered the treat to them. The mother was initially suspicious, but took it with an understanding smile when Lyssa confided her date had bought it for her but she was lactose intolerant and didn't want to hurt his feelings.

She had to suppress the urge to go shop with him. He'd told her what he was going to get. Like most things which concerned Jacob, she'd been impressed by the appropriateness of the choices. Particularly since all she'd seen him in other than the costume hose were T-shirts and jeans that had seen better days. Even tonight, once they'd gotten to the mall, he'd shed the dress shirt, showing he was wearing a T-shirt beneath it. It was a very appealing look on him, but she was looking forward to seeing him in the dark pair of slacks and midnight blue shirt he'd described.

When she rose and wandered around the back of the fountain, curious to see what animals decorated that side, she was delighted to find a very lifelike cougar. A moment later, Jacob was at her shoulder, without his purchases.

"You disappeared on me, my lady."

"As I will occasionally do." She cocked her head, inserted one finger in the pocket of his jeans and tugged at the seam with an indulgent smile, too pleased by her surroundings to get cross with his overprotectiveness. "At night, unless I specifically request it, I don't need my human servant to be a bodyguard. He guards his Mistress's well-being, yes. Helps her scout out danger upon her request, watches over her daytime repose. But when I'm awake at night, I'm fully capable of protecting myself. You've done all the right things to ensure we won't run into problems. If we do, they'll be the type of problem up to me to handle."

"They'll have to come through me."

"No, they won't." Now her tone did sharpen. "I absolutely forbid you to engage a vampire in an attack. It will only interfere with my handling of him." At his stubborn look, she chose a different tack. "I might get killed trying to protect *you*."

"I was able to anticipate your movements the other night," he said defensively. "I've hunted vampires."

"So have I. I can promise you, the power and cunning of a vampire that would come after me will be more than you've ever faced. Otherwise you'd have been dead, and we wouldn't be having this conversation." Before he could open his mouth to argue, she placed a finger on that appealing bottom lip. "Plus, I had no intention of hurting or killing you the other night. It makes a difference." She peered at him over her glasses. "Go get your clothes and stop hovering. You're annoying me." Even though he wasn't.

Giving her a bemused look, he reached out, pushed the bridge of the eyewear so they settled back on the bridge of her nose. "With respect, lady, you weren't able to protect yourself the other night when we met."

She frowned. "You took care of me when I lost consciousness. I am quite fully awake now. Shoo."

She turned her back on him, tilting her head to look to the top of the mountain, conveying quite bluntly that the conversation was over. Even gave a little flip of her hand to underscore the command. The sound of his breath leaving him in an exasperated huff like a disgruntled adolescent almost made her smile.

Ouch. Her hand clapped over her left buttock, a reaction to sharp pain. Astounded, she spun on her heel, glaring at him. He'd *pinched* her. Hard. On her ass.

Already several paces away, he threw her a rakish look over his shoulder. She closed her mouth. He was the most outrageous man. One moment properly deferential, a blink later, acting like . . . an annoyed lover. Teasing her like she was some girl he had out on a date.

With exaggerated casualness, she wandered back around the mountain display. Back inside the store, he was studying a rack of belts. A salesgirl had just approached to assist him. Or to ogle the muscles in his arms defined by the stretched fabric of his short sleeves. While Lyssa watched, the girl reached out to casually touch one of those arms as she pointed out the section of the belts with his size. As if the man was not perfectly capable of determining that for himself. He could figure out her accounts, order about landscapers and repair her woodshed. He knew how to pick out his own belt.

Or perhaps he did need some help.

As she closed in on him, stepping into the store, she slipped her hands in her back pockets to enhance the sway of her hips as she walked. It pushed the jeans down low enough that her hip bones were revealed in the front.

Her eyelashes didn't even flicker as a male sales associate tripped over a display and went sprawling within ten feet of her.

"Oh." The girl left Jacob with a word of apology and hurried to help her coworker with the wrecked display and his bruised dignity.

Jacob barely acknowledged her, his eyes all on Lyssa as she approached. She'd noted he'd registered her entry the moment she'd stepped over the threshold. His mouth had twitched at the sales associate's reaction.

"Something you needed, my lady?" Despite their disguises, she hadn't encouraged him to call her anything else, so he kept his tone low on the address, giving his voice that sensual cadence.

She could tell he was smart enough to be wary. Male enough he couldn't keep his eyes off the low ride of the waistband, the jut of her unbound breasts beneath the kitten T-shirt.

"I decided to come in and help. Choosing belts?"

The trousers and shirts he intended to purchase lay over his arm, apparently retrieved when he came back in the store. "Do you have a preference?" he asked. He already had his hand on one, a simple black strap with a silver buckle, handsome but not overly ornamental. Very much to the taste of the man. Pursing her lips, she picked up one studded with pewter stars at two inch intervals on a wider strap. A look of alarm crossed his face as his grip tightened on the belt he'd originally chosen.

"My lady, I'm not certain if that style is my—"

She wondered how he would feel if she ordered him to wear women's clothes in public. There were so many ways a vampire could torment her servant.

Considering, she cocked her head, surveying the store. There was a married couple several feet away. The two store clerks were restoring the display. A group of teenagers clustered around the discount sales rack at the back of the store.

At the sound of a loud crack, they all turned, scanning the store and the walking area out in front.

Someone with a gift for recalling details might have remembered that the beautiful young woman casually standing with her boyfriend by the belts had held one of them loosely by the buckle in the opposite hand only a blink earlier.

They might also remember the man hadn't been standing rigid, his teeth clenched as if someone had just punched him in the jaw. Or as if he were ready to strangle someone.

19

LYSSA released the tongue of the doubled-over belt with pewter stars, letting it dangle along the line of her thigh.

"Son of a . . ." Jacob closed his eyes, a veritable flood of fire writhing across his left buttock where she'd struck him with it. He swore the imprint of those pewter stars would be tattooed there for all time. If he hadn't been wearing the jeans, he'd be sure of it.

Her jade eyes watched his every expression as he fought not to clamp his hand over his ass like a chastised three-year-old about to wail. Sliding the other belt out of his hand, she took them and the clothes he held over to the male salesclerk. "We want both of these," Lyssa said. She returned to Jacob's side and slid her hand into his back pocket, finding the wallet holding her credit cards and his own. His lips pressed together as she caressed the part of him she'd abused. She had to struggle against the desire to cup her other hand over the generous package of testicles and cock brushing against her thigh, separated only by two thin layers of denim. She wanted to feel him harden under her touch while his ass stung from her punishment.

"I used less effort to do that than you use to breathe, Jacob," she observed. "Think I can't handle myself?"

"I don't know. Breathing is not easy at the moment, my lady."

"Let me make it harder then." Slipping in front of him, she rose on her toes and captured his lips. "Double entendre intended."

His response was immediate. Banding his arms around her, he brought her full against his body, his lengthening cock rubbing insistently over her abdomen. Nipping at her, he muttered a curse into her mouth. She curled her fingers in his hair, tugged hard.

It was the salesclerk's question that had Jacob blinking, breaking free of the kiss.

"Is there anything else you need?"

Lyssa startled him by making a little hop and wrapping her legs around his waist with lithe strength, settling her crotch and ass right on his groin. She increased the pressure there by leaning back to the full reach of her arms with her hands on his shoulders. Dropping her head back, she looked at the mural of clouds painted on the store ceiling.

"Flying clothes, made to look like birds. Interesting."

She was certainly in a mood.

"Does it look like I need anything else?" Jacob asked.

The salesman grinned. Lyssa reeled herself back up and whispered in his ear. Jacob sighed, brushing his cheek against hers as he held her with one arm around her back.

"Socks. I do need two pairs of black dress socks. Thank you, my lady." He brought his attention back to her. "You're not going to make me wear that belt."

"No." Her expression was feline, the green eyes glowing. "I like the one you picked out. I like the other one for other reasons."

"That what I'm afraid of."

"Just think of it this way. Instead of being angry about having to stand behind my chair for dinner, now you'll be grateful you don't have to sit. Don't you ever pinch my ass again." With that, she unhooked her legs and slid down his body. Wiggling free, she wandered back out of the store without a backward glance, torturing him with the swiveling sight of her tight, entirely pinchable ass.

He was beginning to understand it did no good to ponder how she could piss a man off and make him rock hard at the same time. It was a gift far surpassing a man's understanding. When he rejoined her outside, she scampered ahead, stopping at a cluster of children watching a double-level carousel. When she looked over her shoulder at him, it took his breath. The way the straight hair of the wig fluttered back and feathered revealed the dangling earrings he'd chosen for her. They pattered against her delicate neck, drawing his attention to the curve of ear as well as the mystery of what expression her sunglasses hid.

Thomas had said his lady had a wicked sense of humor, a rapier wit that could cut someone down to size in a moment, but he'd never hinted at this playfulness. Had he uncovered a side Thomas hadn't known about? Ground they'd never shared together? The idea gave him a ridiculous rush of pleasure.

He snapped out of that self-indulgent thought when he noted the sales associate's attention to her was being mirrored by many other men in the mall. She didn't tend to blend, his lady, and it reminded him his primary responsibility was protecting her anonymity.

When he reached her, he put an arm around her shoulders, imitating the many pairs of college students and teenagers they'd seen moving in the flood of people around them.

His lady was quick. After a contemplative moment where he felt her narrowed gaze upon him, even through the shaded glasses, she lifted her left hand to his on her shoulder, linking their fingers loosely so their hands were joined in a suggestive arch over the top of her breast. Sliding her other arm around his waist, she hooked her thumb in his waistband, the tips of her fingers in the top of his back pocket, squeezing the area she'd so recently abused.

"You after my wallet again?"

She slanted him a glance. "I've had you thoroughly investigated, Jacob Green. As of Monday morning, you had a grand total of eighteen hundred and twelve dollars and six cents in your savings account, nine hundred and two dollars and thirteen cents in your checking account. You live paycheck to paycheck, with no long-term savings or investment plan, a ridiculous way for a thirty-year-old man to live."

"I'm not quite thirty. Plus I'm working this gig to become the kept servant of a rich vampire. That should take care of me for the next three centuries or so."

When he'd helped her with her makeup earlier, he'd wet her lips with cherry lip gloss. He realized that had been a mistake, because when she smiled he smelled it and wanted to lick it off. He resisted the urge to get close, brush his lips along her temple, the fair cheek, but he couldn't stop his thumb from tracing a discreet line along the top of her breast under the linked bridge of their hands.

"A gold digger. My rose garden is fertilized by the bodies of men after my money."

"And beautiful roses they are. Would you like to ride this, my lady? It's slowing down."

"Which horse do I want to ride?"

"The black one," he said automatically. With that mysteriously satisfied smile, she darted through the turnstile, sliding her grip to his hand so she yanked him onto the platform with her. Putting his bag of purchases down on a bench flanked by two swans, he placed his hands on her waist to lift her onto the black horse, which had stopped on the upward rise. "Since levitating would cause too much attention," he pointed out.

She kept her grip on one of his shoulders. "I think you use any excuse to touch me."

"Every excuse and any situation I can create," he agreed. "There's a midnight movie here. A vampire cult classic, *Fright Night*. I'll take you if you promise to throw yourself in my arms at the scary parts."

She laughed, such a powerfully seductive note it reached out and turned the head of every man within hearing distance. Not wanting to do anything to ruin this carefree side of her nature, nevertheless he stepped closer, helping her guide her leg over the horse's withers. He kept his tone light, careful.

"Are you certain you're not using those pheromones, my lady? You're about to embarrass some of these lads in front of their dates. Get them in all sorts of trouble."

"Perhaps a little," she said, startling him. She removed the sunglasses, hooking them in her jeans pocket. When he raised his gaze, Jacob found her green eyes had the ability to mesmerize him like a snake, seducing him to self-destruction. "Perhaps I don't think you're besotted enough with me, Sir Vagabond."

Perhaps everything tonight was an act. She could be sitting deep inside the casually dressed body, behind the screen of her flirting, calculating her next test of his mettle. Or maybe she was being true.

All he could offer her was his honesty. He pressed closer. "I'm hard as a rock, my lady, and my heart is fair bursting with the heat of your smile. I'd worship every inch of you in whatever manner you wish if you'd give me the privilege." His voice lowered, and he let her hear the raw desire in his voice. "If you'd let me, I'd drag you off into a dark forest, spread you beneath me and fuck you until you screamed and raked my back with your beautiful nails. You'd have trouble walking afterwards, vampire recuperative powers or no."

On that note, he withdrew, taking the white unicorn next to her. Lyssa tipped her head back to watch the mirrors and baroque depictions of cherubs and goblins spin above as the carousel started. It gave her blood time to settle from the images his declaration evoked in her mind, far more dangerous than he could know. When she finally trusted herself to look at him, it didn't help.

From the snug pull of the denim over his crotch from the astride position, she could tell he wanted her. It made saliva gather under her tongue. She wondered what it would be like to see that powerful body synchronized with the motion of a flesh and blood horse. She suspected it was something worth seeing.

"You have a natural seat."

"Jouster, remember." He gave her a strained smile.

As she held the pommel to keep her balance, the curl of her fingers could not help but make Jacob think of her hand curled around him. It was a bitch to ride a horse with a confined erection.

"I'd like to have you show me your horsemanship sometime." She surprised him, reaching out and taking his hand, her grip sure and strong. She even smiled throughout the ride, amused but persistent as they had to let their hands slide from grip to a brush of fingertips and back to a grip again as their horses rose and fell counter to one another.

He decided it wasn't an act, simply because he didn't want it to be.

When the carousel stopped, he brought his leg back over and slid off his mount to give her a hand. Lyssa didn't need it of course, but she liked the courtesy, his hands on her waist, his eyes coursing over her breasts and throat, lingering on her face.

She was going to break her fast. She would take him to her bed tonight and feed on him. The intensity of his blue eyes, the brief tightening of his hands on her waist, told her he knew it as well. Somehow she'd resist giving him the second mark. She wanted him. He'd earned her attentions tonight, after all.

They strolled onward, not saying much now, but she allowed herself to slide her arm back around his waist as before, leaning into him as he resettled his arm over her shoulders. "The Ferris wheel, my lady?" he asked. "Or are there other things you want to see?"

"The tea shop. I want to try a couple of the new flavors I saw through the window. But . . . oh, look at that."

She stopped in front of the wishing pool that was the centerpiece of this leg of the mall. The fountain jetted out sprays of water in graceful arcs, splashing over the faces and bodies of a group of young women sculpted in ceramic. They held their skirts up, baring their thighs. Pushed wet hair from their faces. Some of the expressions were animated, as if they were calling out to their friends. Others were pensive, their eyes closed, heads tilted to the spray. In an act of whimsy, there was a dog, droplets of water cleverly emitting from him, enhancing the impression he was shaking the water off. The nearest sculpted woman held her hand out as if to block him, and she was laughing. The women's clothes clung to them without vulgar display, but it was sensuous, playful, reflecting the fantastical adult landscape the mall attempted to create. The lagoon the walled pool emulated backed up to a tall moss-covered rock. About ten feet up, water poured from an invisible source into the lagoon. A fog system at the base created misting clouds where the water dove into the main pool.

"I want to go in, Jacob." Lyssa turned to face him. "Carry me. I want to feel the waterfall on my body."

He displayed no self-consciousness, not even hesitation. Stepping over the wall into the pool, the water rising to his upper calves, he swung her up into his arms in the same movement.

Cold. She could tell the water was vibrantly cold, possibly with just a trickle of heat from the lights beneath the water's surface that spotlighted the sculptures and made the water glitter. She shivered as he moved through the sculptures, turning her as needed to keep her feet from hitting them. When she stretched out an arm to feel the water on her palm, he moved her directly under the fall as she'd requested, drenching her cotton shirt. As she clamped her hand around his neck, he spun her in a circle, knowing that was what she wanted. Her precognitive servant who didn't know he was precognitive, who hadn't even stopped to consider his answer when she'd asked what horse she wanted to ride.

Water was everywhere, a flood of sound and diamond crystal, blinding her with the pleasure of it.

It was foolish, she knew it was. But she didn't let that stop her. Trusting him to hold her, she spread out both arms, letting the magic gather and flow from her fingertips. It reached out like the water, only the marble wall couldn't contain it. It wrapped around and embraced the young people pointing and laughing at them, pressing up closer to the barrier. They were already bolstered by Jacob and Lyssa's audacity. They wanted to follow, teetering on the edge of the decision. It even reached out to older adults who had slowed to watch, who were unsure how to react. Disapprove? Or wish they had the courage to be like the younger ones?

One additional push, barely a blink of effort, and suddenly they were not alone. A cadre of teenagers splashed in, shouting, sending sheets of water at one another. Some of the boys even scooped up their girlfriends as Jacob had done to hold them in front of the small shoots of water striking the sculptures, eliciting shrieks and giggles, giving them the excuse to hold onto the girls even more tightly. Even one mother with a little girl came in. As her mother held her on her hip, the child tried to pet the dog, shielding her face with one tiny hand from the spray of droplets.

The sheer life of it washed over Lyssa. A moment like this had the nourishing strength of blood. A magic springing from the source of all magic, like life from a womb. Such a memory was strong enough to last a decade, making everything horrible seem not so terrible. Not against the power of this.

Reaching up, she stroked Jacob's hair from his forehead, enjoying the sleek copper highlights of it, the wet strands in her fingers, the strong broadness of his forehead, the slope of cheekbone to jaw. Her fingers slipped down, gripping the neckline of his shirt. A breath later, she tore it like paper, giving her fingers access to the pectoral, the nipple drawn hard and tight from the cold. As the water splashed down on them, he moved them so they were behind the curtain of the fall, a small area just big enough for the two of them standing close together, the heavy sheet of water making them disappear from view of the others, closing them into their own world. He let her go so her body slid down his, though he still held her fast about the waist with his other hand. When she dipped her head, he caught her chin.

"No pheromones. Or anything you release to make it more pleasurable."

"You're already wet, my knight. You think anyone will notice the stain of your seed?"

Color stained his cheeks, but he slid his fingers beneath the wig at the nape, into the nest of her pinned hair. "It's not that, my lady. I want you to know my responses are true ones." His eyes searched her face, his words stilling everything in her mind. The roar of the water and the wavering curtain of it behind his shoulders put them in a place in the universe where there wasn't room for anything else to intrude. "I want to feel the pain as well as the pleasure of belonging to you."

Gods, but what the man's words could do to her. She caught her hand in the tattered neck of the shirt and completely ripped the front of it, raking him with her nails as she did. In one movement she turned, slamming him up against the stone behind the fountain. She was aware of laughter and shrieking behind the wall of water, telling her that even more people had plunged into the fountain. The residual tendrils of her magic still spun her web, creating a screen of humanity, a buffer as effective as the water to keep them from discovery.

She sank her teeth into the left nipple, deep into the areola, knowing the pain there for a man was excruciating. He stiffened and arched into her, a hoarse cry coming from his lips as his hand became a hard fist in her dark locks, tearing the wig away and bringing her hair tumbling down as he held her locked to him. His other hand hooked in her back waistband, his thumb pressed against the tattoo she couldn't see but which seemed to intrigue him so much. His other fingers dug into her buttock, holding her tight against him as she suckled the hot source of his life, his heart thundering so close, separated from her by nothing but her own restraint and a fragile network of ribs.

How many times had she told herself she would make him wait for that second mark, make him earn it by at least first putting him through his paces at the planned dinner? And how little did it mean now, when she had him beneath her hands, the sound of his blood pumping so close, his heat enveloping her? She knew her lack of restraint was absurd, inexplicable, as well as she knew she was going to ignore everything she'd resolved and do it anyway, right here, right now.

She'd said she'd put her second mark on his thigh, but this was too tempting. Despite the empty scream of protest from somewhere inside of her, something even deeper let go. As the blood flowed into her, the secretion flowed into him.

While the first mark burned, the second was a detonation, convulsing the body as shields and gates to the mind were destroyed. He bucked against her, gasping as her mind flooded through the rubble left by the explosion. Fearless, she plunged into the dark tunnel of his mind the way he had plunged his fingers into her hair to create a bond, an anchor.

All the inhabitants—thoughts, people, emotions—surrounded her. Feelings, family, childhood, a tidal wave of images that would give her everything she wanted to know about him, now and forever. But right now she had a single purpose, one set of images and reactions only.

Putting one hand down to cup him, she wrenched open his jeans to find him enormous, not at all affected by the cold water. She gripped him, insisting, pumping him. His desire to feel everything fully notwithstanding, the climax would make the binding easier. But she also wanted the dark pleasure of his loss of control not just in her hand but in his thoughts. The base male response during the descent into orgasm, which was nothing but a morass of primitive words. She wanted the visceral drive of it, the savagery.

Fuck . . . fuck her . . . God . . . cock . . . in her wet cunt . . . ram it into her . . .

The muscles of his throat were working, his whole body shuddering, his hands clamped on her, bruising.

It had not been this way with Thomas. The second mark had been quiet, almost gentle. She'd been amused by his scholarly attempts to mark every transition as she pushed through the shields of his mind. He'd acted almost as if he was going to prepare a paper on it for a science periodical.

This was pure possession. She obliterated Jacob's shields, bludgeoned them into tiny pieces that became a part of the blood she took into her body. From here forward, she could plunge into this jungle whenever she chose to do so. She knew it would test her. His thoughts would make her feel things she'd never felt before.

She made it brutal. He was right. She reveled in the war between his desire to submit and his need to challenge her invasion. She felt his primitive urge to take back control by invading her mind as she was invading his. While she knew he couldn't do that without her permission, she found she didn't know where her mind ended and his began at the moment.

When she raised her head, he clamped his mouth over hers, sucking his blood off her lips, using his teeth to score her as she brought him to violent climax. His hot seed jetted over her wrist and arm, even the front of her shirt, the warmth contrasting with the cold shower of water.

She savored the insistent rock of his body against her as she drained him and he came to a jerky halt. Against her lips, he cursed her for not letting him fuck her. But even as he did so, his hands gentled and he raised his head to let his gaze sweep her face. There was a wonder there, a reverent awe mixed with an expression that made her feel he was seeing something in herself she'd never seen. Raising his thumb, he brushed blood off her lip and held it there. Slowly, she licked at his fingers with the tip of her tongue, feeling like she'd gone from raging lioness to wary kitten in a blink. These moments, which should be inequitable matches of physical prowess, kept ending up on a playing field where she wasn't so certain she was the victor. Or if it was a playing field at all.

The din outside the waterfall was receding, stern shouts and a whistle indicating mall security was clearing out the rowdy teens, dispersing them from the fountain. Jacob refastened his jeans, working up the zipper. Her fingers whispered over his knuckles as he did it, earning a heated look from him. Taking her hand, he twined it with his a moment before she freed herself to slide the torn shirt off him. Her palms molded over the rounded curves of his shoulders, nails pressing into the muscles of his upper arms. Water beaded on his pale lips and the intensity of his eyes warmed her as she folded the shirt like a towel and laid it over his left shoulder, covering the nipple area where she'd bitten him.

She wasn't alone. He was within and without. As she enjoyed his body, his mind was there, all its rooms and the thoughts that filled them. A never-ending maze of chambers she could explore to whatever depths she chose. He'd given her the gift willingly, as much as he could understand what it was he was offering to her.

Most servants were prepped as he'd been, but until the mark was actually given, they didn't realize the power and vulnerability of it. There were vampires so drunk on that power they plumbed their servant's mind until they drove them mad, goading the rooms holding dark fears and secrets to the surface, giving the servant nowhere to be private with his own soul. Since vampires could exchange a similar mark, and she'd offered it to Rex foolishly, she had a personal insight into the dangers of such probing. It became a battle of wills to keep him locked out, leaving her exhausted.

A human did not have the ability to lock her out once marked, but she was not that kind of Mistress. It was most often used as a functional link, a way to exchange information over distances or in front of others. However, as she'd just shown Jacob, depending on the relationship with the servant, it could become far more. If she chose, she could invite him into her own inner chambers. Of course, delving into her deepest chambers might indeed drive him to madness. Her own sanity stayed only within the barest grasp of her fingertips these days as it was.

Pushing that thought away, she moved gently among his thoughts without really examining them, just letting him know she was there. It was enough for now to see the realization of it in his eyes, feel the tight grip of his hands and let him get used to it.

She'd done the second mark the way she'd done the first, on pure impulse. Was she losing the battle with her own will and loneliness? Was her rational need for a servant leveraging her desire to fully bond with him before he understood what that meant?

No. This was it. Two marks. No more.

Gods, please help me keep that resolve. If you will not do it for me, do it for him.

20

He'd parked his bike near the opera house earlier in the week and hitched back to a convenience store where he was supposed to meet Ingram in a regular car. From there the man was going to drive him the rest of the way back to Lyssa's house.

An elderly woman picked him up. She informed him she was turning eighty on Saturday, could barely see, and too many cars on the road made her nervous. After she asked him to take the wheel until they got to their destination, she talked him into stopping at the drugstore for her prescription and the grocery store for three soft pears and several cans of soup. When they finally got to Ingram, he'd had the man follow him while he drove her back to her house. He ignored Elijah's grin when the woman gave him a kiss on the cheek and two pieces of peach cobbler.

He could have lectured her on the foolishness of picking up someone who could easily overpower her and turning over the car to him to boot. However, he'd learned it wasn't necessarily a lack of common sense that made women act that way.

"A woman knows she's safe with you, Jacob. She just knows." It was Milah, one of the circus tumblers he regularly tossed in the air, who'd first pointed it out to him. "Don't get me wrong. You're not a harmless puppy dog. But you can tell you'd break your own hand before you'd let it hurt a woman."

He definitely wasn't feeling harmless at the moment. When Lyssa's fangs sank into him, she'd entered his consciousness on so many levels he'd almost shoved her away in panic. Instead, he turned that energy to holding steady, getting a grip. A fierce grip with both hands, his hold on her waist tightening as her invasion spread into every corner of his mind, deep into wells of his soul where even he didn't go.

His awareness of her was heightened beyond anything he'd imagined. When Thomas had talked about being connected this way, he'd imagined something like schizophrenia, with voices in his head. He had a certain ability to anticipate someone's needs, an uncanny intuition that had served him well throughout his life, but this went far beyond that. When they left the fountain, he stopped at the hallway leading to the restroom because he knew she wanted to wring out her shirt and re-pin her hair. They'd put the wig in one of his bags. He knew she wanted him to wait here, at the entrance to the hall. So he did as she left him without a word, just a brush of contact on his arm. Since no matter how often he'd studied it tonight he couldn't help watching that tempting little ass, he watched it until it disappeared into the restroom and was startled when she let him feel her pleasure at his regard. Her amusement.

He leaned against the wall, resting his head against the cool tile to ease the odd buzzing sensation. From here he could see the Ferris wheel, the way it tilted on its axis like a top. Somewhat the way his mind was doing, trying to find its balance now that someone was riding it with him.

Could she really read it all? Everything he thought or felt? For some reason, he'd never really considered her access to his thoughts below the surface layers. Now it was dawning on him, how many things she would know about him. Things she'd know about him almost before he had the thought himself. He didn't regret it, but damn if it wasn't an uncomfortable idea, making him self-conscious, as if everything about him was under a spotlight for her perusal. Not "as if." It *was.*

I can leave no stone unturned, if I so choose.

She'd returned, was standing there next to him, but she'd spoken inside his head. Her lips had not moved at all. He suspected she'd intended to come upon him unawares, to underscore what Thomas had told him. *The marks are two-way, but only when she allows it.*

As if her invasion into his mind had opened up some of the rooms he himself couldn't open, for the first time he understood his own conflict better. She was a queen, a liege lady, in truth. He was her servant, while his soul burned to give her everything, just for a smile. His sense of honor would keep him at her side even when she drove him mad. But what would keep him protecting and serving her beyond every torment of hell was something she'd be shocked to know, maybe even offended—

His attention snapped to her face as she watched him, her jade green eyes filled with things he didn't understand and didn't want to interpret. Maybe it was good he couldn't read her mind. He couldn't bear her scorn at this moment.

"You consider me yours. No other man's." She voiced the thought he hadn't intended to share. "Be careful, Jacob. You are right. You are my servant. I am your Mistress. Our relationship may be far more intense than that of human lovers, but it is far less equitable, I promise you."

It was like catching mice running out of a cage. He didn't know which thought to chase down and try to slap back into the cage, but it was futile regardless. The bars were gone. There was nowhere to put them. The noise of the mall closed in on him as he struggled with it, and suddenly there seemed to be a lot less oxygen.

"Jacob." Her hand was on his arm. "Breathe deep, Sir Vagabond. Be calm." Her fingers climbed to his biceps, squeezed. "Sshh . . ."

"I can't . . . get a handle on it."

"Nothing to get a handle on. That's where you're making a mistake." Her touch stroked, soothed. "It's like . . . do you believe in the Christian version of God? It's like that, the way they say He is in your thoughts at all times."

"No one really believes that, though." He tried to respond to her gentle teasing in kind, not let the first anxiety attack he'd ever had in his life overcome him. "No one thinks God's in there 24/7, listening to what you're going to eat for breakfast, or watching sitcom reruns at two in the morning with you."

"I won't be, either," she said with a smile. Cupping his face, she brought his eyes to her. When they steadied, focused, she nodded her approval, though she kept stroking his hair from his temples, helping him stay calm as he struggled for his bearings. "Yes, I'll know your thoughts if I'm listening at the time you have them. The main purpose of the mind link is to communicate without using our voices, and to communicate over distance."

You can handle this, Jacob. You can do this.

Her voice or his? His, but she could hear him if she chose to do so.

"I may choose to eavesdrop," she said quietly. "But when I do, most of the time you won't even know I'm there. I've never claimed or desired to be an easy Mistress to serve. If you curse my name, I may hear it, but as long as you act toward me with respect, most of the time I'll allow you the illusion of privacy, the normal range of emotions and personal thoughts inside your head without disruptive intrusion, even when I choose to be there. I don't expect you to be less than human. As Thomas may have told you, over time you'll become far less conscious of it."

Until you lose it. As he weakened, Thomas had spoken of things a man confessed on his deathbed, the staggering sense of loss he'd felt when she blocked their link so effectively he could no longer sense it anymore. It had been like the removal of a vital organ, the severing of a limb.

When Lyssa's eyes darkened with pain, Jacob wished he could have thought about something else, anything else.

"My lady—"

"No." She shook her head, drew away from him. "At least you won't have to worry about that, Jacob. I'll never give you the third mark."

At first he wasn't sure he'd heard her correctly. She was walking, and he had to take a couple of fast strides to catch up, take her arm to stop her. "What do you mean? I don't understand. Have I displeased you somehow?"

She looked away, her body tense, wanting to move. "The second mark isn't a guarantee of the third, and it's not necessary for how I need you to serve me."

"My lady, why do you insist on shutting—"

"Jacob," she snapped. The admonition silenced him, but Lyssa saw the anger in his eyes, the hurt confusion. *To have come so far, worked so hard, and she isn't going to even give me the chance. . . . What the hell? She can't mean it. She—*

She shut down her awareness of his thoughts, unwilling to hear the things that fueled her own frustration. It angered her, his presumption. Almost as much as her desire to do what he wanted.

Coldness invaded her vitals, cutting short the surge of temper. The hair rose on the back of her neck and she went still, surveying her immediate surroundings and then farther out, reaching and looking for the source. Pain rushed in her temples, sudden enough that she froze, caught in the grip of it. *No, not now.* Setting her teeth, she fought to look past it, to push down the nausea rising in her throat. Perhaps it was caused by what she was sensing, not an impending attack. She didn't know which was preferable.

"My lady." He had her arm, his touch gentle but firm. "I should have brought us a car. Do you need your medicine?"

"No." Lyssa blinked, clearing the haze over her eyes. It was an effort, but she made herself straighten. "We should go, though."

Without prompting, he slid an arm around her, bringing her in to his side so they could walk through the mall, blending with the other young lovers who moved in trilling, giggling packs. Noise bounced off the walls. Thankful for the sunglasses, she closed her eyes, curled her fingers into Jacob's flesh. She heard him tell a security guard they were on their way out when he was admonished for not wearing his shirt. She didn't hear the response, but she was sure it was a male security guard. No woman would have required someone looking like Jacob to wear a shirt unless she was insane.

Where was it? She could feel the presence like a poison seeping through the walls, coating the tile floor, trying to come in contact with her. The source of it would not be inside the mall, however. It would wait in the shadows, knowing she'd sensed it. Staying in the mall would appear as weakness, and she refused to show weakness to this one, even if the effort killed her. It would be equally debilitating to let the creature believe it could get under her skin. Either way, she wouldn't permit it to have an advantage. Couldn't.

Jacob.

She spoke his name in her mind, and was reassured when he tightened his arm around her. He could hear her then.

Before they stepped out the parking deck entrance, she straightened, took his elbow in a more formal gesture. He gave her a glance, but said nothing as they moved into the deck area. He was alert, picking up on her mood, his eyes darting everywhere. She knew they wouldn't see her quarry, though. This one had to be flushed.

"Show yourself, Carnal. Unless you're planning to jump out of the shadows and say 'boo.'"

Jacob stiffened and she touched him with her mind. *Follow my lead, and do not disobey me.*

The vampire who stepped out was as tall as Jacob, perhaps taller. Emanating a vampire's physical perfection, he'd honed it to a razor-sharp attraction to draw whatever prey to him he chose. His long dark hair had once been short, but apparently he'd realized the style emphasized too well the precisely cut lines of his face, making the cruelty more easily noticed. His eyes, gray and piercing as an ice pick, were mesmerizing enough to seduce, but lacked the warmth for it. His lean body exhibited a tensile strength suggesting a fencer about to step into a ring.

When his eyes swept Jacob, the vampire dismissed him so quickly Jacob wasn't sure he'd even seen him.

His lady stepped in front of him, he noted with displeasure. He'd have corrected that, but her voice erupted in his mind again. Being such a new sensation, he had to take precious seconds to orient himself to it, focus enough to understand the message she was communicating.

Stay behind me. It's inappropriate for a servant to stand equal with his vampire Mistress. Even worse to insult her by standing in front of her. Speak only when spoken to. A servant never speaks when two vampires are conversing.

As she issued her terse instructions, Carnal's gaze was roving every inch of her in slow, deliberate appraisal, lingering in a way that made Jacob itch for a wooden stake. He tried to remain as impassive as his Mistress, but there was something about the way Lyssa held herself that suggested she was anticipating ugliness from this encounter. Jacob had never let a woman stand between him and danger. He didn't care for the feeling one bit.

"This is a new look for you, Lyssa." His voice was smooth, well-pitched. A cross between a radio personality and a torturer for the Inquisition. "I came by your house, intending to leave my calling card, only to find no servant to meet me. I decided to amuse myself in the area until your return and was fortunate enough to be close enough to this place"—his lip curled distastefully—"to detect the most delicious perfume on the air. You." He cocked his head. "Even in your own Region, I'm surprised you would send out such an obvious beacon like that. Your powerful compulsion magic has stirred up quite a few creatures of the night."

"I've no concern about my enemies, Carnal. They're far more confident of themselves than they should be."

Carnal gave a half bow, his dark hair falling forward over his shoulders. "I hope for your happiness and long life it is so. There are many these days who resist the Council and their pro-human laws. Taking down the vampire queen who helped implement them . . . That would be a powerful victory for them, a catalyst for irrevocable change."

"An era of more bloodshed. It seems some never tire of it."

"Blood is nothing, Lyssa. It is power that drives your enemies. Didn't Rex always say that? Have you forgotten his wisdom?"

Lyssa's posture did not change. From what little of her profile Jacob could see, she didn't even alter her expression. But he sensed Carnal had fired the first arrow when her tone went to frost.

"It seems you've forgotten proper etiquette. We've received no missive from you or a servant. You are to announce your presence before entering my Region."

A flash of something went through the steely eyes, too fast for Jacob to give it a name, though he suspected it was hostility.

"My apologies," the vampire said lightly. "I didn't think old friends needed such formalities. Perhaps you might consider sharing your dinner dalliance with me to break some of the ice between us?"

It took Jacob a moment to realize Carnal was referring to him, for he didn't look in his direction. He focused on Lyssa as if he were trying to peel the skin from her bones with the scalpel of his gaze.

"He isn't food. I'm training him as a new servant."

Curiosity swept the vampire's features and his attention shifted back toward Jacob.

Lower your gaze.

The night he'd brought Lyssa home, Jacob recalled Thomas had advised him to avoid eye contact with Bran and not challenge the dog's dominance. Jacob had refused to do it. *I'm here to take care of her, mate. That's the end of it.*

He'd trained for months on the proper etiquette when a human servant met another vampire. But even with that and his Mistress's sharp admonition in his mind, Jacob faced the vampire's thorough assessment head-on, blue eyes clashing with gray as Carnal registered his existence for the first time.

Carnal's lip curled slightly at the left corner, exposing a fang. Jacob didn't find it anywhere near as intimidating as Bran's upper set, which seemed at the time like it could have graced the model of a saber-toothed tiger at the Smithsonian. Jacob detected a glimmer of red in the man's eyes, but he kept that creepy flat tone, even as he held Jacob's gaze, acknowledging the challenge. "So the rumor is true. You dispatched your scabrous scholar."

"I couldn't bear to have him near me after Rex's death." Lyssa shifted between the two men, breaking the stalemate. Carnal's gaze shot quickly to her, a predator registering the slightest movement of prey that might try to escape him.

"You were merciful. I would have tortured him for months."

"I don't have your lust for blood."

The expression on Carnal's face altered, became more drawn. "Your distance wounds me, Lyssa. I've missed Rex, too."

The arrogance dropped from his voice, making it become more vulnerable. There was a disturbing rawness contrasting with the smooth menace. Strangely, Jacob sensed this was a more honest side to the creature confronting them.

"Things aren't the same without Rex. I was hoping . . . You and I loved him best. All I wanted was to spend time with you remembering him. To come to your home and feel the lingering sense of his presence. I was afraid you'd say no if I asked first. Please forgive me for taunting you. Truly, grief makes me a bastard."

He dropped to one knee as Lyssa remained motionless, her back straight as one of the concrete pillars on the parking deck. When he lifted his head, his gaze returned to Jacob.

"Come, share the blood of your servant with me. He seems young and not yet broken in. The experience of being shared will do him good. He's a fine specimen." Calculation gleamed in his now darkening eyes, reminding Jacob of twin rat holes. "I've no interest in his cock, but it's a particular pleasure to fuck a straight male while feeding. Their humiliation, their rage . . . Throw in a little pain, and it's an incredible taste. This one needs to learn humility."

"I don't share the blood of my servant. Why would I be so foolish as to give you a connection to myself?"

"You were foolish enough to unleash your unique magic in this crowded place, Lyssa," he pointed out, rising to his feet and squaring with her again.

"My husband gave you leave to call me familiar," she said softly. "I never did. Since he's dead, the invitation is rescinded."

Jacob tensed as the air heated around them, impending violence thrumming in the air. Carnal's pale lips curled back. "You weren't so formal when I was ramming my cock into you and you were screaming. Do you know how often I've thought of that? The way my cock was bathed in your blood when I pulled out of your tight ass? After I spilled my come into your body? Perhaps if Rex had let me fuck your frigid cunt we might now be celebrating our heir."

Jacob stepped forward, intending murder. Instead, he was knocked to his knees. Lyssa's hand was in his hair, holding him fast, her eyes cold and remote as she stared down at him in the subjugated pose. "Behave."

She turned her attention back to Carnal, who arrested his forward motion as she pinned him with her gaze. "As you see, I can teach my servant about humility myself. I need nothing from you except to observe the proper courtesies. Go back to your territory. Jacob will contact you when I have decided on the date you may attend me at my home and perform the correct formalities. Then you may travel through my Region. Otherwise I'll place a complaint with your Region Master."

A muscle in his jaw flexed, but he performed a mocking bow. "As you wish. If my inconvenience serves your desires, then I will suffer it gladly. Far be it from me to disregard the all-important bureaucratic rules of the Council."

She inclined her head, not rising to the bait. His gaze swept her. "I hope to see you in your normal attire on that date. This doesn't suit your great beauty at all. Good luck with your servant. I suspect he won't live long."

Turning on his heel, he walked across the parking deck, his hard-soled shoes crisp and sharp on the concrete. Lyssa's nails dug into Jacob's scalp as her eyes remained on her adversary. His knees ached from the impact with the unyielding cement and his chest was tight with anger and embarrassment, but he forced himself to stay still, do nothing further she would perceive as defiance of her wishes.

When he reached the edge of the deck, Carnal stopped. "Do you even miss him, *Lady* Lyssa?" He turned his head, showing his profile. His lip curled, giving the impression he was spitting on the title, but Jacob saw the vulnerability had returned to his expression.

It was a long moment, but Lyssa replied at last, one hollow syllable that echoed, rebounding on ugly gray walls. "Yes."

"And me?"

"You were my husband's friend, Carnal. Not mine. You'll visit my home due to my respect for your Region Master and in honor of my husband's memory, but I do not desire your friendship. Don't seek it further from me."

With a snarl, he disappeared into the darkness. Lyssa waited. Jacob watched her face, realizing she was listening, all her senses extended to determine if they were alone. Her grip eased somewhat, her thumb stroking a lock of his hair from his forehead, easing the strain on his neck her hold had created. It didn't abate his fury, however. He wanted to tell her to let go, to never again make him take a second seat to her in a dangerous situation. Or treat him like a recalcitrant child.

When she turned her gaze to him at last, her green eyes were hard and cold. She backhanded him in the face.

Pain exploded in the bridge of his nose, his jaw and cheek area. The impact knocked him to the concrete. He knew she'd used restraint because he was alive, but he tasted blood in his mouth where his teeth had snapped onto his tongue.

"When I give you an order, you'll obey it. If I tell you to stand behind me, that's where you will stay. Without movement, without a word. Do you understand me?"

He scrambled to his feet almost as soon as she hit him. But before he could regain his balance, she struck him again, the opposite side, knocking him back down, making it clear she could do it all night long. He'd never be able to touch her, not even a slap worthy of two girls squabbling on a playground.

This wasn't being treated like a child. He was being treated like a slave, someone's property, prohibited by the laws of her existence from correcting that notion.

If you want to be in my world, that is what you are. What you must accept.

The presence of her in his mind, the things she had been trying to tell him and things Thomas had hinted at, suddenly made a cohesive, frightening picture. A picture she was forcing him to look at more closely than he'd done before.

Was she the answer to his destiny he'd sought for so long, or was Gideon right? Was he indulging in romanticized wishful thinking rather than truth? As Jacob pushed himself back on his heels, she turned her back on him, a strike more painful than the physical blows.

He didn't have to take it. He could take her home, walk away. Of course he'd walk away with two marks binding him permanently to her, but she would let him go. He swiped at his lips with the back of his hand, came up with blood.

Only moments ago, he'd known down to the depths of his soul he'd never walk away from her. He'd known it even when he took the oath, otherwise he wouldn't have taken it, for to him an oath was sacred, unbreakable.

It will guide you when everything else seems cloudy. Thomas had said that, comparing it to the sacredness that attended the oath of marriage. *For better or worse . . . Our hearts know what is true, Jacob, and need no oath. It's our minds that need it, to help us stay the course through the rough patches. You will need the oath, I promise you. She will make nothing easy.*

He spat blood. Well, this seemed to qualify as one of those rough patches.

He struggled to find *it,* the elusive something that could right his course again, and he remembered that first night, the naked pain in her gaze after Ingram had left and it was just the two of them.

I can't bear to lose another servant . . .

She had no servant. No one to indulge her need to casually reach out, touch and stroke. No one to hold her close, surprising her with the offer of comfort. No one to make her smile, banish shadows from her eyes. No one to kick around and treat like dog shit.

She spoke, her voice quiet, tired. "I release you from your oath, Jacob. You don't have to stay. You can go now. I'll find my way home. He's gone."

Damn it, remembering she could read his mind was a pain in the ass. But for all its drawbacks, the link could introduce an intimacy to their relationship that couldn't be duplicated in mortal interactions. He didn't have to guard words with her, he didn't have to do anything but be exactly who he was. There was a freedom to that.

Thomas, insisting he take that oath, had understood the fundamental essence of who Jacob was, what he wanted above all else.

He moved. One step after another as she remained still, her back to him. A pace behind her, he dropped to one knee, reached out and took her hand. Brought it to his lips before he lifted her knuckles, pressed them against his face where she'd struck him.

Lyssa had tuned out of his mind after hearing the bent of his thoughts. Lost in thoughts of her own, his touch startled her. As she turned toward him, she could feel all the conflict in him, all the reasons to walk away milling in his mind. There was fury simmering there, and yet still he touched her with courtesy and reassurance. Reading his mind was not the same as reading his heart, but this gesture provided the answer to the jumbled chaos of her own needs.

"He may be gone, my lady. But I'm not."

21

HER eyes had been so full of pain when she'd turned toward him. Now she straddled the motorcycle behind him, cheek pressed to his back and arms around his waist. He drove through the light traffic of early morning, his face aching, his mind going over the pieces of the puzzles, the images Carnal had painted, the words she had spoken. Despite his best efforts to accept and get past it, even the way she'd struck him and how both vampires had treated him kept intruding.

He'd scoped out several routes from the mall, and he took the shortcut through a new neighborhood behind the shopping area. It would connect to a main thoroughfare, but instead of taking the turn to it, he went a different way on impulse, speeding down a darkened street with as-yet-unbuilt lots that dead-ended into a service road, currently barricaded off with an iron pole gate to keep out cars. He swung wide and bypassed it, taking the pedestrian path through a proposed forest park area. As they left the tree cover and came out into a clear meadow, the winter grass had turned silver in the moonlight. He cut his headlight and turned off the engine so they could look at the tranquil view. When she turned her head so her other cheek was pressed against his back, he knew she was looking as he was at the varying shadows playing across the field, since the moon had dipped just below the tree line. She kept her arms around his waist as he braced his feet on the ground on either side of the bike.

He could hear nothing but his own thoughts, and realized there was a sense of "other" when she was in his mind. Just a shadow, like when she was following him around the house. It made him feel alone, knowing she wasn't in his mind right now, and yet she'd only marked him an hour or two ago. It made him wonder how Thomas had borne the loss after having it for so long. He breathed in the night air, letting the tranquility of the meadow, the sound of crickets and the feel of her arms around his chest soothe and steady him. Taking one of her hands in his own at last, he kissed her knuckles, then held them on his thigh, warming her cold fingers against his own body heat. He wasn't cold at all despite his dampness. She was, though, and he wondered if it was caused by more than her normal low body temperature.

He felt that shadowy presence enter into his awareness and tested his theory. *Would he be out here? Watching us?*

"No." She spoke then, as if knowing he wasn't quite up to long strings of dialogue in his head yet. There was a dry note to her voice. "Carnal is allergic to nature. He's a made vampire. Rex was his sire. Born and bred in the city, not connected to the earth at all. Probably because he senses it's going to open up one day so the bowels of hell can claim him."

Good.

Tugging on her hand, he encouraged her to dismount, seeing her arch look at his one-word answer to Carnal's current and potential future whereabouts. One hand slid from him as she complied, though he retained her other and she didn't pull free or let go. He swung his leg over and walked her into that meadow. The straw-colored grass as fine as a woman's hair, gold in summer but now shining silver, feathered against their legs, whispering. When he stopped, he turned her to face him. Her eye color was almost a pale sea green in this light. He was glad she'd left off the wig. The wind had dried her hair somewhat, but it was snarled and not smooth around her face. He saw the ghosts in her face, the strain around her mouth. She looked almost mortal.

The desire to withdraw from him, to avoid his questions, filled her eyes. Before she could back away, he put his hands on her shoulders, saying nothing, and kissed her.

Not the hard, passion-driven kisses they'd shared until now, infused with dark images and violence. There was a pleasure in that, but this was a different pleasure, a gift he could offer to her.

Her mouth was soft, yielding. She leaned into him, her hands resting on his hips as she kept her face completely still, her eyes half closed as he spread light kisses on her lips. The top, then the bottom, the corner of her mouth, one eyelid then the other. Her cheek. Next to her ear, where when he started to nibble, her hands closed into fists on the waistband of his jeans. Her fingers slid inside to caress his skin at his waist, finding his hip bones then moving around to the sensitive curve of his buttocks, for she preferred him not to wear underwear. He moved to her neck as he found her flesh as well, palming the small of her back, thinking of the tattoo there and tracing the rougher feel of it. She made a murmur of noise, telling him his fascination with it had made her more aroused in that area. So he lingered, teasing it a bit longer until he took the hem of the T-shirt and brought it over her head, leaving her like him, standing just in a pair of jeans, since she'd worn no bra beneath the snug shirt. It had the softness of worn cloth, a tiny tee probably meant to be a sleep tank, but he'd particularly liked it for her, the "not everyone is a morning person" motto. She looked as cute in it as the sleeping kitten on the front.

"Jacob. I am over a millennium old. I am not cute."

He smiled against her skin. "You are to me. Stop listening to my thoughts." Dropping to one knee, he worshipped her breasts with his mouth, his hands, his eyes. Every touch reverent, designed to create a quiet, yearning arousal, a mode just short of climax where the sweet edge of desire could be ridden forever. While he might die of frustration from such a reality, he knew it would be heaven to her, and he wanted to give her heaven.

She rewarded him, cupping his face, her fingers following where she'd struck him, soothing as he nuzzled between her breasts, pressing them together with his hands so he could lick the valley in between, tease the nipples with his thumbs in slow strokes. A sigh left her, her body leaning further into him, the tension slipping off her like a cloak falling to the forest floor. But here, it was all moonlight and silver, the pale gleam of her skin like cream. Her fingers trailed along his bare wide shoulders, learning every point of bone, the straps of lean muscle.

He opened the jeans, guided them off her legs as she increased her grip on his shoulder, bringing her other hand to his hair. He could tell she liked his hair, the way she so often played with it, watching the reddish brown threads drift through her fingers. He liked feeling her touch there, for it was more spontaneous than some of the other ways she touched him. Not the calculated seduction moves wrapped up in the things she felt were so important for him to understand about the etiquette of their relationship. This moment was just them. That was the way he wanted to keep it. Forget about what had just happened, or what might happen after they left the park. *Give me this, my lady*. Moments like this would make those moments easier to bear.

He kissed the line of her lower abdomen, hip bone to hip bone, small touches of his tongue tracing the line of skin over the low rise of the panties, his chin rubbing against her pubic bone. She made a noise of need and he could smell her desire as he laid his hands on both of her thighs, holding her as he stimulated her further. He remembered that first night when she'd marked him with the slick dew from her cunt. His legs, stomach, cock, chest. Would three centuries be long enough to make sure that he'd kissed every inch of her?

But she'd said she wouldn't give him the third mark. And if he couldn't convince her otherwise, he'd have even less time to be sure his lips had touched every part of her, over and over again.

Lifting his gaze to her face, he hooked his fingers in the panties and eased them down her legs. Left them at her ankles as he bent his head and licked her clit.

Her hand convulsed on his shoulder, a lock of his hair trapped beneath her fingers, tugging on his scalp as her body jerked. He did it again, those slow licks on the clit hood with her legs not yet spread enough to get his head all the way between them. He kept his hands on her thighs to tell her he wanted her to stay that way for a few moments longer. He nuzzled her when she bumped against him impatiently, and her nails dug into his skin. She'd draw blood one way or another, for it was her way. He was learning that much. He didn't want this to be about anything she had to do for someone else. He didn't want her to have to make any decisions.

"Just feel," he murmured. Rising, he slid his arms around her waist to lift her, so the last garment fell to the meadow floor and she was fully, blissfully naked against his half-clad but tautly aroused body. Wrapping her arms around his shoulders, she pressed her face into his neck. He could feel her need for this, to lose herself. As he held her in the tight, quiet embrace, she drew in a deep breath, her nostrils flaring against his skin as she inhaled his scent. Her bare feet brushed against his jean-covered calves, goading a fierce surge of reaction in his chest. He would do anything to protect her, to keep her happy.

Maybe it didn't make sense to the whole world, his brother, even himself. Despite her savagery, her cruelty, he felt whole, complete when she trusted him like this. There were no questions now. This was where he was meant to be, the meaning and importance of his whole life held in his arms. Perhaps it was like the first moment when a mother saw her baby. There would be terrible pain. The child often would do everything he or she could to shake that love. But that kind of love was steadfast, inarguable. That was the point, the clear path.

"Jacob—"

"Sshhh. Just let me love you, my lady."

Shifting, he laid her down on their clothes cushioned beneath by the soft meadow grass. Spreading her hair around her, he brought a handful of it to his lips, brushing it there, then over his eyes, his face, loving the feel of it as she watched him, her hand stroking his shoulder. Her other hand touched his knee as he squatted next to her supine form, trailed along the inseam of the denim. Taking her time making her way up his thigh until she reached the hard evidence of his desire, constrained behind the zipper. He rose, her hand trailing downward to his knee as he shucked off the garment. Tossing it on the pile of her clothes, he looked down at her. Her hand had come back to rest on his bare knee now, her eyes traveling up his body, lingering on his turgid cock, the weight of his balls. She'd required him to shave around his genitals for her, and her eyes registered her approval of the closely trimmed pubic area even as she appreciated the line of hair she'd wanted him to keep at his stomach and the light thatch over his chest. Finally, her eyes lifted to his face.

Even with the desire in her face he could feel the need behind it. She wanted, badly. Now. He was hers. All hers.

He heard that thought as clearly as if she'd spoken it. Without further hesitation, he dropped to one knee next to her, laid his hand on her thigh and spread her legs, feeling as if he were opening an angel's wings to reveal the heart of life and its meaning. Easing over her, he felt the brush of her thigh as she raised it, touching his bare hip. She framed his face with her hands as he lowered himself to kiss her, bearing his weight on his arms as he slid slow and deep within her. Easy, so easy.

"Aaahhh . . ." That soft breath from her again. He closed his own eyes, the feel of her wet pussy closing around him in a moment too sacred not to be met with an attitude of devout prayer. He felt her amusement with the thought, mixed with a wave of her own desire. He smiled as well, opening his eyes as he began to move.

He was a well-endowed man. It had never seemed a thing of much consequence to him, except it saved him from locker-room ribbing and he was able to give pleasure to the women who took joy in it. But as she arched and gasped, he filled her tight channel and was glad to be able to give her that gift.

Her nails sliced him anew, so that he increased the power of his strokes, his desire rising. Her lips parted so he couldn't resist bending and covering them with his own. She met him with a hard kiss, her tongue seeking his, her hands now on his head, gripping his hair as her lower body lifted and fell, increasing the power of the impact as they came together more rapidly.

"Yours, my lady," he muttered, echoing her thoughts, and growled as she raked him from shoulder to buttocks, her heels clamping over his hips.

Mine, she agreed, the jade eyes locking with his. Her hand was between them, now resting on the mark over his nipple, which was swollen and stinging like fire, so when she reared up and placed her mouth over it to suckle on him, it speared shards of aching pleasure through him. Her hands gripped his ass, fingers rocking him against her as her hips rose and dropped, driving them higher.

Come for me, Jacob.

You first, my lady. 'Tis not a battle. Give me the gift of seeing you come while I still have a scrap of sanity to enjoy the sight.

"I can feel your cunt tight like a fist over my cock." He whispered it, lying down on her body, his mouth against her ear as he held her pinned to the ground. He slowed his strokes to rub with excruciating small movements against her clit while she quivered spasmodically beneath him.

She could remove him easily, even reverse the position, but instead her arms locked around his shoulders, her legs still around his hips. She pressed her face into his shoulder as he rocked her, pumping her slowly against his cock, reaching beneath her to palm her soft bottom and guide her on him, up, down, deep in, dragging out.

She hesitated, fighting dark images he couldn't see or understand, but he could sense their pull. He wouldn't try to fight those, but he would coax her from their grasp.

"Let your servant please you. You've nothing to fear from me. My life is yours to do with as you will, my lady." His voice was hoarse. He wanted her ears to hear the truth of it as well as her mind.

Neither death . . . nor pain . . . nor loss. Shall I fear. Only my beloved may rend my heart asunder. Burn me to ashes like the rising of the sun. Vampire . . . poet. Sjaran, twelfth century.

"Never, my lady. Never." Daring to tip the scales, he shifted his firm grip on her buttocks, brushed his finger pads around the rim of her rectum, teasing it as he stroked against her clit. Pressing his cock even more deeply inside her, he found the dense area of her sweet spot when he put his lips to her throat, just beneath her ear.

The grip of her arms increased exponentially and she shattered, her body arching, bucking against him convulsively. With her arms and legs tight around him it was a furious wet friction against his cock that snapped his own barely leashed restraint. As she spasmed, muffling her cries in his shoulder, her cunt clutched him, the tissues quivering between her buttocks beneath the probe of his fingers. Finesse had to desert him in the face of such unbearable sensation. His hand slid back to her buttock and gripped her hard as he pounded into her, his cock spurting as her cries grew in volume, her climax increasing in intensity as he tried to enhance it with his movements within her, his touch, the harsh rasp of his breath against her ear.

That delicate ear, as finely made as any flower that grew in the meadow during the first gentle touch of spring. It was his first rational thought as he regained his senses and found his cheek on the meadow floor, his gaze on that beautiful ear, touched by moonlight. Her hair was a pillow for his head, and he took the opportunity to rub his face against it again before he remembered his manners and pushed himself up on his elbows to cup her face, his fingers brushing her lips.

She kissed them, her hand on the back of his neck drawing him down to exchange a kiss between their mouths, and then another, and another. Until he realized she fully intended to get him charged up again and was succeeding. A process that should have been physically impossible to accomplish so quickly, no matter the stimulus.

One of the benefits of the second mark. Record recovery time.

He'd have smiled if he didn't want her again so much already. Semi-erect, he slid back into her still slippery heat and she held him with her muscles there, stroking, rippling.

In a flash, she rolled so she could sit up and ride him, her hair wild and snarled about her. Catching his hands she held them, using them as a resistant counterpoint as she sinuously worked him, drawing him harder and deeper within her, bringing him closer to explosion with internal muscles as supple as her fingers. She controlled every movement, pushing down on him with a force underscoring the difference in their strengths, her reminder that she had all the advantages, that the choices were hers. His cock responded helplessly, spurting for her again in a much briefer time than he'd ever experienced before, his control gone.

He let her have her way, for he'd accomplished his intent, reminding himself why he'd chosen to serve her. It wasn't the soft firmness of her breasts, the wet pull of her cunt, the sweep of her fine hair on his skin, though all those were enough to make a man kill for her. It was the soul of the woman beneath all that he heard calling to him, making it impossible to walk away.

He'd stand by her, no matter what she did to him.

But even as he had the thought, he remembered what Gideon used to tell him. Fate didn't like being dared.

22

WHEN he came, so did Lyssa, once again surprising her with how responsive her body was to him. Particularly in her current state. The demons pounding on the inside of her head had been driven back by the tender lovemaking he'd initiated. When she took control, needing the sense of holding the reins to tilt her world back to the correct axis, they returned like a building storm, their strength increasing the harder and faster she rode him, so even when the orgasm convulsed her body, she had to shut her eyes against the pain.

They dressed in silence. She didn't search his mind, but she sensed his quiet acceptance of her mood, such that he respected her silence, helped her with her clothes that now felt unbearably damp and uncomfortable. When he got her settled on the bike, he pressed his hand briefly over one of hers resting at his hip before he started the engine. He took them home via forest paths and sleeping neighborhoods, putting them on the main roads only briefly before he reached her drive.

By the time he stopped the motorcycle by the fingerprint reader, she was dizzy. She managed to put her thumb up to it, though her body jerked, alarmingly.

He was watching her closely, but she had no energy to spare as she settled back on the bike, pressing her cheek to his back again. Somehow that helped ease the pain roaring through her head, as if he possessed a magnetism opposite to her own that helped open the blood vessels.

He stopped by the kitchen entrance. When Bran bounded out of the darkness followed by his brothers and sisters, she raised a hand to fend off his usual rambunctious attack, but Jacob intervened.

"Bran, no." His tone was sharp, authoritative. The dog stopped in midbound, backing off.

Jacob took her outstretched hand, concerned by the quiver in it as he helped her off the bike. "My lady, are you well? What can I do?"

"Yes." Her voice was muted. Too labored to project. "It was beautiful, Jacob. So perfect. I'm sorry."

"Sorry for—"

Before he could finish the thought, she spun away from him and hunched over, a shudder rolling through her slight frame. When he closed his hands on her shoulders, his palms partially touching her bare skin below the short sleeves, he found she was burning hot to the touch. She began to vomit into the grass, bright red blood, the force of the expulsion yanking her forward. When she cried out, his heart lurched in alarm.

Filled with pain for her, as well as questions he wanted to demand she answer, he held her until she finished. When she did, she was quivering in his arms, weak as any time he'd yet seen her.

"My lady." He pressed his hand over her feverish brow. Her shaking hands rose, clamped down on his to hold it there, either to ease the pain or give her the comparative coolness of his palm, he didn't know. Her veins were beating violently, a migraine like he'd never felt before. "Don't speak, my lady. I'll get you to bed. Just hold on."

~

Thomas had a form of autoimmune blood disease that had mutated in his altered servant's body, accelerating quickly with no hope of cure. Had Thomas known he was giving Jacob yet another invaluable lesson when Jacob had become his primary caregiver during those last terrible months? There'd been no doctor to call, no hospital to visit. Not even a diagnosis of the ailment because it hadn't been logged by modern medicine and never would be, as long as vampires and their servants remained the shadowy stuff of fiction and nightmares. As he had then, Jacob fell back on remedies and first aid he knew, as well as simple things the monks at the monastery had taught him. He wasn't certain if they would work, but that wasn't the main concern hammering in his mind now.

Though the symptoms between his lady and the monk were very different, Jacob had no doubt they were somehow connected. The cold fear in his vitals told him what he could not ignore or drown out any longer. She was dying. Whatever this ailment was, it was going to kill her in the end. The awareness of it was in her eyes, the same way it had been in Thomas's. In fact, now that he'd given a name to the hollow sickness in his gut, he recalled that awareness had been there all along, in many of the things she'd said or done, the silences she'd maintained, the looks she'd given him. Even the way she touched him, as if she wanted to savor each sensation to the fullest. Vampires were sensual creatures, so he'd overlooked the significance of her exceptional desire to dwell on the experience of a single touch, the beauty of one finite moment.

He'd been angry at her bluntly stated refusal to give him the third mark. He'd uncharitably thought it was more of her tests, holding a carrot just beyond his nose. Seeing now what he hadn't wanted to see, he realized she thought she was saving his life.

With a third mark, if the vampire dies, the servant dies with her . . .

A goddess had the full picture of the journey, its goals and obstacles, in a way a mortal did not. Faith was required to follow her lead. As she'd admitted with no apology, vampires in their stunning arrogance imposed the same relationship on their human servants. But she was a woman as well as a vampire queen, and he wanted her to know she didn't have to play at omnipotence to command his loyalty. He'd have done anything at this moment to ease her agony, given anything for the truth to be a lie.

"The pain . . . it went away during . . ." Her voice was a whisper as he laid her on her bed. She'd had him take her to her hidden bedchamber. "But afterward. It was like a flood. So beautiful. I ruined it."

"Ssshh. You did nothing of the kind. I should have paid closer attention. It was my fault."

"See. Told you. I ruined it."

Another shudder racked her. After giving her the vial of medicine he carried, holding her chin to steady her as she took it down, he turned up the gas logs, for now she was shivering, her skin gone from fire to ice. Reluctantly, he went into the bathroom to get what he needed.

So many things about her were human. So many were not. When he'd helped her across the driveway, since she'd initially refused to be carried, a convulsion had seized her. Her hand had flown out, striking the side of the Mercedes, her personal car. It had put a dent deep in the side that tore the metal, cutting her skin. The wound had healed to a thin scar almost before he got her a towel.

How could nothing else hurt her, but this disease take such a toll? He wished like hell for Thomas. The monk's scholarly mind would have put two and two together and figured out the correlation between the two diseases, ways to slow or ease it. Thomas could have done that for himself, but Jacob had sensed the monk was doing only what was necessary to be around long enough to prepare Jacob to serve his Mistress. Without the connection to Lyssa and no hope of it ever being reinstated, Thomas simply hadn't the will to live. On all other subjects, Thomas had filled him in on every detail he could recall. But on the series of events that had given him the terminal disease, he'd said little, not even how he'd contracted it. He'd just noted brusquely it had to do with Rex's punishment and why his Mistress had to shun him.

Jacob wrung out the cloth in the first of the two basins he brought to the bed. The steaming water burned his hands as he laid it on her forehead. "I need to know what this is, my lady. Let me help you."

"I've told you—"

"With respect, I believe the time is past for that." He met her gaze, frustrated by the shuttered look behind the pain. "I have no leverage, no way of compelling you to heed my request. But Thomas trusted me. I think you trust me, too, no matter how uncomfortable that makes you. I insist on knowing, and that's that. I know giving me the third mark will not only help with the issue of trust, it will help me anticipate your state of mind and health better. You can draw strength from mine whenever you have need, even from a distance."

"It's also a death sentence. Much shorter than you'd get as a mortal. Bran would outlive you."

Her confirmation of it made something twist agonizingly in his chest, but he inclined his head. "I'm aware of that."

Her eyes closed. "Why would I be worth such a sacrifice, Jacob? Does it have anything to do with me, or is it that insufferable code of honor you gratify?"

"Both, my lady. And the sex alone is worth dying for."

"Jacob, this is not a joke." If her head was not about to explode, he suspected she would have screamed it. As it was, she choked it out as a snarl. He cupped her face, his thumb stroking, reassuring.

"Sshh, my lady. Sshh. Aye, it's not. What must I do to convince you that you're worth it to me, my lady?"

"It's not worth it to me, Jacob. Please, stop. Just . . . cease."

When she turned her face back into the pillow, shutting him out, her body quivering with pain, he knew he had to let it go. For now.

He began to hum, a soft Gaelic tune. After his parents' death, he'd had to get accustomed to the idea that he would never again feel his mother's hand touch his brow before he went to sleep at night. During those first months he'd often wake in the dark of the night, feeling afraid and alone. As if their mother had left her maternal alarm clock implanted in his body, Gideon would rouse. Jacob would hear the soft shift of his body in the other twin bed, the rustle of pajamas, and feel such relief when his older brother came and sat on the edge of his own bed. He'd rest a hand on Jacob's leg and sing the songs of their mother's people off tune, the soothing tones of a boy's voice too fast changing to a man's.

So he kept up the tune while he cleaned her up, hoping it was providing comfort to them both. He eased her out of her clothes and tucked soft blankets around her. Sitting on the edge of the mattress, he removed the compress and slid an arm under her back, folding her up against his shoulder. Her forehead rested on it as he very gently unpinned her hair and brushed it out, knowing she'd feel more comfortable with it tended. Then he lowered her back to the pillow and replaced the hot compress.

"Was it Carnal that brought this on, my lady? This was not like the last time."

"No. This is new." She kept her eyes closed, though her lips twisted wryly. "I won't say he didn't contribute."

Jacob picked up one of her hands and began to massage between her thumb and forefinger, carefully kneading the pressure point.

Some of the tension in her shoulders eased, the pounding mallets lessening in force. Lyssa cracked open her eyes. "Oh. That helps."

"Acupressure. It's good to know we're not so different in some things."

Lyssa looked at his hands, tan and strong, at the calluses she would never have. At the contrast of her pale skin, paler than he'd ever have unless he was out of the sun long enough to lose the pigment. "You did this with Thomas."

"He taught it to me." He nodded. "My lady, if it doesn't cause you more pain, will you at least tell me how you came to . . . send Thomas away? I know it's somehow related to your sickness. And his."

Lyssa closed her eyes again. Jacob did deserve to know. More important, he needed to know. There'd been something different about Carnal tonight. He was always a mocking son of a bitch, but she'd sensed something brewing in him, a kind of suppressed excitement. Like a boy dying to tell someone a secret, but savoring the smugness of knowing what someone else didn't. Whatever it was, or even if it was just her imagination distorted by her current state, Jacob deserved to have enough knowledge to protect himself against her enemies.

She took deep breaths, absorbing the touch of his hands as much as the compresses, letting the pain wash over her without resistance, hoping it would soon ebb.

"When I was married," she began softly, "it would have been better if I'd had a female servant, but we tend to do better with servants of the opposite sex. But Thomas was a quiet, scholarly man. He was a monk when he became my servant. I exempted him from the sexual ways a servant is expected to submit to his Mistress."

She felt his mind absorb that. As he remembered some of the images from earlier in the night, his visions made a lazy stir in her blood despite her current state. Then she recalled the point of the conversation and her reaction chilled.

"Rex didn't understand it. He'd thought of so many twisted things to do to a man who'd taken a vow of celibacy. My husband was not an easy vampire, not ever. He and Thomas did not get along well, and over time it got worse."

Because Thomas knew he was a sociopathic monster, Jacob thought, then winced as her eyes opened, reminding him his thoughts were no longer guarded. But she kept on without comment.

"I encouraged Thomas to take a short sabbatical to his monastery in Madrid. For all his love and loyalty to me, which I did not credit as I should have, he needed a place from which to draw energy for the nourishment of his own soul. That was the place for Thomas. 'It's just a piece of land, a pile of stone,' he'd say to me. But I knew his heart. I kept encouraging him to go, take some time. Things were well in hand here. No pending threats on our borders, though I suppose I forgot to look within as well as without."

Her fingers closed into balls on her abdomen, and Jacob moved his massaging touch back there, loosening them. He knew he should tell her to rest, but he couldn't ignore his gut, which told him understanding all the pieces to this puzzle were critical to caring for his Mistress. He didn't know how much time he had.

Enough, Jacob. Be easy on that. This will pass.

Lyssa had no way of knowing if he believed she was telling him the truth. The easing of his brow helped reassure her, however, as if drawing him into her illusion gave her confidence, making the lie forgivable and possibly even truth. She would have enough time, damn it. Because nothing else was acceptable. She had to get through the Council Gathering. Once she did that, it would be five years before there would be any close scrutiny on her or her Region.

"Thomas understood, as I have been trying to teach you, that you don't interfere between vampires. We don't view you like children, from whom we will suffer interruption. You are tools, instruments serving as extensions of our will. Thomas, having lived as a monastic, understood better than most the concept of obedient service. He was well suited to the way of life of a human servant." She paused, her fingers whispering along his leg, crooked on the bed as he traded the now cold compress for another hot one.

"Your pardon, my lady." Reluctantly he left her to refill the basin with more hot water.

"You are not," she murmured.

Jacob lifted his gaze to the mirror. Too late, he remembered her reflection would not be there, though his stricken look was, revealing his reaction to her words before he could mask it. The mirror was one-sided, the way she was saying he must accept their relationship to be.

He pushed that away and came back to her to set the next compress while her fingers slid down to play with his bare ankle under the jeans' cuff. He took it as a good sign she was caressing him, though he noticed she wasn't succumbing to sleep the way she had after the first attack he'd witnessed. Perhaps the change in symptoms had made the sedative effect of the powder less effective.

She sighed. "Physical violence was part of our marriage, a part Thomas did not understand and abhorred. But he held his tongue for I bid him to do so, even as Rex became more and more erratic, trying to make our relationship into something it could never be. Then one night Rex tore out my rosebushes in a fit of rage. Thomas came upon me in the garden, trying to replant them." She pressed her lips together, obviously struggling with the memory. "I was crying. I suppose I'd gotten a little frayed on the edges as well."

Reaching out, Jacob cupped her face, drawing her gaze to his face. "My lady."

She shook her head. "My mother died at five hundred, Jacob. Vampires do die for reasons other than murder by staking or cutting off their heads. Immortality is a gift, but it also has its drawbacks. As mortals pass over the threshold of old age, most eventually get past fear and resistance to the idea of death. This acceptance grows with the years, for they see so many cycles . . . life, death, growth, change. They start to see how things remain the same even as the faces change. Because of that, they become less interested in keeping pace with the world. They want to be quiet, to rotate on the axis they've always known, knowing when Death is ready it will come and they will find renewal then."

She touched the compress on her head. "As you pointed out, we have things in common with humans. We can lose interest in life, in seeking change and growth, only we do not die. Unless a vampire figures out how to get past that phase—think of it as a midlife crisis—he loses his sense of meaning. Things stop having lasting value, for you feel as though you've seen and done it all. While you don't acknowledge it directly as such, your immortality becomes a curse, a prison during that time. You rattle those bars or obscure their presence with a haze of excess. Violence, cruelty and lust for power are drugs of choice for the powerful and purposeless. Quick rushes that don't last, and like drugs, you need more and more fixes. More and more excess, as you rail against the fate that you feel has you in thrall."

Jacob watched her gaze drift to the fire. "We call it the Ennui. It is the greatest risk vampires face as they pass the fourth-century mark. Many don't live to see five. They meet the sunrise. Or they are murdered by one of us or human hunters like your brother, because they choose more destructive ways to deal with it. My mother chose to meet the sun. I hadn't seen her in fifty years when she did that."

He tightened his hand on the side of her throat, and she gave him an indulgent look, but there was sorrow under the attempt to shrug off his sentimentality.

"Vampires are predators, and *kind* is not a word to describe us. But predators can be fair, consistent, and have a reliable integrity.

They are not incapable of compassion. Rex was . . . susceptible to excess. He viewed humans differently than I did, did not appreciate your diversity and value except as it served his needs. Many of my kind are like that, but perhaps there was a little more of an edge to his feelings on the matter. I noticed it, it bothered me, but it never went far enough to be more than an irritation between us. But as the world wore on him, that weakness began to become his strength, and it did not stop with humans. Cruel, manipulative games that involved lesser vampires as well as humans absorbed him like a teenager hooked on the worst of the violent computer games. I tried to minimize the damage, keep him under control."

She kept the focus on herself, made herself his most challenging sparring partner. Jacob remembered Thomas's words, but he hadn't had this information to fill in the blanks. He felt the deceptively fragile network of bones and muscle beneath his hand, the line of her throat. When the delicate edge of her jaw brushed the base of his hand so she could rest the side of her face there, he felt an impotent anger at the destination toward which her words were driving them. Her bones would heal, yes. But they could break. Over and over and over. The nervous system of humans and vampires was another common denominator between the two species. Pain was pain.

"He became infatuated with a young man at the turn of the century. Cecil Miles, an innocuous name for one who would never be more than a New York banking clerk, or would not have been except he stumbled on Rex feeding in an alley. Rex turned and saw Cecil standing there, completely fascinated. He became his new playmate. It was as if their meeting was fated by an evil sprite, for Cecil had an unhealthy fascination with pain and suffering. Rex nurtured his burgeoning bloodlust to keep him company in places I refused to go. He petitioned to make Cecil a vampire, and it was permitted. I should have opposed it."

She drew away now and rose from the bed, letting the compress drop away. Moving to the chair by the fire, she sank into it, turning partly away from him. While Jacob was glad for evidence the attack was receding, he could see the weariness in her. He moved to her side, knelt by the chair.

"Cecil learned quickly, but . . . you remember what I said?"

Jacob nodded. "That made vampires are more bloodthirsty, less disciplined."

"He was . . . what was that word you used? A *sociopath* as a mortal. By his cleverness and Rex's influence, after only a hundred years he acquired himself a small territory in Mexico. Not an influential one. We are not complete fools. But it will not be enough. He will always want more."

"Carnal."

She nodded. "It was Rex's pet name for him. At a certain point, it was what he preferred to be called. I'm not so sure if whatever it was that made Rex more susceptible to the Ennui and his own weaknesses enhanced Carnal's bloodlust. Transferred in the blood during the siring."

She shook her head. "Cecil wanted to be fully in control of Rex, and he realized I was his greatest obstacle in that. Over time he guided Rex more and more toward the things where I had to run interference, increasing Rex's frustration and mistrust of me. Carnal also exacerbated the sickness in Rex's mind, feeding it with more and more creative entertainments, which I am selfishly glad I did not know much about." Her lip curled. "I didn't act any differently from a wife married to a serial killer or a pedophile, who denies to herself what is happening. I deserved the punishment of Thomas's loss, but Thomas certainly didn't."

When Jacob reached out, she shook her head, a sharp movement.

"The night it happened, we had a dinner party planned for midnight. I was dressed in a black dress I think you would have liked." An image of her appeared in his mind briefly, standing in this room, putting on her earrings, showing him the low-slung back of the dress, the short skirt with a fringed hem that drew the eye to the exposed lengths of her thighs.

"I like it," he responded, though he couldn't smile.

"I burned it after that night, but it was one of my favorite dresses." Grim humor passed through her gaze. "Rex and I had fought earlier. It doesn't matter about what. It was meaningless. He came to our room, asked my forgiveness. Touched my face and asked if I would bring some cut roses to the dinner table because they always added such a lovely touch of color to the meal." She swallowed. "When I went to the back garden, I discovered he'd torn them all out of the ground. Only then did I realize why his hands had smelled of the earth.

"Thomas came to find me," she said after a brief pause. "Rex knew I cultivated those roses in honor of my father. But I think I was crying because I knew that was going to be the end, that I could tolerate no more. Then it got worse."

She fell silent. Jacob curled his hand on the chair arm, wanting to touch her, offer comfort. Turning her head to look at him, she reached out, touched his face, ran her fingers over his lips. He swayed as images unfolded in his mind, a sensation disconcertingly like a television flipping on. It obscured his vision as he struggled to manage reality against the flashback she'd chosen to show him graphically.

Thomas stroked her hair, then picked up one of the broken branches. "We will make it all right, my lady. I'll go get a shovel."

The pictures apparently were not adequate, however, for the images kept rolling through his mind as she narrated the event which had sealed Thomas's fate.

"Something alerted me. It took a cursed few precious seconds to pick up on the strained tone of his voice, the delicate way he'd picked up the branch, as if it were made of glass and he was afraid his grip would break it. I found the knife later in the kitchen. Imagined him picking it up and slicing off the end of that branch to a pointed angle with one cut, as if he'd been born a samurai. My monk who regularly cut his hands on small steak knives."

Whether it was the power of the images or she was intentionally letting him inside her mind further than he'd expected, Jacob felt the fear she'd felt then. Not for herself, but for Thomas. Her narration ended, and there were only the images, a movie he knew was not going to end well.

~

She didn't bother with the door. She ran toward the house, her gaze on the upper level where the bedroom was, where she knew Rex would have been standing, watching, waiting for her reaction. Anticipating the bitter enjoyment of her pain, her struggle to put the rosebushes in the ground. She leaped, soaring. Vampires could not fly, but like squirrels they were capable of catapulting themselves remarkable distances.

Jacob felt his own stomach lurch with the unfamiliar sensation, flinched as she didn't slow down for the master bedroom window but went through it, a priceless stained glass art depiction of the dragon and St. George. It exploded around her, cutting her skin. He realized she'd never had it recrafted. It was a curtained picture window, one of the few non–stained glass windows in her home.

Thomas had reached the bedroom a single handful of seconds earlier, probably knowing he had little time before she'd realize his intent. Rex had not expected anything. Thomas was already driving the branch of thorns with its sharpened end toward his back.

The vampire spun just before she came through the window, perhaps sensing Thomas's rage-driven attack. The rosebush stake sliced through the shirt and into his skin but went high, shooting upward and tearing muscle rather than stabbing through it.

Lyssa slammed into Thomas. As he was catapulted into the wall by the impact, she took the blow in the face that Rex had intended for Thomas's chest, had the monk had been there a bare second before.

Lyssa spun, grappled with her husband, and they crashed into the bed frame, shattering it and tangling them both in the covers.

"No," she was saying. "No."

She was adamant, fierce. Pleading, but not for Thomas's life, Jacob realized. That wasn't in question. She would not permit Rex that transgression. She was pleading for him not to force the conflict between them to a point of no return.

Rex backed off, his fangs bared, his shirt bloody, the wound visible under the torn fabric. Even now it was mending. Lyssa watched him warily, her body tense and ready, moving to keep herself between him and the dazed Thomas, struggling to get to his feet.

"I will send him away, Rex. But you cannot kill him. I won't permit it."

"Your loyalty is to him?" Rex snarled. "He intended to murder me."

"You've been trying to murder my soul for so long it knows not how to draw a deep breath anymore," she said in a terrible voice. "You don't see me piteously whining about it, the way you are about a mere human's scratch."

Fury flashed through his eyes, but now she straightened, her expression assuming that dispassionate calm Jacob already knew well. "Thomas," she said without taking her attention from Rex. "Go and pack. You'll go to your monastery in Madrid until I bid you return."

"Never," Rex spat. "He shall never return. Because I will hunt him the moment your back is turned and kill him. Torture him slowly and let you feel every moment of his pain. You'll have to kill me. Show everyone your pathetic weakness, that you would choose a human over your husband."

Lyssa studied him for a long moment. Jacob wondered what thoughts were going through her, for that was something her vision did not reveal. Thomas had made it to his feet, was holding his ribs, his spectacles gone. His hands were shaking, but the fury was still in his eyes. He was even insane enough to dart a quick look around for the sharpened branch, though his face fell when he saw it had rolled under the bed behind Rex.

Lyssa took a step forward, drawing Rex's attention. "A human can't last long under torture. Is that what you want? A blink of distraction, followed by the quick grunt of a snapped neck, the gurgle of a heart being ripped out? Wouldn't you prefer the sweetness of my cries? That's what this is always about, isn't it?"

"My lady, no." Thomas stepped forward, and her hand shot up, pointed like the finger of God toward the door.

"Get out of my sight, servant. I will not permit your death, but I will not tolerate an attack on my husband. Your punishment is banishment. Go," she snapped. "Obey me." She looked toward him, and Jacob saw the crumpling of Thomas's expression as she dealt him a mortal blow with her thoughts. *You've brought this upon me. If you have any love for me at all, you'll go before you make it more than I can bear.*

He stumbled from the room as she shrugged out of her sexy sequined dress as casually as she might before preparing for a shower. Stripping off underwear, tossing it aside so she was completely naked, completely vulnerable. Rex, his eyes already alight with anticipation in a way that elicited nausea in Jacob's belly, drew a bullwhip from a baroque armoire. It was the type of whip Jacob had seen used on elephants in the circus.

"Thomas." She stopped her servant at the door, her voice as cool and remote as ever. "Remember to contact our dinner guests on your way out and let them know we will reschedule."

The vision evaporated, snapped off like a television, her mind closing the door before he could see more. His mind could imagine it too well, however. Thomas's heart had broken that day. Jacob knew it, because he'd seen it in the man's eyes whenever he'd even hinted at what had driven him from his Mistress's service. The wound her words created had not been the shattering blow, however. Jacob suspected it had been her screams coming through the walls as he stood in the servants' quarters, folding socks, placing shirts in a suitcase with his trembling hands.

23

"So he went to Madrid. With the third mark, a vampire can't shield her mind from her servant when she's under great duress," his lady explained. "It's a protection for the vampire, to ensure if she is exposed to sunlight or threatened in a way that makes her insensible, the servant can feel it and come to her aid. But when not under duress, a vampire can sever the link and then, even under duress, until she reactivates it, it cannot be felt."

She met his gaze, reminding him of his unguarded thoughts earlier. "It's a loss beyond measure," she confirmed softly. "To both of us, but at the time I thought it was the best thing. So many things went wrong after that point, I no longer know which one thing or group of things I could have changed to make it turn out differently." She looked down at her hands, an unusually self-conscious gesture for her. "I'm old enough to know wishful thinking is simply pointless."

"No one knows everything, my lady. Thomas never doubted your love for him. Never. You can look into my mind and see the truth of it."

Though she kept her head bowed, he felt her reach out, confirming it. She lifted a shoulder. "That is meager comfort considering everything, but thank you, Jacob."

"He wasn't sick at that point. Neither of you were."

"No."

He didn't want her to stop, but he knew some stories couldn't be told all at once. He had to be appreciative of how much she'd been willing to give him. When he looked at her drawn face, the shuttered eyes, he knew her head could easily begin throbbing again. Reaching out, he ran his knuckles alongside her face. "I want to know, my lady, but not at the cost of draining you. It's been a long night. Perhaps you could tell me later."

She nodded. "But I do need you to understand this, Jacob. Never underestimate Carnal. I did, to my eternal regret. Carnal exploited Rex's struggle with Ennui and poisoned his mind, convincing him the other high-ranking vampires viewed him as little more than a sycophant, living off my riches and the power earned through my title and command of politics."

Shifting to prop her head on the opposite side of the chair, she turned her attention back to the fire. "One of the unfortunate things you learn when you live a long time, Sir Vagabond, is that love can erode. Once it begins to do that, it can be sculpted by the right forces into any manner of vile and evil thing. Carnal was a master sculptor.

"You're right," she said abruptly. "I'm too tired to tell you more. Leave me."

Cursing himself, for he could see the pain back to simmering behind her eyes, he ignored her command. Instead, he left her to fix another compress and came back to her side, kneeling by the chair. Laying his hand over the cloth he placed upon her brow, he wished he could will the pain into himself, lessen the throbbing.

"I thought I told you to leave me."

"Aye, you did. I disobeyed, as you tell me I tend to do."

She had her eyes closed and said no more. Since she didn't order him to go again, he kept vigil quietly at her side, his hand over the compress, his thumb moving slowly over her temple.

As the fire crackled and stillness settled over the room, shadows began to collect in the corners of his mind. Shifting, moving. Becoming figures, voices. Offering him images and thoughts not his own. After a while, they drew his attention so he moved toward them cautiously, a man in the dark learning his way. A startled moment later he realized somehow he was following a misty path from his mind into hers. Suddenly, there was a lurch, and he stepped hip deep into the quicksand of her memories, so squarely he almost jumped at the sensation, for he'd expected more resistance.

Outside of his mind, his lady's lips were tight as she swallowed like a person fighting nausea, her color even paler than usual. Stroking her temples, he hummed the soft Gaelic lullaby. Her brow eased, her fingers reaching for his other hand, drawing it onto his lap to curl her fingers loosely around his. She didn't lift her head or open her eyes. It was a moment of simple pleasures, a stark contrast to the vision straight from Hell into which he'd stumbled.

Rex had taken her down into some part of the mansion Jacob was thankful he hadn't yet seen and hoped had been destroyed. There'd been a rough wooden stock there, something directly out of a medieval village, but the cuffs were lined with some type of substance that burned the skin and made it difficult for a vampire to use her strength to free herself. He'd put her in that stock, gagged her with the bloodstained whip, fastening the two ends to the wood so it stretched her mouth like a horse's bit and kept her head up, her neck at a painful arch where he could see every nuance of her face. Because her beautiful hair was matted on her face, down her back, he gathered it up, twisted it into a knot and then nailed that knot to the wood, wrenching her head to the right. He'd then readjusted the hold of the whip so he could see her windpipe struggling to process air she didn't need but still rasped alarmingly in her throat.

Bloody fucking Christ. With the hair out of the way, Jacob could see Rex had flogged her until her skin hung off her back in strips, the welts so numerous and blood so thick her upper body was a mangled mass, as well as her buttocks. Since he was in her mind, surrounded by the hazy drift of her thoughts, he knew she'd managed to keep from screaming until the very end. She hoped until Thomas had left, despite the fact Jacob thought Rex might have eased off if she'd given in to the urge sooner.

Her teeth bit into the thick blood-soaked braiding while Rex fucked her from behind, digging his hands into the destruction of her back.

Jacob learned then that vampires could not pass out from too much pain. Her muffled cries made an eerie backdrop to the howling of Bran and his siblings. Rex had locked them out, and they were circling the foundation of the house, baying, Bran going mad at being unable to come to her aid.

But even as Jacob watched, horrified and loathing Rex, he was forced to see Rex through her eyes, because these were her memories. He saw in him what she saw. A man with a desperate emptiness taking him over, fixated on the subjugation of his wife as the answer to his need to feel, his ultimate victory that would make everything all right.

One dinner guest had apparently not been dissuaded from coming. Jacob felt his hot rage become ice-cold as Carnal entered the dungeon room, removing the tie of his elegant suit. His eyes greedily drank in the sight of Lyssa's naked and tortured body. He spoke, egging on his sire, telling him he was right to do what he was doing, that she had to understand Rex was the true Master of this Region and of her, now and forever. She was his property . . . his slave to share as he chose.

Jacob saw Rex's hesitation at that. Lyssa did not react to it at first. Apparently, the fact that Carnal had made such a suggestion did not shock her. However, when Rex's face reflected his decision on the matter, her reaction changed.

She'd not been able to hold back her screams, but she hadn't shed any tears. Only when Rex stepped aside and let Carnal take hold of her hips, driving his cock into her rectum with savage ferocity, did she cry. Rex knelt, kissing every tear off her face as if they were jewels he'd won, instead of the rain Jacob knew was washing away all vestiges of the bond they'd shared as husband and wife.

It wasn't the pain, though that was enough that even the residual experience of it made Jacob want to vomit and never eat again. It was the realization Rex was truly lost to her.

Jacob was so deep in her mind now he felt the impact of that in her soul, the searing pain as her heart shattered. But he also witnessed the birth of the ominous realization of what she had to do. She would have to be the catalyst to bring this tragedy to its inevitable conclusion. Only in its infancy then, the idea was a small enough voice to be denied that night. But if she had heeded it then, Thomas would have lived.

And his lady would not be dying.

White-hot pain shot through his mind, shoving him brutally out of her thoughts. Jacob only had a moment to reorient himself to the present before her hand clamped down onto his forearm. His lady twisted ruthlessly, coming out of the chair, slamming him onto his back on the carpet, one leg bent at a painful angle beneath him because of his kneeling position.

Another rough twist, and his forearm snapped under her grip. Agony took the form of fire burning up through his arm to his shoulder, wrenching a hoarse cry from his throat, particularly as she didn't let go, pressing forward, planting her foot on his chest.

"You've no right. No permission." It was a hiss, her eyes glowing red with a menace he'd never seen from her before. "You forget your place, servant. You don't know the meaning of what you just saw. It's something you can't understand so you won't judge it, you hear me? You won't judge me or my husband. I'm done with you tonight. Take your simple cures and be gone."

She caught his other arm and hurled him—there was no other word for the explosion of strength that sent him hurtling toward the incorporeal entrance to this chamber. He closed his eyes, expecting to hit a door. A grunt left him instead as he hit the bedroom floor. The floor of her bedroom on the plane of reality he knew.

When he rolled, trying to regain his feet, he found he was alone with no access to her lower chamber.

"Son of a bitch . . ." He managed it through clenched teeth, cradling his arm. He didn't know whether to curse her or himself and he did both liberally, hoping she was hearing every word he had to say. There was too much pain roiling through him to sense whether she was there or not.

"Ah, Jesus." He pressed his forehead to the carpet.

When she allows it . . .

She hadn't allowed it. Somehow, perhaps because of her illness, she'd been completely unaware he'd been able to walk into her mind, and he'd been unable to resist. Wanting to know, to understand answers she hadn't been ready to offer him. That he'd just told her he wouldn't push her to get. Rationalizing it, he'd figured it would be easier to get them this way, where she wouldn't need to talk about them. But that was hindsight. He hadn't thought at all, just walked through that portal between their minds, fascinated by the ability to use it, feeling that his feelings toward her gave him permission.

Earlier tonight, she'd opened to him, held him close as he made love to her. Touched his face. Everything they'd shared, her smiles at him, the touch of her lips, her body, the pensive look as she remembered things no one should have to remember. Playing in the fountain, letting him put his arm around her as he would a lover . . . It meant something to him. He'd assigned a significance to it that didn't figure on the vampire meter of trust at all.

You forget your place, Jacob.

I thought it was at your side. Your back. Wherever you need me, even if it's hip deep in the quagmire of your fucking psychotic mind.

But it wasn't her voice he heard, only the recollection of her statement and his current response to it. There were no shadows now. He felt her nowhere within him, though the link between them ached like a wound needing the pressure of a bandage.

There was a trembling low in his gut, an element of shock he recognized, and not just from the pain in his arm. He'd never been deliberately hurt by someone he cared about, not physically in the way a mortal enemy would have tried to hurt him. It wasn't just a moment of passion. She'd waited a key moment before she did it, made sure she had his attention so he'd know she'd fully intended to do what she did.

He'd never been treated as a slave. Hadn't that been his thought earlier? She was introducing him to a lot of firsts tonight. So where did that leave him? He couldn't think about it now. He'd do something wrong, something he'd regret later.

She wanted distance. Away from her was the last place he'd wanted to be only minutes before. Now if he didn't get some air he thought he'd try to stake her himself.

Fucking bitch. Broke my fucking arm.

Struggling to one knee, he wondered if he could hitch a ride to the emergency room.

~

"You know, for somebody who isn't in Mrs. Wentworth's employ, I seem to be ferrying you around a lot," Mr. Ingram observed, looking down at the Danish Jacob had bought him from the emergency room vending machines. Feeling a moment of wistfulness, he bit into it.

"Does eating month-old pastry always make you choke up like a little old lady watching greeting card commercials?"

Boy was in a foul mood, but he was paying attention, Ingram noted. The kid watched everybody too close, and didn't know when to leave well enough alone. Probably why he was here. They'd given him some ice to help the pain, but they were backed up, and it would be a while before X-ray could take him.

"Makes me think about my wife, giving me hell for eating this kind of junk."

"You have a wife?" Jacob glanced toward him, brow furrowed. "But—"

"No." Elijah shook his head. "We were only together long enough to produce a baby and then she ran off. Died young of a life she shouldn't have got herself into. Must be genetic, because the boy's tryin' like hell to do the same." He sighed. "But sometimes in my mind I like to paint life the way I wish it could have been. A wife to grow old with. Someone I'd have missed something awful if I'd lost her to cancer or a heart attack. So every time I have something like this, I imagine her old like me, fussing at me about cholesterol or my weight. The way you see people who love each other do. Not a big and flashy first-romance thing, just something you settle down into nice and easy as breathing. As long as you got your breathing, you got the chance to be anything. Without the breathing, it's pretty much over."

Jacob snorted. "And you looked at *me* like I was crazy when you picked me up."

"I'm just imagining the way it could have been with a good woman," Elijah pointed out. "You're sitting over there obsessing about the one who snapped your arm like it was a matchstick. Maybe you'd be better off letting that one go and making up one, like me."

Jacob leaned his head back against the wall, closed his eyes. "I'm tired," he said. "Haven't slept normal hours of late. Maybe I am fucking crazy."

Mr. Ingram made a noncommittal noise. Silence ensued for a few minutes between them.

"Lady's bad sick, isn't she?"

Jacob opened one eye, turned his head without lifting it from the wall. "Yeah," he said.

Elijah nodded. "You know, I had an uncle, come home from the war in a wheelchair. He'd gone off all shiny and strong, everyone's hero. Comes back, okay at first, just quiet. Watching all of us, the way we all watched him. Then he turned into the meanest son of a bitch you'd ever want to meet. Drove off his wife, his kids . . . Ain't no complex psychology to it if you're paying attention. He'd always been invincible to his way of thinking. All of a sudden all the things he felt like people depended on him for were slipping away and he couldn't control it. Couldn't take care of his family no more. Every time he tried to be or do what he used to, something would happen. An infection, a new pain, or he got too tired and couldn't follow through on it."

Jacob lifted his head from the wall then. Ingram took another bite of the pastry, thinking. Swallowed before he continued. Patted at his lips with the napkin.

"People treated him different, thinking because he was a cripple that gave them liberties no one should have without asking. Strangers assumed it was okay to lift him in the truck like a sack of potatoes. Women came up at the church picnic to dump his catheter bottle because his wife or mother said it was okay. Don't need to ask him. It's hard for a man to lose everything he thought made him a man. Don't seem fair for him to have all this potential to serve and then have it taken away. Can't imagine how to reinvent himself. Then he's got everyone acting like he don't have to be treated like a man anymore."

The boy's gaze was steady, but the thoughts were there, running through his head like shit through a goose. Elijah could see it clear enough. He didn't know exactly what had happened between Jacob and the vampire lady. He might just be talking off his head, comparing what happened to one mortal man to what was going on with a woman who claimed to be an ancient vampire, but the boy was free to ignore the thoughts. Mr. Ingram didn't claim to influence no one's will. He certainly didn't have the type of hold Mrs. Wentworth seemed to have on this crazy boy.

Jacob rose abruptly. "We're going to the pharmacy across the street. I'll get a splint and some tape. I don't have time to wait, and if I can't show you how to tape up broken bones after I've seen Gideon do it a hundred times, then I deserve to have it grow back crooked. You don't have to take me back to her. I can hitch."

"I'll get you home, son."

~

After Jacob left, the house had the silence of a tomb and the desolation that came with it. Lyssa, rubbing her forehead, kneading at her neck, moved aimlessly out of her bedroom. Going to her study, she found the day's mail she'd not yet gone through. Jacob had left it in neat stacks as he'd done each day, properly sorted and processed.

She'd told him not to open personal correspondence, whereas he was welcome to open any correspondence from vampires in her Region, invoices from vendors, checks from business interests, things like that. So her eyes focused immediately on the two letters he'd set out separately from the things he'd already handled.

One was from Lord Mason, postmarked from Saudi Arabia. The other was from the monastery in Madrid. Since she paid for all the repairs to the structure and owned the land on which it rested to ensure it would forever remain a sanctuary for Thomas's spirit, she periodically received direct correspondence from Father Gonzalez on various mundane issues. Still, she chose to pick it up with Mason's letter and take them both with her as she moved back out into the hallway. She wasn't really sure of her destination until she arrived at the servants' quarters. Bran moved at her side, his body reassuringly pressed against her thigh. Curling her fingers in his hair, she held onto him to keep herself steady. Colors were still too bright. She suspected she'd tipped over the peak of this particular episode, but things weren't returning to normal as quickly as they had in the past. She had to believe they would, though. Any other answer was unacceptable.

Her head was pounding again, and the hammer seemed to be wielded by the image of Jacob's face as she broke his arm, the feel of the bone giving so easily beneath her touch. Yet perversely she sought to be as close to him as possible by standing here outside of his room. For some reason she was hesitating as if she were an interloper in her own house.

Pushing away the thought and shoving open the door, she viewed the room he used when she didn't command his company in her bed.

She hadn't come in here since he'd moved in. Seeing his few clothes hung in the closet, she put the letters on the dresser so she could run her fingers over the items, like the blue shirt he'd be wearing for the dinner. In the dresser she found neatly folded socks, underwear, spare belt, a few T-shirts and pairs of jeans. It made her chest hurt. But she stood there, the top drawer open, laying her palm on the T-shirt he'd last worn to work in the yard. It had a design from some kind of rock band on it, maybe a concert he'd attended, or maybe just something he'd picked up from a secondhand store. Most of his clothes, while in good shape and well-fitted, seemed likely to have been gotten that way. She ran her fingertips over the jeans, the pockets and front seam, the upper leg, thinking of how his body felt under the worn denim.

When she turned toward the bed, she stopped, nonplussed to find she'd picked up the T-shirt and was holding it in her hand. She brought it to her face and almost moaned as the cool softness of the fabric enveloped her throbbing forehead, her nose and lips buried in the cloth.

Rex had told her about Thomas. Lyssa had not felt well when she rose just before sunset that day. As Rex watched her, something in his eyes crawled into her stomach, making the nausea worse. Vampires never felt sick, but she didn't have energy to spare to worry about that, because he was in one of his erratic, pacing moods. She knew she needed to be alert, needed to appear calm and steady, to handle whatever brutal mischief he might foment. But she was so tired.

It had been a few months since she'd sent Thomas to the monastery. She'd visited him several times there, and she wanted him back. Wanted to stay with him or bring him back. It was time. Rex could stay or go, but she was bringing back her servant.

When Rex started talking about Carnal, she was in no mood to bear it. She retorted as she had countless times before. Carnal was simply using him, wanting to advance himself on Rex's power.

"He told me you'd say something like that." Rex stared at her. She remembered a time when the dark eyes on either side of that aquiline nose had been provocative and mesmerizing to her. "You try to poison me against him. But I'm smarter than you. You tried to poison my heart, but I've done it to you first. And to your pious monk."

She laid her brush down, stared at him. "What are you talking about?"

"You haven't been visiting your monk's mind lately. He's been very naughty." Rex grinned, propping an arm on the windowsill. He was distracted, watching for the sun to set through the crack. He and Carnal would go out tonight and she would be blissfully alone for the evening, but at the moment she needed his mind here.

"Rex, what are you talking about?"

But she thought she knew. On one of her visits, Thomas had tried to make her smile. Told her of a dream he'd had of a young girl bringing him a bouquet of wildflowers, begging for his help. Her brother was dying and had asked for the Last Rites. "You must come, Father. Right now. Please . . ."

"In my dream, my lady, I went to her room, though I tried to explain I was not a priest. There was no brother there. She put her back against the door and removed her blouse. She had beautiful black hair, generous hips, a full bosom . . ."

"Ah, this is sounding nothing like your skinny Mistress, my monk."

Thomas had smiled, taken her hand. "I could not resist her in my dreams, my lady. She knew me, took me places I have not been in a while. I awoke here. It has been a long time since I'd had such a dream."

Rex was talking. "There's an herb with a white and gold flower, one of those long names no one can pronounce. It acts like a hallucinogen. Carnal told me of it. He has a great deal of wisdom for such a young vampire. Of course, I think he keeps questionable company. He likes to play with vampire hunters. But he doesn't know how I used the knowledge he gave me. That's between you and me."

On her last visit, Thomas had not felt well. A flu bug, so she'd not fed from him as she had during times past. She was getting her blood elsewhere of course, but they'd both wanted the connection, the reminder of the bond they shared that must sustain them over a distance. That last time, she'd felt his hot forehead and simply held his hand, sitting in the garden at the monastery, talking about things they enjoyed, not talking about things too painful to discuss. When she'd left, she told him she was going to bring him home, even if she had to throw Rex out.

"You fed from him, didn't you?" Rex turned from the window, studied her. "Each time you go to see that human you love more than me, you feed from him, while you have denied me your blood as well as your body since the night he tried to take my life. Well, you may go to him, die together."

She thought her heart had been ripped out the night Rex had allowed Carnal to rape her. But whenever a person thought she'd been scarred to the depths of her soul, there were even deeper wells to plumb.

If he'd only poisoned her, perhaps she wouldn't have done what she did. After what he'd allowed Carnal to do, she knew there was nothing left of the love between them. But Thomas . . . He'd taken Thomas from her, made Thomas suffer only for the crime of loving her too much. She hadn't deserved Thomas, but Thomas deserved justice.

A quiet calm had stolen over her, and she'd known it was time. In fact, since the night in the dungeon, it had been a countdown, and perhaps the nausea in her stomach was just the timer going off, telling her. She'd risen up from the chair, taken two steps . . .

A moment later, there was just a body on the floor, a crushed heart in her hand. Rex's empty eyes stared at her in disbelief as she drew back the curtains and stood back, watching the last of him turn to ash on a carpet she would burn.

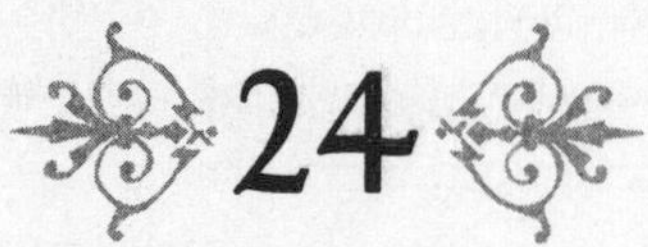

24

No matter her reputation, the Council would have had to act against such a transgression. At the least, her Region would have been taken from her. It was Thomas who had suggested the course of action.

I'm dying, my lady. Tell them I killed Rex when he was off guard. They all knew we did not get along well. They also all knew he'd gotten unstable, no matter what they claimed to your face. Tell them you killed me.

She'd thought of a hundred other options, none of which would have adequately protected the three hundred vampires in her territory. Things were too unstable. Thomas had been right, and she'd hated the truth of his words even as she'd finally capitulated. She severed their link and laid the blame for Rex's death square on the shoulders of the man who'd served her loyally to the end. She'd put magical protection on the monastery, made it effectively disappear from the sight of the vampire world until Thomas's death in case Rex had ever told anyone like Carnal its location, but that had seemed woefully inadequate compared to her servant's last gift of sacrifice.

Perhaps the burning of souls wasn't punishment. Perhaps it was Hell's way of doing what she had done, taken something forever ruined and removed it from existence, as if that could fix anything. If only the memories could be burned with the body.

She sank down on Jacob's bed, lying down. Bran showed his familiarity with the room by jumping up behind her and lying along her back, a comfortable bulwark. Turning her face into the pillow, she smelled Jacob. His aftershave, the striped soap he used with the clean scent it said it had in the commercials. The smell of his skin. Her joints were aching, keeping up an alternating staccato with the drumming in her head.

Thomas had gone on to his God. Cleansed, pure, the painful fire in his blood likely rinsed away with the cool touch of holy water.

When she broke his arm, had Jacob seen a light in her eyes like she'd seen in Rex's? Was it coming to that? Was she becoming so lost in this disease she no longer could see past it? Was she making up her own reality, her own idea of what was a threat? Perhaps there was nothing left for her to do and she could go. Maybe everyone wanted her to go. Maybe it didn't matter. Maybe it just needed to be over.

Opening Mason's letter, she unfolded it, still lying on her side so the creased paper sat on the mattress and she could skim it with half-closed eyes.

He wished her well, the desert vampire rarely seen by any of his own kind. This was the first missive she'd had from him in over twenty years. They'd once been close, long before Rex. But Mason hadn't believed in the dream of Council and civilized behavior for vampires. He didn't care enough to try anything different either, and so they'd parted ways. He just wanted to be left alone in his barren world.

Typical for Mason, he cut right to the purpose of the letter:

You and Rex were the monarchy of us all for nearly a century. You, not Rex, helped set up the Council with its rules, because you know a king and queen are only as good as the two individuals involved. But you are still a queen, Lady Lyssa. I will tell you now what I should have told you long ago. I consider you my liege. If our world forever could be ruled under your justice, there would be no need of Councils and elaborate laws. Rex had deteriorated to the point his passing was a blessing, however it occurred. If I could absolve you of any guilt you carry, I would. Give you a penance or a rosary to say so you would worry on it no more.

I know pressure on you to remarry will be fierce, my fellow vampires crudely thinking their seed might find fertile soil. I do not think you are barren, my lady, if I may be so bold. I simply think there is no man on this earth who is worthy of being a father to a child of your making and your body knows it. I also know a threat is brewing against all you have built, though I've not yet pinpointed the shape of it. I have come out of my sandbox, as you always call it, and am keeping my ears open.

If I may make amends for the ignorance and apathy I showed to your noble cause years ago, if it would be of use to you, I offer myself to you however you need me, even if it is to relieve the crass pressure of matrimony.

You know I do not seek power or even your physical affections if you do not wish to share them. I just offer it as proof of my support of what you value. Even if I cannot believe in it as you do, I know what is valuable in this world. You. You are the Council's strength and they are still too young to be without that. I will stand behind you.

As long as you believe in what we can be, I can believe in your conviction. That is probably as close to a faith as I will ever have.

Mason's senses had a far reach. He obviously had detected the same dark undercurrent of vampire politics she herself had been picking up on of late. Those opposed to the civilized constraints imposed on them by Council code were becoming more vocal, and more numerous. The younger vampires, the ambitious made ones like Carnal. It was important that leadership be strong and unwavering to hold the commitment of the many who stood on the fence. Those were the ones who could upset the balance of power if they turned to apathy instead of cautious support for order.

Her lips twisted. But perhaps the attempt at civility had run its cycle. She'd lived centuries and seen governments rise and fall, philosophies change and die, be reborn and called something else. If the majority opposed the current structure, and the minority could not hold it against their onslaught, change would happen. But a world overrun by the brutality of a host of Carnals . . .

Closing her eyes, she placed her hand on Mason's strong script. Perhaps this was another sign. Mason at last had made a commitment. He would step into the breach. He wouldn't really need her. That had been the root of her disappointment so long ago. If Mason had committed to their cause, nothing would have stopped him from seeing it become a reality. He cared not for diplomacy, but he was good at it, as good as he was at being a benevolent or sometimes not-so-benevolent dictator. He had no problem with totalitarianism as long as the ruler was just. But then, therein lay the problem with absolute monarchy, didn't it? It only worked as long as the person in the crown made it work. But if Mason stood for her, it would be all right. He would not thank her for leaving him with the responsibility, but his word was good.

Bran whined as Lyssa pressed her mouth into the pillow, fought the heaving of her stomach. *I will not throw up. I am tired of that, you hear me? Stop it.*

The wave passed sullenly, and she blinked watering eyes as she opened the letter from the monastery. A smaller envelope fell out of it. An envelope that bore Thomas's seal.

She stared at it for a moment, then her gaze flitted to the short handwritten note in the abbot's script.

Mrs. Wentworth, Brother Thomas gave this to me several weeks before his passing. He asked that I send it to you on this date specifically. I hope it contains words that bring you comfort. We are glad he has finally been accepted into God's House, though he is greatly missed. Thank you for your continued patronage.

Why didn't Jacob bring it? Perhaps it had been additional surety, if Jacob had failed to gain an audience with her. She turned it over in her hands, studied the seal, then broke it open.

My Lady,

By now, I'm sure you've cursed my presumption a hundred times, and I am feeling the lick of flames from the sins I've committed to ensure Jacob was accepted in your service. But I cannot feel shame in at last saying my love for you and my love for God have always been as one, interchangeable in my heart. On good days, I hoped that was just an indication my service to you also served God's will. On bad days, I thought I was perhaps deluding myself and the last hundred and fifty years of my life had been a war between Lucifer and God for my soul, though I cannot imagine I would be of such importance.

I tire easily, and I could not dictate this to Jacob or anyone else, so I will speak frankly. By now I suspect you are confused and torn in your feelings, wondering why you want him so much, this man you've barely just met. For I have no doubt that Jacob succeeded in being accepted into your service, both because of the will of the man and because of what I believe him to be.

Despite a surge of dizziness, Lyssa sat up on the bed, gripping the paper harder.

I know the prejudices of your world, certainly. You know I do. But hear me as I tell you that Jacob is the other part of your soul. You probably gave him the first and second marks with barely a hesitation, startling yourself. Now you are held from giving him the third only for fear of sentencing him to an early death. Did you think I didn't know you were infected and dying when you never came back again? When you sent me your last missive, severing our ties completely? Do you think I know so little of you?

Tears stung her eyes, and she blinked them back. "Foolish monk," she whispered.

Knowing that has only strengthened my belief in the things I will write to you about in this letter. Remember that life is a finite, precious thing, but what makes it precious is what we do with it. You have always treated humans as inferior to your species, though with respect and humaneness. Jacob confuses you because he fills a part of you which you thought could only be filled by an equal. Ergo, he is an equal.

I know you had little patience for my spiritual explorations, but in tracing your long and colorful history, and through other methods also likely to damn my soul, I believe—fully and completely—that Jacob has served you before, in two previous lives.

Do you remember the knight who saved your caravan from vampire hunter attack during the Crusades? He was only with you a short time before he continued his quest, but you remembered him so vividly . . . that was Jacob. Then there was the samurai guard assigned to you as a child. The one who was killed protecting your retreat when your father's house was overrun by his enemies. You are shaking your head . . .

Lyssa stopped the motion, frowning.

but now that I have planted the seeds, you will start remembering many things, including the things these two men have in common with the man in your service now. Jacob knows my theories on this, and though he too has some of your skepticism, he cannot deny his inexplicable compulsion to serve you. Please hear me, my lady. His soul will not survive being parted from you again. Let him make his own choice before you try to make it for him.

I would have liked to have ended my life at your side. That would have been my last wish. But by sending me away from you, it told me God had another plan. To find Jacob for you and give you the soul mate you've always deserved, the love of a man that will fill the emptiness of your woman's heart. That's something you've never had, not in all your many years of life.

I puzzled over why it was that his spirit served you as the samurai guard and the knight, two lifetimes that were within two centuries of each other, but did not cross your path again until now. Unfortunately, I believe it is because he comes to you whenever your life is truly, genuinely in danger. Bless your extraordinary abilities, that has only been three times. God gifts the strong sparingly, only when they have grave need.

As I said in my introduction, Jacob is the last gift I can help God give to you. Please trust your heart, for it is the strongest part of you, even if you do not believe that. You are the most remarkable woman I have ever met. You will always have my love, and I believe you have God's love as well.

Your faithful servant
Thomas

Bran lifted his head, laid it on her hip as she sank back down on the pillow, fisting the letter in one hand, the pillowcase in the other as she turned her face into where Jacob laid his head.

No. Thomas had been a sick man, deluded by his illness, imagining he could give her something that didn't exist, a romantic fantasy. If she believed it, she would kill Jacob with her own selfishness and desires. Perhaps like Mason's letter, it was a sign. A sign she needed to end it before she left another body in her wake.

~

Jacob got home a handful of moments before dawn. Urgency was gnawing at him so hard during the last few miles that without knowing why he asked Elijah to speed it up. The man glanced over at him and flattened the gas pedal. When he wasn't driving a limo Elijah drove a serviceable pickup that was practically antique. However, he had some skill with engines, because it jumped up to ninety with no problem.

Bran was waiting for him in the gravel driveway, whining. It made his skin turn to ice. Jacob barely managed to thank Mr. Ingram before he was in the kitchen, running down the hall, taking the stairs three at a time, Bran on his heels.

The sun was starting to emerge. She'd broken the east-facing stained glass window in the upper hallway. Her palms were still stained with the blood, though the wounds were healed. She held a large shard of colored glass in either hand as she lay on the floor, right where he knew the sun marked a big square of filtered multicolored light each day. She couldn't walk through it when the sun projected directly on the glass, but she could skirt the edges and enjoy the look of it.

With an oath, he pulled her out of the dangerous area, feeling the touch of the early morning breeze coming through the open hole as he went down on his knees next to her. There was blood on her lips. Black and brown, it was also on her chin and the top of the loose dress she'd donned. She'd thrown up again.

"Lyssa." He gathered her up, lifted her despite the fire that shot through his tightly taped forearm. She stirred, opened her eyes. The grogginess of early morning had her firmly in its grip, and perhaps the effect of the drug he'd given her had kicked in at last. She wouldn't have felt the sun until it had her pinned down and burning, searing her to the bones. He would have found a pile of ash outlining the shape of her. He swallowed, cursing himself as he strode back to the bedroom, laying her down on the top of the covers.

"I won't become Rex," she whispered. "Even if I must abandon my responsibilities. This is the way a vampire's life ends. We know it's time to go, but we cannot die, so we simply place ourselves in the right situation to have it ended."

"No."

Elijah's words and this moment made the truth all too clear for him. For the first time, Jacob understood some of what she'd been trying to teach him. More important, *why* she'd been trying to teach it to him, even if he didn't totally agree with all of it.

Gideon had once told him the wise man knew when to let go of pride to grab hold of wisdom. Raised in a society that held an individual's worth and uniqueness as right, and submission to the will of another as wrong, he'd been fighting the very oath he'd taken from the beginning, putting conditions on it.

He placed his fingers on her lips before she could speak further.

"Forgive me, my lady." Bowing his head, he dropped to one knee by the bed. Guiding her hand, he put it on his head as if she sat on a throne, completely in control and beautiful and unmarred, rather than too weak to sit up, weary and stained with her own blood. "You were right. What I did was unforgivable. I'm your servant, and I never should have entered your mind without permission. You won't have to guard your thoughts against me. Ever. I'll never again try to do that without your leave. I beg your forgiveness for my disrespect, though I shall never deserve it."

He stayed that way for long minutes, determined not to move until she bid him to do so, despite how urgently he wanted to cosset her. Clean her up and take care of her to make her feel more like herself.

Her hand slid off his head to his shoulder. Touched his jaw.

Before the illness, there were no slips. You never could have known so much about me, so quickly. Don't you think that's why? This sickness . . .

There was a particular urgency to her words he wasn't sure how to answer. "Well then, at least there is something about this damnable disease that is a blessing," he murmured. *But I think you're wrong, my lady. We would have known each other this deeply, this quickly, no matter what. The first moment I saw you, I knew I was meant to be with you.*

When he lifted his face, her jade eyes were full of things that confused him as well as tore his insides to shreds. She lowered her touch to his unbroken arm, tugged.

Uncomprehending at first, he rose. She turned away, drawing him onto the bed to curl behind her. Encouraging him to cradle her hips in the curve of his, press his back against hers and lay his head over the top of hers on the pillow. When she let go of his arm, he folded it under his head as she captured his injured forearm, bringing it across her waist so she cradled his hand and wrist against her breasts. She dropped her head and kissed the bandage and splint, nestled her cheek against them.

Sleep, Jacob. You need the sleep.

I need to care for you, my lady.

You do, Sir Vagabond. In ways I can't begin to explain. Obey your Mistress. Sleep. If you can bear my stench.

I would happily join you in a pig wallow, my lady.

The sense of her pained smile eased the knot of tension in his chest, helping him settle in behind her, nuzzle her hair with his nose and lips. She was silent then, for so long he thought she'd drifted off, but then her voice came into his mind once more.

Do you know Bran broke out the basement window that night? It was barred so he couldn't get through, but he charged the glass, rammed his head right through it. His skull and shoulders were bloody. He never stopped trying to protect me. . . . You remind me of him.

"It's a good thing your husband is dead, lady, for nothing would have kept me from killing him. Even if I had to accomplish it from the grave by making a bargain with Satan himself. Some acts don't deserve the mercy of love."

Like this? Her fingertips touched his arm.

He pressed his face into her hair, breathing her in. "That's different. I will bear any pain to be near you, to serve you."

"It's no different. What is it we talked about? Love is raw, not pretty. It's visceral as blood." Another pause. "I'm glad you came back. I didn't think you would. Maybe you shouldn't have."

"Carnal raped you." Jacob stroked her temple, the gentleness in his hands in contrast to the rage he felt in his heart. "He hurt you. I invaded your mind without permission."

"No. You're nothing like him." Her fingers tightened on his hand. "And that night was . . . It's complicated in the vampire world, Jacob. You must understand that."

"My heart does not tell me false, my lady." He gave her words back to her. "I saw it in your eyes when you spoke to him. I even felt it when you clung to me in the woods afterward, my body inside yours. It was a betrayal that was soul deep, a wound inflicted on a part of you that will never heal. You're not allowed to act as if it's a crime worse than murder, but it is, because you must live with the violation forever. And for you, my lady, forever is longer than for most."

"You make forever seem far shorter than I'd want it to be, Sir Vagabond." Her fingers whispered over his bandaged arm. A quiet pause. "I'm sorry, Jacob. It doesn't make up for it, but I'm very sorry."

Her voice was soft, vulnerable, and he couldn't hold any anger against it. "So am I." He straightened the arm beneath his head and slid it under her neck, taking it across her chest to cross it with his other arm, holding her close.

"It will mend quickly, with the second mark," she said quietly. "By the night of our dinner, it should be little more than a twinge."

He fitted his fingers into the spaces between her ribs, feeling the fragile network of bone that guarded her heart. Would her heart press agains those bars and reach for his fingertips, a cautious answer to the great emotion in his own chest?

Leaves fluttered in the early morning breeze, making shadowed patterns on the stained glass window on the north side of her bedroom. "I wonder if I can give you anything," he said. "Even a thought you haven't had."

She turned then, pushing him to his back, and propped herself up on his chest to look down at him thoughtfully. Her hair fell over her shoulders, and he gathered some of it up, spreading it out like a peacock's plumage, holding it like the skeins of time from the Fates' loom. With reverence and respect for the miracle it was, for the ability to touch and influence it in any way.

"Why do you think old people go to the park to sit and watch children play? Part of it is to remember things they might have forgotten with the passage of time. Time and memory are circular. Yes, you accumulate wisdom as you age, if you're open to wisdom and not hardheaded." A smile touched her mouth as she gazed at him. He made a face at her, reading her expression well enough on that count. "But no matter how long I live, and how long you live, we will both look at the same flower and see different things. You embrace life with open joy and a fierceness I've never had, never will have. I'm drawn to that joy like a flower is to the sun. Something I sense I need to nourish me, give me a reason to keep blooming."

He sobered, cupped her delicate face in his much larger hand. "My lady, I don't deserve such words."

She shook her head. "I've seen things, Jacob. I've met Chinese dragons whose whiskers feel like feathers when they brush them across your face. I've seen wars begin and end. Seen people do so many things I didn't expect, and many things I did expect, and dreaded. That is why the Ennui does not affect me. Terrible things always outnumber the good, but the overall power of a single good thing is so much greater."

Reaching down, she traced his lips with her thumb, bowed her head to rub it against the back of his knuckles. "Like this moment."

Her hair tangled in his fingers. As he watched, she took the time to extricate it, making sure she didn't pull on it and hurt his arm. It was a simple, tender courtesy, as gentle as earlier she'd been brutal. Her quiet words stroked him. "Life is never as dramatic as we pretend it is in a normal life. But it can be intensely amazing, or quietly desperate, as Thoreau said. If you woke each day with a genuine awareness which allowed you to appreciate everything as if you were seeing it for the very first time . . . or the last . . ."

She bent down, pressed her lips to his. Lightly, so lightly. Jacob, sensing her intent, remained still, absorbing the way that bare touch felt, spreading out over his skin from head to toe, her jade eyes so close, the slim line of her nose.

"We are so absorbed in ourselves. In each other's creations." She whispered it, eye to eye with him. "An incredible movie, a book, a castle . . . We forget the amazing creations that were not ours—the sky, the tree . . . a man's lips. The feel of his body, of the life that courses through it."

From the growing light in her eyes, she was finding her way back to herself, and he thanked whatever deities there were for having prompted him with the right question to ask.

"Ah, a woman's body is so much more amazing, my lady." Moving his touch down, he cupped her breast, his fingers passing over the nipple, kneading. He didn't have the strength to follow through on it, but he liked being able to do it. She didn't seem to mind either.

Twisting her fingers in his hair with whimsical intent, she held his face still as she coiled the strands over her knuckles. "Do you believe in other lives, Jacob? That you get more than one life?"

He stilled. Had Thomas told her? He couldn't tell from her expression and he thankfully didn't sense her in his mind, seeking his reaction, since he wasn't sure of it himself. "I know there are a lot of people who do, my lady," he said carefully. "I'm not sure I'm one of them, but I can't say the possibility isn't there."

She nodded, propped her chin on his shoulder. "If I could choose any life, I would choose to be a creature in the forest. Moving through each day as part of what goes on there. Nothing earth shattering, nothing more dramatic than the daily search for food and survival."

"I think you would miss having your hair brushed, my lady. Your hour-long baths."

He caught her wrist in his uninjured hand as she tugged his hair, hard.

"Your resolve to be respectful didn't last very long. You delight in teasing me."

"I like your smile, my lady. Your laughter."

"Hmm. You remember at the fountain?" She tucked her head under his chin, laid her arm across his chest as he gathered her to him, held her against his side.

"Yes."

"Carnal was right about that one thing. It was unwise to unleash compulsion that strong where any supernatural being would have felt it, but I looked around at all of them, and thought—why can't you feel it? When you see the fountains in that mall, you know someone felt it and was striving to make a connection to a natural world mortals abandoned so long ago. I wanted to give them that moment, that taste of memory. Do you remember how they responded, Jacob? The way they all splashed in, suddenly not worrying about anything except dancing in the flow of the water, celebrating the life of it?"

"I remember." He remembered how she'd laughed and watched them all, the feel of her hands caressing his neck. Turning, he tugged her to lie face-to-face with him, curling her hand in his, forming a link between them. "I've led a very different life, my lady. At the end of it, I would like to know I've lived it fully. And I need you to know I understand that has nothing to do with time. You're my goal. Without you, I won't have a purpose. If there's anything I can do to help you live to see forever, I will. But if you die, I want to follow you."

A shadow crossed her gaze. Before she could open her mouth, he slid his arms around her back, ignored the pain to bring her close to him again, tuck her head back down against his chest. "You don't need to say anything. I just wanted you to know. I was wrong, what I did tonight. I'll do better at trying to understand what it means to serve you, but there are things I won't give up on. You're one of them, even if you order me to do so."

There was a long silence, where he sensed things he didn't understand affecting her above and beyond his words. "You are a pain in my ass," she said.

"It doesn't seem to have affected it adversely, my lady. I'm quite fond of looking at it." He brushed his hand over it. Not a sexual demand, just enjoying the feel of the soft curve and wanting her to know she had his desire. As well as everything else.

"Impertinent knight."

He nodded against her skull. He knew it was time to let her sleep, but he wanted to say one more thing, let her take it into her dreams.

"If it had been me, and I knew I was losing my mind, I would have taken my life before ever causing you pain, my lady. Should I have hurt you even once before I realized I was capable of doing so, I wouldn't have allowed myself to live to see the next sunset."

"Yes, you would have," she said. "For I would never allow you to leave me like that. God help you."

Before he could respond to that startling statement, her even breath told him she'd succumbed to the dawn. While he had much to think about, the drain of the night had taken its toll. He surrendered to it, following her into dreams, hoping he could defend her there better than he'd done this night.

25

The chandelier lights lowered to a dim setting supplemented the candlelight throughout the dining room. Flatware and crystal shone softly, providing a sense of intimate warmth. Instead of a candelabra or candleholders as a center piece, he'd used an old breadboard, the wood cracked and the color of deep chestnut. He'd formed a pyramid of pillar candles upon it in deep burgundy, rose and pink hues. As they burned, their wax ran down the sides of the pyramid, forming twining designs of the colors and blending in pools within the cupped sides of the board.

The catering staff was quiet and efficient. Her guests had been pleased with the artful display of the salad in the plates chosen, the tiny bouquets he'd put at each place setting. Lyssa noticed she had a slightly larger bouquet, a more delicate arrangement of flowers. He'd also cut several of her garden roses and inserted them. The whole thing was tied with a trailing ribbon arranged in a swirl across her plate until the first course was brought. Since the catering company was operated by one of the vampires in her Region, there was nothing they would see or hear tonight that would alarm them. They did not blink as they came to collect the salads from which only a mouthful or two had been consumed, to return with soups that would be barely touched.

But watching the way her guests inhaled the fragrances and took the one or two tastes they could, absorbing the beauty and smell of the food, Lyssa thought vampires actually enjoyed the food more than a human would if it had been placed before him. After all, while she preferred her blood in certain ways, it had a functional quality that couldn't be overlooked.

However, as her gaze flicked to Jacob, she admitted she did sometimes appreciate the way her blood was presented. She'd always chosen her food carefully. Perhaps that was part of what had rankled her at first, Thomas choosing for her. But he'd left the final decision to her, and of course Jacob was turning out in just a short time to be many intriguing things. Functional as well as something to savor.

When he moved to take up his position behind her chair, his attentiveness warmed her back, the nape of her neck. The flow of his thoughts was like mulled wine slipping down her throat. She kept her awareness of it to a quiet murmur while she focused her attention on her guests. It was like the comforting but blurred sound of someone else's voice in the house when one didn't want to feel entirely alone.

Tara Beauchamps and Richard Carlyle, the overlords of the Alabama territory, were both made vampires, but fortunately with more sturdy constitutions than many of the made vampires she'd met. Though she'd changed her name, Tara had been born and made in the Middle East. Part of a Bedouin tribe, she'd gotten separated from them during a sandstorm and found a cavern inhabited by a solitary vampire. Mason had turned her out of loneliness, groomed her, and then brought her into the world for a few years. When he tired of vampire politics and again returned to his caves, he gave Tara freedom from his side. Having been part of a world where she'd had no rights, no value at all except as it was defined by others, treated little better than a pack mule, she was highly cognizant of accumulating power and influence and was accomplished at both with her exotic looks. Dark almond eyes, straight dark hair, eyebrows like slips of silk, and features refined by her vampirism to mesmerizing.

Mason had shown little interest in Tara since he'd let her go, or she in him. Perhaps he sensed it would take centuries to exorcise Tara's fear of being inconsequential again, enough to let her discover the potential depth of character she had. Lyssa was inclined to agree, but she'd seen other, lesser miracles occur. She also liked Tara's wit and sharp mind, even if her ambition required a close eye.

Lyssa still hadn't decided if her pairing with Richard was a fortunate turn of events or not. He seemed compatible with her, unexpectedly. Richard had an austere formality about him, tempered with a dry humor and keen intellect. With a good command of diplomacy while always looking for opportunity, he was a master politician and likely would rise to Council in time. All vampires were blessed with good looks, but his were particularly appealing in their uniqueness, because he was made in his forties. Therefore he had handsome silver threading in his chestnut hair to compliment his gray eyes, as well as the interesting character that lines of age created around them.

Tara and Richard had been together a handful of decades. Most vampires did not marry. If it was difficult enough to make a human marriage work over forty or so years, it was nigh impossible for vampires. Younger, made vampires sometimes married under human law out of nostalgic sentiment despite having to deal with the difficulties of eradicating the paper trail. After all, one couldn't get divorced at a hundred and twenty years old and not raise some eyebrows. Older vampires who married did so under vampire law, which was more like a civil ceremony with no spirituality to it. She and Rex had been a political match. The bond of any vampire marriage could be dissolved by appeal to the Vampire Council. Another attempt to appear civilized. She supposed she and Rex had adhered to more of the human ideal, in a macabre fashion. *Until death do us part . . .*

No illusions of great love there, but there was a fondness between Tara and Richard, and they ran their territory very well. As long as Lyssa made her expectations clear, they followed her mandates. Occasionally they did indulge in some excesses, but that was simply the nature of the vampire. A driving, primal lust to exercise their power, to enjoy its many fruits, sensual or painful.

They were typical of the middle echelon vampire hierarchy. Usually smart enough to know when to choose wisdom over blood lust, and that making fair decisions was in their best interest as long as they were in Lyssa's Region. Another decade and it might even come naturally to them. They might enjoy being wise instead of brutal leaders and recognize the respect and devotion it could earn them. Another advantage of immortality. To the intelligent, open-minded vampire, there was usually time to change.

However, for now they would no doubt exercise every possible way to know all of Brian Morris's weaknesses and strengths and exploit them. She shifted her gaze to him. Young, just over eighty years old, but with a brilliant scientific mind, Brian had already acquired multiple degrees in different fields. One of the attractions of her area was a research facility in the Tuscaloosa area that focused on issues related to vampires behind its façade of an engineering research company.

The other thing that afforded him a measure of regard and rank he wouldn't have otherwise to protect him was that he was a born vampire. A half-breed, with a vampire father and human mother. As she'd told Jacob, his father was an important Master of a Region in Britain. The human mother was the vampire father's servant. Most couplings between humans and vampires did not result in offspring. The rarely occurring child was always a vampire, however.

Brian had an earnest intensity reminding her of a young Thomas. His thirst for learning and ability to think beyond the lines of known scientific thought meant he had a good chance of achieving and even surpassing Lyssa's age.

While his neatly cut blond hair and pleasant hazel eyes suggested an easy mark, the solidly cut chin and the shrewdness of his gaze as he assessed and measured Tara and Richard told Lyssa the vampire who tried to intimidate him would be making a mistake. He might not be as worldly and experienced as the two overlords of the Alabama territory, but he could think on his feet. His father had apparently taught the boy well.

Boy. She almost winced. She thought of the eighty-year-old Brian as a "boy," but Jacob, fifty years his junior, elicited no such maternal compulsions.

"I understand Carnal was in your Region recently." Richard was addressing her. "Do you suspect he's of a matrimonial bent?"

"He'll be disappointed if so," Lyssa replied neutrally. "I won't marry again."

Richard and Tara exchanged glances. "But it was assumed—"

"Yes. But I won't. There's no one of royal blood left, not a direct descendant. Rex was only distantly connected at best, and no one would expect me to condescend to marry beneath my station."

"There are some Council members—"

"They've accumulated their wealth and standing through power, not blood. So what is the research project you will be doing in our area, Brian?" Lyssa pointedly made the subject change.

I think Lord Richard is mightily disappointed, my lady. I suspect he would have liked you to entertain a suit from him.

I was lucky enough to survive one marriage in a millennium. I'm not strong enough to survive two.

You're very strong, my lady. I have the bruises.

She'd kept part of her mind open to Jacob for much of this night so he could follow her thoughts and understand more about her guests and the politics involved. He'd been quiet and listening without comment for the most part, but now she bit the inside of her cheek to hide a smile. He had an amazing aptitude for the mind play. Thomas had needed far more time to accustom himself to the feel of her in his head, to overcome the seasick feeling. After only a few days, Jacob interacted with her easily on the link. But true to his promise on that vulnerable night, he did not try to probe her mind, so she did not have to expend energy to ensure her shields were holding against him. She knew she could trust his word on that, as much as she knew she could trust he'd rebel against her in other ways because it was in his nature, no matter his resolve.

She looked forward to it.

"I'm working on the Delilah virus."

Lyssa's gaze sharpened on Brian. "I thought you were pursuing your latest degree."

"I am, my lady. But I'm also here to work with the scientists at Tuscaloosa Techco on the virus. We were fortunate. One victim of it—the Russian vampire—agreed to be preserved. I'm bringing his body here because they've agreed at Techco to help with the research. Truth, I may get so immersed in it, I may put off the degree another decade. Thirteen vampires in five years . . ." He looked pensively into his blood-laced wine. "There are not many of us. It strikes without discretion. It can take someone as exalted as yourself, my lady." He sketched a bow in Lyssa's direction. "Or someone barely out of boyhood that no one would miss, like myself."

Tara lifted a brow. "Sounds more like those thirteen should have been far more careful. Why should we expend effort on vampires who have unscrupulous and careless dietary habits? It's a weeding out, in my opinion. Darwinian."

Brian's expression hardened, but before he could find words, Richard spoke. "Easy to say, love, until you have it. I visited with Antonio a month before he succumbed. Headaches, vomiting of blood, sudden weakness at very inopportune and unpredictable moments. Those aren't even the worst of the symptoms at the end." He grimaced. "I can only imagine what that body you're carrying looks like."

Jacob, I think we need more wine.

There's not an empty glass, my lady.

Go to the kitchen.

No.

"Jacob," she spoke out loud, drawing their attention. "We're ready for the next course. Only I've decided I'd like it on the Tannen plates instead of the Dresden. Please go supervise that personally. You know how particular I am about the Tannen."

She was fairly certain she heard his teeth grind together. Richard raised a brow. While she assumed her servant hadn't reached out to choke her, there apparently was some evidence in Jacob's face of the struggle going on between them. She would not attempt to cover it or dissemble. That would be worse, suggesting she thought she needed to cover his disobedience rather than handle it.

"Jacob." A ripple of menace emanated from her. "I will not ask twice."

Her coldness swept over her guests. The vampires were old enough to weather it, though they immediately became still, watchful. Richard's servant, a tall black woman named Seanna who'd been with him thirty years but looked as if he'd made her his servant when she was barely out of girlhood, shuddered, but fought to control the reaction and remain impassive. Liam, the blond male behind Tara, almost mirrored her. However, the two of them stilled almost simultaneously, likely steadied by a mind touch from their Master and Mistress. Brian's servant Debra was a thin blonde woman who looked as if her main purpose was to serve as his lab assistant. She appeared the most shaken of the three, telling Lyssa she was the youngest, or that Brian kept her sequestered in labs more than he took her to ritual duties at vampire functions.

"My lady." Jacob's voice was cordial, no inflection, but the anger and frustration in his mind hit her like the blast from a furnace. *But you do yourself no service, hiding this from me.*

She met his gaze as he came around her chair and bowed, his blue eyes cool. He left them for the kitchen.

"I can't believe you chose an Irishman, Lady Lyssa," Tara commented. "Overly sentimental one moment. Absolutely bullheaded the next. They take everything too seriously or not at all. Laugh and cry equally easily. He's not really appropriate material for a human servant, is he? Though I will say, he's very easy on the eyes. I can understand your desire to have something for bedsport, as dynamic as Rex was."

Lyssa noted she did not mention Thomas at all. Carnal's reference to him at the mall had been considered highly inappropriate, but of course Carnal's entire presence had been inappropriate. It would be assumed Lyssa wouldn't wish to speak or even think about the servant who had purportedly killed her husband. However, most vampires also wouldn't venture into the subject of her preferences in the bedroom so directly. It wasn't the first time Tara had sought a more intimate footing. Sometimes Lyssa wondered if the woman simply desired friendship with another female vampire, not having much opportunity for a peer in her own territory. But it was far more likely that Tara was seeking the advantages of a familiarity with someone of Lyssa's rank.

"He is appropriate to my needs," Lyssa said mildly. "Just very young. He doesn't understand his place yet. We all know how easy it can be to forget that sometimes."

The woman stopped, her wineglass poised just below her lips. As Lyssa waited silently, she swallowed, set down the glass. "My apologies, Lady Lyssa, if my comments were too familiar."

Lyssa turned her attention back to Brian. "Have there been any advances with Delilah?"

"The lab I worked in out of Egypt had some very intriguing results. That's another reason I've come here. The Tuscaloosa lab has some correlating data. We think if we run some tests together . . . Well, we'll see. If it's successful, we hope to have a cautiously optimistic report for the Council Gathering. Having the preserved body gives us a unique situation. We can study many things about ourselves we haven't resolved yet. Sensitivity to sunlight, our need to sleep during daylight hours. What our internal organs are like, the composition of our blood . . . There's more to be gained than just insight into the virus."

"I wish you well, then. Humans are our food source, Tara." Lyssa glanced toward the woman as the catering staff returned to replace the soup bowls with the main course, suitably arranged on the Tannen. Out of the corner of her eye she saw Jacob reenter the room and take his position behind her again. "If we can't rely on them without worry of this disease, then we must address the issue before it threatens our extinction. There are only a few thousand of us in the entire world, that we know about."

She could have raised the issue that born vampires had been declining in percentage with each decade, which came with the implication of the weaknesses of made vampires. But given that she sat at the table with two made vampires who already felt a mild competitiveness toward Brian because of the privileges his origin afforded him, she decided to curb that thought. After all, it was intended to be an amicable gathering.

"Richard, Tara. Have you made arrangements for Brian?"

For the next few moments, she listened to them explain how he would be quartered in Tuscaloosa, in enough detail to assure her they'd prepared adequately to integrate him into the community. As they discussed that and other matters mostly related to their mutual business interests, she watched Tara and Richard shift, exchange looks, giving appraising looks to Brian's young servant. And to Lyssa's.

They understood there was a ritual to such events. The formality of a meal, conversation, an update on business concerns. Then, as the moon began to wax, there would be the desire for a performance. For pleasure.

She'd also noticed Tara and Richard's servants studying Jacob closely. She knew there was a kinship between human servants of sorts, and a new one in the upper ranks was always of interest. Brian's servant was too young to understand the nuances. In fact, she wasn't sure Brian himself understood the rituals involved in a vampire social event like this, but she was about to enlighten him and his young servant, for Jacob needed the lesson as well.

The desserts were laid out. Jacob's choice of brownies with raspberry sauce, timed to come out of the oven right now with their wonderful aroma, unwittingly stoked the anticipation of sensual delights. Tara inhaled the brownie and put the raspberry sauce on the tip of her tongue with an expression of absolute reverence that made Lyssa smile. Decadence, chocolate. Candlelight flickering and four very attractive servants awaiting their bidding. One who had openly defied her, giving her the perfect opening to segue into the entertainment the vampires would expect.

Richard watched Tara with similar amusement. "I think the female relationship with chocolate transcends the species barrier. I have a German shepherd at home, a bitch that adores it. Her mate has no interest in it at all." Tara made a face at him, and he smiled affectionately in return before he shifted his attention to Brian. "Lady Lyssa is being very diplomatic tonight, Dr. Morris. From past conversations I've had with her, I don't think she necessarily believes in researching vampire weaknesses."

Richard enjoyed teasing Lyssa on her politics, and she'd known him long enough that he'd earned the right, but it didn't stop her from narrowing her eyes at him. He was less affected than Tara, however, and just gave her a charming grin as he signaled one of the caterers for more wine.

"You don't believe it's important to research things like the effect of sunlight on our bodies, Lady Lyssa? Or Ennui?" Brian asked, his expression earnest and puzzled. "If we could discover a chemical way to curtail it, to retain the zest for life? What if we could figure out a way to walk in daylight? Wouldn't you like to feel the warmth of the sun on your body without pain? Or discard the lethargy that comes upon us when the sun is at its zenith?"

Goodness, he was overflowing with enthusiasm for his work. She had to suppress amusement, for she knew he'd think she was laughing at him.

"I believe there's a balance." Lyssa placed a bite of the brownie in her mouth. The taste exploded through all of her senses. The desire to chew, swallow and keep eating more was almost unbearable, even though she knew she couldn't digest it, would never feel full or satisfied from it. Jacob's pleasure in her approval of it was satisfying on a different, more disturbing level. She put down her fork. "As far as we know, vampires are immortal. If nothing adverse happens to them, they live forever. Again, as far as we know. Yet at a certain age, many begin to lose the will, the interest in life. Who's to say that's not Divinity's way of telling us it's our time to die? That we are mortal, just not in the way that other species are? Perhaps we're more like the members of aboriginal tribes who simply know when it's time to lie down and let the soul go. We do fancy ourselves enlightened, after all."

"But you've not experienced the Ennui, Lady Lyssa." Richard tapped his fingers on the table. "Again, no disrespect, but perhaps as I told my Tara, it's easy to shrug off the need for a cure when you don't have the disease. Not having experienced when the soul of you wants to live, but the rest of you is heedless."

"Perhaps," she said in a neutral tone. "But while survival is important, it should never be considered more important than other things. Honor, integrity. Dignity. As any of us at this table know, a species that abandons those priorities in favor of survival becomes a mob with no rules but savagery. That savagery can run rampant in a lab even more quickly than in a dark alley, because it can be more quickly justified as being for the greater good."

Brian frowned, but before he could speak, Richard chuckled. "I won't argue with the convictions of our greatest matriarch, even if I think her ideas might be a bit old-fashioned." He winked at Lyssa as she arched a brow. "Regardless, my timing is pathetic. It's dessert and time to enjoy ourselves, not darken our minds with these types of thoughts. Lady Lyssa, are you up to a game of challenge or am I now out of favor, rushing your itinerary for our evening?"

"I'm quite ready for it, Lord Richard. You are only out of favor insomuch as your implication of a woman's age. I expect you to make amends with your challenge. Let's address the last piece of business before us, which I think will dovetail nicely into that. Brian, are you willing to accept my mark to remain in my Region, knowing it will always be with you?"

Brian hesitated, which immediately captured her attention and sharpened the focus of the other two vampires at the table. "I am, my lady," he spoke carefully. "But first I must ask. Do you approve of the work I'm here to do?"

A shrewd mind as she'd said, and no pushover. She considered him long enough that she saw him question the wisdom of his conditioned response, but then his jaw firmed and he met her gaze squarely. She smiled.

"Dr. Morris, I believe in the quest for knowledge. I believe that in itself is the cure for Ennui. It only requires the will of the vampire to take advantage of it."

"But all vampires are not strong enough to do that," he argued.

"Then they have decided it is their time to die," she said matter-of-factly. "A form of Tara's Darwinism, I know, but one I believe to be appropriate. I respect that. I don't fear death, and I don't feel my fellow vampires should either. Faith and morality must be the foundation for the quest for knowledge, always governing our actions with regard to it. If we don't disagree too stringently on that, then no, I don't disagree with the work you've come here to do. You are most welcome in my Region."

As she let him think that through, Lyssa took a sip of her wine, tasting the metallic fragrance of Jacob's blood mixed in with the fruits of the vintage. She typically had limitless patience for these moments, but she hoped Brian would finish his deliberations soon.

Since their mental altercation, she could feel Jacob's restlessness increasing. For most of the evening he'd remained virtually motionless when behind her chair, determined to live up to her description of other servants. To a physically active man like him, being compelled to stand still in an environment like this was probably akin to torture. But his internal restlessness made her edgy as well. She could feel the heat of his body. He'd gotten his hair cut, brushed it out so it was like fine copper silk, the tips grazing the broad shoulders covered with the midnight blue shirt. Thinking of his strong lean thighs planted and slightly spread, his arms linked behind his back in a pose of waiting was more than distracting, especially now that her guests' minds were turning to the same type of thoughts. But she was the hostess. She would exercise control.

Even if those black slacks did mold his ass perfectly. When he'd moved out of the hallway to the kitchen, her attention had lingered on his waist, the fit of the belt. Reminding her of the other belt and the mark she'd put on his ass. It had taken several days to heal, giving her the distinct pleasure of viewing where she'd landed the blow. The second mark didn't give him the almost instantaneous healing powers of the third, but the repair was exponentially more rapid than he experienced as a human. There was no evidence of where she'd struck him in the face as well. Even the bone in his forearm had knitted quickly, as she'd said it would, such that he didn't even wear a wrist brace tonight. He was favoring it, but had used the hand of that arm several times to lift plates without any obvious discomfort.

"Then I am ready to accept your mark, gracious lady." Brian inclined his head at last. "Though I know it is a requirement of being in your Region, and I have a keen desire to work at Techco, I want you to know I trust you as I do my father. I will be honored by your mark."

"Well said," she responded, impressed despite herself. "Then come to me and prove it so."

26

Carefully putting down his napkin, Brian rose, walked to her and dropped to one knee. With courtly formality, he raised his chin and turned his head away, exposing his throat to her.

Lyssa put her hand on his shoulder, brushing his ear with her fingertips to confirm those blond strands were in fact almost as soft as a child's. But this was a grown man. She could feel hunger rising around the table just from watching them. Putting her hand to his jaw, she held him immobilized, letting him feel her strength as she leaned forward and gently penetrated his neck with her fangs, tasting him. His hand gripped her chair arm.

It was perhaps his first time being marked. It was a significant act of trust from his father, to give her the right to know his son's whereabouts in perpetuity. She knew Richard and Tara would be highly cognizant of that honor from the British Region Master. While Brian might be too young and too immersed in his quest for scientific discovery to be aware of it, he was apparently digesting some of it from the gravity of their audience and the surge of sensation accompanying the bite. She deliberately used the pheromones this time to ease the pain, and to torment the servant who had openly defied her.

Brian's other hand came to rest on her knee. She could feel him fighting the impropriety of it, but he was unable to deny the primal urge at such stimulation. Scientist he might be, but he was a man and a vampire, and there were certain things difficult for him to resist on either level. She knew Tara and Richard would expose him to it much more brutally, amused by his innocence.

Good sense kept his hand where it was, quivering on her leg as she took what she needed to claim him as hers while in her Region, an aura others would know and respect.

There was a slow, sensual pleasure to it, having a man on his knees to her, overwhelming him, feeling his instinctive struggle with his surrender. It wasn't the battle of wills it was with Jacob. Even when he surrendered, there was a defiance that fed her lust. Brian's capitulation was intended, a well-defined ritual.

Knowing she was playing with fire, something that would easily become a conflagration if she fed it fuel, she nevertheless opened herself up to the kindling of what was going on in her servant's mind.

Anger. Control. Discipline. A white-hot desire to pull Brian away from her and break the fingers touching her, even as his rational mind told him what she was doing was a planned part of the dinner, the type of business she regularly conducted. Like finalizing a contract.

But she's taking her bloody fucking time signing the dotted line.

She let her amusement flood him. *Caught that, did you? Would you kiss the taste of his blood off my lips, my obedient servant? He's fair close to exploding in his neatly pressed trousers. As you well know, I can push him to it with barely a thought. What if I wrapped my fist on his cock—*

Pray, cease, lady.

And let him dampen my hand? What if I made you lick his essence off my palm? Prove your loyalty and obedience?

Command me anything but that, my lady.

Dark satisfaction swept her. She looked toward Jacob as she lifted her mouth from Brian's neck, knew his blood was on her lips as she delicately collected it off her bottom lip with her tongue. Through some miracle of sheer will, Jacob was keeping his expression impassive, but she felt as if the focused blue of those clear eyes could burn her like lasers.

She leaned back from Brian, supporting his jaw with her hand as his head stayed bowed in his obvious struggle to master his body and mind's reaction.

"Is it . . . is it always like that?" he managed, low. The scientist trying to find answers he could grasp. Handle.

"No." It was Tara who spoke, her voice thick. Her eyes met Lyssa's, reflecting her remembrance of when Lyssa and Rex had marked her. They'd laid her down on this very table, sweeping away glassware to let the marking ceremony become a far more sensual experience. She'd climaxed again and again and Rex, unable to resist, had at last fucked her while Lyssa stood at her head, her hair wrapped in one restraining hand while she stroked her breasts with the other. As she lightly scored Tara with her nails, Lyssa channeled the magical heat through all three of them in a spiraling flow, increasing the intensity. That had been a small bit of Fey magic, passing easily as a variant on compulsion.

"It's something different with a vampire as ancient as Lady Lyssa, Dr. Morris. It's an honor to be in her home, a privilege of the highest order to receive her mark and serve her." Tara raised her cup. "To what we all aspire to be, but most of us never will. Your secrets inspire us and comfort us as often as they bring us despair at our failure to live up to them."

She must be getting far too old and sentimental if a temporary flash of sincerity could move her. Lyssa kept her expression impassive, but bowed in Tara's direction instead of nodding, enough of a physical response to let the woman know she was pleased.

Brian took his hand from her knee. With a glance for permission, he brushed a kiss on her hand resting on that same knee, just above where his hand had been. "My thanks, Lady Lyssa."

"The pleasure is mine. You are a sweet, welcome addition to my world." She gave him a fond look as he flushed. "You may return to your chair, Brian."

His hesitation told her they were indeed dealing with an innocent on such matters. Perhaps because he was a born vampire and his parents would be in charge of initiating such things, it had been avoided. Or his research had kept him far removed from where he would be initiated into this side of vampire life. As the other two recognized the depth of his inexperience, it sharpened the hunger she felt in the air to a razor's edge.

"Don't be embarrassed by your arousal. Indulgence of sensual pleasure is one of the most important parts of a vampire social occasion. In fact, I suspect even one such as I could not get attendance to matters of business without it." She let a light, practiced smile play over her face at Richard's chuckle, but the gesture showed the tips of her fangs.

"I intend to ensure you are all well-sated before the evening is over. You were the appetizer to get us started. Now please take your seat, and take your time getting there. We'll all enjoy the sight of your cock straining against your trousers, wanting more."

As she purred the words, letting the blatant sexual teasing stroke through the air of the room, she felt Jacob's reaction roll over her. An equally blatant wanting of *her*, part possession, part need. She wanted to feed on that wanting . . . wanted to feel it in her blood.

I'll be more than happy to show you how much I want you right here, my lady.

"Richard." She leaned back in her chair. "You spoke of a challenge. I accept. Tell us your desire."

His eyes glowed with calculated pleasure. Lifting his wineglass, he rose as Brian took his seat, attempting to assume the same nonchalant attitude as the other vampires at the table, leaning back in his chair and making a discreet adjustment. Though Lyssa noted when he laid his hand on the table his fingers curled tensely around the base of his own glass, his eyes focused on Richard.

As Richard rose, he turned to Seanna. Bending, he kissed the top of her breast as the black woman remained immobile, her eyes ahead, possibly meeting Jacob's. Her lips parted at the stimulation, though. Since she wore a strapless corset, Richard casually reached in, scooped one full breast out of the tight confines and manipulated the nipple before his audience. She remained completely still despite the increase in her pulse they could all sense, telegraphing her arousal. When he left her a moment later, he left the breast exposed.

The overlord moved in a slow, thoughtful circle around the room. The vampires waited patiently, but Lyssa could feel the tension rising for all the servants as he paused behind each. Liam was well used to the overlord's preferences and so, like Seanna, appeared to be stimulated primarily at the idea of the night's entertainment as Richard gave his nape an affectionate fondle.

"He's so dramatic," Tara commented. "He should have done stage."

"A flair for the dramatic can make for more interesting presentation," Lyssa responded. She adjusted her chair to an angle so she could see him step behind her own servant, examining him thoroughly. She knew that particular view was a delightful one, though most views of Jacob were well worth the time.

"You may feel free to touch my servant if it suits your purpose, Richard. Jacob will remain still."

Jacob's aversion to the thought was instant, but he stayed motionless, his jaw rigid as Richard went right for gold, palming his ass, giving it a hard squeeze. Lyssa followed the movement of Richard's long-fingered hand as he stepped closer to reach around Jacob to his groin area. He propped his other wrist on her servant's shoulder, the base of the wineglass he held pressed against Jacob's upper chest, the half-full contents near his jawline. He moved his own hips against Jacob's trousered backside, apparently letting him feel the pressure of his own arousal.

"A nicely sized cock," he observed, cupping Jacob firmly and running his thumb along the cock beneath the clothes. "It will pleasure some lucky human servant well tonight. But which one? What is your servant capable of, Lady Lyssa?"

How about breaking his fingers if he doesn't get them off my dick? And make him eat that wineglass a piece at a time?

"I have full confidence in Jacob's capabilities." She met his furious blue gaze, showing only cool amusement in her own. "Whatever your challenge."

"He doesn't like the touch of a man. That's obvious. You couldn't get a crowbar up his ass at the moment." Richard chuckled, ran the glass along the side of Jacob's face playfully. "He's lucky I'm not in the mood to teach him his likes and dislikes mean little here. I suspect making him fuck Tara's young man would be a pleasure for us all to watch."

Lyssa watched the quiver run down Jacob's arm, the fingers of his right hand curl slightly. Violence was surging up through his blood, the only thing stopping it his obedience to her will. What he likely didn't know was that everyone in this room knew what was going on, could see it. Richard was enjoying this, seeing how far it could go.

"Not Liam fucking him, my sweet?" Tara asked.

Richard shook his head. "Too easy. He could say he had to submit for his Mistress. If he has to arouse himself enough to fuck a man, shoot his seed into him, that's a whole other level of self-discovery."

He stepped away from Jacob, moved toward Debra. "However, as fun as that sounds, I've something in mind for my own selfish pleasure. I'm impressed by his restraint, so it makes me curious how far it extends." He stopped behind Debra. "So my challenge is this. He'll fuck Seanna and bring Debra to orgasm by whatever method he chooses, but he must understand their bodies and tailor his actions to ensure they come at exactly the same time." He caught Debra around the waist, eliciting a gasp of shock from her. Fondling her breasts through the white shirt, he nipped at her throat while she closed her eyes and trembled, trying to stay still, not as adept as Jacob at remaining impassive.

"What say you, lady?" Richard lifted his head, looked toward Lyssa. "The rosebush of your choice, of any color, from any part of the world, if he succeeds. If he fails, then Tara will get her wish. Liam will fuck him and show him what it is to have a man bring him to climax." His voice dropped to a murmur as he met Jacob's gaze with predatory intent. "Because he will. He will shame that heterosexual predilection of yours, show you that your cock cares nothing for gender, only for pleasure."

My lady, don't—

"Done." Lyssa tilted her head back to look at her servant. "I want my rosebush, Jacob. And I can promise you that you want me to have it, too. I've seen Liam's cock. It's not something a virgin ass would wish to take for his first time."

"Ah, Lyssa, you're cruel. If I'd known he was a virgin to that—"

"Next time, do better research," Lyssa responded, with a smile in her voice, though her gaze on Jacob held no humor. Just ruthless intent.

Anything I command. You said as much.

My lady, why are you doing this?

You defied me. This is the price. But more than that, it will bring me pleasure. This is as much a part of being a human servant as anything you've done tonight.

He closed his eyes, bowed his head. Because Lyssa knew all their eyes were on him, she didn't tease him further. They all knew he was young, new. Being present the first time a servant was initiated into the demands of a vampire social event was a special gift. Being present when a servant of such high rank was broken in was a particular honor, and Tara and Richard knew it. Though Lyssa had been unaware of Debra's innocence, it was a double boon to have two servants in the same situation, at the same social event. The anticipation surged through the room, spurring the lust quotient for every vampire present.

In the meantime, she felt the conflict roiling within Jacob, the mores of a lifetime fighting with his oath to serve her. He'd built another foundation out of what he believed to be true about their relationship, and she was once again smashing it to rubble.

Open yourself, Jacob. Get past all you know. Don't think. Feel. Look at them. Two women, both beautiful, all yours to pleasure while I watch. While we all watch. You'll be able to find release in them while our hunger simply builds and builds. Your submission will pleasure us all, but particularly your Mistress. You think I do it just to prove my will over you, but there is more going on here, something that will benefit you as well. This is a lesson you need to learn, but it's more than that. It's the essence of what we are.

He raised his head then, but instead of looking at the two women, he looked at her. There was desperation in his gaze, but as her attention slid down, he almost groaned as she visibly appreciated the reaction growing there despite his resistance to it.

"Obey me, Jacob. Nothing pleases me more than your obedience." *It nourishes me like blood.*

27

Jacob shifted his attention to Richard. He'd moved back behind Tara and his hand was on her shoulder, tracing the top of her breast visible in her low-cut dress with a fingertip he'd dipped into the wine. She watched the interplay intently, though her head tilted, acknowledging her enjoyment of the touch. Liam had taken a respectful step back, his face bland. Jacob wondered if he felt anger at his Mistress being touched by another as he'd felt at Brian's hand on his own Mistress. Or maybe he was some kind of aberration in the vampire world, as his Mistress kept implying.

"All three of you," Richard said. "Strip now, where you are." He glanced negligently over at Jacob. "Then the stage is yours, servant."

Jacob noted no one asked Brian his opinion of the proceedings. The man had looked startled at first, but the lust Lyssa's actions had roused in him apparently left few obstacles in the way for his acquiescence. He moved his chair now to get a better view of the two women. When Debra hesitated, he did rise and remove her glasses, giving her cheek a light caress with his knuckles. But that was all. He sat back down, his expression otherwise detached.

Seanna began to comply the moment the words left her Master's lips. She loosened the corset, her breasts thrust out, the exposed one joined now by its mate at the drawn back position of her shoulders. The loosened corset slithered down her hips and then she peeled away the snug hip-hugging skirt she'd worn beneath it. She wore a black thong with garters. With a slight smile, she turned her back to the table and bent low to slide it off, giving Jacob a view of her dusky pussy and the generous globes of her mocha-colored buttocks.

His gaze went to Debra, unbuttoning the tailored silk blouse Richard had half pulled out of her slacks. She'd worn the type of outfit she'd have worn to a dinner at a business conference, underscoring her lack of experience with this type of gathering. Apparently using her Master's burning gaze to fortify her, she raised her chin and unfastened the slacks, let them slide down her legs to draw them off over her practical heels. They were the shoes a research assistant would wear, a bit worn, probably from parking-lot gravel at the university. Her underwear was silky material, but a modest bikini. Her bra had just a touch of lace. With her blonde hair pulled back in a barrette, showing the strain of her expression, it was obvious this was not something she'd expected or been asked to do before. Yet Brian was willing to explore this new territory. He sat waiting with avid interest and no obvious sympathy for her feelings in the matter. No more than Lyssa had shown to him. It was an isolating, desolate feeling.

Only if you don't realize how connected we feel to you. Look at Seanna, her pleasure in pleasing her Master.

Debra hesitated on the bra, her fingers trembling enough to make her fumble the task. She struggled for the strap as Seanna smirked.

Jacob moved, sending a fierce message to his Mistress that did not bear repeating. Her jade eyes glittered, but she didn't respond, merely watched him as he defied Richard and walked around the table to

Debra. She didn't turn, keeping her gaze desperately fastened on Brian's throat, now unable to meet even his eyes. She flinched as Jacob touched her shoulders, gently brushing her hands away.

"'S all right, lass," he murmured, deliberately letting the Irish rise in his tone. He unhooked the bra, touching the tender area between her shoulder blades with his fingers, showing her he intended to be gentle. Sliding the straps down her arms, he dropped the garment onto her other clothes. "You'll come to no harm with me. I'll give you pleasure for your Master's enjoyment. Just relax."

When she nodded, he was sure she'd firmed her jaw to keep her teeth from chattering. She obviously hadn't been a servant anywhere near as long as Seanna or Liam. This was not something to do to a young woman. He felt a vicious anger at all of them for it. Easing the underwear down her legs, he steadied her as she stepped out of them. He had her step back into her shoes, but otherwise she was now naked.

"You." He nodded at Seanna. "Put your heels back on as well." He stepped back from Debra then unbuttoned his shirt, finding himself in line with Tara so that he had to watch her avid gaze cover every expanse of skin he was exposing. He couldn't do this. Couldn't fucking do it.

Look at me.

Gladly, he thought, shifting his gaze a moment before he thought to wonder if Lyssa's request was to ease his discomfort—not likely—or to satisfy some possessive need of her own. Either possibility might help him make it through this, though.

She'd shifted to the side in her pushed-back chair, her legs crossed, hand lying over her lap, the other resting on the table as her fingers stroked the stem of her wineglass. Casually imperious, hostess and highest ranking member of this assembly. Irresistible, her hair poured like silk over her shoulder, lips moist from the wine. She'd worn a man's poet shirt tonight, the full lace at the end of the sleeves draping her fingers, the loosely laced neckline revealing the curves of her breasts. She'd sashed it in over a black skirt.

The black and white outfit and the mascara she wore enhanced the depth of her eyes as he met her gaze, trying not to focus on the fact he was undressing in front of strangers to perform like a sexual gladiator with two women he didn't even know. Richard was now standing to his right, his brows raised, following Jacob's every move.

"I suspect this is not the first time your human servant has given you a reason to punish him, Lady Lyssa."

"There is pleasure in punishment, Richard, as you well know. For us both, though Jacob is yet learning that."

Do not speak unless invited to speak. He remembered the rule, had to bite off the pressing need to retort. He wanted the male vampire to give him another few feet of personal space. Hell, if he was out of the room and in the driveway he wouldn't be far enough. If he didn't stop staring at his ass . . .

He stripped off the pants viciously. The air in the room felt like weight on every part of his exposed skin. He was somewhat mollified when Tara drew in a startled breath and Richard took one step back. Jacob bent and removed the two wooden stakes neatly strapped to one calf and tossed them on the pile of his clothing.

He inclined his head, baring his teeth in a smile. "Part of my job is to protect and care for my Mistress, no?"

Richard's attention turned to Lyssa. His lady's expression was unreadable.

"Jacob, a challenge is on the table. Both of them to climax at once. Don't disappoint me."

It brought his attention back to the unimaginable thing he was being asked to do, and to her.

"And Jacob . . ." She paused, considering him, her eyes wandering with a blatant appreciation that made his cock grow harder, responding to the attention like a mindlessly loyal golden retriever. "I command you to come as well. If at the same time, that will certainly be impressive, but if you cannot come within five minutes afterward, then I will make you stand before us and masturbate until you do."

"Vampires are very patient," Tara observed.

"Perhaps if he can't come within those five minutes, we should let Liam take charge of it."

"No." Lyssa shook her head at Richard. "That's only if he fails your challenge, not mine. Come, don't sulk, Richard. Most vampire males couldn't achieve such a feat as you've given him without the crutch of pheromones." Tara snorted with laughter. "He'll likely fail, though I suspect Debra and Seanna will still get pleasure from the experience."

"As will we." Tara chuckled. "Seanna loves such games. She will be working against you, Jacob. Trying to come before or after young Debra. It will take a commanding touch to make her mind."

"You give him tips, my love." Richard shot her a warning glance. "Cease."

"Well then, Tara, that's where an alpha servant can be handy," Lyssa said smoothly.

If I fail, the only way that smirking blond son of a bitch is going to fuck me is if that vamp bastard holds me down by force.

You think that isn't what Richard intends? What better show could he demand than two strong men struggling for sexual mastery over one another?

You would allow a vampire to hold me down to let another man rape me?

He met her gaze. Shadows flickered there, but there was no indication of her thoughts except what she spoke in his mind.

My world is not the human world, Jacob. Time is passing. Obey me and remember this as my punishment if you think to defy me again. As my punishments go, this one is gentler than most.

As the moments ticked by and the locked gazes of the hostess and her servant made it clear a battle of wills was ensuing, Jacob felt a dangerous energy gathering in the room. When he shifted his attention at last to Tara's cool expression and Richard's calculating one, it occurred to him the option to walk out no longer existed. He was in a room with three vampires who seemed entirely convinced the humans here would serve whatever need or drive they had, and if they didn't, they would be forced to do so.

As proof of it, three of them already stood unclothed. Seanna looked toward him expectantly. Debra had her eyes lowered, staring at Brian's feet.

Jacob reached out and took the young woman's cold hand. He drew her toward the end of the table where Seanna waited, watching them from behind Richard's empty chair.

"My lord, I'm commandeering your space for the pleasure of all viewers." Jacob cast a contemptuous glance toward the male vampire a moment before he used his arm to sweep off the place setting, sending the dessert plate, silverware, place mat, bouquet and water glass spinning off the table. The china bounced onto the floor and shattered, spraying raspberry sauce over his ankle, the Aubusson carpet and chair legs.

Tara and Debra jumped. Everyone showed some adverse reaction except his lady, who could have been a statue as she watched him.

"Easy, lass." Taking Debra by the forearm and elbow, he moved her before him so she was facing Lyssa. He glanced at Seanna, pointed to bring her to within a step from him. "You watch for now. No touching either of us, but you watch everything we do."

Her dark eyes met his. She was almost his height, and he'd noted the slight parting of her lips at his words. His order. She liked a man to come on strong. And she liked to watch.

"It's a good thing you commanded them to keep on their shoes," Tara noted, lifting her chin to take in the debris on the far side. "Thinking ahead to protect their feet."

Jacob inclined his head. "There's that. But mainly I like fucking a woman when all she's wearing are those little skinny heels."

He pressed his body up against Debra's back, taking both of her hands, guiding them down before her, down to her mons. "Play with your pussy for them," he murmured against her ear as he bent to her neck. "Look toward your Master. Touch yourself for him, as you would if the two of you were alone. It's just you and him."

"I've never . . ."

"But it's something he's always wanted you to do. Look at him, lass. Every man likes seeing his woman touch herself. It makes him hard, makes him want to take you, even as you take yourself to completion while he watches."

When she continued to hesitate he guided her, taking her fingers down, down, then resting his own fingertips between the spaces of hers on the soft blonde curls. He brushed his fingertips on her clit, earned a tremor, did it again, bringing her fingers into it while he took his other hand up to her breast. As he did, her pale lashes lifted. Following instinct, he nipped her slim throat and earned an instant reaction. An arching into his body, a gasp. Brian's eyes flared with response.

As Jacob worked down her shoulder, he rubbed himself slowly against her tense buttocks and watched his lady. Imagined it was her dark hair against his nose, his lips, her smooth petals growing wet against his fingertips. He thought about the way he'd driven hard into her cunt while she spread open for him on the kitchen table, her fangs sunk deep into him.

Power was building in the room, feeding on the response he was stoking and enhancing, provoking him further. Seanna's fingers brushed his flank. Without looking at her, he caught her hand, yanked, turned her so her ass was pressed against his hip, his arm pinning her arms to her sides by holding her across the breastbone, his hand clamped onto her opposite shoulder, which now brushed Debra's. He rubbed the side of his thigh against the cleft of Seanna's generous buttocks as he kissed his way back up to Debra's ear again, registering the way her breathing was starting to go shallow from arousal. He kept his arm firm just over Seanna's full breasts, letting her feel the pressure so close to the nipples, but it was Debra's nipples he pinched with his other hand, tugging as Seanna arched in involuntary invitation to do the same.

Instead, he kept her firmly anchored to him and sensed her surprise when she realized she couldn't shake him, not even to turn. She'd expected her strength as a servant would be enough to match him, but apparently two marks and his male human physique were enough to let him hold his own.

He pressed his hard cock against Debra's ass and felt her tense again. "Sshh, girl," he murmured to her. "Nothing going in that way. Just let me tease you a bit. Spread your thighs out for me."

When she did, he slid his cock between them, rubbing between her labia lips, teasing her clit with his hand as she leaned back further into him, her fingers now not only playing over her own clit, but making whispering, shy caresses on his broad head when he pushed through to her touch and withdrew, a repetitious stroking he could feel melting her tension and self-consciousness into halting, aroused response.

Bringing any woman to orgasm at the right moment was challenging. Synchronizing two was almost impossible, as Lyssa had implied. But he wasn't accepting the possibility of failure. It was just a matter of gauging the way they each responded, and what stimulated them the most.

Releasing Seanna, he shoved her down onto her belly on the smooth table surface. "Like to play games, do you, love? You'll play no games with me. Spread your legs and show me your cunt. Lift up that fine ass so I can see clear what I'm going to fuck."

At the same moment, before Debra could tremble at his rough tone, he turned her gently. He moved close enough to lift her up by the waist, holding her in a short embrace, giving her a reassuring squeeze before he palmed her bottom and sat her on the table. Letting her hold onto his hand and wrist with one hand, he lowered her to her back next to Seanna, even as he roughly fondled the dark skin of that one's buttocks. He made his focus his own pleasure, conveying he didn't give a damn if his grip was too rough. If he wanted to leave fingerprints on her ass, that's what he'd do. As a result, she was dripping, her trembling thighs wide and ass lifted, inviting more.

"Lyssa, I think your man is proving that men can indeed multitask," Tara commented, but Jacob barely heard her, caught in the flood of energy.

Gentle and rough. Tenderness and cruelty. Two sides of the coin, pleasures as light and dark as the women's contrasting skin, and with permutations of all the shades between. He couldn't deny the allure of it. Within him, as he suspected it was for most men, were the gentle lover and the demanding, primal animal. Here he was allowed to indulge and unleash both. Over it all was the watchful presence of his Mistress who'd compelled him to this course, which added an indefinable but no less arousing ingredient to it. The stimulation he felt was a synergy of all the arousal in the room. Instead of two women, he was arousing all of them. The power of it swept over him. While it drained some of the force of his anger, it left a sharp edge that only fed the hunger in himself.

Covering the side of Debra's left breast with one hand, he let the fingers of his other drift down her body, down to her mound. Tugging at those simple, delicate curls, he feathered over the pink lips that peeked from them, inviting the pads of his fingers. At the same time, when Seanna spread her legs wider, bumping Debra's leg, he startled her with a hard flat-handed slap on those wet lips, causing a gasp. It distracted Debra enough he had no trouble inserting a finger up to the second knuckle into her, drawing her attention back to him immediately. He worked the finger just inside her opening, letting her feel the sucking wetness as he used his thumb to put pressure on her clit.

"Oh . . ." A little breath left her and her head tilted toward Brian. Her Master was a tense statue at his place setting, watching her with avid interest. A flush tinged her cheeks at the intensity of his expression.

Jacob turned Seanna over on her back. "Link your arms," he commanded. Debra looked confused, but Seanna slid her arm through the space between the other girl's elbow and body.

"Lift them over your head."

When Seanna did, Debra's trembling increased. Because the women were of similar height, it drew them closer together as he'd expected, pressing left breast against the side of the right.

Removing his fingers from Debra, he commanded them to do the same with their legs and then he straddled that linked pair of limbs, pressing his thighs against the pussy of each woman. He bent, cupping Debra's breast in one hand and Seanna's in the other. He began to suckle them, administer random teasing licks with his tongue. Because their arms and legs were linked, the movements of their bodies responding to him rubbed him harder against them so their slickness marked his upper thighs. The tip of his cock was wet and marked Debra's hip in return, for her leg was on top.

Richard was kneading Tara's breasts in earnest, and he'd bent to her neck, sharply nipping her. Brian reached forward impulsively and grasped Debra's unencumbered breast, his knuckles brushing Jacob's. Debra cried out in reaction to his touch.

Still the Lady Lyssa just watched. No expression on her perfect face.

If I crawled under the table and pressed my face to your knees, my lady, would you part them for me? Would I find you soaking wet, your clit aching for the suckling of my lips?

28

SHE didn't respond, but neither did her eyes leave him. By the slight press of her moist lips together he knew she'd heard him clearly enough. Keeping his gaze on her, he caught Seanna's arm, rolled her over onto Debra so she lay upon her as a man would. Jacob grasped Debra's legs, lifted them so she had her heels on his back, her thighs alongside Seanna's hips. Only then did he drive his cock into Seanna, into a deep well of pussy so slick and hot it almost made him lose his focus. He held Debra's legs against the black woman's thighs and moved the three of them, pounding hard into Seanna, knowing every stroke rubbed her clit against Debra's as she held herself over her, their nipples brushing, breasts bumping into each other.

It was enough to break Richard's control. He pulled Tara out of the chair, rucked up her tight skirt, tore away her panties and sank into her from behind at the same moment he gripped her shoulder with his fangs. Brian put his hand to Debra's chin, tilted her head back at an angle just short of breaking her neck and claimed her lips, growling into her mouth as she whimpered her need.

Seanna could go at any time, but Jacob's gut told him Debra wasn't quite there. His fevered gaze fell on the untouched dessert on Brian's plate and he reached for it, grabbing a fistful of the sauce and brownie together. Lifting Seanna with a firm hand at her throat, he massaged the sauce and moist brownie into those chocolate-colored breasts. When Brian moved down to her throat, Debra watched, mesmerized by the play of Jacob's paler hands against the firm dark skin, the deep brown nipples. The raspberry sauce slid down over them, giving the appearance of blood to hungry, nonhuman eyes.

Keeping one hand below Seanna's jawline, Jacob moved the other down to Debra's clit. He passed his thumb over the sensitive nub before he slid two fingers deep inside of her and began to work her again, his thumb shuttling back and forth across the clit as she bucked beneath his ministrations. Brian bit her.

Her clit spasmed against Jacob's palm. *Thank you, Lord Brian.* Working his cock in Seanna, Jacob increased his hold on her throat so he was restricting her air, punishing her. Demanding.

"Come for me, you arrogant bitch," he whispered. Fierce triumph flooded him as she cursed . . . and her body began to shudder. She cried out, her muscles milking him. He let himself feel it, though he didn't want to. He wanted to stand away from it and remain in control of the situation entirely, but his Mistress had anticipated that when she required he come as well. She would leave him nothing. But he'd succeeded where she'd expected him to fail.

Oh, you're quite wrong about that, Sir Vagabond. I knew you wouldn't fail.

Lifting his attention back to her now, he saw her lips were parted, her fingers frozen on the stem of her wineglass. The way she was turned in the poet's shirt showed him almost all of the curve of her left breast. There was a tiny pen and ink stencil of a rose on it. She'd made him do it, forcing him to discuss with her the more mundane details of the week's domestic duties while he did it. Treating him as casually as if he were a lady's maid, disinterested in a lady's breasts, all the while knowing it was all he could do to keep himself from smearing the ink with the pads of his fingers to grasp her, take his fill of her weight and shape. He was growing accustomed to her small torments, but he realized now they were just preparatory exercises for things like this.

He watched the rose petals flutter with the reaction she was masking so well from the others. But when it came to her, it was as if he couldn't overlook the slightest detail. What others might need time-lapse photography to see . . . the tiny breath, the slight tremor . . . he saw and felt it all in a rush of scalding heat through his body. He tortured himself with every feature, every gesture, but it wasn't enough.

He needed something to bring this tableau to a close. As the thought entered his mind, he was afraid she'd withhold it just to enjoy watching him masturbate in front of them all. But he took the leap and tried to ask instead of demand. Even his thoughts felt raw with need, as his voice would have been if he spoke out loud what he was thinking now.

Command me to come, my lady. Only your lips can compel me.

Charming courtier. But the intensity of her expression increased, telling him he'd touched her. *Surely your cock is hard enough the stroke of Seanna's cunt would make it explode.*

Only the stroke of your words will do that, my lady. My cock aches to explode for you. Within you.

Within every part of her in fact. That soft wet pussy, between her moist lips, in her tight ass . . .

Perhaps he should not have had those thoughts, because a spark of fire came into her expression. The women were convulsing in aftershocks, still responding to his touch and the feel of his cock, but they were coming down. Her gaze lifted to the grandfather clock ticking in the corner next to the china cabinet.

I have three and a half more minutes to make up my mind, don't I? If you come before then, I'll know your words were just empty flattery, an attempt to hold onto control, rather than the gift of your full surrender.

Seanna's muscles rippled, her ass pushing back into him.

"Lick the sauce off of her," Tara purred. She had her cheek to the table, her arm extended under it like a lazy cat. Richard sat in her chair now, and had his hands on her thighs, holding them open as he ate at her pussy, making her jerk as she spoke breathlessly. "Turn her over."

Seanna's flexibility would be enough to make most men lose control. As he began to lift her, she simply rose up on her hands and twisted over, turning on his cock like a pin, holding onto his shoulders so he could lift her off Debra, step unsteadily to the side to lay her back on the table. In a smooth movement, he was full hilt in her again. She tilted up, offering her breasts with her cupped hands as she tightened her legs on him, drawing him deeper, making him feel the lock of her legs across his buttocks, the squeeze of her inside. Christ, she was bloody strong. As if she knew what was going on between him and his Mistress, the light of challenge was in her eye. But there was reviving desire there as well, even as her body still quivered with the climax he'd given her.

"You've got a nice cock, Irishman," she said. "I want to feel it spill inside me."

He wanted to tell her to shut her mouth, as if she'd said something obscene to him. Instead, he bent over her and put his lips to the curve of her other breast, feeling her arms come around his shoulders, cover his hair in a surprisingly romantic move, reminiscent of his lady's touch . . . but it wasn't her.

He wanted to throw her off, but instead it gave him an idea. He raised his gaze as he licked the raspberry sauce slowly off the brown swell of breast, suckling then covering her nipple with his mouth, tugging it in, showing his lady by demonstration. He wouldn't think about the clock now. That was irrelevant. Either she was going to be merciful or she was going to be cruel. He had to await her pleasure either way.

Her gaze flickered, acknowledging the truth of that thought. He rubbed his lips in the raspberry sauce then brought his face to Seanna, keeping his attention locked on his lady as she nibbled and nuzzled at his mouth, scoring him with her teeth. He didn't kiss her back, keeping his lips firm and unyielding, but it didn't seem to bother her. If anything, his indifference seemed to goad her to greater efforts. She was lifting her hips from the table, stroking herself on his cock and driving herself back to orgasm even as she yanked him toward the same cliff's edge with the slow pumping motion inside her soaked tissues. He'd kept his hand on Debra's abdomen, a reassuring touch, not wanting to just abandon her, but now Brian pulled her off the table away from him, curling her up in his arms. He laved the punctures in her neck, his hand between her bare legs, penetrating her wetness.

Jacob returned to suckling the sauce off the generous breasts of Richard's servant, noting that her Master watched even as he busied himself at Tara's pussy, his lips slick with her juices, his grip tightening as she began to writhe. Games of power. Who held the reins, and who only thought they did. As his lady watched all of it, Jacob suspected she missed no nuance of what was happening. What the relationships here truly were.

What is it she truly needs me to be? Her mouth says one thing, her mind another. Her heart and soul hold the truth of it, but she holds those out of reach . . .

He couldn't help his thoughts, even knowing she was in his mind where she could hear them. She rose, a slow glide. Keeping his eyes on her, he framed Seanna's breasts in both hands, lashing at her nipples, using some of his own strength to drive her up again. Her nails were raking his shoulders, drawing blood, so much like his lady he had to stifle a groan.

Lyssa was a slow, sensuous shadow behind the flames of the dim candlelight. She trailed her hand on Brian's shoulder as she passed him, a mild reminder of her ownership. The scientist stilled momentarily to watch her, then was drawn back into his fascination with his own servant.

Seanna gasped as Jacob changed angle and kept the pace at his own desire. He was getting precariously close, but he knew it wasn't Seanna's welcoming cunt. It was his lady's approach. As Seanna went over that cliff, she left him behind, proving the point. Expectant pulsing energy rushed to his cock as Lyssa moved behind him. Her hand whispered along his shoulder as it had Brian's, only it changed track, descended. He kept moving as he felt she desired him to do, his upper body flexing, muscles rippling under her touch as he fucked a stranger at her command. Her nails passed over where Seanna had scored him and he shuddered as he felt his lady's lips touch there, her skirt brush the back of his legs. Her hands came to rest on his hips. Pressing against his buttocks, she moved with him, her mound rubbing at the seam of his ass, lower, the tops of his thighs.

"Mistress . . . my lady . . ." His desire became explosive, his need for release ratcheted up to blazing. He could have gone now, but still he waited. . . . He was following her hands as she tightened on him, released, driving him in and out more slowly, tormenting him not from the dragging friction of Seanna's cunt, but from the control her slender hands were imposing on him. Fondling, directing him, working him as intimately as if she were fucking him. When he licked at Seanna's breasts with all the focus of a blind man, the hair on his forehead brushing the base of her throat, he heard the breath of sound behind him. His lady's breasts, loose in the soft shirt, brushed his back. The hint of a taut nipple, the rough lacings at odds with the silken mounds beneath as she kissed his neck.

Would you like to come for me, Jacob?

Yes, my lady. God, yes.

Then you may. You have three seconds—

It exploded from him before she could complete the sentence. It was all his body had needed. All that mattered was she'd required it, commanded it. He had no ability to explain why he'd made that so important, such that every temptation couldn't push him over the way the whisper of her voice in his mind did now, like a lever flipping.

He rammed Seanna hard against the table, taking her aftershocks up to the intensity of a climax, her body arching impossibly as she screamed. There was pleasure in knowing he didn't have to be gentle, that he could give her pain to assuage some of the shadows snarling in his soul. Relentlessly he kept fucking her, spiraling himself into a darkness he didn't know, at the behest of the darkness behind him.

At the moment he came, it pushed Tara over as well. She screamed, drawing Jacob's attention to see Richard had turned over the oral play to Liam. The blond servant tongued his Mistress frenetically while bent over the dining room chair so Richard could drive into his muscular ass. Liam's guttural response was muffled in Tara's cunt, but it was obvious Richard was not going to be outdone. Both male servants came at the same time. Jacob shifted his gaze away, closed his eyes and thought only of his Mistress. He had no desire to bond with the man who might have been ordered to fuck him. Or that he would have had to fuck the way Richard was doing now. Pleasure and disgust warred within him, but he could not deny his Mistress her pleasure, even to save his own pride.

As Jacob came, Lyssa moved with him, her body firm against his back, hips curved to his. He dropped to one elbow on the table over Seanna. The two women worked him together until he was sure they'd drained every drop he had. When at last they slowed, he had to stay where he was, head bowed, breathing hard, sides shuddering.

"Magnificent," Richard murmured. "Lady Lyssa, you've outdone yourself this night."

Jacob felt his lady touch his hair, a lingering contact gone before he could turn his lips to it. She left him as if he were Bran and she'd just made him perform some type of trick. As if the intimacy, the melding of their minds that had driven him to the powerful public climax, had never existed.

When he had the composure to raise his head, Richard sat in Tara's chair again and Liam straddled his knee, facing outward as Richard played with the man's cock. Tara sat on the table, kissing her servant. Liam held her waist as Richard fondled him. Jacob could envision she would eventually straddle the servant and wrap her legs around Richard. Debra was writhing under Brian's touch and softly begging for permission to come, quiet whimpers like a pleading kitten. Brian was absorbed in her response, shaking his head to deny her as he continued to work his fingers on her clit, his fingers wet with her arousal.

Lyssa placed her hands on the back of her chair, as if using the ornately carved wood as a shield for her body.

"I think he met the challenge quite adequately, wouldn't you say, Lord Richard?"

"He's magnificent, Lady Lyssa," Richard acknowledged. "I'll look forward to tripping him up another time, another way. I'd love to see him and Liam wrestle for the right of who gets to fuck whom." Amusement crossed his features. "Though I still think he'd be more dismayed by winning than losing."

"Indeed." Lyssa studied Jacob. "Jacob, clean yourself up and get dressed. You've served me well tonight. Please make sure the floor gets cleaned up. We'll take our coffee in the library."

"Yes, Mistress." Jacob pushed himself up, his mind too disoriented from the climax to offer more than the automatic response. Until he realized what he'd called her. His gaze flitted to her to find her green eyes alive with something beyond pleasure, something it oddly seemed she didn't want him to see. She immediately shifted her attention to what Richard was saying.

Somewhere in his fogged brain he knew that was a good thing. Because he wasn't at all certain he wanted to focus too much on what had just happened.

The guests began to rise, apparently responding to her cue and intending to continue their sensual pursuits in the library. Brian lifted Debra's quivering body off him, guiding her as she clutched his arm, her breath shallow with arousal. When Richard took Liam and Tara out the door just behind the couple, Jacob noted he didn't spare any attention for Seanna. Perhaps he was displeased with her for losing his wager. Or he was more involved with Tara and Liam at the moment and wouldn't give thought to Seanna until he wanted something from her again. When he did, he of course would assume she'd be close at hand, a well-trained pet.

Seanna's eyes widened when Jacob took her by the arm, easing her to her feet. Bending, he picked up her clothes and offered them to her. "There's a bathroom just down the corridor. If you'd like to wash up, there are towels there." He kept his hand at her elbow as she got her bearings. "Are you all right?"

She nodded, then started as Jacob lifted a cloth napkin, pressed it between her legs just as his seed began to tumble from her, keeping it from traveling down her legs. She shuddered at the light touch.

"You're a strange one, Jacob Green," she observed.

When Jacob glanced at her, he found her expression almost open and friendly. She surprised him by touching the side of his face the way a much wiser, older sister would have done. Closing her hand over the cloth, she took it from him. "I'll take advantage of that bathroom now. My Master will have need of me again before long. He tends to like to release his cock only between my lips."

Nudity in the dressing area of the circus was one thing. This open carnality was something entirely different and new to him. His lady had known that, fully exploited it tonight. He'd responded to her challenge because it wasn't in his nature to back down, but he found himself somewhat shell-shocked to think about what he'd done. How aroused he'd been by it. By his lady's pleasure in his performance.

You know what a sexual submissive is, Jacob? He remembered her words, uncomfortably.

"It's been a pleasure, Irishman." A slight smile crossed Seanna's face as she drew his attention back to the present. She ran her fingertips over the flush that had risen on his neck at her bald words. "I fully expect you to be eaten by wolves before I see you again, but I hope I'm wrong."

As she walked away, her lush hips swayed with such natural sensuality he knew it wasn't feigned. Jacob bent, picked up his clothing. When he looked up, he found his lady standing in the doorway.

The length of the room was between them, the images of what had just happened here. Crockery shattered on the floor, swept there by his temper. He couldn't think of anything to say. Anything he wanted to say.

He gave a clumsy, short bow, eager to head for the kitchen and blessed privacy.

"You think you'll ever have privacy again, Jacob?" she asked softly.

A muscle ticked along his jaw. He felt his teeth grind together. "I have what my Mis—my lady sees fit for me to have." *Damn it.*

"Tell me, is that what bothers you the most?" she asked after a pause that made the air in the room feel exponentially warmer. "The fact that heeding my will made you harder than you've ever been in your life, or that your cock wouldn't release without my command?"

Maybe what bothers me the most is how you keep refusing to admit what you really want, my lady.

With a curl of his lip that could only be called a snarl, he turned on his heel and headed for the kitchen, leaving her alone in the dining area. He'd intended the insult, but knew she wouldn't call him on it, because they both knew she'd won that round.

The answer to her question had been painfully clear, so that not even a mental response had been necessary.

29

THEIR guests left at a courteous time for vampires, half past three in the morning. It had been a successful event, all her formal intentions accomplished, including teaching her servant another vital aspect of the role he was expected to play. He'd exceeded her expectations. Indeed, probably everyone's. Brian had learned a good deal as well. She suspected Debra would be reaping the benefits of that again before the pull of dawn claimed him. He was a handsome boy who tended to approach a new experience with thorough intensity.

So why did she stand here in her bedchamber, feeling empty? She was in the lower one, but she'd left the passageway to it open. She hadn't commanded Jacob to come to her, though.

When she last saw him, he'd been finishing up with the catering group. As she stood before the fire warming her hands, turning them over and over, watching the firelight play on her palms, her knuckles, she occasionally reached out with her mind to locate him.

In the kitchen and dining room, helping with cleanup. Then out back, giving Bran and his pack scraps. The smile that curved her lips felt like a stretched wound as he helped the all-female catering staff get the crates of supplies back to their van. He had such an easy way with women. She was sure he was unintentionally giving them all sorts of fantasies. Any one of them would take him to her bed with little encouragement. Probably two or three at once. She should probably push him that way, allow him to release his frustration. Give him some time and space to get his mind around what had happened tonight.

She tried to avoid dipping into anything more than the surface layers of his mind. But as she watched the women make any excuse to brush against him, touch his hands when they transferred the crates, she felt his politeness coupled with a complete absence of interest. Nothing toward them. But as she risked it, went deeper, she found there was something explosive below the nothing. It scalded her body, warming it even more than the aura of the flame flickering shadows over her hands.

The force of restless, dark desire and the simmering lust had only one objective. Her. With each moment he drew closer to finishing his tasks for the evening, it was building. The anticipation of it expanded proportionately in herself.

She thought of him taking Seanna and bringing Debra to climax, meeting the challenge before him with an erotic creativity she'd not realized he had. Laying Debra out on the table as he held Seanna from behind, his pale body against Seanna's dark skin, his fingers wet from Debra's cunt as he took them to his lips, tasted . . . During all of it, he had rarely let his eyes leave his Mistress's face.

She shuddered, making herself stay by the fire. Waiting to see what he would do with all that lust mixed with anger. Not once when buried in either woman had that singular focus on her wavered. He'd climaxed with her image firmly before him, and she knew it had been to prove something to her. Something that rose up in her now, tearing at her with savage claws, telling her there was no way in hell she would push him toward another woman's arms. Not now. Maybe not ever.

She tried but couldn't brush it off as the obsession of a vampire with her new servant. She'd never experienced this feeling with one before. Not in all her long life. Not even with Rex. He'd called her Mistress . . .

The grip of that remarkable realization paralyzed her as she felt him enter the bedroom above. He'd see that hazy outline to this chamber, beckoning him closer to her.

She closed her eyes, a soft gasp of response leaving her as he didn't hesitate, didn't even pause to wonder if he needed permission. Linked with his mind now as if she was the one unable to break the link, she knew he didn't give a damn. All that easy courtesy had vanished, and he had one intent, growing with every stride down the illusory steps.

She didn't turn from the fire, a straight, indifferent pose. Even though his approach was swift, even though she felt his intention as hard as an urgent cock in her hand, she was not entirely prepared for the way he came up behind her. His hands closed on her shoulders, slid down and increased the tension of his hold so her arms were drawn back. Her fingertips grazed his thighs, planted on either side of her, the hardness of his cock pressed against her hips. She sought a grip in the soft stuff of his slacks as he pulled her back against him and released one of her hands to grip her hair, tilt her head and claim her lips.

Keep your hands on my legs.

She sucked in a trembling breath as he savaged her mind with the command the way he was savaging her mouth. He knew she didn't have to obey, that he didn't have the strength to make her obey. And yet . . . she sensed the certainty in his mind that he could seduce her to his will and would, by God.

She thought of those long, clever fingers deep in Debra's pussy, her cries as she writhed. Brian had seized her throat, bending down to suckle her breasts, overwhelmed by the tableau such that he had to be a part of it. Jacob had taken them all to the edge of the cliff. But all along, his eyes had promised she was the only one he intended to take over it with him.

She couldn't keep up, his teeth biting her lips, mouth sucking the air out of hers, his tongue stroking and caressing it as deeply as he would caress her cunt. When his hand closed over her throat, a growl broke from her lips, vibrated against his. His other hand left hers on his thigh and pushed under the waistband of her skirt. Seizing a handful of her panties in the front, he rubbed the silky fabric against her crotch, making her writhe as the back dug deeper into her cleft, bringing her up to her toes. She wanted . . .

Show me how he fucked you. The way you liked it best.

The question was so shockingly intimate she didn't think to block the image that flashed through her mind until it was too late.

The answer evoked a specific memory. Rex, pushing her down on her hands and knees before the fire. He'd massaged her with oil, leaving no expanse of skin uncovered until she'd gleamed in the firelight like a creature of water. He'd even run it through her hair, slicking it down on her skull. Holding a hand on her neck to press her cheek to the rug, he'd slid into her, teased her until her hands stretched out, tugging at the long hairs of the carpet. Her whole body quivered with every stroke, aching for release. He told her he loved her that night, a break in his voice. His hold had been ruthless, his touch gentle. He'd shattered her with his merciless tenderness.

Jacob stilled, his breath on her temple. His fingers rested on her mound still, making soft strokes over her clit, which increased the bittersweet yearning. As he nuzzled her hair, she saw him struggling to get his mind around the revelation. "You did love him."

"Yes. I did. Very much. Despite all the wisdom of the world that told me I was a fool for it." She pressed her temple to his upper arm as his hand continued to hold her throat. She took comfort in that touch, his hair brushing her eyelashes as she closed her eyes. "You can love someone whose cruelty you could not bear otherwise," she murmured. "Every time you leave, you think you won't want back into hell, yet there's something about those fires you miss. As if there was a secret to them you never truly understood. But you wanted to understand it, enough to burn for the comprehension."

His hand lifted and slipped inside the panties to move down, making her feel every millimeter slide of his fingertips as he reached the clean soft skin of her mound, her clit hood and even lower, taking possession of her labia, positioning his knuckles on either side of the clit, applying a knowledgeable pressure that made her moan quietly.

I understand, my lady. Jesus, but you're teaching me to understand.

It was an unkind observation, but one she couldn't argue. Nor could she move away, not when his angry thoughts were seductive murmured offerings in her mind, matching his movements without. He unfastened the skirt, let it fall to her ankles, then nudged her arm up to remove the oversized silk poet's shirt she'd worn. She'd removed the sash earlier. When he'd come into the room, she'd seen in his mind his reaction to her standing before the fire, the shadow of her curves and nipples outlined through the fabric. It had goaded his cock, but not as much as her haughty and remote posture had.

This was his shirt.

Yes. Tara and Richard knew it. It sent a message.

"It helped you assume his mantle. Made them feel a part of him was still in the room, reinforcing your authority."

"Very good. Yes."

He stripped off the shirt, deliberately balled it up and sent it across the room. She stayed motionless, turned away from him. She listened to the sounds of him removing his own clothes, unzipping the slacks, kicking it all away from him. His knee nudged the seam of her thighs, his arm sliding around her waist. With relentless pressure, he took her down to her knees on the rug before the fire, his body hard and strong and now bare behind her, the heat of his cock pressing against her left buttock. He spread kisses on her neck and shoulders like flower petals drifting over her skin. Romantic, stirring. Fantastical. He eased her back up so she was sitting on her heels. Lifting her hair, he unpinned it, then cupped it in his hands, letting it spill down her back again and again. Dropping her head back, she enjoyed his desire to stroke her hair, feel it pour between his fingers. She closed her eyes, filled with pleasure at the joy he was taking in it, even as his body moved against her, reminding her how empty it was between her legs.

"Jacob . . ."

"Sshhh, my lady. You obey my will now. You'll let me pleasure you at my own pace, surrender to my desires. I have many desires when it comes to you."

I shouldn't do this. You'll be like a dog I've allowed to misbehave. I'll have to be that much more stern tomorrow to reestablish my authority.

"You relish that, my lady. You like giving me punishment. Your pleasure brings me pleasure. But let me show you what it is to accept my desire for now."

How could she resist him, when he'd done so many things to rouse her tonight? He'd performed to perfection on every level. When he'd defied her, he'd twisted the consequences of his actions with such delectable proficiency she knew Tara, Richard and Brian would not soon forget the evening, and would look forward to the next invitation. They would spread the word, talk about Lady Lyssa's new servant, enhance the impression that she'd not lost an ounce of her allure or power.

But now, despite the fact she'd taken him from fury to humiliation to climax, here he was, seducing her with a tender form of dominance she'd never experienced before. She had the disturbing thought she might truly be helpless to him at the moment.

He kissed his way down her spine, slowly pushing her until she dipped forward on her hands again. He spread kisses over her buttocks, his thumb probing her between, the heated entrance that unleashed so many powerful longings.

"Down on your elbows, my lady. I want to see your perfect ass in the air, your thighs spread and your pussy glistening, hungry for my cock."

He wound his hand in her hair, that clever bondage she would only be able to resist if she overcame vanity, and he knew her too well. She complied, gracefully spreading herself, butterflies quivering in her stomach remarkably at the tension on her hair like a restraint. She knew she was in no physical danger from him. But everything deep within was shaking as if he were threatening the very heart of who she was. All the guards she usually posted to protect her were gone. Her thoughts literally suspended as the tip of him found her and slowly, slowly eased in. Deeper, deeper, and she curved up, meeting him, a cry emerging from her lips as he filled her completely, down into places empty for so long she'd forgotten how vast and dark they could be. Which made it all the more amazing that he filled them. Tightly.

Instead of pinning her the way Rex had done, he dropped over her, his body covering her, hands placed on the outside of her elbows, his hard upper body pressed all along her back and hips, thighs tucked in behind her buttocks. It kept him seated so his testicles pressed against her clit. His breath was on her neck at the top point of her spine. Tumbling her hair over her left shoulder, he tangled it with her fingers, drawing her down lower, shortening the binding he'd made.

He touched his lips to the point of her neck. "You may have the greater strength, my lady."

Now he kissed her shoulder.

"The greater wisdom."

Back to the neck, so that her breath clogged in her throat.

"But tonight you've provoked *my* will, such that you'll be overpowered by it. I'll bring you such pleasure you'll be *my* willing slave."

He'd already accomplished that, and he didn't know it. She would have begged him to move, but one thing she knew from such a long life was never to rush something that felt so good.

Jacob. She said his name softly in her mind. He began to move.

Long, slow strokes. Short strokes to tease her clit, but then back to long and slow interchanging strokes that began to inspire low, guttural noises of demand from her, noises he answered in kind as she began to arch back for him, meeting his thrusts. He picked up the pace and the strength, making those deep strokes harder, deeper, more forceful and punishing. Working her hard, covering her like a male predator, sure of his power, seeking his own pleasure but also seeking to make her acknowledge his claim. She saw it flash through his mind. There'd been Rex, and Thomas, and others he didn't want to know about. There were the things she'd made him endure tonight. Richard's touch. The whole performance, her punishment for his disobedience. Through it all, there'd been one word to help him maintain his control. Hearing him utter it in his mind, she lost hers.

Yours. The way he spoke it was a brand he placed on her soul. It was that which pushed her over, taking away her choice so the ripple of her cunt startled her, a strong, hard reaction seizing her in its grip and tearing a cry from her lips as she threw her head back. Baring her fangs to the firelight, she knew her eyes glinted red as her body rippled with the power of the climax. He anchored himself to her with a hand around her waist, continuing to drive in hard, stretching out the length of the climax so a cry became a scream, her breasts heavy and aching until his hand found one and gripped it, giving her even more anchor for the wild thrusting of her hips. He came as she was riding the second crest, and it pushed her onto the wildly rocking sea of a third, her cunt spasming, her clit so sensitive she screamed when his testicles slapped against it over and over, as he shot his seed into her.

"Yours," he said fiercely in her ear. "Yours, no matter who you force me to fuck to prove your damn dominance. All yours, lady. Heart, soul, mind . . . every drop of my fucking blood is yours."

And every tear, she thought, wondering if he realized that the wetness between his jaw and her cheek came from him.

As Tara had said. Overly sentimental, these Irishmen.

Her Irishman.

30

THEY lay by the fire for the remainder of the night, saying little. She let him doze, knowing he wasn't quite used to her hours yet. It took the human body a long time to adapt to a vampire's schedule.

The third mark made that much easier. The mark she couldn't give him, no matter how strong the compulsion in her to do so was growing. The third mark would give him a much greater level of strength, enhanced senses on many levels. Not to mention the far deeper level of connection. She'd lied to Jacob somewhat on that. While she had been able to disconnect the link between her and Thomas, the awareness of his existence could not be totally blocked from her. She'd known the moment Thomas had died.

What's more, Thomas had known it, because she'd heard his dying words. Perhaps because when she'd felt his life essence slipping, she'd torn away the veil between them, acting on pure emotion, desperately seeking one last touch with him.

Good-bye, my lady.

Then nothing. That chamber of her heart forever empty in a blink, populated with inanimate memories. Dusty bookshops he'd loved, his spectacles sitting on a side table by firelight. Places he'd been with all the evidence of him except his living presence.

Her reverie drifted into a predawn doze, for she woke out of it only as Jacob lifted her, took her to the bed and slid her naked under the covers, arranging them over her.

"You aren't going to lie with me until dawn comes, Sir Vagabond?"

He bent over her, studying her as she reached out. When he pressed his lips to her wrist, she thought she could look at that straight nose, the firm lips and clear, clear blue eyes, for hours. She tangled her fingers in the strands of reddish hair that fell forward over his shoulder. "My lady only has to ask," he murmured as if there was something sleeping in the room he didn't wish to wake. "There's nothing I'll refuse her."

"Until dawn," she murmured back, closing her eyes.

Jacob lay down next to her. She curled against him with the deceptive docility and appeal of a kitten, when a few hours before she'd done everything she could to tear his soul to ribbons. He reflected there was nothing linear about their relationship. They didn't even have the upward consistency of a spiral. He was beginning to sense this was the way she loved, as mercurial as a fairy in truth, choosing by some random path of her own which thought or action she would pursue next. He might as well predict the direction to chase a butterfly through a meadow of wildflowers so colorful he could barely distinguish between the creature he chased and the nodding blooms.

Of course a bat flitting through the night sky after a mosquito was more apt. A smile tugged at his lips. He saw from his watch dawn was minutes away. She'd had a long night and her body was settling. Shaking his head at his own foolishness, he brushed his lips over her ear. "Sleep, my lady. I'll take care of everything aloft."

"I know you will," she said sleepily. "Go now. Let me rest."

Because he knew it was a command, he did, albeit reluctantly.

When he looked back from the top of the stairs, he watched her until the opening slowly faded, taking her and the mystery of her thoughts away from him. Except for the jagged cut of the last drowsy sentence she uttered in his mind.

I won't have need of you tomorrow night.

He'd apparently put in a long day. She found a neat stack of her account books and the usual summary of daily tasks addressed on her credenza in her office when she got up. The routine she preferred when she didn't want his attendance was to rise, review the status of her household and business interests, and then either pursue her evening errands or seek him out on her own time, if at all, if she then had need of him.

The vampires who ran businesses in Lyssa's Region had regular correspondence with her, and she skimmed the report of their requests and questions, noting Jacob had handled most of those as her agent and handled them well. She could tell her servant's intuition was benefiting her interests. He'd noted Jonas of the Savannah territory seemed nervous about his fourth quarter estimated earnings. Myra in Raleigh needed an additional employee but was preferring to work herself to death rather than admit she needed help running the lucrative crystal shop.

The window people had come to replace the piece of plywood he'd put over the window in the upper hall with a new sheet of plate glass until she decided if she wanted to commission a new stained glass work. Despite her preference for a hired limo, she had three cars in her garage. He'd checked them for operating condition and found two in need of work. He'd gotten to one and would handle the other later in the week. Today also had been the cleaning staff's day and he left her a general inventory of what was in the kitchen in case she had any other events planned for the near future. He'd called in a carpet crew to clean the Aubusson in the dining room.

"I ought to take that out of your salary," she observed with amusement.

As the clock ticked and she finished her review, she made herself sit back in her chair, tap her fingers on the desk. One at a time, a ripple of motion. She'd told him he wouldn't see her tonight. After last night by the fire, her own desires meant nothing. She had to rein it back in. They were not lovers. She couldn't let him develop emotional ideas.

"Damn it," she muttered. The tapping became a drumming. Hadn't she as much as said this would happen? *You'll be like a dog I've allowed to misbehave . . .*

Why shouldn't she spend time with him if she wanted to do so? He was *her* servant. She didn't have to justify anything.

Rising abruptly from the desk, she moved into the hallway, headed toward the sound of the television. It was coming from the den area, which she knew was his preferred place for leisure time, though he didn't take much of it. The quick swim in the pool, playtime with the dogs, an occasional movie or news program. He didn't care for idleness, her vagabond knight.

But why would he? He was a strong young man in excellent health, in the prime of his life. Which brought her the image of his arms, muscles taut, in a variety of favorite images. Playing tug-of-war with Bran, replacing a rotted piece of framing board on the second level, the hammer descending in smooth strokes. Drawing her close so that her fingers could whisper over the curves of those firm biceps.

The closer she got, the more her step increased, though she kept her movements silent and blocked Bran's awareness of her approach.

The den library was a sunken area. She sat down on the top of the steps leading into it, preferring to watch the scene unnoticed for a few moments.

Jacob was stretched out on the couch, wearing just a pair of jeans. He had a bowl of popcorn on his bare abdomen, remote in hand as he watched a movie. His feet were propped up on the opposite arm and he was occasionally throwing Bran a piece of the popcorn. The dog was amusing him by catching it in midair, most of the time.

"Don't give me that look. That pitch was not too high," he informed the wolfhound as Bran had to go retrieve a piece that went under the adjacent chair, managing to scoot it back several inches in his hunt. "It does you some good to move. Getting all lazy and fat, lying around watching television."

"From where I'm sitting, that sounds like the pot calling the kettle black," she commented.

Jacob tilted his head, then swung his legs to the floor. She was almost sorry for the change of pose, enjoying the sight of that lean half-naked body on her couch.

"I can turn this off, my lady, if you wish to—"

"No. Leave it." She paused, feeling incomprehensibly awkward.

He considered her. "Did I misunderstand you? I thought you said you wouldn't require me tonight."

"I don't." She rose, smoothed her hands across her skirt.

"Did you want the room? I can go to the servant's quarters to give you privacy."

"No . . . I just need . . ." She shook her head at her inability to express her desire to simply spend some time in his company. She knew it took time, the easy camaraderie she'd had with Thomas. For one thing, he'd had all of her marks. But the friendship, the companionship she sought with Jacob was something different, something which had a certain tension to it that had not existed between her and Thomas. It was underscored when he moved to the stairs and put his hand on the rail, a foot casually on the bottom step, his body so close, eyes so intent, alert . . . reminding her that he was as aware as she was of everything they'd shared the previous night.

Perhaps the right man could make a woman of any age act like an insecure schoolgirl. Except she'd never acted or felt that way with any man. Ever. At any age. "Jacob, I would like to spend some time with you."

He blinked. Then a pleased smile crossed his face, loosening the tension in her stomach. She'd not realized his easy manner could be as effective on her as it was on the landscapers or the dogs. It even seemed to work on Mr. Ingram.

"You do me honor, lady. Do you prefer the couch?"

"I do." When she crossed to it, she spread her skirt and sat at the end, placing the pillow he'd been using on her lap. "I'd like you to lie back down as you were."

He came around the coffee table, sliding the popcorn bowl to the coffee table. Giving her a curious glance, he settled his head in her lap, the pillow between it and her thighs, giving his neck a comfortable brace to watch the television. She toyed with the ends of his hair and glanced toward the muted screen in time to see two swordsmen reach the end of a contemporary battle in a parking deck. One sliced off the other's head, though the camera mercifully cut away.

"What *are* you watching?"

"This is *Highlander*." At her blank look, that infectious smile crossed his face again. "The hero is immortal. There's a whole group of immortals, and each time one cuts off another's head, the winner gets the dead immortal's power. It's all filtering down to the time when there will be only one all-powerful immortal."

She frowned. "How lonely. He'll be the only one of his kind."

"Well, the hero never goes out of his way to pick a fight. It just happens that way. There are lots of evil immortals who want to be the only one."

"Mmmm."

"You might get some tips from this." Jacob propped one bare foot on the top of the other on the opposite arm of the sofa and rocked his knee, drawing her attention to those long thighs as her fingers traced his ears, his temples. His hand dropped down to the floor, his fingers finding her bare ankle and closing around it. "Whenever he meets a woman he wants, he announces he's immortal and can never die, and bam, he gets laid." He cleared his throat. "Excuse me, my lady. He gets his way with them."

She pursed her lips. "They equate immortality with stamina or sexual prowess?"

He chuckled. "I'm just saying it seems like a highly effective pickup line, if you want to use it. Not that I'm encouraging you."

She tugged on his hair in reproof. "You think I need pickup lines?"

"Well, look at me. I fell for the whole I-need-a-human-servant line."

Jacob liked the way she almost smiled at the joke. But even as he enjoyed her touch, was engaged by the play of the lamplight along her cheek, limning the fine line of it, the resentments he'd buried beneath a frenzy of activity today couldn't help rising.

Was this what being her servant would be like? The most incredibly powerful experiences of his life mixed with indifference or outright rejection? Was he just supposed to accept it? "I won't have need of you today" versus "Come here so I can fuck your brains out"? Perhaps a servant was just a different version of her relationship with Bran. Put his head in her lap to be stroked, keeping her company when it suited her? A pet who could also perform tasks that required opposing digits?

Her lashes slowly rose, the brilliant green eyes fastening on his, and he silently cursed at her expression.

"You know, I keep forgetting you can do that."

"Would it make a difference if you didn't?" she said icily. "It takes self-control to block your own thoughts, Jacob. You don't have too much of that."

When she began to rise, push him off her, he twisted, laid an arm over her thighs. "Please don't go, my lady. I didn't mean to offend you. If you can read my thoughts, you know that."

Blowing out a frustrated breath, he lunged up from the couch, paced to the television, and snapped it off. Raking a hand through his hair, he turned, faced her. "Damn it, I don't know how to deal with this, how to deal with you. Thomas taught me how to winterize your houses and take care of your accounts, but it's like one moment you're . . . everything inside of me. And then the next moment, you take it away. I don't know if you're getting off on it, or if you're as torn up about it as I am, or if I'm just losing my fucking mind."

She looked down. She noted she had her hands pressed hard on her thighs, conveying her tension, but she didn't know how to relax them. "I knew last night was a mistake. I owe you an apology, Jacob."

"No. Don't you do that." Taking two steps back to her, he knelt and covered her hands with his own, tightening when she made to draw away. He was so tall he was eye level with her, and Lyssa found she had difficulty meeting his gaze. She'd met the gazes of vampires who wanted to tear her to pieces, but she couldn't handle those blue eyes, the way they made her feel.

"My lady." His fingers touched her chin, curling so his knuckles feathered over her skin, then straightened again to trace her ear, a lock of her hair. When she finally managed to meet his gaze, there was something in his that caused a lump in her throat.

"I'm going to take a huge leap here and say I think this confuses you as much as it does me. You don't have to confirm or deny it, but I don't think any less of you for that being the truth. I just . . ." He blew out another breath, gave her a half smile. "How about we do this? I am truly, deeply honored that you want to spend time with me tonight. Will you forgive my thoughts and consent to stay awhile?"

When she studied him a long moment, knowing her expression was remote at best, still masking a hurt she didn't deserve to feel, he gave her an arch look. "I'm only human, you know. And male, to boot."

She allowed herself a small, tight smile. "Show me something to make it worth my while to stay. Something Bran can't do for me."

Relief crossed his features, soothing her wounded feelings, but again she had no right to feel wounded. There was nothing he'd thought she could have challenged. That had annoyed her as much as him having the thought in the first place.

"Come here." She urged him to lay back down with his head in her lap. He complied, but his brow was furrowed as he considered her demand.

"No listening in," he warned. "I want to surprise you." As he thought, he indulged in a stretch, bending his arms over his head so he caught the edge of the couch on the other side of her lap. The exercise pressed his shoulders into her thigh and tempted her to run her hand down the center of his chest to his flat stomach. Perhaps even lower, to the waistband of the jeans and the tempting curve of groin displayed. He was the most unconsciously sensual man she'd ever met, his somewhat bohemian mannerisms and dress making him even more appealing. She followed the urge, smoothing her palm over him, feeling the muscles tense and relax in response as she reached, pressing her breast into his shoulder as she leaned over. As she brushed his stomach with her knuckles, letting one finger play just under the silver fastener of the jeans, his gaze rose.

"I'm just occupying myself while waiting," she informed him. "I can promise you this is something I never do with Bran."

"My relief on that knows no bounds, my lady. But come to think of it, that's something that Bran doesn't do for you . . ."

31

"Oh no." She shook her head, even as she continued teasing with one finger, enjoying the feel of his hard waist, the fit of his jeans starting to constrict, the crossed position of his ankles making it all the more pleasurable to watch his reaction. "Too easy."

"All right, then. I've got it." With a regretful look, part courtesy and all genuine, leaving her own arousal simmering, he rose from the couch. Taking her hand briefly, he brushed his lips across it before he went to the entertainment center. Selecting a piece of music from her extensive collection, he inserted it into her player.

Turning around, waiting for the music to start, he began to crack his knuckles meditatively as if he was using the process to review what he had in his mind. "Are you familiar with soft-shoe, my lady?"

Whatever she'd been expecting, it hadn't been that. "Not really."

"Soft-shoe is a type of tap dancing," he said. "Only it's done with soft-soled shoes, hence the name. Or in bare feet." He glanced down at his own with a smile. She watched, fascinated, as he took each finger in hand, cracked and dislocated each knuckle, then restored it with a chilling pop of noise.

"It was first introduced by George Primrose in minstrel shows in the early part of the twentieth century. The key to it is the lightness of the tapping, performed at a smooth and leisurely cadence. It was also called the sand dance. I don't remember why, though sometimes I think it's because there's something soothing about it, like a lullaby."

He adjusted the angle of the floor lamp, turning it so it was behind him. Picking up the baseball cap he'd apparently donned earlier and then casually thrown on the coffee table, he spun it, using two fingers of his right hand. "No thumbs," he pointed out.

"Duly noted," she nodded. Quietly enchanted.

He started the music. The piano tune was a sad piece from the 1920s like the fading sounds of a carnival, appropriate as he began to perform the spare, smooth movements of the routine for her, with the sweeps and turns of the entertainers of that era. His shadow was thrown up on the wall by the lamp. If she focused on that image, he could have been any of those long-ago men who'd charmed children and made men and women long for experiences never as good as they seemed in their memories. The true definition of nostalgia.

He did eventually use his thumbs with the cap, but that was all right with her. It was a dance style made for a man, with the wide wheeling of the arms, the leaps in the same place, reminding her of Gaelic warriors preparing for battle, dancing in firelight. Trying to connect to something that would make them everything good men hoped they could be.

She could have watched him do it for hours, the man and his shadow dancing for one another, mesmerizing her with the poignancy of it. When the piece came to an end, he did a spin to complete it. The hat rolled down his arm to his fingers as he finished in a low bow and then straightened, a little breathless, his lips curved.

As he came across the floor back to her, his thumb cracked when he dropped the hat on the table. Grimacing, he pulled on the lowest joint to dislocate and reset it again.

Lyssa bolted straight up on the couch, her eyes widening. "That's how you do it." She pointed at his hand accusingly. "That's how you get out of restraints."

He winced. "Busted. If it makes you feel any better, old wives' tales say I'm supposed to suffer terrible arthritis when I get older." He considered her. "Of course, that was one of the major draws of the whole human servant gig, avoiding that."

"You . . ." She shook her head at him. "I thought the attraction was spending an eternity exposed to my charming and sweet disposition."

"That, too," he agreed. She noticed he was studying her more closely. Dropping to one knee beside her again, he reached out, cupped her face. "You're hungry, my lady."

He was beginning to detect the minute pallor changes of her skin that indicated she was ready for nourishment. It had taken several months for Thomas to pick up on it, and while she knew Thomas could have described it to him, somehow she knew he hadn't. Jacob was just that attuned to her needs.

"May I offer you . . . something? It's part of my job, isn't it?"

"Yes." She inclined her head, which tucked her jaw into the curve of his hand.

"Would you prefer it in wine, or . . ."

She could tell he was braced for her to reject him since she'd gone back to her mode of establishing emotional distance between them. An attempt that was beginning to seem like a pointless exercise when something as simple as a dance could make her wonder why she deprived herself of his company for any length of time.

She shook her head. "When it comes to you, Jacob, I prefer the source."

Most of the time she'd taken her blood in wine from Thomas. He'd simply prepared it for her, cutting his arm and mixing his life source in the wine that diluted it and gave it a variety of tastes, depending on what vintage she was in the mood to taste. With Jacob, she suspected it would be a long, long time before she'd relinquish her right to put her lips directly to his skin, feel his shudder as she pierced him. If she had a long time, which she didn't. Which made it even more important to her.

"I'll take it directly from my servant's throat," she said.

Nodding, he rose, his mind projecting what he was about to do so he knew he didn't have to hesitate and wait for a sign of approval. She was intrigued by the decision, in the way he constantly surprised her with his impulsive, assertive actions when it came to her. Of course the majority of her surprise had to do with her reaction, the fact she liked his impulses enough not to forbid them.

When he slid his arms under her, she linked hers around his neck. Turning, he took his seat on the couch with her cradled in his lap, her arm naturally sliding along his back, the other holding to his shoulder.

"I've noticed you like the places that are the most life-threatening, my lady. The carotid artery, the femoral. I think you don't want me to forget my life is yours for the taking."

An intuitive man. She let the thought whisper through his mind like the hint of danger. As if he sensed her hunger rising hard and fast to the surface, he tightened his arm around her back, drawing her closer while the music continued to play. His glance went pointedly to the remote next to his thigh.

There are some men who think sex and watching cable TV at the same time is the closest thing to heaven on earth.

Touch it and I shall remind you immediately your life is mine for the taking.

I didn't say I was one of them, my lady. The warmth of his smile touched her face as she closed her eyes, placed her mouth over him and bit, digging in as she would for the anticipation of sweet fruit waiting behind a firm rind. She knew he now understood she liked him to feel pain at the entry, that she'd been glad he didn't want her to use her secretions to desensitize the experience. She was stirred by how aroused he got without them, stoked by the stimulation of their two energies.

He stroked her back with his one hand, his other lying over her legs, palm resting on her hip. His arousal grew beneath her, but from his mind she knew he also understood that when she fed it might or might not lead to that. Sometimes the taking of what he was willing to surrender to her was something of its own to savor. It had a deep intensity to it she didn't want to mesh with sex, like not mixing two equally good foods together so as not to dull the nuances of each.

Plus he was enjoying the simple feeling of being in a state of wanting her, letting that yearning build but holding it in check for her pleasure, for when she called for it. Which ratcheted up her own desire. During the dinner, without prompting he'd startled himself by calling her Mistress. Closing her eyes, she savored the sweet taste of blood, the disturbing though exultant realization he was beginning to understand what serving a Mistress truly meant.

He wasn't a natural sexual submissive by a long shot, but by pledging his heart, mind and soul to serve her, whether it be her pleasure or need for companionship, or as her protector, he'd opened up the path in himself. He was learning what pleasured her soul could create pleasure in his own, taking him places he'd never considered arousing before. For her and her alone he would submit, and that made his submission all the more potent.

Pressing her breasts against his chest, she dug in her grip on his arm. His own hand fisted the fabric of her skirt into a ball as he communicated back the same passion, his fingers flexing in a rhythm with her nursing at his throat, her generous swallows of his blood.

At length, she drew back, pressing and holding her lips on the wound as she'd done in the past, waiting for the blood to clot from the agents in her mouth, enjoying the taste of him settling on her tongue as she did so. He was still hard beneath her, and she rubbed herself against him, a passing stroke. His head dropped back to the sofa as he eyed her, his hand coming up to her face, threading his fingers into her hair. "I want you," he said in a quiet voice. His thumb moved to her lips, to the fang that was still somewhat elongated. Pressing so it punctured, he gave her another taste. She took it into her mouth, suckling on his thumb as his fingers fanned out over her lashes, her nose, her lips. Nuzzling against his touch, she closed her eyes, taking the thumb deeper so his large hand masked her face. As she let him draw his thumb out slowly, she flicked her tongue against it, opened her eyes so she could watch the images rolling through his mind reflect in his expression.

"Would you like your cock in my mouth, Sir Vagabond?"

He swallowed. "I'm sure you can read my mind, my lady. But I would never presume to—"

"Tell me." Her voice was low. She knew her eyes were bright, harsh demand and desire projecting in her voice, compelling him to respond in kind.

"Yes, my lady. I want my cock in your mouth. I want to feel your lips, your teeth on me. I want you to swallow my come. Hold you on me with my hands fisted in your hair, watching my cock stretch your beautiful, perfect mouth. But there's something I want even more than that."

He showed her in his mind, in great detail, such that she trembled and moisture gathered between her legs, feeling the images almost as if he were doing it.

"You've picked up on the advantages of this form of communication far more quickly than Thomas."

"Well, my mind is far less pure."

She tugged his hair so his head obligingly dipped. "Thomas was a man as well as a monk. He had thoughts."

"You enjoyed teasing him."

"At times," she admitted, no apology in her tone. In fact, Jacob noted there was laughter there, one of the first times he'd heard her speak of the man without sadness. He'd apparently found a memory that didn't overlap with the tragedy which had taken him from her. As much as his body wanted to push them forward on the roller coaster he'd just initiated, he forced himself to patience to get an answer to the question that had been plaguing him. He suspected she might be in a mood to answer.

"When Thomas became my servant, I did require him to lie with me at least once," she confessed what he asked in his mind. "I required proof of his loyalty, that his devotion to me would supersede his oath to God."

"You tread in dangerous waters, my lady. Even vampires answer to a higher power."

She nodded. "There are those who believe the folk tales, that we're already damned. But I'm not one of them. A vampire is part of creation, like a man, dog or mosquito, trees or rivers, and our souls are as up for grabs as any. But men create religion, not gods. I personally believe Divinity could care less if we indulge in carnal knowledge of one another."

In fact, there was a spiritual power to it so overwhelming, Lyssa thought the religions that used it as a form of worship made more sense than those that called it a sin. "A man's integrity, his morality, his sense of right and wrong and the choices they compel him to make, that's his connection to God. While I have no problem testing that connection for my own purposes, I respect it for the most part when its strength is true. That's why I only asked for it once." Something like humor danced through her gaze. "I do admit to the occasional flirtation, a teasing and provocative image injected in his mind at the right moment to distract him from a task." She sobered. "But with Thomas, his faith was unbreakable. He never did anything to shame himself before his God, no matter what he himself thought about it."

She considered the copper strands of his hair tangled with her fingers, the beauty of Jacob's eyes. Those firm, sensual lips.

"One thing I do understand is the power of devotion and loyalty. While I might not believe whatever we call God requires us to give up sex, since that was something Thomas did to prove his loyalty to Him or Her, it demanded my respect. Any deity, or queen for that matter," she allowed herself a small smile, "would appreciate a servant who gives up a significant natural desire to prove his love and dedication to her service. I might ask someone to choose between their conscience and my desires, but as you have pointed out before, Sir Vagabond, the choice remains in the realm of that person's soul. If the soul is strong enough, I can't take the choice away unless I use a level of duress that damns my own soul, not theirs. I'm not like some of my brethren."

At last, she gave him the answer she knew he'd been seeking, and her eyes were intent on his, underscoring she understood the significance of her answer. "If I ask you to make a choice, there is a strong and urgent need for it. Not because I just enjoy taunting you and breaking your soul into pieces, bit by bit. I swear it."

Jacob nodded, his hand finding her other one and holding it, his fingers closing around hers. "Then I will trust you, my lady, even if I don't always agree. Did he please you?"

She cocked her head, met his gaze with an amused look. "He did. He was a gentle, thorough lover who made me regret my decision to demand it of him only once."

"Really."

She laughed at him then. She knew it couldn't be compared to the volatile couplings she'd had with Jacob. They encompassed a whole spectrum of reactions and action. In their few joinings, Jacob had been gentle, thorough. Also passionate, demanding. Surprisingly inventive and intuitive, never forgetting or leaving her heart and mind out of the equation when their two bodies came together. He was powerful in the arts of charm and seduction for that reason, all the more so because he used them for their mutual pleasure, never with a thought to manipulate. He brought an adventurous innocence to it she also appreciated, learning all the dark paths a body could take for sexual pleasure. He elicited unexpected responses from her, like now when she heard the faint territorial note enter his voice. He didn't like talking about other men that had been with her, even one like Thomas.

"What about you, Jacob? You are too at ease around a woman's body for me to think you don't remember fondly one or two . . . dozen."

He chuckled. In one of those unexpected moves, even as she knew his thoughts, he lifted her as easily as he would a child, shifting her and guiding her legs so she sat astride him, her legs curved and overlapped behind his hips, between his body and the couch. He snugged her up to him with those large, capable palms on her hips and backside. She drew in a little breath when he accurately put the pressure of his cock against her clit, his fingers holding her buttocks, kneading. "You've driven them all out of my mind, my lady. And before you try to make a liar out of me . . ." She had the snippet of a thought as she dove in, trying to do just that, before he put his hand on the back of her neck and brought his mouth to hers to delve into her in a sense that was far more physical. It did, however, accomplish the objective of driving anything else from her mind for the moment.

Brash, impulsive . . . Tara's words came back to her, and all Lyssa could think was, "Thank God." He knew her power, but it still didn't stop him from these impossibly forward moments she welcomed like a drug. Somehow they carried her away from a need to control everything, to worry about his place and her place . . .

Putting his hands on either side of her face, he held her as he kissed her, caressing her neck, making her need him inside her suddenly, desperately. Reaching in between them, she found his jeans and opened them, his lower body lifting to allow her to move them down to his thighs. She moved her hands to herself, but he guided them to his shoulders, coaxing her to let him be the one who gathered her skirt, bringing her bare skin in contact with his hard stomach, the thrust of his cock, the feel of crumpled denim next to her calves. He murmured a sound of appreciation as he only found her beneath the cloth. His hands were sure as he took her down on him, holding her steady. He slid deep into her with the torturously pleasurable ease of watching a sunset melt on the horizon, the heat spreading out, the beauty of it taking over and surrounding all the senses.

Oh God, he was perfect. She wished she could let him into her mind to tell him . . . and then she did. She gave him the images in her head, letting him see how she was seeing him, how she was feeling him, wanting him . . . harder. Wanting him whispering to her, all barriers and rules gone, at least at this level.

He pulled the pins from her hair, letting them clatter to the floor as he gripped her hair, used it to pull her down on him even more powerfully, his eyes darkening, pupils widening as he drank even more of her in.

"Fuck me," he demanded. "Fuck me."

God . . . yes. That was what she wanted, that guttural desire that was all hers. A natural part of him to take over a woman, held in check as he served her until she tore off the bridle as she did now, giving him his head and feeling all that power surging under her, wild and unfettered as it was meant to be.

"I'm going to make you come, my lady," he growled, his hands dropping to seize her hips, forcing her down on him, her clit smacking against his pubic area each time, a blow that shuddered through her system even as he stretched her further, took her deeper, widened her thighs to open up her cunt, bring the labia and clit in closer contact with his hot skin. "Fuck you until you're screaming my name, until none of it matters. Until you know you're mine. That you can trust me with everything, forever."

His. It was insane. But she felt so intertwined with him now, she didn't have any energy to argue, could only ride as he was compelling her to do with the grip of his hands, the jerk and thrust of his hips. The orgasm swelled up hard and fast and still he was taking her down in those relentless strokes, spreading her wide. He curled his arm around her waist as she began to climax, pulling her down with one arm as he found her clit with his thumb, held her slightly off of him and used his hips to piston into her, holding her immobile as he worked her, in and out, his thumb working that tiny bud of flesh. The climax battered her as she writhed, holding tightly to his shoulder, one hand gripped in his hair as the pressure became too overwhelming and she screamed as he said she would.

With a sound of fierce triumph, he shot his seed into her, his powerful shoulders flexing under her hands, his head pressing down against her sternum. She held her jaw to him, biting down on her lips as she hoarsely cried his name, whispered it as her cries became whimpers and her clutching hands eased into short, jerky movements on him. To stroking, light touches of amazement.

When he leaned back on the sofa, he framed her face in his hands again, keeping her balanced on his loins. The dinner, the things she'd told him over and over . . . the broken arm. Those were the things that were supposed to make sense. This was supposed to be confusing. But right now it was just the opposite. The possession by the fire, this, every time he smiled at her or kept on serving her even as he rebelled against her . . . those things were all so clear, though she couldn't describe or encapsulate them with words to explain exactly *what* was so clear.

"My lady?" With a half smile of exhaustion, he tapped her forehead then drew her down so she was comfortably wrapped in his arms. "Turn it off. Let's watch the movie together."

"I'll watch the movie, and you'll fall asleep," she said against his skin. His laughter rumbled against her cheek.

"You're likely right about that. I guess I'll just have to trust a mere lass to keep me safe while I sleep, no?"

The affected brogue came easily to him, and made things shiver up her spine even as she snorted. *Mere lass.* "Yes. I'll keep you safe. I promise."

He was silent for a moment, then startled her with a drowsy comment. "It was curious to me that you didn't know about the soft-shoe, my lady. I guess I expect you to know everything."

She rubbed her face against his chest. "Weren't you listening the other night, Sir Vagabond? Just because I'm as old as I am doesn't mean I've reached this state of all-encompassing wisdom where I just sit on the top of a mountain soaked in enlightenment. Good for you, too, because you'd go insane with the inactivity." When he chuckled, she closed her eyes at the thrill it gave her to feel him vibrate against her body again. "I know a lot of things by experience humans will never live long enough to understand, including yourself. But one thing I've learned is we don't overcome our nature. It's so much a part of us, I'd say it's maybe half of our souls."

When Bran raised his head, she looked at the dog, wishing she could have his simple acceptance of life. "If our nature is to want to love and be loved," she said softly, "we don't overcome that, get past it. On the same note, I could live ten thousand years and not understand why we do the things we do to each other."

She waited for his response, but his even breath told her he had succumbed in her embrace, the taking of his blood and the climax too much to keep him conscious. He'd drifted off on the soothing notes of her voice, trusting he'd not come to any harm with her.

When the total lack of sense she was using could well be the death of him.

If she dared, she would have said more.

Or why, knowing I shouldn't have you at all, I want you so much. Reaching up, she touched his face, brushing his brow. *All the wisdom in the world doesn't make me immune to the way you desire me.*

With regret she rose and covered him with a lap blanket, leaving him to dream alone. Though her mind mocked her, she had to keep making the attempt to teach him what being a servant to a vampire queen truly meant. Her heart called her a coward, running from her desperate wish to stay in those arms all night long. Maybe even beyond that.

But they had to get through the Council Gathering. *She* had to get through it. If nothing else, she'd at last acknowledged she would need Jacob to do that. It was time to focus on what needed to be done. Time was too short to indulge her heart.

32

He hadn't seen her directly for several days, but Jacob tried to accept it, rationalize it. She was fighting her own feelings for him. Therefore, in an odd way these repetitive absences were gratifying. Frustrating as hell, yes. Particularly when he felt her presence so close it was like the yearning left in the aftermath of an erotic dream.

Oh hell. He wished he were as stubborn as she thought he was, too stubborn to let any doubts filter into his mind and heart. He couldn't help thinking about her words, things she'd said and what she didn't say. The things that had happened during the short time in her service. Maybe she could influence his mind, and she was using this absence and her ability to manipulate his thoughts to make his doubts build, because one thing in particular kept needling his consciousness.

Her conflict, the physical and emotional pain she seemed to be confronting. Was he contributing to it?

It was as if they were back on that damn merry-go-round, or maybe they'd been on it the whole time, circling around, again and again, dealing with the same conflicts and issues. He'd had his sense of himself challenged over and over. What he wanted, what he would endure to have it, whether his willingness to do that was right or wrong. That had been his focus. How *he* was handling things. But now all the things Gideon had told him, all the flaws in his character repeatedly pointed out, rose more prominently in his mind as each day passed.

What about her? What did she really need?

She'd said it. So had Tara, even Carnal. Every time a vampire was around him, his formidable Mistress included, he felt swamped by their years of knowledge, so much greater than his. Their surety, based on experience, for what was right and true.

Not suitable to be a servant. Thomas had been sure, but with all the debris between now and his memories of his time with Thomas, the certainty the man had instilled in him was flagging. Had it been the desperation of a sick and dying man, hoping a coincidence had given him a way to perform one last significant service for his lady? Jacob thought of Lyssa lying in the hallway, seeking her own death. The anger he'd evoked in her, the frustration. Had she accepted him or had he forced the issue? *Was* he the best man to be her servant? Yes, she had a will of iron, but the Irish were stubborn enough to wear down iron.

It even crossed his mind that the compulsion to be with her could just be the pathetic cliché of a human drawn to a vampire's magnetism. Maybe he'd just been trying to spin the elusive threads of a wishful dream into the fabric of reality.

On the third night, he lay on the grass of her back lawn, staring up at the stars in the night sky. A child had told the emperor he was naked. A fool had brought a king back from despair by the simplicity of his worldview. He'd chosen to accept the role of human servant to Lady Lyssa because his gut had told him it was where he was supposed to be. The moment he'd seen her at Eldar's Salon, he'd known it with a deep conviction he couldn't shake even now. He'd known it at the bullfight, though he hadn't known what to call the compulsion then.

He wasn't certain if he was cut out to be a human servant. What he knew for certain was he was meant to serve her. What the hell that meant, he didn't know. Did he need to step out of the way to let someone more suitable take care of her?

"Oh, this is such *bullshit*. I'm sick of it."

At the fork of each road in his life he'd gone on his gut when every external source of information told him it was the wrong direction. He'd have to trust it.

He rolled to his feet, strode determinedly into the house. It took all of several minutes to stuff everything in his duffel, shoulder it and head for the kitchen entrance and the garage where he kept his motorcycle. Bran kept pace, following him with a stiff-legged stately stride that said the dog knew something significant was occurring.

When he rolled the bike out, he strapped the bag and the weapons tote on the back rack. Stood there, breathing deep. Swung his leg over to straddle the motorcycle, feel it between his thighs, ready to roar to life and take him wherever he wanted to go. She wouldn't hold him, would shut down the link between them, though she'd always know where he was and what he was thinking if she chose to do so. Wanted to do so. Sometimes in a weak moment, maybe he'd hear a whisper of her own thoughts in his dreams, her touch.

He would feel her. Know she was close, watching him. She could even be standing directly behind him now, where the bike's exhaust would make her skirt tremble around her legs when he started it up.

He stayed where he was a long time, straddling the gap between two decisions, somehow knowing whichever way he went on it, it was the last time he'd struggle with it. No matter what any of her kind or his own had to say about it. Even her.

"What's stronger than blood, Jacob?" His brother's voice, angry and hurt, when he'd left him. *"What the hell is stronger than that?"*

My feet have grown heavy and clumsy. . . . I'd trip over them and fall flat on my face if I got more than a hundred paces from you. . . .

I'm not as good as you think. I'm no saint, and I'm far from harmless.

He hadn't had an answer for his brother then. He did now.

The heart. That's what.

Bran sat a foot away from the bike, alert, gazing at him steadily. He'd wondered before how she'd taught him not to give away her presence when she was near. It was a question he hadn't had a chance to ask her. One of the many things he'd like a lifetime to find out. She didn't have a lifetime, though. Not even the length of a human lifetime left to her. Or a dog's.

He thought of her all the ways he'd seen or experienced her. Vulnerable. But not the sickness. She would have expelled him long before now if she'd thought for a moment the main reason he was here was pity, so he didn't waste any concern on that. She had the kind of pride that would make her die in her bed alone, no matter how tortured by the symptoms of her illness, rather than compel someone to her side to be her caretaker alone.

He thought about her mannerisms during the vampire dinner, when she forced him to couple with two women he didn't know before the cruel eyes of strangers. Her threat at the salon to dismember him, which was an affectionate, lighthearted memory in comparison. The way she watched him with such close attention as if she were fascinated not only by his words, but every minute change of facial expression or body language. Knowing that close scrutiny was coupled with the ability to hear his thoughts made him feel exposed and inextricably bound to her at once, a sense of infinite belonging. Yes, he was what they called an alpha male. But he wouldn't deny he belonged to Lady Lyssa, nor did it bother him anymore to realize it. It didn't change anything that already existed to give it names.

He was acknowledging what was already there, a part of their relationship that like so much of it couldn't be adequately explained. Even by the two people who were a part of it.

In his mind were the good images. Fewer but far more powerful than the not-so-good, as she'd said. Like making love before the fire, after the dinner. When she waited for him, wanted him. Letting him take her down and have her, sweep them both into a realm where politics and their status in her world or his did not matter.

Swinging his leg back off the bike, he set down the weapons bag and duffel. He would stay because she needed him, but more than that, he would stay because he was in love with her. Perversely, he realized that was what had caused the wave of doubt. Because he loved her with everything he was, he'd finally gotten beyond himself, the need to prove himself, to what *she* needed. While he was sure that there were many others who could be a better human servant to her, his gut told him in his inability to start that engine, she needed him. How or why wasn't important. He was going to be here for her.

Bran gave him a doleful look as Jacob started to shoulder the bags to return to the house. "Thought I was going to go for a spin and let you give chase, did you?" He paused as the dog cocked his head. "Well, I suppose someone has to keep you and your worthless brothers and sisters in shape."

~

A moment later, Lyssa watched while he kicked the bike into gear and sped down the mile-long driveway, Bran in hot pursuit, his brothers and sisters materializing from all parts of the grounds to join in the fun. When he got to the end, he put a foot down and deftly spun the bike in a circle, spitting out gravel to make the dogs jump excitedly just beyond range as he gunned it to shoot back up the drive. As he did, she saw him laughing, the weight of his thoughts lifted now that he'd made peace with them. The image before her shimmered, and suddenly she saw him coming across the field at full gallop, his sword drawn, coming to the aid of a woman he'd never met, whose caravan was under attack . . .

Startled, she blinked and the image disappeared, but the vividness of it, like her dream of the knight the first evening Jacob was in her home, lingered. Of course what woman *didn't* dream of her knight in shining armor? But then, there was much to be said of a knight in a snug T-shirt and worn jeans, handling a powerful motorcycle with callused hands and the grip of his thighs as deftly as he might a warhorse.

She'd heard his thoughts, had experienced myriad emotions herself as he sorted through his own. A few of his thoughts had almost tempted her to break the silence she'd imposed between them. Watching Bran and his family give chase to the bike with that intensity that quickly brought to mind their heritage of pulling down deer or tracking wolves, she knew it wouldn't change her mind about her next course of action.

She just wished she could predict it would accomplish her intention, instead of skittering off into some altogether different direction, as her interactions with Jacob seemed to do.

There was no hope for that. The Council Gathering was approaching. She would make a last attempt to teach him the one lesson she'd been trying to teach him from the beginning, the one most crucial to his survival. From there forward, he would serve her, but Fate would be his true Mistress.

Damn it, Lyssa wasn't going to give him up to any other woman without a fight. She couldn't let him be another Thomas.

Open your mind, Jacob. Be ready to learn.

~

Five days later, she left him a message.

"It's time to test your skills for the Council. Meet me at the forest edge at full dark. Wear black clothing that allows you to move quickly. Bring your preferred weapons for fighting vampires."

Jacob enjoyed the idle fantasy they were going after Carnal, but since she'd said to meet her where the thickly forested nature preserve started behind her house, he doubted that was the case.

The security company that regularly patrolled the outside perimeter of the fenced preserve handled detection not prevention, for she knew no human methods would prevent a vampire from entering and only result in loss of human life. But a vampire would have a very difficult time getting onto her property undetected, which was what mattered to her.

She was waiting when he got there. His heart leaped foolishly at that first sight of her in a week. Standing in front of the tree line, she almost blended into it, an innate part of the woods. Her hair was loose, surprising him, but when he reached her side he saw it fit the wildness that seemed so close to the surface in her tonight. With no light out here save for the sliver of moonlight, her expression was in shadow.

"Have you ever played tag, Jacob?"

"I have." He wished he could see her face. Her voice rasped in a manner different than he'd ever heard it before, a creature he wasn't entirely sure he knew, and she was a mystery on most days. Even the dogs were acting differently. Not as house pets. Snarling occasionally at each other, reinforcing the pack's pecking order. Circling, impatient, they'd reverted to a primeval behavior he didn't know they remembered, but it called to mind the wilds of Ireland. As they brushed his legs he didn't pet them, knowing instinctively it wasn't appropriate and likely would lose him a hand. "Is that what we're doing?"

"The rules are essentially the same. I'll give you fifteen minutes to put distance between yourself and me. See if you can confuse me with your trail. I won't be using the mark to find you, only my vampire senses. Confuse me as best you may."

She tugged the dress off herself, a hard rip rather than taking it off, underscoring the primitive nature of the game she intended to play. She wore nothing under it. Dropping to a crouch in bare feet, she rested her fingers on the dirt and considered him, her head cocked, fangs catching the moonlight.

"Once I find you"—he noted she apparently had no doubt of this—"you'll try to stop me from running you to ground, using every weapon or method you've learned. I want to see what your brother has taught you. See if you can evade me, thwart my intent."

"What intent is that, my lady?"

A flash of her eyes in the night, and Bran whined, the sound evolving into a half growl. "To treat you as prey. Capture you as I would if I was doing it on speed and intelligence alone. No seductive games. No glamour. Tonight you see my true face, Jacob. I will see how you survive it."

He considered that. "And the dogs?"

"They'll run with the hunt, like the Fey riders at night, for it's their nature. They like to run. But they won't help find you. This is between you and me only."

He inclined his head and began to remove the wooden arrows from the wrist gauntlet.

"What are you doing?"

"Preparing for the game you've proposed, my lady." He removed the gun from his back waistband. Then a knife with its leg sheath, several hidden stakes and the small crossbow he carried, making a tidy pile of the weapons between them.

"I told you to bring those for a reason."

"Which would be?" He blinked at her.

"You realize playing dumb means absolutely nothing when the person you're trying to irritate can read your mind?"

"Then I suspect whether I state the obvious or not, you're quite capable of being irritated. I won't draw a weapon against you, my lady. Not now. Not ever."

"My point is to show your weapons will be useless against me."

"As they've been against other vampires my brother and I have hunted and killed?" Now his temper flared, and he saw her green eyes fire in response. "Perhaps one day I'll show you I'm not nearly as impotent against your enemies as you believe me to be. But I won't use you as an example. As formidable as you are, my lady, I won't risk you being wrong."

He removed another knife from the harness on his back, flipped and staked it into the dirt two feet from her before he dropped the harness to the ground as well. "Good hunting, my lady. Perhaps it's best you won't be listening to my thoughts for a while."

He moved into the forest, letting its darkness swallow him. He'd run the trails with Bran and already knew where many of them were, since he'd explored the width and breadth of her property in the daytime hours. That she would catch up to him quickly, he'd no doubt. Vampire senses were keen. Hearing, sight, and of course she knew the property even better than he did. With only a fifteen-minute lead, he'd leave enough of a scent she'd pick up lingering traces of that as well. So he thought about an open area where she'd have to slow her approach, take time to search, and knew just the place.

Damnable, aggravating woman. Sometimes the similarities between her and Gideon were far too marked, their propensity for always assuming they knew what was best.

What does it gain to prove a man impotent, to convince him without a doubt he's helpless? A parent will still rush into a burning building to save his child, knowing they'll both die. Is it an act of futility, or a noble choice imbued with its own power because of the love that drives it?

His anger surged up, driving out philosophy in favor of raw reaction.

I'm not Thomas, damn it. Did you ever hold fast to his arm at night to keep him close to you in your dreams? Perhaps this isn't about proving Carnal can rip me limb from limb or that I'm ready for politics at the Council Gathering, but that you have control over a situation and feelings already far beyond your control. You're afraid of recreating a situation that broke your heart. But I am not him. And I am definitely not your fucking husband.

Pain shot through his temple, causing a brief sense of dizziness that made him stumble. His jaw flexed.

No cheating, my lady.

A sense of infuriated woman, heat and fire, and she was gone, pulling out so fast he felt somewhat sick to his stomach. He had no doubt her purpose was to hear what was going through his head, not to find him. But by catching her there, he'd won a point. She was not invulnerable and unaffected by him. No one was invulnerable. Not vampires, humans or wolfhounds. Grudgingly he admitted only the dogs seemed to accept that with good grace.

Twelve minutes later he found the glade he sought. About twenty-five-feet in diameter, it was surrounded by an interlocking circle of live oaks, pines and maples, their branches a tapestry against the night sky. There was a good amount of undergrowth as well. If she moved rapidly, she'd give herself away. She could leap up into the trees, travel that way. But while vampires could leap to extraordinary heights, they couldn't fly, so she wouldn't be able to soar over the trees. He squatted on his heels, putting his back against one of the large oaks growing so closely to the pines he was enclosed on three sides. Even more important, he was shadowed. Crossing his arms, he bowed his head to his breast, closing his eyes so he wouldn't rely on them. Vision was a hindrance when it came to vampires. The human eye could not follow them, and yet it would try to, draining energy and focus from other senses he'd found more useful.

Concealed at his hip was the only weapon he hadn't dropped from his arsenal. He'd use it to prove his point, if he could. It was the vampires' assumption of human weakness that got them killed. How often had he and Gideon used one of the team as bait, leading the vampire into a trap, distracting him, taking him out with an error in judgment? Yes, Gideon had lost people, because vampires weren't stupid. Their senses could detect danger in ways humans were not as honed to pick up, except with exceedingly high effort and practice.

But he made every effort to do so now. Listening, his nostrils flared, body tense but loose at once. Alert and ready to move.

There were a variety of sounds. Leaves and branches making contact as the breeze moved through them. One of the nocturnal animals scratching at something. A bark in the distance as one of the dogs found something of interest and warned one of his more aggressive brethren back because he wasn't finished examining it to his satisfaction. He could hear the quiet sound of his own breath. His heartbeat. *Thud. Thud.*

She'd hear that when she got close enough, but she'd have to pinpoint its location. You didn't often escape a vampire. Gideon taught him that early. Once they were on your trail, your only chance was to turn to the offensive, set them up to surprise them and take them out. Was she moving quietly through the wood now? Those bare feet pressing precisely into the earth, disturbing no undergrowth, her body flowing through it, letting the foliage pass across her bare skin, branches leaving tiny red scrapes that would vanish in a blink? The moonlight would turn her pale skin to milky gray, all that dark loose hair cloaking her. A creature of the night. Why had she undressed? To show that with nothing but her bare hands she could take him down? Or to distract him with those curves, the pale folds of her sex she'd revealed with a primal immodesty as she crouched in her feral pose, watching him discard his weapons. His body burned at the deprivation. His cock had no sense at all when it came to her, but he ruefully acknowledged no other part of him seemed to, either. His heart ached to hold her in his arms.

Slowly he raised his head, opening his eyes as he braced the back of his head on the tree trunk. The branches of the large live oak across from him stretched out like the gnarled arms of a giant.

It took a blink for him to realize there was something not part of the expected picture. When he scrolled his gaze back, at first he thought he might be in a Faustian dream. Perhaps there were other reasons Lyssa had the forest perimeter patrolled. Not only to give her warning of vampire intruders, but to protect creatures humans only dreamed about in surrealistic nightmares or whimsical fantasy.

Then shock coursed through his blood, freezing him. He was looking at his Mistress.

She crouched on a tree limb the way she'd been squatting on the ground when he left her. It was this position that suggested the amazing possibility to him. Her bare toes curled into the limb, elongated so they were more like a bird's claws, holding her balance. It seemed she'd broadened and thickened in the shoulders with the transformation, but as he continued to study her, he was reminded of the gargoyles at Notre Dame. Winged gargoyles.

Her skin was silver gray now. Her hair was gone, her small skull as delicate as a child's, the ears pointed, fangs pronounced and curving out over her bottom lip. Yes, that was a tail wrapped around the branch several times, helping her remain still. It had a barbed tip. Her fingers were talons. The smooth sleekness of her was like an animal, no womanly softness. Even the discernable mounds of her breasts were part of the sleek musculature. Yet he found her incredibly feminine. He'd have known she was female even without the male curiosity that caused him to seek evidence of her bosom, her sex. Her eyes had gotten larger, rounded, more widely spaced like a doe's, with long lashes and no irises or whites, just pure darkness. The skin did not look scaled, but tough, like a seal's skin.

Despite the legends, he'd never known a vampire who could shape-shift. Their affinity for caverns associated them with bats, their affinity for predatory animals like Bran gave rise to the idea they could become all sorts of things, stories he'd always known were untrue. Vampires had exceptional, deadly talents. Speed, strength, seductive illusion. Transforming into something else was not one of them. What he was looking at had to be another mysterious power of his lady's Fey parentage.

She couldn't see him, but she apparently knew he was in this glade, for from slight movements of her head he knew she was traversing it with her gaze. Shadowed by the three trees, he was safe for the moment. He'd been fortunate to move his head when she was looking elsewhere. As widely spaced as her eyes were, they weren't quite wide enough to have caught the movement.

The position of her head, the slight tilt, told him she was now focusing on where he was. Jacob remained motionless. She kept staring. She knew he was there, but she couldn't separate him from the shadows of his cover. It had been an excellent choice, but he suspected he had only a series of seconds before its usefulness would expire.

Less than that. She exploded from the branch, swooping down. She thought she could flush him with panic or intimidation. He held fast as she plunged toward his spot, marking the best time to move even as a part of him marveled at the fascinating sight. The thin body, ribs as pronounced as a greyhound's. The leather-like wings, extended so he could see the curved talon at the elbow joint, were nearly ten feet wide, tip to tip. She looked like a fallen angel, one of God's outcasts coming from the bowels of hell seeking souls for Lucifer. Or a fairy bathed in blood so often she had brought sensual beauty and horror together in the same form.

She should have looked frightening, unappealing, but there was a precise elegance to her, the sparing movements he'd know in any form.

Closing his eyes, he waited until he sensed she was almost upon him. He threw himself out of the alcove as the sweep of her wings passed over him, her talons grazing his back, tearing his shirt. He ducked under her reach, spun and leaped on her back, snugging his arm around her throat below her jaw, taking the teeth out of the equation.

They tumbled, but she used the powerful wings to take her from the ground with him still holding on. Six feet in the air she executed a flip, which slapped her wings through the grass of the glade. It threw his weight in an unexpected direction, disorienting him. He lost his grip and two blinks later found himself on his back, his wind knocked from him and her sitting on his chest. Just as she had sat in the tree, her bare feet flat on his stomach, knees bent up to her bosom, protecting herself. Her wings were half outstretched to balance herself, those dark eyes focused on him. This close up, he could see far more of Lyssa in her features, though he had no lingering doubt he was in the presence of his lady.

Of course she appeared impassive right now, but he read other things. The tension in her body indicated an overwhelming energy, barely suppressed. It could be bloodlust, or just plain lust. Or something else, something more unguarded this form allowed more free play than her vampire form did.

She had him effectively pinned. At these close quarters, her strength and speed would counter anything he did. Testing, he lifted one arm and it was immediately seized in her grip, the talons overlapping so he felt them scrape against his skin. Pressing forward, he communicated intent instead of struggle, keeping his gaze steady on those dark eyes.

She'd not yet spoken, and he didn't know if she could speak in this form, at least in a way he would understand. But he didn't feel a need for it, lying beneath this beautiful, fascinating creature who could destroy him without a thought. He felt certain her power over him was not as absolute as she thought it was. But proving that was no longer as important to him as touching her face.

While she granted his desire, she kept her grip on his wrist. When he brushed the firm gray skin of her cheek, her eyes, those large dark pools, remained unblinking, watching him. As he pressed a fingertip along the prominent cheekbone, there was a silver sheen to her skin, a type of oil that set off a ripple of glittering reaction, like static rippling in tiny starbursts along a woman's skirt as she moved. This had an electrical tingle to it but no pain. The area on either side of the bridge of the nose and under the eyes was drawn taut in three symmetrical folds. They gave her eyes a further depth, a sorrowful mystery, and his heart tightened as he passed his thumb over them, wondering at the track shedding tears would take. Or if she could cry in this form. Now he moved on to her ear, twice as long as an elf's and yet standing just as upright, giving her the appearance of small horns. He traced up to the point, rising up on one elbow to do so. She tilted her head down toward him, making a soft crooning noise, a noise of pleasure as he dipped into the shell of it.

He couldn't help but marvel at the precise artistry of her. Her neck was long, giving her better reach to look over her shoulder when flying and execute maneuvers like he'd just experienced. He wanted to caress the line of it, but first he wanted this. He moved from her ear to cup her head, the bare skull under his palm. It was smooth and silken like her body when it had been brushed with a lustrous powder. There was an exotic, different scent to her as well, almost a hint of vanilla cream. Tantalizing.

At his touch on her skull, she made another of those soft noises, this time with a slight growl. He kept doing it, even as it became a low rumble and he knew he was arousing her with the stroking.

Hunger. She was hungry.

Raising his chin, he tilted back his head. Inviting. Offering.

33

SHE looked startled, making him wonder if she even realized she'd been projecting the thought.

He understood an inkling of the bond that could grow between mother and child when the child was dependent on his mother's sustenance for life. While his feelings for Lyssa were not maternal in any sense, when she lowered her head and found his throat, allowing him to slide his arm over her shoulder, rest his hand on the crest of one wing, he knew the fierce, protective connection was the same, the sense that this was the most important thing he'd done or would ever do in his life, caring for her. Committing himself to her. Nurturing her whenever, however she needed it. He was also aware that hunger encompassed several different things for her.

He moved his other hand up her hip to the stark indentation of her waist and along the ripples of her rib cage, his thumb grazing the base of her breast. Stroking her, just feeling the slope of her. Her breath touched his jaw as she released his wrist to curve around his throat and shoulder, tilting his head up to an even more straining arch, making him aware of the rush of blood through the arteries, the vulnerability of his windpipe that could be crushed with the pressure of her thumb, the clamp of her jaw. Closing his eyes, he moved his other hand along her thigh as she changed her position and straddled him, pressing her bare sex down against his pelvis and eliciting a groan of pleasure as the movement confirmed he was hard and erect for her. Her wings moved, stretching out and then folding over both of them like the curtains of a bed, closing them into even greater darkness where he could just make out the line of her shoulder, feel the press of the elbow talon against his side.

He didn't want to do it, knew it was the wrong thing to do, but he had to.

My lady, a vampire's confidence in her superiority can be a fatal mistake.

He'd counted on her not using the mind link between them, but when he made the comment in his mind, she lifted her head, her fangs an inch away from his throat. He increased his grip on the slender stake he had pressed firmly between her ribs. In one blink, he could have sent it spearing into the heart beneath.

When one gave a shot to a horse, one thumped and poked the powerful muscle repeatedly. Once the animal was used to the rapping, one tossed the needle like a dart into the spot. The pressure and teasing of his fingers had served the same purpose.

As she rose above him, straightening, he gripped the shaft between them, broke it and let it fall to the earth beside him. "I'm not easily killed, my lady. I may be driven by anger when you are in danger, or distressed by that monster who pretended to be your husband's friend, but I never stop using my brain."

Except when I'm sunk deep into your body.

As she continued to stare at him, not speaking, he knew he might lose her in a blink, her capricious moods dictating she withdraw at his unexpected move and disappear into the shadows of the forest, leaving him a hollow victory. In fact, making his heart lurch with the loss, she suddenly stood five feet away from him, her back straight, that tail following the line of her hip, curled around the front of her feet. With her taloned fingers slightly curled, wings at half spread, she looked like a demonic angel.

"Don't go, my lady." He whispered it, sitting up and extending a hand toward her silhouette, not wanting her to fade into the darkness. "I beg you. Appease your hunger in whatever manner your body demands of me."

The wind kicked up, making the branches of the live oaks creak, the pines whisper secrets. The night creatures had stilled, sensing a predator in their midst.

He used his eyes now, keeping them clamped on her outline as if that could compel her to stay. Then she began to move back toward him. Slowly. One step, two. When she stepped over him, he settled his hands on the outside of her thighs, his thumbs caressing her flesh. Bending forward, he laid his lips on her upper thigh, close to the tight folds of flesh hiding her sex. If the emotions driving the gesture had physical force, color, perhaps he would have left the imprint of a tiny bloodred rose on her leg, a permanent reminder of the kiss and all it meant.

Her hands came to rest on his shoulders, pushed at him, eased him to his back as she straddled him again, pinning his shoulders to the ground before she sat back and continued to study him, as if confused by the type of prey she'd found.

He felt like her dark eyes were gazing into his soul, making it yearn to be a part of her, connected to her forever. The need surged up in him. While his rational mind argued with him not to voice it, not to ruin this moment, his heart was fiercely sure it needed to happen. Right now. This was the time. The turning point.

Go with your gut.

"I've no doubt you're my Mistress." Reaching up, he stroked his knuckles along the line of her cheek, his thumb against the corner of her dark eye. He moved back to her ear, down to the side of her throat, following her windpipe, feeling her swallow. When he increased his grip, her eyes flickered to him. "I'm your servant, my lady. Please, let me serve you. Don't doubt me or yourself. I've proven my loyalty to you. My skill. Believe in me and give me my own choice."

Why do you force me to play games? All of you, even Thomas. Can't I have one person whom I don't have to force to do my bidding for their own good?

So she could communicate in this form. Hearing her voice in his head sounding as it usually did was startling with the contrast of this winged transformation, but he recovered quickly.

Perhaps you need to stop feeling you have to make those choices for us. Old you are, my lady, he teased her gently. *But God you are not. Even God gave us free will.*

He was an idiot that day. A weak moment that has caused more pain and aggravation in the world than can be measured.

Something shimmered in her expression, something that turned into a hard quiver running through her body. He was astonished to see moisture collect in the corner of one large dark eye, become a glittering tear. A moment later he knew what track a tear would take in this form. The diamond shape of it was split into three trails by the overlapping folds, dampening her face. Catching the moisture with his finger, he carefully wiped it away. "Don't cry. Please, my lady."

He began to rise, intending comfort. As unexpectedly as a lightning strike out of a clear sky, she seized his hand, pulled back on her haunches and twisted him so she rolled him over. Forced him to his stomach where he could not see her and his arm was pressed at an uncomfortable angle behind his back. With his cheek pressed into the dirt and grass of the forest floor, he could only see her in his peripheral vision. Just brief impressions, shadows, though she was very solidly real, the way she anchored herself on his body. She stood on his thighs now in her birdlike crouch so that her sharp toenails pressed into his muscles. Using her other hand, she pushed away his torn T-shirt, baring the strip of skin just above the waistband of his jeans. He turned his pinned wrist to twine his fingers with the claws holding his arm to his back. While she accepted the contact, it did not ease the strength of her grip. When she bent to him, the tip of her tongue touched him, a tongue that felt forked and a bit longer than it had been. He felt the scrape of a fang.

Use your free hand and reach under yourself. Unzip your jeans.

It took a bit of effort. This form was not much heavier, but with her weight on his upper thighs and pressed on his lower back, she didn't give him much maneuvering room. He sensed her pleasure in the necessary flexing of his muscles and buttocks to rise up the amount needed to do her bidding. Since she was completely naked, it stood to reason she would desire him in the same state, though lying prone on a bare erection was not the most comfortable position in the world. The unbidden image of her impaling herself on him as he lay on his back, his arms drawn to straining over his head by vines dangling from the trees above, tortured him further.

Hold on a second. He wouldn't envision himself bound. But the next image was the sultry glide of her slick cunt down his length . . . one inch . . . two inches . . . She was offering him her fantasies, goading him with her own desires. It was like the intense eroticism of watching a woman masturbate, only he was getting to see it from inside of her head, the visions she conjured to stimulate herself.

He managed to complete the task and struggled to get his shoes off in the same fashion, inspiring her to run her hand over his buttocks as they shifted to accomplish the task. Once the shoes were gone, she pulled the jeans off him in a quick move that took his lower body off the ground, dragging him a couple feet. He gripped at the earth, seeking balance, but before he could find it she was back on top of him again. She guided his arms back so the elbows were bent at right angles, his hands gripping his forearms to form a square on his lower back. Then she manacled his overlapping wrists with one long-fingered hand, the talons snicking together like the sound of a lock, scraping against his skin.

Why are you afraid to let me be free, my lady?

Why are you afraid of surrendering, Jacob?

With her free hand, she flicked a claw across the top of his thigh, raking him, taking flesh, drawing blood.

It stung like nettles, the fire racing over the back of his leg, telling him she carried some type of venom in those razor tips, hopefully just a temporary measure to distract prey. But Jesus, it burned. He couldn't help his spasmodic twitching. But she showed mercy, leaning down and blowing on the area, bringing the feel of a cool mist across desert sands, easing the feeling. So flooded with relief, he wasn't prepared at all when she eased two fingers deep into his backside. He jerked immediately after though, struggling against her. He clenched around her invasion, creating a different burning sensation, almost as uncomfortable.

Easy, Jacob. Breathe deeply and relax. She held him down effortlessly. It made him fight even harder, his mind overcome by panic at the physical and emotional reactions that surged through him at the uninvited penetration. There were no inanimate manacles he could slip. She moved effortlessly with him as he thrashed, and the predatory pleasure he sensed from her at his struggle only made his reaction harder to control.

A virgin in this area entirely, aren't you? Never even allowed a woman to tease your rim, though you go for mine often enough. I know you've enjoyed the pleasure of a woman's tight hole.

While he was sure his rectum was going to simply erupt into flames, he was cognizant that before she'd invaded she'd transformed her fingers back to human form, for there was no feeling of cutting sharpness, just a woman's fingers, lubricated with that oil he'd felt on her skin. Maybe also from oils lower down. Perhaps she had actually touched herself when he'd envisioned her masturbating.

Easy, Sir Vagabond. Be my slave. Submit to my pleasure. Leaning over him now, she pressed her thighs against the outside of his, her mons brushing the base of his ass just below where her fingers were penetrating. *Though I admit I love to watch you fight me, your muscles rippling along your back and shoulders, that delectably tight ass. I love your power, Jacob, knowing you're a strong man who will resist even when you know you're irrevocably caught. But as much as that arouses me, I love when you give me all that power as a gift.*

You also like taking it, my lady.

He felt her dangerous amusement. *Yes, I do. Did you know, from the first time I saw you at the Eldar, to every second you've been in my house, there hasn't been a single moment I haven't wanted to taste you, smell you, fuck you? Eat you alive. You're a hunger I seem unable to appease.*

She was doing it again, putting images in his brain that were making his cock into a painful iron bar against the ground. She worked her fingers inside of him in a way that had him pushing himself mindlessly against the earth as if it were her pussy he was plunging into. He was working a furrow into the forest floor that was getting warmer from the heat of his body, making the dirt and packed leaves moist from the arousal leaking from him.

You're trying to change the subject, my lady. Turn us away from the course you know is inevitable. It won't work.

Shut up, slave.

She leaned farther forward, putting more straining pressure on his arms. She'd turned completely back to human form except that one hand holding him, for he felt the difference in her weight distribution. Her hair fell against his shoulder blades. The skin of her thighs had become silky smooth and soft like her breasts as they pressed against the top of his folded arms. Putting her teeth to the juncture of shoulder and neck, she bit deep, her nose and cheek along his jawline.

She drank with her body on top of his, her fingers far too cleverly pumping in his ass. As she drew sustenance from him, using him completely for her pleasure and nourishment but offering him nothing beyond that, it shattered him into pieces. His mind simply stopped functioning. She tightened her thighs on him rhythmically, matching her cadence with her drinking. As she rocked, she pressed her pubic bone against the loose curl of her hand in a way that bumped her fingers more deeply into his ass, as if she had a cock and her curled knuckles were the scrotal sac slapping against him. He thought there might be four fingers in him now, stretching him past bearing with the physical pleasure and emotional turmoil.

He didn't have any interest in being fucked by a man, never had, but this image, of his delicate, sexy Mistress using the illusion of a cock to force him to climax, overwhelmed him in a way he didn't expect. Hadn't Thomas told him she would force him to explore places in himself he'd never even thought to look?

His cock was pulsing hard. "My lady . . . Mistress . . ."

"You'll come for me, now. Now," she repeated it sharply, and he groaned, a sound that wrenched from him as a snarling growl, evolving into a roar as his insides drew taut and he spurted like a hot geyser. He slammed his hips into the ground, the earth nowhere close to the slickness of her cunt, but it didn't matter to his frenetically humping cock. He could imagine it, for she was filling his head with it. She was remembering their first night, when he had the taste of her in his mouth, her grinding against his face, her thighs gripping his skull.

It spurred an orgasm that had already reached an intensity level he'd never known existed. If she'd used pheromones, he was sure it would have killed him.

When he roared at the intensity, somewhere out in the night he heard Bran howl. He thought he even felt vibration beneath him when his seed fertilized the ground. As if the Earth Herself had responded to the energy rolling over him like an avalanche.

She didn't let her fangs slide out of him until he at last slowed, breathing hard. Even then she kept her tongue and lips on the wound, her soft breath in his ear.

As he tried to steady himself in the aftermath, she stretched out on him, her body quivering with her own reaction. The curve of her pelvis fitted over his buttocks, her stomach against the small of his back as she mashed her breasts pleasantly into the upper broadness of it. Her now completely restored hands folded over the base of his neck, her fingers tangling in his hair as she laid her cheek partly on them, partly on him, her lips nuzzling his flesh. Her bare toes rested against one of his calves, one knee planted between his thighs, close enough to put the weight of her thigh against his temporarily depleted testicles as she draped over him.

"You haven't let me give you pleasure." His voice was hoarse.

"You've given me more pleasure than I've felt in a long time," she corrected softly. "Just be still and quiet for me now. Let me lie upon you and believe, at least for a little while, that the world is a place where I could love you the way I want to."

The words startled him, but her hair whispered over his shoulder as the breeze picked up again, the strands drifting across his lips as if trying to underscore her desire for silence.

What you were worrying about a couple days ago . . . You are *wrong in so many ways to be a human servant. But I want you in a way I've not wanted anything in a very long time. I keep intending to send you away, and I just can't.*

I wouldn't go, my lady. You can't make me.

"Yes, I—" She stopped, and he felt her smile against his hair. He'd smile back if he wasn't so exhausted, his body drained, his emotions a maze. "We'll argue about it later."

"All right."

The trees rustled above, the earth a comforting smell beneath him, a restful bed. He drifted and dozed awhile with her lying upon him, her body shifting on his. All of it integrated into the languid pleasure of providing her a bed, his body recuperating from the explosive orgasm. From the effort of offering her all she'd demanded and everything he wanted to give, and having it rejected again. But he was here.

I'll never leave you, my lady . . .

At length, he surfaced. It might have been a half hour later, perhaps an hour. He was aware of an aura of needy energy sinking into his body from the heat of hers. As his senses sharpened, he became aware of the sensual rub of her lips on the back of his neck, the alternating tensing and relaxing of her hips as she stimulated her clit on the curve of his buttocks.

He put a hand under him, began to rise as she held onto him. Slowly he turned, tumbling her to her back, completing a full circle so he was lying on top of her. She was curiously docile through it all, watching him. Reaching down between them, he found her clit and teased it, making her shudder as his cock hardened at her reaction. Shifting, he moved down her body to frame her petite breasts with tender reverence before he began to suckle, creating a blush on her fair skin with the stubble of his jaw. Her legs rose, holding him around the hips as his stiffening member found her, eased its way naturally in as it grew harder and he continued laving her breasts. The soft nipples were not so soft now, the plump weight of her swelling in his hand. He felt the press of her body all along his. He wanted her to tremble in his arms, climax over his cock. He wanted to feel her small pussy grip him tightly like the illusion of a fulfilled promise. It would not sate the longing in his heart, but maybe it would ease the yearning for a moment or two.

He wasn't afraid of her sending him away. He was afraid of losing her altogether. The thought of it built in his mind and he couldn't bear it, the knowledge that it would become reality. So he kissed and suckled her fiercely, trying to serve her even as tears gathered in his eyes and he couldn't blink them back.

Something shuddered through her mind as if the thoughts running through his mind had found a resounding echo in her own.

This is as close as I can get to what I truly desire . . . still only a shallow substitute for what I miss so keenly. But how can I miss something so much that I've never had . . .

When he raised his head, her eyes were full of pain, so torn that they'd almost transformed back to the eyes of the creature hidden within herself, the pupils dark and taking over all the lighter areas. Her hand touched his face, giving him comfort even as her other hand clutched his arm, holding on as if he was her only hope to keep her from falling over the edge of an abyss.

He moved within her, keeping his gaze on her. He would seduce her with his body even as he told her with his tears he loved her. More than anything. More than his own life.

She tried to turn her face away, press her cheek to the earth, but he caught her chin. "No. Don't you pull back. Mark me, my lady. Give me the third mark, and I'll never leave you alone. Not ever. It's what I want. Have mercy, my lady. Please . . . don't leave me alone to grieve you."

Lyssa stared up at him, at the implacable resolve in his blue eyes. She wondered how her heart could hurt so much and not crack into a hundred pieces.

There had been a postscript to Thomas's note, put in as an afterthought. Neither the sentence structure nor the writing had been smooth, as if he'd been about to suffer an attack right before he completed the letter and feared he might not emerge from the other side of it to complete the correspondence.

> *You have been together before. . . . Let him make his own decision. . . . He will seem impossibly young to you, and he is, in so many charming ways. It will help keep you young, but he is also*

an old, old soul. Don't deny him his own wisdom, unique and separate from yours.

"I shouldn't. It's wrong."

"Yes, you should. Please."

He'd moved his hand so now it cupped the side of her face, cradling the weight of her skull. It made her remember the days she was so weary from her battles with Rex she couldn't even raise her head to acknowledge the presence of the moon, greet the night, see the petals of her roses gleam. All she'd wanted as she'd sat there, head bowed, was to feel his touch on her face. When a man touched your face first, lingered there, studying you—as Jacob was studying her now, as if he wanted to look at her just that way forever—it meant he loved you. Or at least it made a woman think he loved her. Enough that she was willing to give anything. Sacrifice anything.

Only this time, Jacob was the one willing to give it all. Sacrifice everything. In the depths of his love for her, he considered it a gift, not a sacrifice at all.

When she curled her arm around his neck, he understood, using the tension in his fine stomach muscles to lift them up so she straddled him, his body still linked to hers. Holding her hand on his neck, she knew her whole world had become his blue eyes. Steady. Pure.

"You'll need to bite my throat, here. Over the artery." She brought his hand to it, and hers was shaking. He squeezed her, reassuring, even as he trembled, too. "Try to use your canines. It helps with the puncturing. But don't hesitate and worry about hurting me. Bite down as hard as you can, and drink my blood. I'll let you know when to stop."

He stared at her, barely breathing, and yet she couldn't deny she felt almost the same way, swept with paralyzing shock by what she was about to do, no matter all the reasons not to do it. The only words or actions she seemed capable of were those that would put them on a course where there was no turning back.

He threaded his hand through her hair. As she helped, pulling the thick strands of it to the opposite shoulder, he leaned in. But before he went to her neck, he pressed his lips to hers, keeping his eyes open, the two of them watching each other, the moment so heavy with intent and change, she couldn't speak.

No. She wouldn't do this to him.

His cognitive ability denied her the change of heart. He sensed it a moment before she had the thought, because even as she had it, he'd wrapped his hand in her hair, yanked her head to the side and clamped down on her with the savage clumsiness of a young wolf making his first kill. But on a vampire, the blood exchange of a third mark was far from the terror a deer might feel beneath the jaws of a predator.

Every time he'd nipped at her or let her feel the pressure of his teeth she'd felt a surge of intense erotic reaction for just this reason. It set off an explosive sensation that rocketed through her the moment his teeth punctured through, finding her blood.

He stilled as her blood filled his mouth, getting used to it, and then his throat worked as he swallowed. Once . . . twice . . . three times. Before the second mark, it would not have gone down with such eager ease, but those two marks gave him the intuitive desire, the hunger for it.

Drawing his hand from the side of her face, she dipped her head. Not to dislodge him, just giving her better access to his wrist. In comparison to the other times she'd bitten him she pricked him almost delicately, letting her grip sink in rather than forcing it in among the strands of veins and arteries. Her jaw trembled, her body on the pinnacle of decision. His cock was deeply embedded in her body, holding her there.

I love you, my lady. Do it. No regrets. Not now, not ever. If you die tomorrow, I will follow you with only gratitude for the honor of being your servant forever . . . your slave, if it's your pleasure to call me that.

She'd held a drop of it on her finger once, the fluid that made the third mark possible. Gleaming silver, reminding her of a ribbon of lightning with the way it glowed. As she released it now and let it flow into his wrist vein, she closed her eyes and let the reaction unfold and enfold the both of them, spinning out the energy that would link them. She would not feel alone or be alone again. For some reason it felt like the first time in her life she could feel that way, believe it for certain.

It was like it had been with Thomas, but so different as well, as if the soul merging itself into hers was one she'd always known as intimately as her own. He'd just committed everything to her, so how could she not give him the same? For this moment at least, as the third mark bound them, she let everything be open, her heart, soul and mind where he could read and see anything. Feel how very significant this was to her, the fulfillment she'd missed so much and yet felt as if she was experiencing it in an amazing new way.

He cried out hoarsely against her skin as the quicksilver ribbon manifested itself another way, a way she hadn't warned him about, for of course she'd never expected to do this. Her hands slipped to his back, feeling the change in the skin, the burning of the individual design that would display to all that he carried the third mark. Her mark specifically.

When we first met, you said a tattoo is something you get when you're sure you'll stand by that belief or commitment forever.

So I did . . . Gods, my lady . . .

She was crying and moving on him at once, riding him again, going up through a spiraling tunnel, charging into a star-strewn universe that contained just the two of them, nothing to fear, nothing else but this moment.

She saw the knight in her mind. The quicksilver flash of a samurai's blade against the gleam of chain mail, the tunic of the Crusades. Lotus blossoms and red roses. Hard muscles pressed against her woman's body. Gentle hands on her face when she'd been a child, his dark hair loose and curling in her small fingers. He'd sung to comfort her then, too, only in a Japanese tongue.

He's served you twice before. He will not bear being parted from you a third time. . . .

As she began to feel lightheaded, she pulled out of the swirling depths of the memories. Putting her fingers to his lips, she reached out to him with her mind.

Enough, love. That's plenty. Though even to her, it felt like it would never be enough.

Jacob withdrew slowly, licking her, holding his mouth over her, feeling the way the wound slowly closed beneath his tongue. His hands slipped to her hips, anchoring her, and she dropped her head on her shoulders, emitting a wild, low cry as the first crest of the climax hit her like an unexpected rainstorm. His mouth was on her breasts, and she saw a smear of her blood there. Catching his jaw, she sealed her own mouth over his, pulling deep and hard, the same as he was doing to her. Their minds revolved together as if dancing, all the pieces of one another mixing up until she wasn't sure which memories were his and which ones were hers.

She was giving him too much of herself. The bad as well as the good were swirling in this cycle of energy, but his mind reached through it all to reassure her.

I want it all, my lady. Don't fear I can't handle it.

Thomas's words resounded in her head. *Your soul mate.*

Catching two handfuls of her hair, Jacob pressed his face into it, tangled her wrists in it, then his fingers with hers, rolling them over so she was on her back again, staring at the sky and the silhouette of his face over hers. His body pressed her to the earth, stroking her even more deeply so she tilted up, opened to him even more. Her body was shuddering with every wave of the orgasm and needing more, more, more. . . . His eyes were taking in everything, within and without them, trying to hold onto this moment forever. But she knew its temporal nature was what gave it so much sweetness. How could it become a memory to sustain her heart if it never ended?

"Let go with me," she rasped against his ear as she squeezed him within. And he did, holding closer to her, his hips suddenly jerking, his thighs flexing, drawing her up with him into another shuddering peak.

She felt everything he felt, the sense of release on so many levels. And one of those levels startled her with its intensity, so deep it clogged her throat with tears.

All of the worry and fears he'd had, his doubts . . . he let them all go, his heart easing to the point the climax was a true release, a purging. She felt a wave of relief from him as powerful as exhaustion. She would not shut him out, would let him offer her every resource he had to serve her.

Like a multidimensional collage, she saw an ocean of overlapping memories, his lifelong quest to find his sense of purpose, his resting place. The home where he was always meant to be. Her.

So worried about taking from him what she shouldn't ask, she hadn't realized how much it would mean to him to have her take the gift he'd been freely offering from the beginning.

There would be no more questions for him, no matter where they went or what they had to do. And because she felt the truth of that flood her with the power of his jetting seed, she felt her heart ease as well. At least for now.

Damn if you weren't right in the end, you wily old monk.

Reaching up, she touched her servant's face in wonder. *I love you, Jacob Green.* Then she said it to him, to prolong her joy in the fierce reaction that filled his expression. "I love you." She managed a smile through tears. "But don't expect that to change anything. Who you are, who I am. I won't be any easier to live with."

He kissed the curve of her mouth. Holding his lips there motionless for a long moment, he pressed his forehead to hers, his eyes closed, hands framing her face. The night moved around them and there was just this moment, the beat of his heart, the mingling of their breaths.

When at last he raised his head, he'd regained his composure. His blue eyes held a trace of the mischief she knew so well, though his voice trembled. "My lady, I just received the miracle of a lifetime. It's a greedy and unwise man that would ask for two, particularly on the very same night."

As she thumped his chest with a light fist, he caught her hand, but she sobered.

"I'm dying, Jacob," she said quietly, freeing herself to put her fingers to his lips so he wouldn't interrupt her. "There's nothing you can do about that. Nothing that can change it. What matters now is that I protect those who depend on me. Whenever it comes to a choice between that and my personal well-being, you must promise me you will always put the former first. Swear it."

His eyes held hers but he did not speak. She pushed him off her. "Turn around."

When he obeyed, her fingers traced the design, letting him feel it. From a distance, it appeared as a sinuous prehistoric snake, but also like an etching of his spine, representing his ability to move, to act, to think—all at her command.

As she held her touch there, she waited.

"Your goals shall be mine, my lady," he said at last. "Though I will strive to protect you."

There was the Council Gathering to face. Carnal. The end of her life and all she must do to prepare for it. Tasks she must handle, using him to help her. She would have to be ruthless to serve her duty, which meant if she had to be cruel to him, crueler than he'd yet been able to imagine, she would be.

When he turned, took her beneath him again, she saw him register her thoughts. His elbows pressed to the earth on either side of her head, keeping her gazing up into his face.

"My love for you means nothing in the world in which I must live. You understand that, Jacob?"

Jacob touched her face with his free hand. Her mind was still open to him, whether she knew it or not, so he felt her fears and worries, as well as her indomitable resolve. He matched it with his own.

"It means everything to me, my lady. That's all that matters. No matter what you need, I'll be at your side."

Stay tuned for the conclusion of
Jacob and Lyssa's story in

The Mark of The Vampire Queen